BEAUTIFUL BUT STRANGE

THE ENTIRE SERIES

J J SOREL

BOOKS BY J J SOREL

THORNHILL TRILOGY

Entrance

Enlighten

Enfold

THE IMPORTANCE OF BEING WILD

THE IMPORTANCE OF BEING BELLA

TAKE MY HEART

BEAUTIFUL BUT STRANGE

Flooded

Flirted

Flourished

DARK DESCENT INTO DESIRE

(Out 2020)

www.jjsorel.com

Cover http://www.wolfsparrowcovers.com/

Edited by Red Adept - Kim Husband

ISBN 9781694889058

"Why, sometimes I've believed as many as six impossible things before breakfast."

Alice in Wonderland - Lewis Carroll

Flooded

Book One

JUNIPER

I looked up at the devil in a suit, a good-looking one at that. But hell, he wasn't going to chop down my oak tree, charming smile or not.

Boasting wildflowers, butterflies, and bird life that always made a drab day exceptional, that land, which resembled a green oasis, had been in my family for decades. Originally owned by my great-grandmother, it had been the setting to my magical spells when at the immature age of thirteen I'd gone all Harry Potter and started making spells, imagining that the wise old oak that I'd named Oscar had magical powers. Swapping my magic wand for lipstick, I'd had my first kiss under that tree. I'd also shed tears there after Owen Mitchell broke my heart by confessing that it was my brother he wanted to hook up with.

"Sam? What kind of name is that for a murderer?" I asked.

He stood with his big arms crossed. His dark eyes sparkled with amusement. "Murderer's a tad dramatic, isn't it?"

"Well, that's what you are." I pointed at him.

"It's a tree, not a human being."

"They're just as important," I snapped.

"And what's wrong with my name, anyway?" he asked, tilting his head with a hint of a smirk.

"Nothing, I suppose." Desperate for a pee, I shifted my weight. Perched against the tree since morning, I had been about to unchain myself when Mr. Developer From Hell turned up.

If it hadn't been for earlier rain, Oscar would have been felled already. I'd only caught sight of the harvester machine earlier that day. The shock of seeing that incongruous beast of a machine among wildflowers and glistening greenery made my veins freeze. I decided to ride back home furiously, seeking answers. My father wasn't there. It was Cam, our neighbor, that had supplied me with a chain, and with no time to lose, I'd rushed back and wrapped it around the thick trunk.

Up in the sky, dark-gray clouds, looking equally as agitated as me, threatened to dump a month's worth of rain again. Nevertheless, I chose to remain chained to the tree.

"You don't seem comfortable. Why don't you unchain yourself? Here…" He extended his arm. "Let me help you. You must be needing some lunch."

Jerking back, I snapped, "Get away from me. I'm not going anywhere. Not while that evil machinery remains. You're not going to touch Oscar. That will only happen over my dead body."

His frown ironed out, and I noticed his lips curling slightly. I had to look away. This was not a friendly exchange. We were enemies.

"Oscar? The tree's got a name?"

His surprised drawl nearly made me want to laugh. But I held my ground. "Yeah. And so? Oscar's a beautiful, living, breathing being. He's been here for me all my life."

"He?" He cocked his head.

"Well, look at him. He's majestic and powerful and he's a he. I just know it."

"Okay. I'll take your word for it." He raked his fingers through his dark waves. "I didn't get your name."

"I didn't tell you. And you didn't ask," I said.

"No, I didn't, and that was rude of me." In any other circumstances, his respectful tone would have endeared him to me, for even though he belonged to the enemy, I struggled to dislike him. But then again, it could have been a smooth front honed to manipulate.

"My name's Juni." I moved onto my other butt cheek, the sponginess of which I appreciated for once. It was one of the only benefits of possessing a big ass.

"Is that short for June?"

"No, Juniper."

He studied me a while. His eyes landed right on mine, mesmerizing me. I had to look away. Sam had warm, chocolatey eyes that bordered on hypnotic.

A line formed between his dark eyebrows. "Like the bush?"

"Yeah. And what's more, our last name is Berry."

"Juniper Berry." A deep laugh resonated from his chest. "It suits you."

"Are you making fun of me?" I narrowed my eyes.

"No. I meant it as a compliment."

My cheeks burned under his unshifting gaze, which bordered on inappropriate because it penetrated so deeply. I had to look away in order to concentrate and remain firm.

When he lowered himself to the ground, I flinched at his sudden informality. "Aren't you going to dirty that suit?"

He shrugged. "A little grime here and there never hurt anybody. And I like getting a bit dirty." A slow, cheeky smile spread across his face.

"I bet you do," I said under my breath.

"I heard that, Juniper."

"Now listen, Sam. If you think you can charm me into unchaining myself, you are seriously mistaken. I'm here for the long haul. That big ugly beast over there is not coming anywhere near Oscar. You'll have to take me first."

"Is that an invitation?" he asked, cocking his handsome head.

I rolled my eyes in defiance. "Look, Sam, if you're trying to hit on me, forget it. You're not my type."

"How do you know?" He smirked.

"Well…look at you." I pointed at his head. "With that poisonous hair product in your hair. And I bet that expensive designer suit could feed an entire village in Africa."

A husky, infectious laugh erupted from him. Being a hopeless giggler, I had to squeeze my lips together in order to remain cool.

"For starters, I use a natural product in my hair, because believe it or not, Ms. Environmentalist, I too share your concern for the planet." I opened my mouth to comment, but he continued, "My question was not about me being your type but why you think I'm hitting on you."

"Mm…" His challenging grin made me want to slap those dimpled cheeks. "Look, Mr. Strong and Almighty Developer, I'm in need of a toilet break. So can you go away and give me some privacy? And, take him with you." I pointed to the machine.

SAM

After a small puddle splashed over my Italian leather shoes, I carefully avoided a mud patch by taking a wide stride. Looking up, I noticed dark, roiling clouds. There was more rain in store.

Recent downpours had promoted an abundance of growth. The bushes were flourishing, and the fertile lushness radiated that pleasant damp-grass scent.

The block was set in the middle of Oakland, a highly sought-after area for real estate. I could understand Juni's desire to protect it. But it wasn't my decision to make. I was just doing my father's dirty work.

I moved away to give her some privacy.

The novelty of the situation had added a bit of zing to my otherwise dull existence. Although working for my father had given me the type of lifestyle that many my age would have walked some weirdo's pet crocodile for, I had an itch for something more meaningful in my life that didn't involve overseeing the felling of impressive old trees.

As I stood a hundred or so yards away from that hippie angel, I found myself questioning my convictions in general. I knew what I really wanted to do. The trouble was that my father, who could turn water into ice by shouting vitriol, had other plans for me, his only son. I was "the son" in Chalmer and Son—which should have read Chalmer and Daughter, because

Julia, my sister, had more business acumen in her little manicured fingernail than I could ever hope to possess. Acquisitions and mergers did not float my boat, so to speak, nor did dividing and conquering. That gene must have gone to my sister.

Even though I'd inherited a more curious nature than what was fitting for someone peddling his father's wares, I possessed enough pragmatism to understand that in order to survive in a family like mine, I needed to toe the line.

I returned my attention to the pretty—no, not pretty, beautiful—but strange girl chained to the tree. I could have played dirty and stopped her from chaining herself up again, but I was enjoying myself too much. I would gently cajole Juniper, and that way, at least, she wouldn't completely hate me. And who knows, she might even accept a conciliatory drink or two. But then again, judging by the defiance and condemnation firing out of those pretty green eyes, I was dreaming.

"Hello, Rosie," I heard from behind. Expecting to find that someone else had arrived, I turned around and discovered Juniper talking to a bird.

I sighed. Before me stood a goddess, albeit a slightly kooky one.

The sun filtered through her dress, revealing an abundance of curves. Hers was my type of figure: no bones knocking into each other, just soft, warm deliciousness to slink my hands over.

Even though I tried not to stare, I couldn't help it.

As I strode over, finding it that little more difficult to move suddenly, the robin flew away.

"You frightened her."

"Her?" I asked.

"Are you still here?" Her eyes widened with indignation.

"You have this uncanny way with nature, haven't you? Like guessing the gender of trees and birds."

"And so what if I can?" She lifted her chin.

"Look Juniper, I'm not here to cause trouble. And in many ways, I'm just as fond of this tree as you are."

"Well then, take that beastly machine and be gone." She fluttered her hand in the air.

Looking very medieval in that long skirt, her blonde hair swept up in a bun, Juni possessed the kind of natural beauty that my eyes and body craved. But seeing Juni with her hands on her hips and that cute scowl on her face, I sensed that I had more chance of brokering peace in the Middle East than of taking her to bed.

"You shouldn't be here, anyway. This land belongs to my family."

"Not according to our records."

"That's bullshit," she blurted.

"Juniper, there's no need for bad language."

"That's not bad language. I can do better than that." Her face glowed with insolence—feistiness that only added to her already considerable sex appeal.

"Can I get you some food, then? Let me do that."

"I've got all the food I need." She pointed to her backpack.

"How is it that you're here alone? I would have thought your boyfriend would be here supporting you."

A little smirk claimed her full lips. "Oh… good try, mister."

"Now listen, Juniper Berry." I stopped myself there. Suddenly it felt as if I were in a cartoon or something just as ludicrous. "I never thought I'd hear myself calling anyone that."

"Are you making fun of me?" She reached into her backpack and grabbed a stainless-steel water bottle.

"I'd never do that."

"Hm…" She sipped before wiping her rosy lips with the back of her hand.

"Why are you staring?" she asked.

I shrugged. "I'm not sure. I guess I find you rather fascinating, if not a bit frustrating. And in any case, I'm still waiting for an answer. Why are you here fighting this out alone?"

She grabbed a cookie from a container and munched on it. "I'd offer you one, but then, that would encourage you."

"It's okay. I'm off sugar."

"So am I," she said in the most genial tone so far.

"Really?" I looked down at her cookie with surprise.

"It has dates in it."

"Oh." I nodded, lowering myself to the ground again so that I was at eye level. "You still haven't answered me."

"No one was around. And I don't have a boyfriend. Even though that's none of your business."

"You're right. It's none of my business. But I'm allowed to be curious." I had raised a brow and paused for a response when a buzz in my pocket broke the spell. "Excuse me." I peered down at my cell.

The message read: *Have you moved that greenie, yet?*

I typed: *It may take some time.*

A rumble startled both of us. I looked up at the sky. "I think there's a storm coming, Juniper."

"I don't mind. I love them."

"Yes. I get that. From a balcony staring out to sea, I can't think of anything better."

Her brows puckered slightly.

I shook my head. "What?"

"You surprise me a little," she said, munching on her cookie.

"There's a lot about me that you may find surprising." I stared deeply into her eyes. This time she held my gaze before looking away. "Juniper, it's dangerous to sit under a tree when there's lightning about. I think you know that."

"I do. But I'm willing to die for Oscar."

My eyebrows gathered tightly. "You're a woman of conviction. I like that. But dying for a tree?"

"Why not? People have died for all kinds of causes."

"You're too young and beautiful to be a martyr, Juniper."

JUNI

"Are you suggesting that only ugly, hairy-lipped women make martyrs?"

He stared at me with amusement twinkling away in those large dark eyes, which teased a tiny smile out of me. As I realized how ridiculous that last comment sounded, my lips trembled into a grin.

Sam's compliment wasn't lost on me either. I mean, who doesn't like being thought of as beautiful?

The air between us filled with that infectious husky laugh of his, and I had to summon every inch of will to stifle a giggle.

"That's not what I meant, Juniper. Although…" He studied my face closely while wearing a smirk, which told me he was about to poke fun again. Pointing, he added, "I think I see what looks like the makings of a mustache."

"What?" My face burned with indignation. I knew too well of those fine little hairs. But they were fair and therefore unnoticeable, I'd always supposed. "I do not…" My voice went up in pitch.

He laughed. "I'm only playing with you, Juniper." His scrutiny continued, however, making me jumpy. I had a pimple forming, and suddenly his gaze made it throb.

I hated vanity and strove to ignore such trivialities. I even made a point of going makeup-free most of the time. But as we locked eyes, Sam's unshifting attention seemed to have magnified my flaws.

"Stop looking at me so closely. It's inappropriate."

"What? I can't stare at the prettiest set of eyes I've seen in a long while, if ever?"

I frowned. "Ever?" came out of nowhere.

Flirtatious banter, although fun, wasn't something I should've shared with the enemy. "Look, Sam, if you're trying to hit on me, then you're on the wrong side. And you're not my type, anyway."

"The wrong side?" He cocked his handsome head. "I'm into recycling. I have solar panels at home. I like—no, I love—nature. Should I continue?"

I shook my head.

He held his dimpled chin. "Now, let me guess your type: He's a skinny, bearded dude who does yoga, loves kale, listens to folk music, and hates wearing shoes."

Resentment churned away, as a tirade knotted around my vocal cords. "Fuck off, Sam."

What Sam didn't know, even though he'd managed to annoy the crap out of me, was that he'd just described Callum, my sort-of ex. "Sort of" because we never consummated anything.

I couldn't help but take umbrage, not so much because Sam was acting like a smug dick but because he'd reminded me that Callum, who kept calling me, was as alluring as a bowl of oatmeal— wholesome and good but lacking in mouth-watering deliciousness.

Sam pulled a face of amused surprise. "I've hit a sore spot."

Just as I was about to argue that point, the sky lit up with a strike of lightning.

Sam stared down at his Rolex while the roar of thunder made me jump.

"Five seconds. That means one mile away. Too close. Look, Juniper. There's a storm and it's about to rain. There'll be nothing happening here today." He took his cell out of his pocket. "I'll call them. You can listen on speaker. Okay?"

"No need. I believe you. But you go first, and then I'll unchain myself and leave. But," I pointed at him, "I'll be back. Oscar remains here for another hundred years at least."

He crossed his heart. "Nothing will happen to Oscar."

"Ever?"

"One can never say ever." He opened his large hands. "But at least while the weather's like this."

I had to accept that, given that rain had started pelting down and a puddle had formed at my feet.

"Can I get your number?" Sam asked. His eyes softened.

He was the enemy, that voice of reason reminded me. "No," I uttered coldly.

"I just thought that if I heard something about the land, I could save you going through all of this again."

"Well, if that's the reason, then here," I said, holding out my hand for his cell.

He handed it over, and as he watched me enter my number, Sam asked, "Did you think I wanted to ask you out?"

I looked up at him and half expected to see that little cheeky smirk he wore so well. Instead, his expression remained neutral.

"I'm not sure what I thought," I said with a tight voice.

"I mean, I wouldn't mind…" He stopped short as the rain doubled in strength. "Let me help you. It's really coming down thick."

He wasn't kidding. My bun had collapsed, and my hair fell over my shoulders. I pushed it away from my eyes as rain splashed over my lashes, blurring my sight.

I searched frantically for the key. I'd used it to unchain myself to pee, but I'd forgotten where I'd placed it. I unzipped every compartment of my backpack searching for it.

"Where's the key, Juniper?"

"I don't know. It should be here somewhere. Maybe I left it over there." I pointed.

Sam sloshed through the mud. His designer shoes, which I'd earlier noted for their shininess, were now submerged in sludge.

He got down on his knees, running his hands through clumps of submerged grass.

"You go. I'll figure something out," I said, crossing my arms and trembling. I grabbed my cell to call my dad, but just to add insult to injury, the battery was flat. My chest collapsed with frustration as I turned my frazzled brain inside out trying to remember my parents' number.

Sam looked up at the sky. "It's here to stay. And this is low-lying land." He ran his hands through his soaked hair. "Shit. When it rains, it really fucking rains."

"Hello… climate change."

"Yeah, well, that's indisputable," he said almost to himself.

"It's because people like you are clearing land and putting down slabs of concrete."

"Juni… this is no time for politics. And I have nothing to do with climate change." He reached for his cell and pressed some keys. "Josh… Yeah good, no, I mean not so… anyway, look… there's an emergency. I need some bolt-cutters, like now. It's pouring down here. We'll be flooded for sure."

His face contorted, which only added to my own sudden fear, given that the rain had already created a pond splashing around my shins. My heart skipped a beat as I recalled the last deluge, a year back when the land had turned into a lake.

Finishing his call, Sam pushed back his dark hair, which kept falling over his forehead.

His frown jittered my nerves. "What's happening?" I asked.

"Apparently, the levy's broken. Downtown's flooded. The roads are closed."

"Shit. So quickly?" I looked Sam squarely in the face. "You don't have to stay."

SAM

"Are you fucking kidding me? I'm not leaving you here." I pressed Josh's number again. "Hey, get a boat here. Now."

"How do I do that?"

"Emergency Services. Call them right now. We don't have much time. And make sure they bring those bolt cutters."

"I'm onto it."

I tucked my cell into the inner pocket of my jacket. Studying the tree, I could see that it would be easy enough to climb. But what about Juni?

"How long's that chain?"

Juni stepped away from the tree and extended the chain fastened around her waist. She had a yard at the most between herself and the tree.

"Shit, Juniper…"

"Call me Juni, please."

I studied her for a moment. She was calm and collected, which made me admire her but also incited the desire to place her over my lap and spank her for being so fucking stubborn and for losing that key.

She was soaking. And just to make matters worse for my overactive male glands, her dress had gone transparent, revealing a body that would remain etched in my erotic memory for life.

How could I think of my dick at such a moment? Perhaps that theory that men think of sex every seven seconds had something to do with it. Only in my case, I thought of fucking Juni every twenty seconds, given that she was in danger of drowning.

My cell pinged. "Josh." Adrenaline pumped through me.

"I've called them. They'll be there as soon as they can. They're pretty flat out."

"I can imagine." I exhaled a tight breath. "Okay. Thanks."

Juni crossed her arms. I was grateful for that. My eyes, with a mind of their own, kept lingering inappropriately on her spiked nipples and that barely-there bra, which held the nicest set of tits I'd ever laid eyes on.

"I'm sorry about this, Sam." Noticing her eyes pooling with tears, I just wanted to take her into my arms and reassure her. Instead, I pushed a thick lock of saturated hair away from her face.

"Don't worry. I won't let anything happen to you."

Shivering, she gripped her arms.

We leaned against the tree to get as much cover from the rain as we could, even though we were already drenched.

It didn't take long for the water to rise to Juni's waist. She was around a foot shorter than me.

Juni's eyes looked into mine, and I fell into deep green pools of anxiety.

"Don't worry." My voice remained low and calm. "I won't let anything happen to you. Even if you have to stand on my shoulders."

"You'd drown for me?" Her forehead creased.

"Well, I'd do everything not to, of course." I sniffed. "I'm sure they'll be here soon. And in any case, I can float and hold you up at the same time."

"With this heavy chain?" Juni stared at my arms.

"You're a lot lighter than the weights I'm used to lifting."

A smile grew on her face, which lightened my mood instantly. "Now you're bragging. And it's such a waste of time for a bit of vanity."

Although her mood flip was jarring, I welcomed the banter. "It will come in handy now. If I had weak arms, I wouldn't be able to lift you."

She shrugged. "Mm… I suppose. But why do you do that? Is it to attract girls?"

Was she taunting me? I wondered, noticing a hint of playfulness in her gaze. "Probably. It's what most women like, isn't it? A strong male physique."

"Mm… It takes more than muscles to attract me."

"Let me guess, you go more for the geeky type?" I asked, talking loudly as the rain bucketed down.

"I don't have a type as such. But intelligence is pretty up there."

"Then we share that in common," I said.

"Oh… then you like intelligent men?" A teasing smile formed on her wet lips.

"No. I'm not gay. I'm into women. The more intelligent, the feistier, the better." I stared deeply into her eyes to make a point.

The rain had moved up to her stomach area. And although that little banter was a welcome distraction, panic had returned to Juni's eyes.

A voice within reassured that the boat would turn up any moment, even though each second felt more like ten minutes. Survival instinct burned through my veins, especially as the growing river started to swallow our bodies.

"Let's try this." I bent down and lifted the muddy chain. The water, having reached my pelvis, shriveled my balls to the size of peanuts.

I wrapped the slack part of the chain around the trunk. Holding onto the chain so that it didn't drag her in tight, I tugged, channeling herculean strength in a bid to pry apart a link.

After a few loud heaves, my muscles slumped. "It's a pity you opted for the thickest chain known to mankind," I yelled, deafened by the thunderous rain.

"I had to," she yelled back. "Otherwise you would have freed me."

I relaxed my grip on the chain, my hands burning from where the metal had cut in. "Wouldn't that have been too bad," I muttered.

"You don't have to stay, you know." Her eyes lit up with anger, although behind that flicker of defiance, uncertainty loomed close. "I'm not asking you to put your life on the line." She pointed. "You should go. I'll wait for the boat myself."

"I'm not going anywhere, Juni." Sweat poured down my neck. While my lower half shivered, my upper body dripped with cold sweat.

An overpowering urge to take Juni into my arms swept through me, mainly to help ease her trembling. Her teeth chattered, although any sound was inaudible against the roar of the furious downpour, and I could see her mouth quivering.

Just as I reached toward her, we heard an engine.

Our heads turned sharply and nearly banged into each other. I smiled, and so did Juni, whose body, like mine, collapsed with relief.

A FEW HOURS LATER

Although my eyes had a mind of their own, I had to look anywhere but at Juni's saturated cotton dress, with those delectable curves provoking dirty thoughts.

"What do you mean you have no other rooms?" she demanded.

For a hippie, Juni was fiery. But then, I hadn't really met any other hippies in my life, so my opinion was based on that clichéd notion of someone who chanted "om" in the mornings and greeted people with "Peace, man."

That did not fit Juni at all.

"Sorry ma'am, but with the floods and all, we're all booked out."

I stood by fighting a grin. The bad boy in me extracted pleasure from watching Juni spit venom, as disrespectful as garnering entertainment from a person's frustration was.

Gripping at the counter and looking annoyed, Juni rolled her eyes.

The concierge looked over at me with a shrug. Somewhere behind those spectacles, I read, "You're one hell of a lucky son of a bitch. She's going to have to bunk up with you." At least, that's what I would have thought.

"Juni, it's all good. My suite's large enough to house a family."

She let out a long, resigned breath. "I have little choice." She regarded the man behind the reception desk again. "Are you sure the roads are flooded?"

"You won't be going anywhere. There's also more rain on the way."

Juni looked at me. Her expressive rosebud lips formed a tight line. "Lead the way, then."

The elevator dropped us right into the room I'd booked for a couple of nights, which was fortuitous. I could have driven back downtown, but having an early call, I'd decided to stay there instead.

I made way for Juni to enter.

"Freaking hell, this is rather lavish," she said, turning around in a circle. "It smells of synthetic perfumes." She scrunched her face. "This room's awash with carcinogens."

I shrugged. "There's not much I can do about that right now. Why don't you get out of those wet clothes and have a hot shower? I'll arrange for some dry clothes."

She stood there crossing her arms, which only made her large chest bigger, which I had to work overtime not to ogle.

"Where are you going to find those?"

I grinned. "Oh… I have my ways."

She studied me for a moment, her eyes narrowing slightly.

"Now what?" I asked, getting closer and closer to wanting to place her over my knees and sink my hand onto her curvy ass for a little spank. Not that BDSM floated my boat. But Juni's defiance and ridiculous stubbornness pushed a few buttons. I had to keep biting my tongue to avoid reacting.

The angel came through, occasionally. Especially as we had sat on the boat after being rescued. Juni's eyes had pooled with tears, as she thanked me for saving her. Taking her hand and squeezing it gently, I had to fight the urge to hold her in my arms and kiss her. Although we'd been through a trial together, it hardly seemed appropriate. Having gotten that out of her system, Juni had then pleaded with the exhausted driver to drop her home. He explained more than once that their services were stretched to the limits, and he had to follow orders by transporting people to the closest safe ground.

"I hope you're not going to try and seduce me."

I'd just turned away when my head did a sharp double take. "What?"

She knitted her slender fingers and stared down at her hands.

"That's not my style, Juni. I mean, you're a beautiful girl. But I'd never try and force myself on you. I've never had to resort to forcing myself on any woman." An edge sharpened my tone.

"Now you're bragging again."

"Again?" I tilted my head.

She rolled her eyes. "How goddamn predictable you men are."

I sighed. "You're pretty predictable yourself, Juni. And in any case, I'm not that desperate that I would take advantage of you."

Her forehead creased. "But you only just said I was…"

"Beautiful," I interjected. "You are, but I need more than that to seduce someone."

I left her hanging and headed for the bathroom to run water. Once the temperature was right, I strolled back out and said, "The shower's nice and hot."

As Juni headed to the bathroom, I asked, "What size are you?"

Her brow lowered. "That's kind of personal."

"Is it?" I shrugged it off. "Then I promise not to tell anyone."

"Now you're making fun of me."

I studied her for a moment and turned away. "Whatever." I went into the bedroom.

She followed me in, wearing a questioning frown. I could see Juni was out of her comfort zone. I should have been more sympathetic, given that some women were sensitive about their dress size.

I opened up my luggage and handed her a T-shirt. “You need to get out of those clothes. I can arrange to have them washed and dried.”

“Why did you want my size?”

“I was going to ring the staff to pick up some items for you.”

“Promise you won’t poke fun at me if I tell you?” she asked.

“Are we talking about dress size or something more personal here?”

“A woman’s size is personal.”

“As you’ve already said.” I paused, having lost my train of thought, mainly because Juni stretched my T-shirt against her considerable chest to see if it would fit. “To be honest, I don’t know the difference between a size eight or sixteen.”

“One is fat; the other is skinny,” she replied dryly.

“You’re neither of those.”

“I’m a size fourteen.”

I nodded. “Good.”

“Which is fat,” she replied.

Her defensiveness surprised me, given that I wouldn’t have taken her for someone who cared about her weight.

“That’s bullshit,” I said, picking up the receiver.

JUNI

"Ah..." exhaled from my lips. My tense, cold flesh rippled with delight as hot water cascaded over me. Suddenly life felt good again. I picked up the body wash, and although I couldn't read the ingredients, I sniffed it and detected essential oils. I pumped the jasmine-scented liquid onto a sea sponge and sighed with approval as foam slid over my thawing flesh. I pumped some shampoo onto my palm and massaged it into my hair. For some reason, I saw Sam's thick dark waves that sat messily on his handsome head.

Sam had stayed.

Holding me up effortlessly, he'd dropped the funny-guy act. Instead, his eyes had shone with concern for me, a hostile stranger.

If that dinghy hadn't arrived, we might have even died together.

First a devil, then a flirt, and finally a hero. That was Sam. And I couldn't hate him anymore. Not that I had ever really hated him. Who could with those sweet, mischievous eyes smiling back?

As I massaged shampoo vigorously through my hair, a guilty knot formed in my belly. I'd done nothing but bicker with him. *He must think I'm an ungrateful bitch.*

Stepping out of the large glass cubicle, I selected a thick, warm bath towel from the heated towel rack. My body melted into its warmth as I rubbed myself dry.

Feeling revived and refreshed, I appreciated the comfort that luxury brought. Although my home life was anything but luxurious, I didn't crave that kind of manicured opulence, as I had everything I needed in life. In any case, my family was wealthy. They hadn't designed it that way. It had just happened.

Having removed his shirt and oozing sex, Sam sipped from a bottle of water, the sinews in his forearms flexing as he clasped the bottle. Standing by the tall windows, he looked out over the balcony. His thick dark hair had been combed back away from his handsome face. And as he turned to set his bottle down, I copped an eyeful of a torso that could have been carved by Michelangelo.

He looked at me and smiled so sweetly, that I almost wanted to drop my don't-come-near-me-or-I'll-scream act.

Running his hands over his hair, he said, "Hope everything was to your liking."

"It was, thank you. You have good taste in body wash and shampoo. Organic and essential oils."

"I wouldn't dream of anything else." As always, his twinkling eyes tickled my senses. "Where I can manage it, all my products are organic and natural."

My eyebrows squeezed in tight. "They are?"

He laughed. "You're not the only one who's concerned about chemicals and their effect on us and the environment." I was about to respond, but he distracted me by pointing at the sofa. "There are some things for you to change into."

My eyes widened. "My God, where did all these come from?"

"There's a boutique connected to the hotel."

"You bought all of these in fifteen minutes?"

"I didn't. One of the staff brought them up."

I picked up a pair of jeans that I wouldn't be seen dead in. "I hate denim."

He shrugged. "I just told her to pick up some clothes for a young woman sized fourteen."

"I'm not that young," I said.

"Whatever." He headed for the bathroom. "I'm having a shower."

Sam's dismissive tone, although justified, made me shrink. I really needed to start showing some gratitude.

I removed the wet battery charger from my backpack along with all the other sodden items, including my sketchpad with all my recently doodled designs and laid them on my bath towel. I dried the charger before plugging it into a socket.

I needed to call my parents as soon as possible.

My attention returned to a pink, slinky dress that slithered over my fingers as I lifted it. Predictably, it was so synthetic that one could've melted it down to make a car tire. Studying it as a young girl would her first pair of crystal slippers, I walked into the bedroom and held it up against my body. Peering into the mirror, I could see the color suited my pale features.

I placed the dress on a chair and distractedly looked around the very large bedroom, which housed a bed that could comfortably sleep four. Despite the room's lack of ornament, an all-encompassing view dominated. The room lived in the sky, it seemed. Grayish cloud mass drifted along in the foreground of a black, inscrutable sky. Even with that impenetrable darkness before me, after everything we'd been through, I felt safe.

I thought about the rescue mission, which had involved Sam pulling the chain away from my waist carefully as John, our rescuer, cut into it, taking care not to hurt me, but hurrying as the water reached my shoulders. All in all, it was the most danger I'd ever been in. God knows what I would've done had Sam not been there. Devil or not, he had saved my life. But I might not have lost that key were he not there, given how much he distracted me.

But that was now pointless speculation because Sam had risked his life for me.

Was there another bedroom somewhere? I wondered, returning to the couch in order to check out the other bits and pieces. I picked up a slinky nightie that looked more like a negligee. My jaw dropped as I studied the underwear: a tiny piece of fabric, destined to stretch over my big ass, dangled from my fingers.

Sam came out with a towel wrapped around his waist. My body, with a mind of its own, let out a silent sigh of approval. How could it not? I was female after all.

He stood before me with that golden torso and looked at the panties dangling from my hand. "Let me guess, too synthetic?"

"Yes… and too small."

He studied me for a moment with a hint of a grin. "It's all the rage."

I rolled my eyes. And then, goodness knows why, but my eyes settled on his thigh, where a slight tenting took place. Sam quickly turned away to hide what looked like a very big hard-on, obviously aroused by the slinky lingerie that remained limp in my hand.

Inflamed in a way that I couldn't understand, I wasn't immune to this sudden heat between us either. While my head told me that Sam wasn't my type, my body had other ideas. Taking a deep breath, I hoped that he wouldn't notice my burning cheeks.

SAM

I would have grumbled through every brainless reality show inflicted on humankind just to see Juni in those small pieces of fabric. Of course, they would never have been my choice, at least not for someone like Juni, not because she had that organic-cotton-only vibe about her but because we'd only just met. I'd never shopped for lingerie before, although not from the lack of desire, given my fetish for lace, especially lace stretched over feminine curves. I couldn't decide whether to thank or reprimand the person responsible for buying them.

Swearing at myself under my breath for being so damn horny, I even considered taking a cold shower, which would have seemed crazy since I'd only just had one. This was hardly the time to be aroused. But hell, I was a man. Besides, it had been a while since I'd touched a woman, so my appendage did what any hot-blooded, self-respecting dick would do: it sprang to attention.

I quickly left Juni to make her choices and went into the bedroom to change. I'd never been shy around women before. But then, Juni wasn't just any woman. And she had me figured all wrong. I wasn't that money-hungry land clearer she kept blustering on about.

Buttoning up my shirt, I almost felt normal again, especially after having been soaked to the skin. The day's events kept flashing in my mind. While the water had risen around us and we waited for help, thoughts had swept through me, arriving as thick and fast as the rain itself. At first, harnessing the confidence a privileged life brings, I had believed that everything would be fine. But when the water level reached my belly and Juni's shoulders, my heart had started to race. I'd never been exposed to that kind of danger before. While Juni's hand had squeezed the life out of mine, all I could think of was love and how I'd never been in love before, which really surprised me upon reflection, because I hadn't exactly given love much thought in my life. If anything, I didn't expect it would happen to me. A part of me thought perhaps I'd become a recluse or a raging bachelor who drank too much and dated every pretty girl in town. The thought of this, on a deeper level, felt like junk food—enjoyable at first but sickening by the end.

"Are you dressed? Can I enter?" I asked.

After she responded with a "yes," I entered the living room.

When I saw Juni standing in front of the mirrored wall, her head looking over her shoulder as she studied her curvy butt, a silent gasp left me. I had to squeeze my lips tight to stop the saliva from exiting. I thought I'd stopped drooling twenty-five years ago.

She turned, and her eyes wandered over my body. "You look different in casual gear."

I smoothed down my green shirt, and a rare streak of self-consciousness cast its shadow over me. Another new experience. Normally, I didn't really give a shit about my clothes, opting for comfort over fashion, but that hint of a smirk on Juni's pretty face did make me wonder. "You don't approve?" I asked.

"It's not my place to approve or disapprove. Green's a favorite of mine, though."

I nodded slowly. "Ah… yes. That makes sense for a tree hugger."

"I do other things too. I don't just sit under trees," she said with enough feistiness to make my lips curl.

"Is that so, Juniper?"

She pulled at the body-hugging pink dress that had a nice low cut around the bustline, enabling her considerable cleavage to provoke me.

I made a mental note to tip the buyer.

"This is a bit revealing," she said, trying to lift the dress to cover her protruding flesh that had my lower regions doing gymnastics.

"You'd look great in anything, Juniper," I said.

She twisted her head again to check that ass, which had already launched a thousand fantasies.

"It doesn't look big," I said with a hint of a smile.

Juni turned sharply, and we locked eyes for what seemed a long time. I wasn't going anywhere.

"Was I being inappropriate?" I asked.

"Mm… maybe," she said almost to herself as she continued to pull at the dress.

I removed a credit card from my wallet and offered it to Juni. "Hey, why don't you go down and select some clothes that you'd prefer to wear. Mind you, I'm not sure if they stock organic cotton." The last bit I uttered quietly, but a grin still found its way onto my face.

Her eyebrows squeezed tightly. I waited for another blasting, but then her face relaxed. "I do prefer cotton, but this is kind of nice."

"It's more than nice. It looks spectacular, and pink really suits you."

She nodded, and a gentle smile touched her.

As our eyes held again, she looked away first, which had become the normal pattern between us. Where beauty was concerned, I stood my ground. Life was too short to rob my eyes of someone as gorgeous as Juni.

Juni checked her charging phone and unplugged it. "I have to call my parents."

"You sure do. You could have used mine, earlier. They'll be worried sick, won't they?"

She nodded while scrolling down the screen. "I can't remember the number. They've only recently had it changed."

"Oh," I said, leaving to give her some privacy.

"Right then. Food. I must eat. How would you like to do this?" I asked.

Shrugging, she gazed up at me almost submissively. "Whatever... only..."

"Let me guess, you're a vegetarian and insist I don't eat meat around you?"

"Ha?" She shook her head. "Now why would you think that?"

"Well... I just thought...going on..." My stammering only added to how stupid I sounded.

"Just because I was sitting under a tree..."

"Chained to a tree," I interjected with a raised brow.

"You think I'm some kind of hippie?"

"One need not be a hippie to be a vegetarian," I added. Juni kept glaring at me. "Sorry if I've hit a raw nerve there. And anyway, I don't have a problem with you being a hippie."

"Well, thank you, Mr. Corporate-Slash-and-Burn."

I held my hands up in self-defense. "I just wrongly assumed you were vegetarian, that's all." I took a deep breath and headed for the fridge to grab a beer.

Pâté, Camembert cheese, and ham smiled back at me, making my stomach rumble. One by one, I placed the packages on the island in the kitchen.

Twisting the cap off a locally brewed beer, I took a thirsty gulp. "Can I offer you anything?" I asked.

She pointed to the beer in my hand. "I'll have one of those too if you have enough."

I took care not to show surprise, even though it was not what I expected.

"I've got plenty." I smiled sweetly. "I bought a whole carton of it from a local brewery."

I shook my head. "Why that frown, Juni?"

"You don't strike me as a man who supports local breweries."

"What? Evil developers aren't meant to like beer?" I twisted off another cap and grabbed a glass.

"No glass. I'll drink it from the bottle, thanks. My dad brews his own beer."

I wiped my lips. "Really? What's the label? It's one of my passions, you know, going to boutique breweries and buying local." Juni's head pushed back. "I'm a surprising man in many ways."

"I'm sure you are."

Her dry tone, bordering on sarcasm, wasn't lost on me, but instead of defending myself, I chuckled. I was having too much fun.

JUNI

"My dad sells his beer at the local farmers market. It's called Haight Ash Berry Ale."

Once again, Sam pulled that puzzled amused expression that seemed permanently etched on his tanned features. "Where have I heard that name before?"

"My grandparents named my dad and his twin Haight and Ash. Hence that label. It's really popular and sells well."

"Your father's name is Hate?"

I laughed at his wide-eyed expression. "Yeah… it's kind of weird, I know. Dad prefers Harry. He tried to pronounce it like 'height' instead. But I guess everyone knows about that area in San Francisco, which is an important part of sixties hippie folklore."

"So let me guess, your grandfather was a hippie."

"Yep. Sure was. He's still alive and doing well. He lives in a commune."

"With nine wives?" He cocked his head slightly, and that grin that he wore too well made his eyes flicker with humor.

I could do little else but smile. "Ha ha ha. He's happily married, thank you very much."

"That's sweet."

"To a man," I said, falling onto the soft leather couch.

"Oh…" He nodded pensively. "Was your father adopted?"

I shook my head. "Nope. After Grandma died, he ended up with Ginsberg."

"Allen Ginsberg?" He ran his hands through his thick wave of dark hair.

"He's dead," I said.

"I know that."

I stared at Sam, trying to figure him out.

"Why are you staring at me like that, Juni?" he asked yet again.

"You've heard of the Beat poet, Allen Ginsberg?"

He sauntered over to the kitchen, where he removed the wrapper from the Camembert cheese and placed it on a plate. "I have, Juni. I majored in twentieth-century American literature."

If Sam hoped to impress me, he had. "Really? What was your favorite book?" I decided to test him, anyway.

"Now that's not so easy to answer." He paused to reflect. "I enjoyed *Catcher in the Rye* and *To Kill a Mockingbird…* But I really love Steinbeck. I also have a soft spot for Edgar Allan Poe."

"He's not twentieth century, though," I challenged, hiding my ignorance because I hadn't heard of Steinbeck.

"No…true… But just because I majored in modern literature doesn't mean I haven't read the classics." He held up a plate with cheese and pâté. "Here are some snacks." Sam took out a packet of rice crackers and poured the contents into a bowl.

He placed everything on the table, and gesturing, he said, "Why don't you sit and eat while we discuss what could be a complex subject."

His dry tone made me giggle. "I'm not that hard to please."

"We are talking about food?" His eyebrow arched.

I couldn't decide whether I wanted to slap or kiss him. Both, I thought.

I threw him a smirk and took to a cracker with creamy cheese like someone who hadn't eaten for a week. It slithered down my throat, and I sighed with approval.

"That good, eh?" Sam sat across the table and joined me.

We devoured the wheel of creamy cheese silently. It was a comfortable silence, interrupted only by the sound of crunching and the occasional smile and locking of eyes.

It should have felt uncomfortable, but in reality, I felt quite at ease, and the novelty of lolling about in an opulent penthouse wasn't lost on me. That was after I got over the synthetic fragrances hijacking my nasal passages.

"You do realize this place is awash with so many chemicals it could make you sterile," I said. When it came to editing thoughts, I'd missed that gene.

Sam looked at me with amused wonder. "I'll make a note next time I stay in a hotel to demand only essential oils."

"That's a really good plan. I'm only thinking of your health here."

"Well, thank you, ma'am."

I had to laugh at his drawl.

"So, Juniper… Dinner?"

"Call me Juni." I pointed at the window. "We won't be able to leave because the streets are flooded."

"That's true." Sam rose and headed for the phone. He lifted the receiver. "Hi. Just calling to check what's on the menu?" He nodded. "Right. Sure. I thought that much. I'll get back to you in a moment."

Sam said, "There's a limited menu because the flood's prevented deliveries. They're going to have to fly in supplies."

"Shit. This could turn into a dystopian nightmare where we end up eating each other," I said, creeping myself out more than anything.

Sam shook his head. "I think you've been watching too many movies."

"I don't have a TV," I said.

"Then… well…." He looked at me. "Really?"

"Yeah. My parents wouldn't let us watch TV, and I've gotten used to it."

"But you have internet, don't you?"

"I do," I said.

"YouTube?"

I nodded guiltily. "Don't tell my dad."

He licked his finger and held it in the air. “Promise.” He held my gaze again. “There’s chicken, salad, chips, roast veggies. What would you like? It’s room service only, I’m afraid. The restaurant downstairs is blocked off with sandbags.”

I stared out the window again. “It has that end-of-the-world look about it.”

“You have a dramatic take on things, for a…”

“For a what?” I cut in.

“An earth angel.” His eyes plowed into mine, and I felt my cheeks fire up.

“I expected you to call me a hippie,” I said.

“You’re too individual for that,” he said, settling down at the table.

“I’ll take that as a compliment,” I said playing with my fingers.

“You should,” he said.

SAM

"Is it cage-free?" she asked.

I was at the fridge debating whether to open the chardonnay or another beer when I turned to stare at Juni with a scrunched forehead, which was getting a good work-out around her. "The chicken, you mean?"

"Yeah."

"I didn't ask." I scratched my head. "So, you won't have any if it's not?"

She bit into her cheek. I could see Juni was seriously challenged by her staunch beliefs in clean living. "Just ask them. And maybe ask if they know where it was farmed."

"Are you serious?" I looked for signs of humor, but Juni's straight face contradicted that.

"Well, they pump hormones and antibiotics into chickens, and I for one want to have healthy babies."

Now it was my turn to bite into my cheek. "Okay. Good to know you aspire to a big family. The planet will appreciate that." My tone was so dry my palate stuck to my tongue.

"You're making fun of my views. Views"—she pointed—"that are about creating a healthier environment."

I held my hands up in self-defense. "Okay, I get it." I strode over to the phone and steadied my voice. "Hey, can you tell me where the chicken comes from?"

After a moment of justified silence, the operator uttered, "Excuse me?"

"Can you ask the kitchen staff where they source their chickens, please?" Even though my tone was constrained, I nodded reassuringly to Juni, who reflected the kind of encouragement one gave someone before jumping into rough waters to save an otter.

"One moment, please," he said.

I heard mumbles in the background. "Sorry for keeping you waiting. Ah… the person who buys the supplies isn't in. Although the chef assures me that it's quality meat, just like all the produce supplied to the hotel."

"Okay. Thanks."

"Are you still wishing to place an order?"

"Just one moment." I set down the receiver and approached Juni, who was drying objects she'd removed from her backpack with a towel, including a strange furry thing that resembled a rodent.

Noticing Juni rubbing the furry thing, I asked, "What's that?"

She looked up, and her face lit up like a child's. Again, I lost my train of thought. Juni seemed so sweet and innocent, which I was sure she wasn't. Seeing her in that dress had all kinds of fantasies bubbling away. Like having her against a wall with my hands smothering those curves while ravaging that smirk off her lips.

"That's Elwood, my rabbit. He's my lucky charm. My great-grandfather, a fighter pilot, made him."

She lifted the furry thing, which still looked more like a drowned rat.

"I see." I nodded slowly. "They don't know where the chicken's from. Do you want me to order just fries and veggies, salad?"

She thought about it for a moment. "No. I'm good."

"So, is that a yes or a no?" I asked.

"I'll have whatever you're having," she replied with a sweet smile.

I nodded.

After I ordered, I joined Juni on the balcony. The street below, normally a bustling shopping strip, resembled a somber, murky river.

We stood there silently watching boats buzzing up and down.

"It's so surreal. It really does resemble something dystopian," said Juni.

"You seem engrossed in the doom and gloom, Juniper."

She turned and studied me for a moment as if trying to read me properly. She pointed to the sky. "It's bleak up there."

"It is. But it will clear. And then there'll be sunshine, pretty flowers, and the beach."

"Is that your life?" she asked.

I shrugged. "I do have a fondness for summer."

"I bet you've got a big beach house somewhere," she said.

"Uh-huh. In Malibu."

"Let me guess." Juni held her chin. "A big modern white box. All windows, clean lines, and stainless-steel appliances."

"Nope. It's classic Italianate, cluttered with collectibles, a garden that's been there for over a hundred years, and charming cobbled steps down to the beach."

"Your own private beach, I suppose," she said.

"Yes. But you're welcome to stay," I said with a raised eyebrow. Her mouth opened to respond when I added, "And you can even bring Elwood, and your boyfriend if you like."

She fought off a smile. "I don't have a boyfriend, as you already know."

"Just playing, Juniper." Once again, we locked eyes. "The food shouldn't take long, I hope."

"Great. I'm starving," she said, checking out some wet items lying on towels.

"I can get the staff to dry those for you if you like," I said.

"No need."

I returned to the drenched ball of fur. "What about Elwood?"

"Oh, he's okay." Juni asked, "Why are you looking at me like that?"

"How?"

"I don't know, as if you're trying to figure me out."

"I am. I mean, why were you stroking your good-luck charm?"

Juni shrugged. "I asked him to make it stop raining."

"Does he normally grant your wishes?"

"He does."

Juni's messy bun, which sat on top of her head, had started to sag. Even though it shouldn't have, it added to her sexiness. I was so spellbound that I jumped when my cell buzzed.

JUNI

Dressed in cream-colored pants that showed off his muscular thighs, Sam had the easygoing stride of a male model combined with a hint of swagger, which could have easily placed him on a sporting field.

I stared down dejectedly at the soggy drawing pad with my latest designs and headed into the bathroom to dry them with the hairdryer. I'd come up with a nice reversible skirt that could turn into a wraparound dress and more, with one piece of fabric creating four wearable items. I envisaged it being great for traveling. I'd already been selling a blouse I'd created from hemp and cotton blend online. The orders had banked up. The thought of that made my shoulders tense. I had no idea how I'd manage. When I'd started selling my clothes, I never expected that level of interest. Initially, I was just happy to sell at the local artisans' market, but that soon grew when some of my customers showed off my creations on Facebook.

A knock came at the door. I waited for a moment, but Sam was on his phone in the other room, so I answered it myself. A tantalizing aroma teased my nose as I stared down at the trolley carrying our dinner.

"Where would you like this, ma'am?" the man asked, wheeling in the feast.

"Ah… here is fine, thanks," I said.

Sam sauntered back in and rubbed his hands together. “Great. I’m starved.”

He tipped the waiter, who left with a big smile.

Sam turned to me. “Would you like some wine with that? I have a nice Chardonnay or a Merlot?”

“Chardonnay, thanks,” I replied.

Pointing at the table, Sam said, “Just sit wherever you want.”

When I reached to take the plates off the trolley, Sam stopped me. “I’ll do that. Just sit and relax.”

After the wine was poured, Sam carved up the chicken. “Leg or breast?” He tilted his head.

“I’m easy,” I said. “Which would you prefer?” Although it was unintended, that question suddenly had a sexual connotation, probably due to Sam, and that knowing grin he wore too well.

“I like both. But if I had to choose, I suppose the breast.”

“We are talking about the chicken?” I asked.

“But of course. What else did you think I meant?” He cocked his head.

I rolled my eyes. But as the delicious aroma wafted up, eating became my sole interest.

The chicken was so delicious, I polished the plate.

“I wouldn’t have taken you for a carnivore.” Sam wiped his lips with a cloth napkin.

“I’m what’s known as an omnivore,” I replied.

“And so am I. There’s not much I won’t eat.”

“Really? Snails, frog’s legs?” I challenged.

“I ate those when I was in Spain and France.”

“You’ve traveled?”

“I have.” Sam lifted the bottle of wine. “Refill?”

Although I felt tipsy, I nodded. The novelty of the experience justified relaxing my normal moderate approach to alcohol.

“And you?” Sam asked.

I shook my head. "Not yet. I'd love to, though. I'd love to go to Italy and France. I'm keen on fashion design." I might as well have said I slew dragons. Shaking my head, I asked, "Why that puzzled look?"

"For someone who hates synthetic fabric, like that pretty dress you're wearing…" He drifted off as his eyes plowed into mine again.

Breaking away from his stare, I asked, "You were saying?"

"Sorry. You're looking very beautiful at the moment with your hair down, and pink's really your color."

"Thanks for the compliment, Sam. But you're not my type."

"So you've said. I wasn't hitting on you." His tone cooled. "And in any case, perhaps you're not my type."

"Out of curiosity, what is your type?" I tilted my head with a challenging grin.

He rose and ambled over to the balcony, where he stood by the window, watching rain blur the view.

"I like women that are cultured and intelligent."

"Right, let me guess… Long-legged beauties that spend most of their time in spas and museums?"

He chuckled at my mocking tone. "Nope. I'm rather partial to petite, curvy girls that give as good as they get." He stared me square in the face as if to make a point.

"That doesn't sound very refined to me," I said rather dismissively, which was a ruse because, on a deeper level, I smiled.

Dusk had arrived. On the horizon, choppy waves from the bay reminded me that it was a moving body of water and not an extension of the sky.

Sam turned to look at me again. "Tell me more about the clothes you design."

"I'm working with hemp and cotton blends and use natural dyes."

"You do your own sewing too?" he asked.

I nodded.

"That's very creative. Did you major in design?" he asked, sitting down at the table again.

I shook my head while biting into a nail. It was a moot point. Being self-taught, I didn't think I belonged to that hallowed world of designers. "I was homeschooled."

Boyish wonder painted Sam's face. "Really? Now that's fascinating. So you taught yourself to design and sew?"

The way his eyes shone with admiration, I might as well have invented the wheel, which made my lips curl into a tight smile. I nodded. "I started with dolls' clothes when I was little. Then Dad bartered for a sewing machine from the neighbors, and I went from there."

"Your family had to barter?" he asked.

"Hey… it wasn't like that. My dad's super rich. Ridiculously so."

Sam's forehead lowered sharply. "Okay. Well, that's good, I suppose."

"He calls himself an accidental billionaire."

Sam laughed. "That's novel. Although I'm sure a few lottery winners could be known as that."

"Mom and Dad have always been into self-sufficiency. Everything we ate we grew. Born largely out of my dad's hatred for the capitalist system he bartered."

"Then he's a communist?"

"No. He doesn't go for that either. Dad will rant on and on about how Russia made a mess of communism and that Karl Marx was full of bullshit."

What started as a smile turned into an infectious belly laugh. Sam said, "I'm dying to meet him."

Sam would have been the devil incarnate in my father's eyes, but I kept that to myself.

"But now the anti-capitalist's a billionaire." Sam's amusement at my eccentric father's expense was infectious instead of grating. I had to bite my lips to not giggle.

I shrugged. "I know it's strange."

"He's not still bartering though, is he?"

"He is."

"But why?" Sam asked.

"He just loves the game. Dad's a classic wheeler and dealer. In more ways than one."

"But then, why are you still sewing on an old machine? And why aren't you in Paris following that dream?"

"Dad wants me to do things organically. Learn the business from the ground up. I sell my creations at the artisans' market here, and during the day, I sew."

"But you could scale up. I mean, you could set up a warehouse and employ staff."

"Yeah, I know." I bit into another nail.

Studying me for a moment, Sam relaxed his tone. "You seem a little stressed."

"I am." A sigh of frustration exited my mouth. "I've taken so many orders and have fallen seriously behind." My lips wobbled as I tried to suppress tears.

"Hey." Sam took my hand and leaned over. "It's okay. The rain will stop soon. We've still got the internet. Why don't you send your customers a note of apology? Or if you like, I can help you with refunds. That way you can set yourself up properly before going into a full-scale operation."

Our eyes locked, and a tear slid down my cheek. I quickly wiped it with my finger. "Thanks. That's very generous. I haven't spent their money. It's still sitting in PayPal. I think I'll do just that. It would at least help me relax."

"Let's draft a letter explaining the circumstances and give them the option to either wait a few weeks or accept a refund. It's important for your reputation that you act professionally and honestly."

I leaned my chin down on my tented fingers. "That's sound advice. And I love what I do."

SAM

"There," I said, closing my laptop. "All done."

Juni leaned back on the chair. Her bun was about to collapse. She looked like she'd been in a windstorm as she scratched at her tummy and shifted about.

"Are you okay?"

Tugging at her clingy dress, Juni said, "This is itching the hell out of me. I knew I'd grow to hate it."

I rose and picked up the receiver. "Can you find out if the clothes sent to be washed and dried are ready yet, please?"

"Immediately, sir."

Replacing the receiver, I looked over at Juni with a reassuring smile.

It felt as though we'd known each other longer than six hours. Juni made me feel at ease. Even though the thought of having to convince my father not to flatten that land was anything but relaxing, especially now that I'd promised Juni I'd do my utmost to hold off felling Oscar.

My cell buzzed, and speak of the devil, my dad's stern face flashed on my screen, setting off a spasm in my neck.

"Hey," I said, taking the call to the bedroom.

"Your mother was expecting you for dinner. And Marie's here waiting."

"It's a river out here. I'm not going to be able to make it."

"We could arrange a boat for you," he said.

I thought about the boat ride with Juni and how she'd huddled close, with her natural fragrance doing inappropriate things to me.

A dinner party with a bunch of filthy rich snobs—one of which, if my father had any say, was to be my wife—could wait.

"Not necessary. Just apologize to Marie on my behalf."

"You should at least do that, Sam. For Christ's sake." His voice, gruff from years of cigars and bourbon, scraped at me.

"Put her on, then," I said, taking a deep breath.

"That tree's coming down as soon as the land drains. I hope that blonde greenie hasn't gotten into your ear or dick."

I winced at my father's natural crassness. "How do you know what she looks like?"

"It's all over the news: an image of a drenched, chubby girl nearly sitting on top of you in a boat. Is she there with you at that hotel?"

My mother had jumped on the phone. "Darling, are you okay? I was hoping you'd come to see us."

I sighed. "I know. Just convey my apologies."

"Who's that girl? Is she staying with you?"

"She is. But only because there are no other rooms available."

I thought about my father's rude comment. "And she's not fat, by the way."

"Who said that?" she asked.

"He just did. Look, Mom, I have to go."

"Now listen, Sam." My father seized the phone. "That tree's coming down. ASAP."

"So, you keep saying. What about if I pay him out?" I asked.

"Are you kidding me? It would be my money. And I won't allow it."

"I've got my own stash."

"Over my dead body. That's prime land there."

"We'll talk about it tomorrow," I said, coldly. His bossy tone made my fists tighten.

"What will I tell Marie? She was here when the news bulletin came up. You were looking pretty cozy with that chubby blonde."

"She's *not* chubby," I snapped.

"Marie's joining this family if I have to drag you down that aisle."

"Don't tell me what to do." I poked violently at the end button.

I rubbed my neck. The conversation would have descended into my father threatening to cut me out of the Chalmer fortune. I didn't really care. I had enough to keep the fire of life burning away for probably more than one's natural lifetime.

A deep breath shot out of my mouth. I remained there for a moment, composing myself. Marie Carter. Oh, God. I could have done worse in that she was a stunner, but she was also a control freak and empty-headed. I recalled her insisting on that first date that I ditch the blue silk shirt I'd picked up in Paris.

I headed to the bar for a stiff bourbon.

Juni, who had changed back into her own dress, looked up at me and shook her head. "You look like you've been in combat with a lion."

An ironic chuckle tickled my throat. "How did you guess?" I gulped back a swig and held up the bottle. "Can I offer you one?"

She shook her head. "Your neck's gone all red. You sure look ruffled."

"I've just been talking to my ball-crushing father."

A slow smile turned into a giggle. "He jumps up and down on your collection of balls at home?"

I scratched my head. "Um… no." I kept looking at her, trying to work out if she really thought that. "It's just a figure of speech, Juni. Excuse me for being coarse."

"Hey, it's cool. I got it the first time. Just making fun."

"I see you've changed back."

Juni touched her floral skirt. "It's nice and clean. Although it stinks."

"Really?"

"That horrible washing powder fragrance. I can't get it out of my nose."

Her green eyes widened, something she did when ranting about some uncontrollable problem in the world. Instead of it annoying me, I wanted to stroke her arm and offer to fix it. Even if it required superhero strength.

"Mm… I'm sorry," was the best I could offer. "I prefer you in that skirt. It's more you."

"Really?" Her eyes narrowed slightly. "You're just saying that to be nice."

"No. I'm serious. I like women in floral dresses."

"This is a skirt," she corrected. "I thought you'd go for more revealing choices."

"You don't know me," I said, moving over to the glass doors that opened out onto the balcony. Night had fallen and rain continued to splash against the glass.

She smiled tightly and continued to gaze at me as if trying to figure me out again. "I take it you don't get on with your dad?"

I nodded slowly and let out a frustrated sigh.

"Is he forcing you to clear our land?"

"Juni, it's not your land." I bit my lip. This was not a discussion I wanted to have.

"Last time I spoke to my father, he said it was ours."

"Nothing's going to happen for a while, at least. So can we not talk about this?"

"Your father's calling the shots, isn't he?"

"You could say that. I'm the 'son' in Chalmer and Son."

"Charmer." Juni giggled. "How apt."

"That's Chalmer with an l," I corrected.

She fell back onto the couch. I wanted to join her and stare into those big playful eyes while stroking her milky white arms teasingly close to those swelling breasts.

"I'm not one of those." I sat down at the other end of the three-seater red leather sofa, leaving one cushion between us.

She turned to face me squarely. "I disagree. You are a charmer."

"How?" I opened out my hands. "In my book, being a charmer is a euphemism for a sleaze, which I am not."

"I meant it as a compliment, Sam. Otherwise, I would've insisted on sleeping in the hotel's store cupboard."

I laughed. "How uncomfortable: broom handles poking into you and buckets falling on your head."

She giggled before reverting to seriousness. "So why do you have to work for your father?"

Was I ready for a psychology session? I'd had enough of paying a bespectacled professional whose insights did nothing to unravel the confusion about me and my life plan.

"He wants to mold me into himself. His father did it before him. Chalmer and Son has been a company for two hundred years. They built those hotels by the railway line."

"Those heritage buildings in old Oakland?" Juni asked.

I nodded. A streak of pride touched me because I loved those buildings too. They were a golden mark on the Chalmer name, a true achievement in my book.

"I think my mom might have marched to save them from being demolished," she said.

I sniffed at the irony of it all. Having created buildings that people fought to save, Chalmer and Son were now in the business of demolishing them and building cheap condos.

It was a lightbulb moment for Juni, whose face lit up as if she'd discovered some profound meaning to a baffling issue. "I wonder how your forefathers would have felt knowing that you're now knocking things down."

"Juni, I imagine they felled an entire forest to build those pretty edifices that you now justifiably so admire."

"Mmm… I suppose you're right." She studied me for a long while. "So if you're not happy working for your father, what is it you really like to do?"

JUNI

Boy, I might have just asked Sam if he could recite the Bible cover to cover. It was a simple enough question, I thought. But judging by his guttural sigh, I'd entered a battlefield.

He rose from the sofa. "Can I get you anything. Water, wine, tequila?"

"Tequila? You've got that?" I asked.

I shrugged. "I caught up with a buddy last night, and he brought over a bottle."

"And you didn't finish it?"

"I'm not an alcoholic." He ruffled his hair, something Sam did regularly and unconsciously. And the more his dark waves stuck up, the more my attraction increased. Each time I looked at Sam, he showed another face. The trouble was, he was so fucking handsome, I couldn't look at him without breaking out into a heat rash.

"Scotty was in town for a conference, and we met up here. He'd been to Mexico and brought over a bottle." He headed for the kitchen area, and standing at the island, he lifted the crystal bottle. "Would you like a shot?"

"Okay. Although I do prefer margaritas."

That golden smile stretched across his tanned face. "Done. That's what we had. I'm not into straight shots, either."

He went about squeezing lemons and pouring salt on a plate.

"You have that cocktail barman look about you." I leaned on my elbow, watching him with amusement.

"Mm… maybe I missed my calling."

"You're, what, thirty or so. You could still do that." I figured he was a bit younger but decided to poke at his ego.

He looked up at me, and a grin touched his lips. "I'm actually forty-five. I've got a really good cosmetic surgeon."

"Bullshit," I said.

His gaze slid up to mine with a smirk before he returned to mixing our drinks. He looked up again. "Why are you staring at me like that?"

"I'm just interested in knowing how old you are," I said.

"I'm twenty-eight going on fifty."

"Huh?" My head pushed back. "You mean fifteen, don't you?"

He came toward me, careful not to spill my drink, which he set down on the glass-topped table by my side.

"Occasionally fifteen, but mostly fifty, I think."

"I wouldn't have taken you for an old soul," I said.

"I think I am. I'm heavily into retro. And history fascinates me."

"You're not a fan of modernity?" I asked. I was a serious retro freak myself, so we shared that in common.

"I'm not such a fan." He sipped his margarita. "Mm… that's quite good."

I took a sip, and the lemony liquor left a pleasant flavor behind as it burned down my windpipe. I licked the salt from my lips. "Mm… that is yummy. So, you were saying?"

He shrugged. "Just that I have a thing for antiques and books, and I'm not your typical…"

"Mogul," I finished.

Sam shook his head while continuing to drink pensively.

"Why choose this place to stay?" I asked.

"I wanted to stay in the old area in one of those hotels my great-grandfather built, but it was booked out. There's a convention in town, apparently."

Three margaritas later…

Holding onto my stomach, I laughed and laughed. We'd decided to play charades. Sam, the clown, pulled a Jim Carrey face and had me in stitches.

"*Mask*," I yelled out.

Defeated, Sam fell onto the couch. "For someone who grew up without a TV, how is it you know all these films?"

"I'm a cinema junkie. I go to the movies all the time."

Sam pulled that trying-to-figure-me-out frown again. "With your boyfriend, I suppose."

"I don't have one of those."

"So you said. I meant teenage sweetheart. You must've had one of those," he said, stretching his big arm along the ridge of the couch while crossing his legs.

"Did you have one?" I asked.

"Didn't everyone?" Responding to my smirk, he shook his head. "What?"

"You always get this red streak on your neck whenever you're thrown a sticky question."

Touching his neck, Sam said, "I didn't realize I was so transparent." After a pause to reflect, he added, "When I was young, I went out with my high school sweetheart for a while. That was before she decided to change sides."

I sat up. "She became a lesbian?"

He nodded wistfully. "Uh-huh."

"Then she didn't really cheat, I suppose."

"I obviously didn't perform glowingly on behalf of the male population though," said Sam, revealing an element of insecurity that I could never have imagined a man like him possessing.

Shaking my head vehemently, I said, "That's not true. She was obviously born that way." My eyes softened with sympathy. "You still did it though. Didn't you?"

He nodded slowly. "Unsurprisingly, Mel wasn't easy to excite." He raised a brow.

"That makes sense, considering. And in any case, women aren't as easy to excite as men are in that department."

He turned and faced me. A glimmer of a smile touched his fleshy lips. "And which department are we referring to?"

I recrossed my legs. "You know what I mean."

"No… Spell it out. I'm a man who's lost his way."

My brows squeezed tight. "You come across as confident to me."

"Why would you think that?" hc asked.

I looked for a hint of a smile, but his lips formed a tight line.

"You've got that kind of swagger that good-looking men have."

His head pushed back. "Swagger? What is that anyway?"

I got up and strutted about with my shoulders pulled back and my legs slightly apart. It was harder than I imagined, and Sam responded with a deep belly laugh that made me giggle too.

"You look ridiculous. I hope I don't get around like that. I look like a man who's lost his horse."

I fell onto the couch, laughing. "I channeled a cowboy."

He turned to face me. "You're crazy, Juniper Berry. And I think you're stereotyping me a little."

I held my hands up in self-defense. "Men do that all the time to women."

"I'm not like those men. I have nothing but respect for women."

"Mm…" was the best I could say to that.

His smile melted away. "Anyway, getting back to what you were saying earlier that women aren't as easy to please. I'm new to this. Enlighten me."

"I find that hard to believe."

"I'm not a player." He nodded as though to emphasize that point. "In any case, you're a very attractive woman. I'm sure you've had your share of male admirers."

Before I had time to edit my thoughts, I blurted, "I've never experienced it before."

Sam shifted his body around to face me fully. "Are we talking about the same thing here?"

"I think so." I squirmed. Although I was tipsy, actually probably more than tipsy, for some reason I wanted to talk to him about it.

"So, let me get this straight: you've never orgasmed. Is that what you mean?"

I bit my lip and shook my head.

"Have you spoken to your friends about it? Isn't that what you girls do? Talk about boys and sex."

"I don't."

"Okay." He nodded thoughtfully. A moment passed, and then he looked at me again. "Have you… I mean…"

"Had sex?"

He nodded.

"Nope." I bit into a fingernail.

"But that doesn't make sense. You're an adult."

"I'm twenty-four. I just haven't met the right guy, I suppose."

"But your parents. The hippie lifestyle… isn't that all about experimenting and openness?"

"My grandparents were into open marriages, but my parents aren't. My mom is more conventional, I suppose. I mean she's kind of eccentric, but she'd be pretty pissed off if Dad played around. He doesn't. He's besotted with Mom. I want that too. I saw what it did to some of my cousins. One got pregnant at eighteen. And all the others were and still are boy crazy. That's all they ever talk about. I don't want to be like that."

A tinge of admiration warmed his expression. "But you're so beautiful. How's that possible?"

I stared down at my hands, mainly because his eyes were burning into mine and making it hard for me to think. "I'm not that beautiful. I'm overweight."

"That's not true. Believe it or not, men like women like you."

The best I could do was shrug. I looked up at him again. “Shit, I can’t believe I just admitted that to you.” I tried not to drown in his gaze again. “And why do you keep looking at me like that?”

He opened his hand. “How am I looking at you?”

“Like I’m some kind of a freak.”

“I don’t think you’re a freak. I just can’t get my head around it, that’s all.”

“Now I hope you’re not getting any ideas here, Sam. I mean, I shouldn’t have opened up about that.” Not giving him time to reply, I continued, “Tell me about all your girlfriends, then.”

SAM

I headed back to the stainless-steel bench, where half a bottle of tequila stood among squeezed lemons and spilled salt, a messy reminder that we'd been hitting it hard. Although Juni didn't seem that drunk, only a little louder.

"That subject requires another drink, I think," I said, exercising my natural evasiveness.

As I mixed the drinks, I couldn't stop thinking about Juni's inexperience with men. Our flirtatious banter had put a buzz in the air. But then had come *that* sobering revelation.

Noticing Juni's empty glass, I asked, "Another?"

Juni had decided to dance to Van Morrison, which was playing in the background. After twirling around, she replied, "Sure, why not? They're yummy." There it was, the child in her. The woman wasn't too far away, though, as her body moved provocatively.

"I love this song," she crooned, singing along in a soprano, which, although in tune, sounded wacky, just like the girl herself. "It's a marvelous night for a moon dance… all the stars…"

Fond of that tune myself, I sang along, knowing how silly we really sounded, but hey, who cared. This was a first for me. Not known for singing in the presence of others, I was that guy who gritted his teeth at karaoke nights.

Juni leapt about, spinning around me like some fairy-witch casting a spell.

"Come on, dance with me," she implored.

"I don't dance," I said.

Grabbing my hand, Juni said, "Don't be shy."

At her urging, I swayed slowly. Then, summoning up waltz steps I had once learned in preparation for a deb's ball, I took her into my arms like a real grown-up.

As I held Juni close, I understood why this was the dance for lovers. My hand pressed gently against the small of her back. Drawing her against me, I felt the graceful undulation of her hips. That pleasant numbness I garnered from drinking had not prevented a fiery bolt of arousal from heading straight to my groin.

I pressed against her and instead of pulling away, Juni remained close. Her arms stretched up, and her knitted fingers clung to my neck. Her cheek rested on my shoulder.

It was a beautiful moment as I inhaled her soft, fragrant hair.

Juni looked up at me. Barefooted, she was about a foot shorter than me. I lifted her chin toward me and bent down. Before either of us could think, my lips landed on hers.

They were feather soft, a little sticky, and lemony flavored. As her warm breath tickled my mouth, I indulged in the sweetest kiss I'd ever tasted.

Her breasts pushed hard against my body while my hands ran up and down her deeply indented waist all the way to her shapely hips. The heat of our bodies melted my brain, and blood surged down to my dick.

My tongue gently parted her lips and entered deeply while I continued to savor her moist, pillowy lips.

We remained entwined after the song had ended. I walked her to the sofa, and we fell onto it.

Then the spell broke. Juni released herself from my arms. "Oh wow, I don't know what happened there. Did we just kiss?"

Exhaling a deep breath, I nodded. "I think we did."

"I shouldn't have done that. Oh, God." She bit into her lip, which only deepened my hunger to get back there.

"I'm sorry." I moved to the other end of the sofa. "Although I think you seemed just as guilty."

She gulped down her margarita as if she was doing some kind of penance. And then those big green eyes looked up at me, and I swear they went a darker shade of sultry. Or was that just my imagination, stimulated by an intense charge of testosterone?

Juni looked down and then slowly lifted her eyes toward me again. A smile grew on her lips. I couldn't look at her without having all sorts of dirty thoughts that the nice guy within tried to fight.

"You're a great kisser," she said.

I moved closer again. "You think so?"

Her smile was peppered with a hint of wickedness. I would've crawled naked through a parasite-infested jungle just to kiss that smirk off her lips.

"And so are you. Spectacularly so," I said, holding her hand.

The fact that she didn't move away encouraged me to slide closer.

As I reached in, she pushed me away. "Stop." She stood up. "We really shouldn't. You're not my type. And this could get ugly."

I took another deep breath in a bid to still the rage of hormones besieging my senses. "That's fine. I won't touch you, promise. It's just…"

I had picked up my drink for a sip when she interjected. "It's just what?"

"You're my type in more ways than I could have understood before today."

She fell onto the sofa again and tilted her beautiful rosy-cheeked face. "Really? That's kind of an interesting thing to say. I'm still trying to work out if it makes sense."

I sniffed. "That makes two of us."

"I'll take it as a compliment," she said, playing with a lock of her golden hair. "You're a little different from what I first thought, too."

Now it was my turn to sit up. "Okay. Let it spill. Your first impression, and be sure to throw in the ugly details. I'm a big boy. I can take it." I grinned.

"Now you're bragging," she said.

"About being a grown-up?" I cocked my head.

"Ha ha ha." She held my gaze for a moment. That mischievous twinkle in her eyes and the few buttons of her blouse, still undone from our hot-and-bothered session earlier, made my dick throb. Her considerable milky cleavage competed with her cat eyes for my attention.

"Why are you looking at me like that?" I asked.

"I'm wondering why a guy like you hasn't got a girlfriend."

"I could ask the same about you, Juni."

"I asked first," she said.

"I suppose I haven't met the right girl."

"That's original," she muttered dryly.

"Well, you're not the only one that's fussy here," I argued.

"But you've had lots of girlfriends, I'm sure."

"Didn't we have this conversation earlier?" I asked.

"Hm… Tell me about yourself then. I mean apart from being a hotshot developer with questionable morals."

I turned sharply to look at her. "Questionable morals? Hey, you seemed a willing participant. I don't force myself on women if that's what you think."

"That's not what I meant. I mean the fact you're working for the devil."

"My father's many things, but the devil's a bit extreme," I said, wavering a little, given that my father had indeed been involved with some seedy transactions in his life, not to mention the cheating, which made me wonder why my sweet mother remained in that marriage.

"Was that your first impression? Getting back to my question," I asked, steering our banter away from my dad, who was never my go-to subject when seeking entertainment.

She drained her glass. I rose. "Another?"

"Are you trying to get me drunk so that you can have your way with me?" She fluttered her eyelashes and put on a ridiculous Southern drawl.

"I've already told you, Juni, I don't force myself on women. If anything, they're the ones that drop me the line, so to speak."

"Now you are bragging." She continued to study me playfully. "So, what do you like to do?"

I shrugged. "I like to do very little if I can."

"You're lazy, then?"

I flinched. That was my father's favorite line. "No. I'm very active."

"Then what are your interests?"

"I like reading, tennis, swimming… learning about crafting beer. Maybe your father can give me a few tips?" I cocked my head.

Her brow pinched. "Brewing beer? Now, that I didn't expect."

"That's my passion. If I had it my way, I'd set up a boutique brewery with Scotty."

"Scotty's a canine?"

I coughed as the liquor went down the wrong way. "No. Now you're being ridiculous. He's my best buddy. We grew up in the same neighborhood."

She nodded thoughtfully.

JUNI

As much as I tried to dislike Sam, I just couldn't.

And that kiss.

Phew.

It took some time for my heart to stop pounding and return to a regular beat. And that charge of heat tingled all the way down. I'd only felt that once before, and that had nothing to do with a living, breathing soul, more to do with reading some of my aunt's smutty romance novels. Sam reminded me of some of the romantic heroes: strong, sensitive, sexy, and a little cocky. Only he was real.

Sam stood at the window. "It's still bucketing down." He turned and looked at me. "Have you called your folks yet?"

"I did earlier, while you were showering," I said.

"What did you tell them? Not wishing to pry, of course."

"I told my father the truth—that I lost the key to the chain, my phone battery went flat, and I couldn't get home because the streets were blocked. And that I was sharing the developer's hotel room."

Sam's eyebrows shot up. "Really?"

I shrugged. "He knows I can look after myself. He's from that 'what doesn't kill you makes you stronger' school of thinking."

"Right." He nodded. "But he's not concerned that you're being put up by a stranger?"

"You're not that much of a stranger, are you?" I tilted my head. "I mean, we've been through a bit together. And here we are, getting drunk."

"I suppose when you put it like that. And I do feel more acquainted with you than most women I've hung out with."

Studying him while he moved about, I replied, "You mustn't have talked much."

He smiled at my raised brow. "Not a lot in common is more like it."

"And we have?" My pitch rose with disbelief.

"You're easy to talk to." He paused for a moment, I supposed to choose his words carefully. "That is… putting aside the fancy footwork I've had to do, proving that I'm not that asshole you thought of me as." He tilted his head.

Pulling a tight smile, I hadn't made it easy for Sam with that quick-to-judge manner of mine. "I just don't like that world you represent. Why don't you just set up your brewery and do what you really love?"

He nodded pensively. "That's the plan. But for now, I'm working with my father. Even though it gives me little pleasure." He paused. "And what about you, Juni? You're still living with your parents, I take it."

I nodded. "I've always lived on the farm."

"That's interesting," Sam responded.

"It has its moments." I sighed, feeling tired all of a sudden. "We have some animals and grow our own food. Like you, I work for my dad. It's pretty busy. In fact, my day flies. By the time I collect the eggs, milk Moonie and Mary, not to mention the cheesemaking and gathering of vegetables, I'm exhausted."

"But what about designing clothes?"

"Oh, I find time for that later in the evenings. I sew sometimes into the early hours."

"God, Juni, you're overworked," he said with genuine concern that touched me for some reason.

"I am. I've told Dad I can't continue doing it. I just want to design and make clothes and have some time to, you know, daydream." I smiled. "That's what I really like to do."

"I'm there with you. Reverie is underrated," he said, sitting down again.

"Reverie?" I repeated.

"It means to muse," he said with a gentle smile.

"It has a nice sound," I said.

"It has. And daydreaming is healthy. That's where great ideas spring from," he said.

I stretched my legs out on the sofa.

"Are you tired?" Sam asked.

"A little. But I'm good."

"What I don't get is, if your father's so rich, why doesn't he employ a farmhand?"

"He's going to. Especially since Lingam joined the world of business and rabid capitalism."

Noticing Sam's eyes firing with amusement, I added, "That's my dad's description."

"Lingam?" Sam's brows pinched.

"My brother. He prefers Lee. Mom and Dad were devotees of Krishna for a while there. It's a symbol of Shiva. Not that I'm into it."

"Are you close to your brother?"

I shook my head. "Not really. We've always been different. As kids, we used to fight a lot, which upset my parents, who were invested in that whole peace-and-love thing."

"Did I catch a hint of cynicism there?" he asked.

"Mm… probably. I'm not convinced by all that, and anyhow, it doesn't make sense culturally speaking. Since I'm Anglo-Saxon, Wicca is probably more fitting as far as spiritual practice is concerned."

"Wicca? As in witchcraft?" Sam asked.

"Yeah. Only don't worry, I'm not practicing. My aunt's the witch in the family."

"You remind me of a fairy." His eyes flickered with warmth.

Having always loved fairies growing up, I took that as the ultimate compliment.

Although the bed was very comfortable, I couldn't stop tossing and turning. We had argued about who should sleep where. Sam won, and there I lay in that huge bed, feeling like Alice in Wonderland after eating that mushroom.

Sam was on the sofa, which I kept reminding myself was comfortable and big enough for a bed. If I was being honest to myself, I was suffering separation anxiety. I wanted Sam in that bed with me. I wanted him to hold me. We'd spent all day and night together.

That was strange when all I had wanted to do was hate him.

Sam was definitely the first man I'd ever kissed, the memory of which still burned on my lips. All the others had been boys, sloppy and inexperienced by comparison.

The air must have been awash with our sexual chemistry because I was so flushed with arousal, I just couldn't sleep.

As I lay there staring at the ceiling, I touched myself, and a strong throb ached through me. The thought of masturbating in Sam's bed flushed me with heat, even though I resisted. I wondered whether I'd see Sam again after we returned to our very different lives.

Lightning lit up the room, making me wince. My leg muscles tightened, anticipating thunder. Then boom. The room almost shook. The heavens were at it again.

SAM

I tossed and turned. Juni had turned me upside down, and my aching erection had me debating whether to tiptoe into the bedroom and grab the lube.

But what would I say if Juni saw me? "Um… I need to jerk off because you're so fucking hot, I'm in agony."

Shuddering through the walls, a crack of thunder took my mind off my dick. The weather was certainly working against us. Or was that for us?

I wouldn't have met Juni otherwise. And I had to admit, in those eight hours or so of getting to know her, I knew one thing: I wanted to see her again.

Marie Carter entered my thoughts, causing my erection to droop—something a potential wife-to-be should not do. My teeth ground at the thought of my father bludgeoning me with that same monologue: "You're a Chalmer. You'll do as I say!" His banging fist would be muted by the leather coating on the same desk that his mother had sat at. The matriarch of the family, my grandmother, who pulled all the strings, and made the Chalmers' squillions.

One look at Juni and my father would make that crash of thunder sound like a baby's fart.

As I entertained raging hormones and cndless thoughts, a silhouette appeared before me.

Stupid me jumped. I mean, who else was it going to be?

I turned on the lamp. I was lying naked under a sheet, and my member stood to attention, much to my horror. Before I could sit up and hide my obvious erection, Juni's eyes popped open. My incurable horniness had been outed.

It was my turn to cop an eyeful of feminine wonderland, because before me stood a curvy goddess. Wearing the silky barely-there nightie that the hotel staff member had dropped off earlier, Juni crossed her arms when noticing my gaze.

"Are you okay?" I asked after what seemed a long pause—which it was because hormones had flooded my thoughts.

The room brightened and a streak of lightning illuminated Juni's face, which scrunched in fear.

"Are you frightened of the storm?"

She bit her lip.

The crash of thunder that followed made her cry out. I sat up and wrapped the sheet around my waist. "I can sit up with you until it passes if you like, only…"

She lowered herself to sit by my side "Only what?"

"You might have to cover up, Juni."

Her tightened features softened into that little adorable smile I couldn't get enough of. "Am I that alluring?"

I tilted my head. "That pretty little piece of fabric is see-through. I'm sorry, but I'm finding it hard to think."

She scratched away at the fabric. "I hate the way it feels, although I do like how it looks." Her lips twitched into a shy smile.

I took a steadying breath.

As lightning lit up the space, Juni moved closer and covered her ears.

"It's okay, Juni." I thought about the storm earlier that day. "You seemed cool about the storm under the tree."

"I know. But night storms have always freaked me out." She looked at me, gnawing on her bottom lip while crossing her arms over her considerable chest, which my eyes battled to avoid.

"You must think I'm being silly."

I shook my head. "No way. I understand. Nature's powerful."

She stared at me and nodded. "Um…" She stared at my naked chest. "Do you have any pajamas here?"

Boy, how I wanted to respond in the negative, but instead, Mr. Do-the-Right-Thing nodded. I rose from the couch and wrapped the sheet more tightly around my waist before heading for the bedroom.

Juni followed me in that tiny little nightie that I couldn't help but take a mental photo of. I even snuck a peek at that curvy ass that I would have sat through ten hours of *Dirty Dancing* on a loop to rub myself against.

She must have sensed my gaze burning a hole into her flesh because Juni turned and asked, "Are you leering at me?"

Painting on a weak, apologetic smile, I admitted, "I wouldn't be a hot-blooded male if I didn't." After she rolled her eyes as a testimony to my lack of control, I added, "Now don't be like that, Juniper. You have to admit there's not a lot of fabric going on there."

"I'm not responsible for this." Her brow lowered. "Hey, did you arrange it this way? Did you ask whoever bought all these items to get the sexiest little negligee available?"

My face crumpled in disbelief. I shook my head in protest. "Now listen, Juni, I might be many things, but underhanded I'm not." I turned away from her and spilled the contents of my suitcase onto the floor. I bent down and dragged out a pajama top. "Here." I handed it to her. "It's comfortable cotton."

Taking it from me, she said, "You sound disappointed."

I rubbed my neck. "Sorry. I'm weak that way. Beauty has got this way of getting under my skin." I arched an eyebrow. "So to speak."

A slow smile grew on her face. "Thanks. And Sam…"

"Mm?"

"I'm sorry for suggesting that you arranged this." She touched the silky fabric of her barely-there nightie, and once again I had to struggle not to look.

"Turn around while I slip into something more comfortable." I had begun to leave when Juni asked, "Where are you going?"

"Back to sleep," I muttered. I'd had enough of this game, and I needed some serious hand relief.

"No… Please."

I stopped and turned just as she was buttoning up the pajama top that had dinosaurs printed all over it. "That really suits you. In many ways I prefer it."

She studied the pattern on the sleeve and giggled. "This is so cute. Dinosaurs. You're such a boy."

I shrugged. "I never quite grew up, I suppose."

"That's cute." Juni smiled, sliding under the covers.

"Okay, then, sweet dreams," I said.

"No… stay." She stared at me imploringly.

Unsure what she expected, I sat on the edge of the bed. "What?" I shook my head. "Do you want me to read you a bedtime story?"

She giggled. "No, stupid. Just get in. I'm not good in strange beds."

"The bed's not that strange. It's standard in many ways. Although it does come with a massage feature." I tilted my head, making light of something that was anything but as I battled with the primitive male within, who at this stage was engorged and blue with desire.

"You're funny. You make me laugh," said Juni. "Jump in. I won't bite."

"That's a shame," I said, ambling over to the other side of the bed.

"You've got a thing for vampires?" Juni asked, rolling over to look at me, just as I let my sheet drop.

Her eyes landed on my throbbing member. "Holy shit."

I bit my lip. "Hey. You're making me feel self-conscious."

She looked away. "Sorry. It's just that…"

Tucking myself in, I asked, "What?"

"You're… you know?"

"Hard?" I asked with a dry tone.

"Yes."

"Blame it on that skimpy little number. And that pajama top isn't exactly easing matters."

Humor gleamed in her eyes.

"It should behave soon. You've got to turn around, and not come too close, though," I warned.

"You don't want me to cuddle you?" she asked.

Now that took me aback. I took another deep breath and did what any self-respecting, hot-blooded male would do. I put my arms around Juni and drew her close.

"You're going to remain naked?" she asked.

I began to rise from the bed, but she stopped me. My God… Juni had this confusing way about her. I couldn't read her at all.

"Do you want me to put on my pajama bottoms?"

"No. It's cool. I've never been in this situation before. It's kind of sexy."

I lifted myself and leaned up on my elbow to study her again. With her golden hair splashed over the pillow and eyes enticingly half closed, Juni was really stretching the limit of my self-control.

When her pink tongue ran along her sensuous lips, my brain kicked in with "What the fuck are you waiting for?"

Before another second lapsed, my hungry mouth was on hers.

Pent-up sexual energy made my lips red hot and hers too. I drew her tightly to me. And the heat coming from her made me remove the comforter. The lights were off, but the streetlights beaming over the walls enabled me to see her glorious form reflecting off the mirrored cupboard doors.

Our lips melded, and as my tongue plunged in deeply, her tongue swirled with mine a tangle.

Juni seemed just as hungry for that kiss as I was.

Undoing the buttons to the pajama top, I ran my hands along her silky-soft skin. Her considerable curves stole my breath.

I'm sure my fingers trembled with anticipation as they traveled up her waist and landed on the fullness of her breasts.

A groan left my throat. My mouth traveled down to her pink, distended nipples as I sucked and teased one at a time gently with my teeth. Puckering and rigid, they poked at my tongue as I savored their sweetness.

Juni writhed in my arms.

"I want to make you come, Juni. Will you let me?"

"Uh-huh," she said with a breathy voice that made my dick cream up.

I took to her sweet mouth and devoured it with the ferocity of someone anticipating the Mount Everest equivalent of pleasure.

Her soft skin smelled of roses as my fingers walked down her curvy, milky thighs. Juni opened them wide, inviting me somewhere sacred. At least it felt like that.

Nobody had ever been there.

Opening the folds of her pussy, my finger trembled slightly. Knowing I had to be as delicate as possible, I gently stroked her clit. I salivated from the need to taste her. The way she opened her legs even wider told me that Juni wanted this as much as I did.

I entered her with my finger and had to fight through a tight wall of muscles. A groan echoed in my chest, imagining how it would feel to enter her. I could barely breathe.

"Do you mind if I place my tongue on your clit?" I murmured.

JUNI

"Yes…" filtered out of my breath.

Sam stopped. He lifted his head, which was near my belly. "You don't want me to?"

"No… I mean yes, please, I do," I said, my brain scattered. Whatever he was doing with that magic touch of his drove me crazy with such desperation, I needed him to take me all the way.

I'm not sure what came over me, but seeing him naked, with that body fit for a Greek god, and those hard, rippling muscles that my fingers couldn't stop sliding over made my body come alive.

And that penis. Oh my God.

Flooded with need, my hands almost pushed his head down between my legs, a move I was certain I'd be embarrassed about later.

Life was way too short to not experience that.

When his tongue settled on my clit, I shuddered from oversensitivity. He swirled it gently around with delicate little flutters that made me moan. Moisture dribbled down my leg as prickling heat pulsated through me.

I'd used my finger before, but this was something else. A cry left my lips as the wave just grew and grew, his tongue moving faster and licking away as if he was eating ice cream.

"Oooh…." I sighed.

He stopped and his dark, sexy eyes looked up at me.

I pressed his head down, almost aggressively. Boy, did I need a release. I knew that it would be huge because I'd already had one golden wave of heat rip through me. And just as I thought that was it, another, even bigger, thundered through me.

Releasing clenched muscles, I fell into a whirlpool, giving way to something hot, and addictive. I moaned and sighed.

But it didn't just stop there.

It just kept growing. It seemed as though I was drowning in pleasure, mushrooming into one big explosion of creamy deliciousness. My heart grew and grew, and I cried out so loudly that my own eardrums reverberated.

When it was over, I relaxed my thighs, and then it suddenly hit me: I'd nearly crushed Sam's head between my legs.

Sam sat up, his full lips glistening and his face red.

"Shit. I'm sorry. Did I hurt you?" I asked, trying to think, even though my wits were still on the ceiling.

"No. It was beautiful. Just like you."

He wiped his lips on his big bicep.

Instead of having reached satiation, a deep need lingered where his tongue had ravaged. I'd become greedy for more, especially after seeing his muscular bicep glistening with my cum.

It was so erotic.

Everything about Sam was. Sex must have been his middle name. That mess of dark hair that I couldn't stop grabbing at, and the fire of hunger in his eyes.

A deep sigh escaped my lips.

He took me into his strong arms, and our lips met tenderly. I tasted myself on him as his tongue entered deeply. I knew I had to go all the way. The blaze in my vagina had intensified.

"Are you okay?" Sam asked.

"Uh-huh," I responded.

"I hope those loud screams were of pleasure," he said.

I nodded. "I hope I wasn't too loud."

"You were. But I liked it."

Sam took me into his arms and held me. I could feel his erection hitting my thigh.

"Did you orgasm too?" I asked. I tentatively stroked his dick, and my palm went sticky.

"Not yet," he said with a strangled tone.

"You're all wet," I said.

"That's pre-cum. Nature's lubrication."

"In readiness for what?" I asked. I knew the answer, but it turned me on to hear him say it.

"For fucking, Juniper."

"I want you to," I said.

Sam pulled away from me and sat up.

Pushing back a wave of hair from his face, he said, "Um…" His brows merged. "You want me to be your first?"

The surprise on his handsome face made me laugh as I removed his ridiculous but very sweet dinosaur pajama top.

His eyes darkened with a hint of lust as they wandered over my breasts, which only added to the throbbing ache below. I'd never felt so sexy.

In many ways, I'd never thought of myself as being very sexual. That was before Sam.

Strange as it seemed, seeing that we'd only just met, and in questionable circumstances, I trusted him.

Sam was kind, if not a little anxious to make sure I was comfortable. I liked that. It was a form of chivalry.

When I nodded, he replied, "Are you sure? I mean, I…" He stroked my arm, and I fell into his embrace again.

I loved feeling the heat of his body against mine.

"Juni, I'm crazy about you. But are you sure?"

Now it was my turn to frown. "How can you know that?"

He shook his head. "What?"

"That you're crazy about me. We've only just met."

He studied me for a moment. "Well… What can I say? You're very beautiful, you make me laugh, and"—he stroked my arm— "you're intelligent, if not a little idealistic and airy. But that's what makes you special."

"But I said all those awful things to you," I challenged.

"I deserved it. That tree's worth fighting for. And you, too, are worth fighting for."

I drew away. "Why would you have to fight for me?"

"Just a figure of speech."

"I want you to fuck me, Sam."

He rubbed his neck, which had gone red. "Okay."

"You don't want to?"

"Hell… There's nothing I want more. Believe me."

"Then?"

He continued to stare at me as if trying to glean more from me. I have to admit my feelings for him only increased, for I could see he understood the seriousness of my decision.

"I just don't want you to think I'm taking advantage of you," he said.

"I can tell you're not. If you don't want to, tell me, Sam. I can put on that cute pajama top of yours and go to sleep."

His dark eyes lingered over me as if trying to find some hidden meaning to my words. "Juni, I want this."

"Then… touch me again," I said.

After his hands had swept over my breasts and he'd almost crushed me in an embrace, he pulled away and said, "Don't move. I'll be back in a minute."

SAM

I fell onto my worn brown leather sofa that had once belonged to my grandfather. Late-afternoon sun poured in through the bay window, exposing dust, reminding me that I needed to arrange for a cleaner.

It was more than dust that was on my mind, however. After having not slept, I could barely remember the drive home to Nob Hill.

For some, it was that visit to the pyramids, while for others it may have been something more salacious but still life-changing, like when a slinky dame lowered herself under the table of a celebrated Montmartre café and sucked their dick. For me, however, it was that last twenty-four hours with Juni.

It was an experience that would remain etched in every region of my being forever. My body still tingled. I'd fallen in love. Or so I thought, given that I'd never felt like that before.

Kicking off my shoes, I exhaled a deep breath as my tired frame sank heavily into the soft cushions. I closed my eyes, and it all came flooding back, literally. My head was abuzz from the four coffees I'd drunk, two of which I'd consumed while watching Juni rearrange her backpack over and over. Unlike me, Juni seemed revved up and ready to conquer her world as she packed in those accomplished designs that she'd salvaged with a hairdryer.

Noticing my unflinching attention, Juni had stopped what she was doing, and from those big inquisitive eyes, I read, "What are we going to do now?"

When birds started chirping and the sky cleared, we knew that reality had finally arrived. So had a boat Juni's father had arranged to pick her up, while Josh from the firm had arranged a boat to take me back to higher ground so that I could return home.

Personally, I could have handled another day or so in that hotel, waiting for the water to subside, but that was why boats were invented. As it was, we didn't get that far. After we passed distressed people wading through water looking for cars that had floated away and shop owners shaking their heads, crying in despair, I realized that we needed to do more than just return to our comfortable lives. Both Josh and I rolled up our sleeves and ended up wading through knee-high murky water, lugging sandbags all day long.

As I adjusted my position on the sofa, my muscles ached. I'd returned at five in the afternoon. I kept seeing Juni's body undulating sensually. It was enough to bring a grown man to tears, the way she'd discovered the joys of riding my cock.

There were a few stops and starts, such as the way Juni watched with wide-eyed innocence while I struggled to sheathe my overly enthusiastic dick in the smaller-sized condoms supplied by the hotel. And there was an unfortunate accident, one that we didn't discuss, for reasons I couldn't explain. Maybe because the icky subject of semen would have pierced our magic bubble.

Her giggles had only made matters worse, but eventually, I managed. I tongued her pussy again, making sure she'd be nice and ready, while she pulled at clumps of my hair. When it came to noisy orgasms, Juni was operatic. I'd even noticed the flicker of a smile in the staff member's eyes when he delivered our breakfast later.

"I want you to enter me," Juni purred.

Wiping my lips with the back of my hand, I said, "Let's take this nice and slow, okay?" My finger entered. "You're extremely tight, Juni. I mean, really tight."

"And that's a problem?"

"Not for me it ain't," I replied.

"It feels nice."

Her soft, sexy voice nearly made me burst out of the rubber sheath. I entered with two fingers, and she squirmed. "Are you okay?"

"I like it. Please, I'm ready." Juni lowered her eyes in anticipation, parting her swollen lips.

One inch at a time, I entered her. Luckily, Juni was still creamy. I slid in, and a deep groan reverberated through my ribcage. Hours of arousal banking up ready to erupt threatened a quick climax.

"Are you okay? I'm not hurting you?"

"You're really big, and it does hurt a little," she said with a small voice.

"Do you want me to stop?"

"Do you want to stop?" she challenged.

"Fuck. No. My God. Juni…" I'd lost my ability to think, let alone talk. When I managed to fill her, she sucked back a sharp intake of air. I stopped.

She squeezed my arms. Her nails dug in as though passing her pain onto me.

"Don't stop, please," she implored.

That was music to my ears. I continued taking it agonizingly slowly. In and out. The friction was so intense, I would have sat through a year of toddlers sawing away at violins to experience her pussy naked without that piece of rubber.

Nevertheless, exquisite was too lame an adjective to describe the sensation.

Her thighs wrapped around me. Gripping my ass, Juni seemed to push me deeper. And happy to deliver, I picked up the pace.

Her cries, which could've been of pleasure or pain, made my movements hesitant. I had to ask her which it was.

"It's both," she declared.

All it took was a gyration of her pelvis, for that girl was a natural, and the explosion was bigger than Vesuvius. I was noisy too. Having always been quiet where orgasms were concerned, I didn't even know I had those agonized groans in me.

I fell into Juni's arms, and after a deep, tender kiss, I murmured, "Thanks."

Juni remained inert, her searching wide gaze burning into me. Was she pissed off with me? Did she feel regret? I wondered.

After I returned from the bathroom, I took Juni into my arms again. "Are you okay?"

"I think so. Can we do that again?"

I pulled away. "Huh?"

JUNI

My dirty mind showed no bounds. Squeezing and pulling away at poor Moonie's teat, all I could think of was Sam's big cock. I'd gone from rolling my eyes at the mention of sex to wanting so desperately to talk endlessly about it. I was no longer the same girl.

Hot, swelling pain thrummed through me, especially as my ass rested on the lumpy stool. While milk poured into a bucket, I swear it wouldn't have taken much to orgasm. Sam had released something inside of me—profoundly erotic, and sensual at the same time. I could barely move without imagining the sensation of Sam's big dick inside of me. Although he'd stretched me to kingdom come, the pleasure just kept burning away.

One day had passed since Sam dropped me off. Wearing a smile that could've melted the ice caps of Greenland, Sam assured me that once the water subsided, he'd have the machine removed and that Oscar would remain standing.

Boy, he had stamina, as did I it seemed. We'd fucked and fucked. I'd lost count of how many times I'd climaxed. Poor Sam ended up with scratches all over his arms. He assured me he loved my nails digging in. I'd also discovered that sweet spot between pleasure and pain. God knows the guy was so big that at times it was painful, but then when my muscles relaxed, the burn was gaspingly delicious.

Moonie mooed, alerting me to the fact that milk spilled out of the bucket and onto my foot. I was sure she knew. Her big eyes bored into me as if to say, “So, Juniper Berry, you’re now a woman.”

I patted her and headed over to milk Mary, our goat.

Back to hard work on the farm. All I wanted to do was sit among the daisies and daydream while reliving Sam fucking me over and over.

When he’d first entered me, it hurt so much, I bit into my lip. For a moment there, I couldn’t make out what all the fuss was about. It was painful. Pure and simple. And then… we did it a second time and… Oh My God… If I thought the man had a golden tongue, then I was about to discover that Sam also had a golden cock of the most persuasive variety. It never seemed to go down.

My throat was hoarse. I felt drugged from endless orgasms, and even my toes ached from gripping. After I couldn’t take anymore, I ended up falling back on the bed with my tongue hanging out.

Sam still found me beautiful, as crazy as that seemed, given my hair looked like I’d been in a Siberian storm and my face had become mysteriously splotchy.

But where was he? He’d promised to call.

It had been twenty-four hours.

Just as he pressed the elevator button for me, a shy smile touched his chiseled tanned features, and I melted into his arms again.

“You’ve got my number, Sammy.”

“Sammy?” His voice lowered into that gravelly drawl that had a direct line to my lower regions.

“Okay. Too soon for cutie names. Call me,” I repeated.

We hugged. We kissed over and over, deeply, his tongue provoking mine. He tasted of mint and sex. As I buried my face in his warm neck, I sniffed his essence in deeply, as I would a heady rose.

His fingers crept under my dress.

"Now why did you go and do that?" he asked while his fingers hovered tormentingly close to my pussy.

"What?" I uttered.

"You haven't got any panties on."

I recalled him ripping them off just after we'd had a coffee and agreed to stop touching each other. "You tore them off. Remember?"

He scratched his neck, and a sly smile touched his lips.

Before I knew what was happening his finger was doing that gentle rotating thing that made my clit swell and my pussy go all creamy. Holding on tight, I let him fuck me with his fingers. He complained that there were no condoms left. And even though Sam said he would've hung upside down on a moving circle as a drunken knife thrower's target to experience skin on skin, he wasn't that irresponsible.

Between giggling and moaning, I surrendered to another orgasm, this time against an elevator wall.

And just as I was coming while squashed up against his big chest, he whispered, "I love you, Juni."

I pulled away and looked at him. It seemed genuine because his eyes had gone dark and serious.

I must have looked stunned.

"Too soon?" he asked.

Nodding very slowly, because what could one say to that? I said, "It is. But hey, Sam, I'm into you."

As lame and kind of unromantic as that sounded, it was all that I could say because my heart had not stopped racing since. This was new. I'd never experienced anything like this before.

I needed a girl to talk to. I'd tried calling Jess, a friend who I knew from the artisans' market, but she'd gone away. It was time to call my nymphomaniac aunt Scarlett.

Floating back into the house, I passed my father. He was negotiating with a couple of bearded guys who'd arrived to pick up a few boxes of Juniper's Nectar, my father's homemade gin, which boasted "special" properties. For a man who'd run through the field naked after taking peyote, my dad had turned into a very successful businessman, although we weren't allowed to call him that.

"Juni, you seem a little pale," he said looking up at me.

The two young guys nodded a greeting. One even stared a little longer than what was socially acceptable. I must have been wearing sex on my sleeve or something.

"I'm just a bit tired, Dad," I said.

"This is Juniper." My father extended his hand.

"Oh wow… man… you named the gin after your daughter, sweet," said the guy who reminded me of Seth Rogen.

My eyes slid to my dad, who, scratching his beard, returned a subtle smile.

"The other way around," I corrected. "My parents named me after the bush."

The visitor extended his arm. "I'm Brandon and this is Mikey." He pointed to his friend, who returned a smile. "So, after a juniper bush?"

My dad said, "Juniper berries make gin."

Brandon nodded slowly, his mouth opening with an "Aah."

"Okay, then, nice meeting you. Must dash." I flashed a quick smile and headed into the adjoining room of our two-story house which had been built by my great-grandfather, known for being a practical man. He could do anything with his hands. As a fighter pilot in the Second World War, he was more John Wayne than Timothy Leary. Since he was the only hero of the family, we had, in his honor, a room upstairs that resembled a small museum filled with medals, photos, and uniforms. As a reminder of that dark period of history, he had made the family promise to keep everything on display.

I had my own space, which was more like a big shed situated on the property but separate from the main house.

Sauntering into my mother's room, I was met by a large Pre-Raphaelite mural. She loved to surround herself with gorgeous things. Spinning wool, my mom had her head bowed while she hummed to Mozart. She'd studied piano at Berkeley, which was where she met my father, who was a guitar student at the time. They both dropped out and traveled instead.

Resembling a classical image in a painting herself, my mother was dressed in a green crushed-velvet gown. Her long blonde braid fell down her chest as she pumped the treadle with a barefoot. As always, whenever I entered that floral-scented room, it felt as though I'd time-traveled into the nineteenth century.

"Hey, Mom," I said.

She looked up, and a sunny expression filled her face. "Darling."

"Is Scarlett back from Europe?"

"Yes. She called a few days ago."

"I need to see her," I said, falling into a floral armchair.

"Oh… boy troubles?" That was my mother. Psychic.

Like her sister, Scarlett, my mom was drawn to the tarot and paganism, although my aunt, a self-proclaimed witch, took it far more seriously.

"Kind of."

"Why don't you tell me about it." Her soft voice, as always, soothed.

Even though I resembled my mother physically, I'd inherited my dad's restless energy, which came in handy, for there was much expected of me on the farm.

My brother Lee was lost to us. He'd shunned my father's way of life from an early age and lived a high-rolling life in LA as a lawyer. That had broken my father up. We hadn't seen him for three years, though not for lack of trying. My mother's calls were the only ones he took.

A mellifluous soprano from the Magic Flute aria uplifted me as sunlight filtered into my pores.

"Is he nice?"

"Um… yeah…" I shifted. "At first, he was my enemy."

"Oh… really. You fought?" She rolled the wool she'd spun into a ball and placed it in a basket at her feet.

"Not so much. But he's working for his father's firm that's developing our land, which according to Sam doesn't belong to our family."

"I see. I'm not sure about the legalities, darling. Your father looks after all of those matters." She smiled tightly.

I sensed something from that evasive comment, given that my mother normally knew everything about our affairs.

"So you got to know each other while staying at the same hotel?"

I nodded. "We shared the room, Mom." I bit my lip.

"Ah… Did you both?"

"We were romantic." I wiggled in the chair, trying to get comfortable.

She nodded. "Are you okay?"

"He told me he loved me." My voice crackled.

Rising from her seat, she came to me and took my hand. "He didn't take advantage of you, did he?"

I shook my head decisively. "No. I wanted to be with him just as much."

"Then what's the matter?"

"He hasn't called."

"You only returned yesterday morning."

"I know. But he promised to call me last night."

She patted my hand. Her eyes shone with that reassuring sweetness I wished I could bottle, for it always managed to relax me. "Sweetie, I'm sure he'll be in touch. He could have been detained. What's his star sign?"

My brows gathered. "I didn't ask."

SAM

I paced about like a restless tiger. Pressed against the counter at the police station were many equally pissed-off victims. Just my luck it had been peak hour for muggers. Some joker named Fagin must've ferried them in and put them to work.

Rubbing my neck, I winced. A sting of pain bit back. The knife had pierced flesh alarmingly close to where my carotid artery had been pumping blood drunk on adrenaline.

As cool steel had touched skin, all I could think of was Juni.

That wasn't unusual, given that she hadn't left my thoughts once. She'd even visited my dreams. And then, when I woke up after having fallen unintentionally asleep on the couch, I realized I hadn't called her as promised.

Muttering endless "fucks," I stumbled about looking for my phone that, just to add to frustration, had gone flat. And if that was not enough to make a grown man scream, I'd also run out of coffee.

I flew down the stairs and hit the sidewalk as a disheveled wreck since I'd barely buttoned my shirt. And wearing the same clothes I'd worn the day before, I was stumbling along, eyes half closed when a couple of kids confronted me. At first, I almost laughed. They couldn't grow fluff on their faces, and their high-pitched demands suggested that their balls hadn't even dropped. But these kids meant business. One stretched as far as he could reach and pressed a knife to my neck. It wasn't until the sharp tip tore skin that I capitulated and gave them my wallet and cell phone.

With the benefit of hindsight, I should've kneed the kid in the groin, but instinct would never have allowed me to hurt a minor. Now, how fucking stupid was that? Misplaced morals had robbed me of Juni's number!

I should've left the phone on the charger, but instead, out of habit, I'd placed it in my pocket, and in what resembled a scene straight out of *Oliver Twist*, my phone was stolen from me.

There I stood on busy California Street. The first thing I remembered was seeing a cable car rattling past and the pressed-to-the-window gapes with "Poor asshole" written all over them.

In a pathetic attempt to raise the alarm, I yelled, "Grab those kids. They've just robbed me!"

Oblivious to my angst, the passing crowds just pushed ahead with heads bowed. I'd nearly pulled my hair out by its roots from frustration when a passer-by finally handed me her phone. After taking a few minutes to recall his number, I finally contacted my father, who grumbled something about the youth of today being forced to join the army. It was only after interrupting him to tell him that I was on a stranger's phone that my father agreed to send someone to meet me at the police station.

An ageing policeman with a veiny, bulbous nose that resembled an ancient map took my statement. His eyes finally made it to my face. Tired and disinterested, he muttered, "That will do."

"What happens now?" I asked.

He puffed out a breath. "Not much."

"Are you telling me that you won't investigate?"

He shook his head slowly.

"But this is ridiculous. This can't be…" I stopped my tirade. His droopy indifference almost put me to sleep. I realized I was flogging a dead horse. I turned away and then sharply did a retake. "Hey, I really need my cell phone. It's got a phone number."

"Try your local pawn shops."

"Shouldn't that be outlawed? I mean, the owners of these shops are only encouraging that behavior."

"I don't make the laws, sir."

Shaking my head at how fucked up the world was, I left the building and met Susan, my father's PA. She handed me an envelope with a credit card and some cash.

"Thanks, Susie," I said, sighing.

She dug around in her bag and handed me a cell phone.

I thanked her again before shuffling off. Two steps later, the cell vibrated. It was my father. I gritted my teeth and answered. "Hey."

"We need to see you to discuss a few matters. Your mother has arranged another dinner. The Carters have been invited. This time, even if there's an earthquake, you'll be there. Tomorrow night."

"Seven, I suppose?"

"Come earlier. We have business matters to discuss."

"Sure." I ended the call.

Along the way, I stopped off at a few pawn shops. They weren't hard to find. Desperate times required desperate measures, as the saying had it. And if anyone rooted for the downtrodden, it was me, something that I'd never admit to my father, who believed we were all created equal.

Having removed the silver spoon from my mouth following a hair-raising visit to Africa, I acknowledged that life was far more complicated than that, even though I hadn't forgiven those little assholes. They'd taken Juni's number. And to add insult to injury, I found every single number I'd stored in that phone but not hers! I even wondered if she had pressed save, because the cloud did not have it listed. I even called numbers of a few girls I'd had little trysts with, only to be either hung up on or told to go fuck myself. Mm… Not nice. Can't say it was something I was proud of, those drunken nights picking up girls who were just as horny and blasé, it seemed, about pursuing anything other than fuck-buddy status. I quickly deleted those numbers.

I stumbled into a café and ordered a coffee. A bottle of Bulleit came into my eye line, and within a breath, I convinced myself that it wasn't too early for a shot.

Delivering my order with an understanding grin, the waiter asked, "A hard night?"

"No… a hard, fucking morning," I mumbled.

The fiery shot hit the right spot, and I took to my double-shot espresso like a man who'd been through the wars.

I googled the name "Juniper Berry" and found nothing but information about gin. There was no profile on an actual person named that, or a Facebook page with her name, which just didn't make sense to me. Then I recalled her father's name and googled Haight Berry, and tried Harry Berry. Nothing came up about sustainable farming or any business with that name. I googled Haight Ash Berry Ale and tried every variation of spelling imaginable. To no avail. I even started to wonder if I'd actually conjured up Juni. For someone who sold her clothes online, I couldn't understand how she didn't have an online presence. I recalled the emails I'd drafted for her orders. My shoulders slumped. I'd deleted them. Or I should say, Juni had deleted them.

There was the artisans' market. I recalled that Juni sold her clothes there. That was the place to start. That weekend.

A smile settled on my tired mouth as I pictured her beautiful, expressive face firing up with enthusiasm when she showed me her drawings. Something had happened in the past two days that had never happened to me before.

I'd lost my heart to a girl name Juniper Berry.

JUNI

I headed down to my Aunt Scarlett's apartment in North Beach. It had been three days, and I still hadn't heard from Sam. I know I could've looked him up and called him, but for some reason, I needed him to call me.

Sea air scraped at my cheek, blowing my hair into my face. The salty air revived me as I walked up the steps to the entrance of my aunt's Edwardian home.

As always, the first thing that hit me when Scarlett opened the door was a mix of floral citrusy aromas that seemed to have seeped into the building, given that my aunt had lived there for years. Wearing a flowing red skirt and a purple silk shirt tied under her braless breasts, Scarlett opened her arms and hugged me.

"Juniper."

I smiled. "Hey, Scarlett. Thanks for letting me come over."

"Anytime. I love having you around."

Scarlett was my mother's older sister by three years, even though she looked much younger than forty-eight. With long, flowing blonde hair and a voluptuous figure, she had that type of beauty that never seemed to fade. Despite possessing an ethereal quality, floating along in her long skirts, Scarlett had fire in her belly and an unapologetic approach to life.

"Can I offer you a tea?"

"Have you got any coffee?" I asked.

"Of course."

I followed her into the kitchen, which was more like a witch's lair. A dark cauldron dangled over an iron furnace, while in the other corner existed the modern trappings of a kitchen. Colored jars sat on ledges, filled with all manner of herbs and ingredients, while overhead, reminiscent of a Victorian apothecary, drying plants hung on hooks. Scarlett insisted that her brews were comparable to modern medicine, if not more effective.

"Javier's here. He's still asleep. We had a big night." Her eyebrows lifted as if she was divulging something taboo.

"Oh. I hope I'm not intruding?"

Twisting the espresso pot apart, Scarlett said, "Never. I love having you here. Anyway, we're like an old couple."

"How long's it been?" Familiar with my aunt's predilection for men half her age, whom she changed as regularly as her bedsheets, I kept my tone neutral.

"About a month." Her face had a glow that I understood all too well because I probably looked that way around Sam. "He's gorgeous."

"Let me guess, he's a student?"

My aunt ran classes in Wicca, astrology, and herb lore. "He's training to be a shaman. We got together at a peyote ritual in the desert."

"Ah…" I should have guessed. Drugs.

Although my mom and dad had stopped tripping long ago, Scarlett, as part of her practice in witchcraft, was an avid participant in all things mind-altering.

The coffee percolated, and as she lifted the pot, Javier sauntered in wearing nothing but a charming smile.

Unsure where to focus, I settled on his tanned face.

Scarlett gave him a hug and said, "We have a guest."

Javier noticed me for the first time, and instead of covering up, he came close and kissed me on the cheek. I stepped away so as to not meet all of him. He didn't seem to notice my stiffness, and I, in turn, went out of my way not to notice his.

"Ah… a relative? I can see a resemblance." He spoke with a heavy Spanish accent.

My gaze remained glued to his dark, smiling eyes.

"Go and pop something on, *mi corazón*. Juni's blushing."

He left the room and returned with a sarong tied around his waist and then stood behind Scarlett. With his hands on her hips, he held her tight as he rubbed himself against her while kissing her neck.

"And good morning to you, too," she said with a chuckle.

"Now be a good boy and go clean the bathroom. We need a little female time." She passed Javier a cup of black coffee, and he sauntered off.

"He's my cleaner," said Scarlett.

"I thought you met at one of your classes?"

"We met at tantra," she said, with a little smile. "But I do have rules." She raised a brow. "In return for staying here, I insist that he helps." Grabbing a cup of coffee, she stretched out her arm. "Let's go outside. It's such a lovely sunny day."

I followed Scarlett. Clasping my cup of coffee, I lowered myself onto a velvet cushion on top of the wrought-iron seat.

"I've met someone," I said.

"Oh. That's nice." Scarlett studied me as if boring into my innermost thoughts. "He's affected you profoundly, I can see."

"He's my first…" I knitted my fingers.

"Oh… that's beautiful."

Scarlett came to me and hugged me. A lump formed in my throat.

After she stepped away, her eyebrows twitched slightly. "Oh darling, you have regrets?"

I shook my head. "It felt incredible. Painful at first, but then…"

"Amazing. I know. It's hard not to love a dick." Scarlett said that almost to herself as if admitting to an affliction. Her face became serious. "What did you do with the sheet?"

That jarred. I was still mulling over her penis comment. "Ha?"

"The sheet with your blood on it."

My lips stretched into a scowl. "I tried to ignore it, to be honest. I was a little uneasy about what the staff might think."

Scarlett's eyes softened with compassion. "Juni, I'm sure they see it all the time. Women do have periods."

"Why would I need to keep the sheet?" I asked. Although I should have been used to my aunt's eccentricities by now, that question fired up curiosity.

"Virgin's blood, especially when mixed with male seed, makes for a potent blend, my love. One can cast magical spells for fertility."

"But I wouldn't want to get pregnant," I said.

"No. But metaphysically speaking, it makes for a fertile coupling, promising happiness and eternal love."

I nodded slowly. "He wore a condom. There was no, you know..." I opened my hand.

Was I really discussing sexual fluids with a relative? All I really wanted was to talk about Sam's dimples when he smiled and that strong, buff body, not whether his cum had mingled with my virgin blood. Although I wouldn't have minded talking about his penis, given that I couldn't stop thinking about how it felt inside of me.

"Sensible, I suppose, if not a little disappointing," she said.

"How?"

"If you really want a man to fall under your spell, he has to soak in your essence."

I thought of Sam's exquisite tongue. "He kind of did that at the other end." Normally honest about many things, and confident when it came to conversation, I found myself stammering.

"Oh... nice. He's a good one. Cunnilingus. Mm... The tongue possesses a powerhouse of pleasure."

"I haven't heard from him, Scarlett." My mouth wobbled.

Her head tilted, and an empathic glint touched her large green eyes. "Oh, sweetheart." Handing me a tissue, Scarlett sat close, holding my hand. "But you did enjoy it, didn't you?"

Blowing my nose, I nodded. "He was the enemy. I was meant to hate him, but instead, we ended up…"

"Fucking." Scarlett ended my sentence. "You're now a woman."

"I'm not sure I like the way I feel. I've kind of fallen for him. Big time."

"Mm… I see. All right then. There's only one thing to do."

I shook my head. "What?"

"A spell," she said with a decisive nod. "Tell me, have you got anything of his?"

Biting my thumbnail nearly off, I shook my head. I couldn't decide whether this was right or not.

Shouldn't Sam want to call me sans fucking spell?

"Come. Let's mix a brew. I'll then teach you a mantra. And during twilight, we'll go out and cast the spell into the sea. That way the winds can send it over to him. Where does he live?"

Lulled by the thought of the sea at twilight and the poetry of casting my heart's desires into the ether, I stared blankly at my rosy-cheeked aunt. "I don't know."

"You didn't do much talking?"

"Yeah, we did. But about all kinds of things." I shook my head. "Freaking hell, I hardly know him."

SAM

Lined with mansion after mansion, the Pacific Heights street slumbered under shadowy lamplight. I drove up the hill to where my parents' home sat boastfully, looking out over the bay. It was a recent acquisition, and I wasn't a big fan of the neo-Georgian house. The exterior was nice enough, but the squeaky-clean interior with its white shiny surfaces seemed sterile and uninviting.

I swung my pride and joy, a '68 convertible Mustang, into the visitors' parking lot. I'd never really grown up in many ways. When I was a boy, my grandfather had owned a garage full of vintage cars: from Chevrolets to Mustangs. There, he'd spend most of his time under their hoods, tweaking carburetors so that engines would purr when idling and roar when fired up. Hanging out with my grease-stained granddad had fostered a love for those glossy, brightly colored cars with smooth leather seats, the smell of which still flooded me with memories of me at the steering wheel, pretending to drive.

My late grandmother, my dad's mother, had been the mover and shaker. She brought the oil fields and subsequent wealth into the family. Much to my father's chagrin, I took after my grandfather in that I also had a taste for beautiful, handcrafted objects that stood out like gleaming gems.

I parked next to my sister's BMW. Despite screaming of success, it looked like any other modern sedan. In comparison, my convertible, with its cream roof and turquoise body, looked sleek and elegant under the moonlight.

As I stood there filling my lungs with salty air, I thought of Marie Carter, the fiancée I didn't want but that my domineering father insisted I marry. Something about old wealth and good breeding. Considering that most of the women in that clique looked the same, I questioned the limited gene pool in those circles, which in my estimation contradicted that notion of good breeding.

Smoothing down my windswept hair, I headed for the entrance and climbed white marble steps flanked by columns. Rocio, who'd been with the family for longer than me, opened the door, and her big, warm smile welcomed me in. "Ah… *como se guapo.*"

By now, I'd become accustomed to her compliments and rather liked them. Coming from a sixty-year-old, they were heartwarming.

I kissed her on the cheek.

Squinting at the shiny marble floor, I missed our old rambling Victorian mansion in Nob Hill. I was grateful that my grandparents, who at one time had owned homes scattered throughout San Francisco, had kept my humble two-story home on California Street.

The house I really loved and looked forward to moving into one day, however, was my grandfather's cherished home in Malibu. I'd recently bought it outright from my sister Julia, who had an aversion to houses that were older than her. Our tastes differed so much that I often wondered if we were even related. Given that Julia resembled me, I had to accept that we came from different batches of genes.

Voices echoed down the hallway. My dad, as always, dominated in the sound waves. As his barrage of words pierced my eardrums, I thought that had my dad possessed a creative bone in that large frame of his, he would have made a fine actor with that booming projection.

I stepped into the dining room, where at the table sat Marie, my parents, Julia, and her latest boyfriend, whose name escaped me. My sister had had so many, I could only assume they'd all failed to measure up to some impossible standard.

"Sam. At last," my father growled. He was a tall man with a thick head of peppery hair and bore that older-man handsomeness that women seemed to love. This was unfortunate for my mother, who turned a blind eye to his predilection for brunettes with ample chests.

"Sorry." A half smile was the best I could offer. "I've had one of those weeks."

I headed over to my mom and kissed her on the cheek. "Hey."

She stroked my arm affectionately. Her large dark eyes, which were like mine, had that warm sheen that soothed. I was desperate to talk to her about Juni. My mother understood me. She was better than any shrink I'd ever visited, even though I hadn't seen that many.

A whiff of strong perfume tickled my nasal passages. As always, I had an allergic reaction to Marie's fragrance and sneezed. Two sneezes later, I managed to plant a half-hearted kiss on her cheek. "Hey, Marie."

"I see your sinuses are still playing up," she said, tapping the empty chair by her side.

Before sitting down this time, having learned from past experiences, I grabbed a box of tissues.

By the time we were onto the main course, I'd nearly gone through the whole box.

My father, who wasn't a very tolerant man, grumbled, "Sam, what's wrong with you?"

I responded with a shrug. He grunted, which was his go-to language around me, before resuming his discussion about the stock market with Julia's guy, who I was reminded was called Steve.

I turned to Marie and whispered, "Do you mind if I sit across the table?"

Despite her frozen forehead battling to frown, I sensed a big "why?" but instead she replied, "No. Of course, not."

I leaned in and whispered, "I think I'm allergic to your perfume."

She grimaced. "But I'm wearing Chanel No.5."

Opening my hands, I said, "I don't know why, but it makes me sneeze."

She rolled her eyes. Was Chanel No. 5 an indelible part of her life? I wondered. Not that I cared that much, given that there was no way that Marie would become my better half, so to speak. Because when all was said and done, the woman I married would be someone I admired, I looked up to and respected. And, of course, someone that made me hot and bothered.

Juni entered my thoughts, which wasn't unusual, considering she'd been residing in the seedy recesses of my mind all week, not to mention in my groin.

After I settled into the chair next to my mom, she touched my hand affectionately and smiled sweetly at me. Miraculously, my sneezing ceased.

My father looked over at me and said, "Next week… we're going back in. That tree's going."

"I'll buy it."

Julia stopped eating. "You want to buy a tree?"

Having taken a sip of wine, I had to stifle a laugh. Unfortunately, the wine ended up going down the wrong way, and a coughing fit followed.

By this stage, my dad, who'd had enough of my bodily noises, growled, "Now listen, Sam, you need to change your life. Look at you. You're a mess."

I shook my head. "Hey. Relax. Liquid went down the wrong way, that's all." Just as he was about to blast me, treating me like that kid he used to slap around, I looked at my sister. "I want to buy that land."

"You can't," my father interjected. "It doesn't belong to the family. I have a silent partner in this. He owns that land. We're doing the building. Remember? We own the construction company." His sarcasm made me cringe. "And, we stand to make a tidy sum from this deal."

"Who's this guy, anyway?" I asked.

"He's from LA," he replied.

"Maybe I can have a word with him?"

Julia said, "Perhaps he'll sell you the tree."

I rolled my eyes at her dig. I sensed that Julia, competitive to a fault, resented that the Y chromosome had headed my way and not hers. Not that I gave a shit. She could run Chalmer and Son in her sleep. She was a freak of nature. And I did admire her intelligence where business was concerned. I wasn't too sure about her choice of boyfriends. I was unimpressed with Steve, her latest. He struck me as one of those "yes" guys, someone she could order about.

Wearing his customary why-aren't-you-like-your-sister sneer, my father demanded, "Why are you going on about this god damn tree?" His bloodshot blue eyes glared back at me.

My fists clenched. I'd never hit my dad, although I'd come close. Suffice to say that the wall in my old bedroom had a few puncture marks. Growing up, it would start with that same glaring scowl before he'd pounce on me and slap me around after I'd refused to sit through boring board meetings. As a teenager, all I wanted to do was hang with Scotty and talk about dinosaurs or drift about smiling at pretty girls. I did take up boxing, though. That was one activity my pugnacious father approved of.

If one could divorce a parent, I would have signed on that dotted line.

As I went into overdrive trying to figure out how I could stop that land from being cleared, my mother whispered, "Do you want to come outside with me so I can have a cigarette?"

Although I hated my mom smoking, I needed a break from all the scrutiny and from Marie, whose high-pitched giggles grated on me.

We went up the stairs to the rooftop terrace. As we stepped out, I stared out over the swimming pool to the sea with watery moonbeam-streaked stairs leading up to the stars.

We positioned ourselves behind a wall in order for the lighter that I held up to her cigarette to work. As the cigarette fired up, I was about to remonstrate with my mother to kick that ugly habit, when she said, "So, tell me about this girl?"

"What girl?" I asked half-heartedly, for I was not good at lying.

"I can see something's come over you, Sam."

"Am I that transparent?"

"I am your mother," she said, turning away to puff out smoke.

Combing back my hair with my hand, I said, "I have met a girl. In odd circumstances."

"That's nice. Tell me about it."

I thought about this for a moment. "Will you promise not to tell him"—I cocked my head— "if I tell you about it?"

"Is she that unusual?"

"Let's put it this way, she's not like Marie."

"I can see Marie's not a good match, Sam. I am doing my best to convince your father."

"Thanks, Mom."

I took a breath and told her everything about how we met: the chain, the flood, which my mother already knew about, and the shared hotel room. I omitted the virgin bit. Sex was not the kind of topic I felt comfortable discussing with my mother.

"And you lost your phone. Oh my. But you know enough about her. At least you know she's from Oakland."

"Who's from Oakland?" I heard from behind. Turning around, I spotted my father and Steve holding cigars.

As the choking, acrid smoke floated up my nostril, I stepped away.

A disapproving grunt exited my father. He hated that I didn't share cigars on important occasions. According to him, all Chalmer men smoked cigars, and my refusing to smoke them was a rebellious contrivance to break that longstanding tradition.

"Nobody. Just… telling Mom about the flood."

"Marie's all alone in there. You're not being very social, Sam," he said.

"Well, I can't help it if I'm allergic to her perfume." I shifted away as a curl of smoke threatened to make me sneeze again.

My mother said, "Sam makes a good point, darling. He's always been allergic to perfumes as far as I can recall."

My dad grunted again. “Hm… he’s not allergic to yours.”

“I’ve taken to wearing those lovely essential-oil-based fragrances I picked up in Paris.”

I stared at my mom, who cast me a subtle wink. She’d become my ally. Especially now that she knew about Juni.

“All that greenie nonsense,” grumbled my father.

Meanwhile, Steve stood by and nodded in agreement to everything that came out of my dad’s mouth.

“What about the beach house in St. Vincent? Last I heard, it was about to be swallowed up by the sea,” I said dryly.

“I’m having it moved,” he responded.

“Sure. There’s an answer for everything when one can buy their way out of environmental disasters,” I responded coolly.

“Now look, Sam, we’re not going to have this climate change debate again. I will not have your greenie attitude corrupting this family.”

Steve looked at me with that resigned don’t-ask-me apathy I so hated in humans, which only empowered men like my father to call the shots.

“Cary, let’s not get into politics,” my mother implored.

Ignoring her pleas, he turned to me and said, “I need a word.” He looked at Steve, who went and joined my mother.

I stretched my neck from side to side to alleviate a spasm in the muscle.

My father looked at me for a moment. “What’s got into you, Sam?”

“Nothing. Why?”

“You’re different. And what’s your issue with this tree?”

“It’s a beautiful tree. And the land itself offers a break from all the development happening in that area. Even the recent flood proved that. It’s low lying, and whoever develops there is going to get into trouble in the future.”

“And you want to buy that land because of that?”

I shook my head in disbelief. My dad just didn’t get it. “Where’s your civic responsibility, Dad?”

"People everywhere are seeking affordable condos. And I mean to deliver. Now if that's not civic duty, I don't know what is."

A frustrated breath left me. How would I keep my promise not to develop on that land?

He studied me long and hard. "There's something you could do."

My brows pinched. "Tell me."

"If you marry Marie Carter, I'll give you that land."

"But you said the land belongs to some dude in LA determined to develop."

"Yes. But money can buy anything. You know that," he said with a smirk that made an icy clump settle on my chest.

As I ruminated over my father's offer, a big chunk of my cheek sat between my teeth. "But I don't love her."

"You know your problem, Sam?" Without waiting for my response, he continued, "You're an idealist. Women like Marie make great wives. She's smitten, which means you can do whatever you like."

"What does that mean exactly? Enlighten me, Father."

"Do I need to spell it out?"

"If you're suggesting I cheat on my future wife, as you do, then you're seriously off the mark. The woman I marry will be one that I adore, and not just because she pleases me in bed but because she's my equal."

Predictably, my father grimaced at what I'm sure he deemed a preposterous notion. He shook his head. "I sent you to the best schools and this is what you've become: a liberal. Please don't tell me you're now voting Democrat. That will have me reaching for my blood-pressure meds."

"That's my business. And my democratic right."

He responded with a gruff snort.

As he was leaving to go back in, he reiterated, "The land's yours. But you must marry Marie Carter."

With that conflict pounding through my head and speaking of the devil, I found Marie sitting up close to Julia, giggling. They were very close. Since they came from similar backgrounds, it made sense.

I must've startled them because both women looked up at me as if were a six-foot-two-inch rabbit.

"Marie, can I have a word?" I said.

Julia gave her a subtle approving nod, which I found odd for some reason.

Marie sashayed over to me wearing a fabricated smile. I sensed that she wasn't as attracted as she made out, or was that because of that permanent blank expression?

"There you are, Sammy," she said, linking her arm in mine.

My head felt like a heavy weight, barely moving into a nod. "We should do dinner."

She squished in tight. "Oh, I thought you'd never ask."

"Marie, if we're going to do this, it's because of our parents."

"Oh… what do you mean?" Her blue eyes had that confused tinge, and then she glanced over at Julia, who was talking to Steve.

"What I mean is that we should do dinner and discuss it." While these words exited my lips, a sinking feeling seized me. How was I going to play this game? I wanted Juni, not Marie. And when it came to bullshitting, I was not that man.

She nodded slowly and cozied up close, and then her perfume traveled up my nasal passages and I sneezed. After I settled down, I said, "Okay, I'll call you."

Leaning in, she kissed my cheek, and then I erupted into a sneezing fit. Marie shook her head as though I had some control over my allergy, just like my father earlier. "You'll have to remember to take some Sudafed."

"Or perhaps don't wear Chanel No.5," I retorted.

I may as well have suggested that Marie wash the floor of some halfway house. Her plumped lips parted and her painted eyebrows twitched. "Are you kidding? I shower in it."

Gritting my teeth, I said, "Then Sudafed it is."

JUNI

Four weeks later...

My period was late. It had only been five weeks since I gave myself, foolishly, to Sam. And I hadn't heard a word from him.

Hell.

I'd always prided myself on being able to read people. Convinced that he was sincere, I had fallen into Sam's big arms, and the rest was history, so to speak. If I ever ran into him again, apart from stomping on his foot, I'd suggest to Sam that he arrange for a screen test in Hollywood.

My hands shook as I ripped open the wrapper of a pregnancy test. I was at my friend Jess's place. She'd suggested that I drop in so that she could hold my hand. Jess screen-printed fabrics. I loved her quirky and interesting designs and was inspired to collaborate with her on a clothing range. While having that discussion, I opened up about my late period.

"But he used a condom," I said at the conclusion of my teary recounting of that night with Sam.

Sympathy coated Jess's dark eyes. "They don't always work."

It was the longest ten minutes I'd ever waited. As the positive line started to grow, my heart squeezed tighter the more defined that line became. I even had to look away. When I turned my head back and focused, the word "positive" punched me in the face.

My heart sank. Tears welled in my eyes. "This couldn't be!" I told myself.

Jess knocked on the door. "Are you okay, sweetie?"

In a trance, I walked out and showed her.

"Shit," she said. "You bought two. Try again. It happened to a friend of mine. They're not always accurate."

An hour later, while sipping a herbal concoction known for its calming properties, we stared down at not two but five plastic sticks, all reading positive.

As the reality of the situation dawned on me, I said, "I'm not ready for this."

Holding my hand, Jess said, "You'll have to tell him, I suppose."

I'd already looked up the number for Chalmer and Son and had even called it a couple of times, but couldn't go through with it. Scarlett admonished me for being so old-fashioned. "This is the noughties," she'd exclaimed. "Women can call men. And in any case, he owes you an explanation."

She was right. But for some reason, I couldn't bring myself to call Sam. It irked me that he hadn't called as promised. It showed that he wasn't interested. Plain. And. Fucking. Simple.

I shook my head. "No. He can go fuck himself. I'll go it alone. I'm not calling that asshole."

"Go, sister." Jess nodded defiantly. "And anyway, I'm here, Juni. I love babies. I wanted to become a midwife. I might still, you know, if this doesn't work." She pointed to her latest run of printed T-shirts.

"They'll sell. They're brilliant, Jess."

After four weeks of absence from the market, I'd decided to revert to my life before Sam messed it up. I'd created a range of wraparound reversible dresses made from organic hemp and cotton blend. Sewing like crazy all month it had been my way of dealing with out-of-control emotions. Every time Sam's twinkling dark eyes entered my thoughts, I pushed down on the accelerator pedal, visualizing sewing over that bone-melting smile of his. I lost count of how many times I nearly sewed over my finger.

Rocking my head to and fro, I studied myself in the mirror wearing one of my creations: a magenta dress trimmed with a turquoise frill.

"I love that dress," said Jess, admiring it in the mirror. "If I make enough sales today, I'm going to buy one."

"No need. I'll swap you for a T-shirt," I said, eyeing one featuring an upside-down tree hanging from the talons of a horned mythical creature, which to me symbolized my predicament: my life changed after I chained myself to Oscar. The upside-down tree represented how seriously fucked up my life had become now that I was pregnant.

My parents would understand. And there was Scarlett, who'd probably want to ritualize the whole birth. Visualizing myself in her sunken bath with rose petals and a cloaked midwife chanting, I almost laughed.

I sat on the edge of my friend's bed with my head in my hands. Jess entered, carrying a cup of coffee. As with most market days, I'd spent the night at Jess's. It was closer to the market. And she didn't own a car, so it helped both of us.

"Hey, sweetie. It will be all right. I'll be here to help."

"I don't even know if I want to keep it."

Jess studied me for a moment. Although her fixed stare conveyed varying emotions, it was empathy and not judgment that I read—a heartwarming reminder of why Jess was my best friend.

"I don't even know the father that well."

"But you spent hours together," she countered.

Apart from Scarlett, Jess was the only one that I'd spoken to about how I'd lost my virginity in a penthouse suite with a man I thought I hated. And like Scarlett, Jess, also a hopeless romantic, had stars in her eyes.

"Yeah." I sighed, replaying that scene for the millionth time—Sam's sweet and understanding manner, those affable chocolate eyes, and his playful ways. "He certainly duped me."

"But you don't know that for sure. He could have been in an accident."

I looked up at Jess. "That thought struck me, too. I mean, how can one make up that much passion?"

"Then why don't you contact him?" she asked. "And, you know what they say: action speaks louder than words." She raised an eyebrow.

"I know, and going by his body language, he couldn't get enough of me. He smothered me with affection." I stopped to take a breath as I thought of Sam's strong arms around me and how his feathery kisses turned into moist, hungry ones. "I might have to contact him, I suppose." I sighed. "You're right. Something might have happened to him."

"I can understand why you're hurting. It's not easy making *that* call. It would be nicer if you heard from him. But you just don't know, Juni." She shrugged. "The baby will be stunning." She smiled encouragingly.

Sam's handsome features entered my thoughts. I'd memorized everything about him. Particularly that unflinching, hooded gaze that smoldered as he stretched me to the point of indescribable ecstasy.

"Mm… Only I hope he or she doesn't take after the father. He deceived me." I erupted like a volcano of despair, drenching Jess's cheek as she comforted me with a hug.

"Remember, you don't have to do this alone. I'm here."

"You're a good friend, Jess." Wiping my tears, I rose from the bed. "Let's get a move on."

We loaded her gear into my car along with my latest collection and headed off to the market.

One of the only joys of getting up early was the pretty dawn that promised a warm summer's day. Inhaling optimism, I marveled at the soft red-pinks bleeding through the translucent turquoise sky.

SAM

I'd talked Scotty into going to the artisans' market with me, which I'd already visited every Saturday without fail for four weeks. It was the only market in that area, and I recalled Juni distinctly telling me that she sold her clothes at a market in Oakland.

As I expected, Scotty would have preferred to hang out at his warehouse or, more accurately, his makeshift dinosaur factory, which was how I described that industrial building he'd moved into. A paleontologist, Scotty was reconstructing a T-Rex, who I'd named Marc Bolan. The name made Scotty return a puzzled look. He'd missed out on seventies pop music. His academic parents' musical tastes had never made it past the nineteenth century, or so he said.

"It will do you good," I said, crossing the main road. "You never get out. You're going to fossilize soon."

He laughed. "I wouldn't have picked you for the market sort of guy, Sam."

"I'm not. But there's a girl."

We stood at the entrance of the bustling market. As it was a warm, sunny day, the crowd was huge.

"Ah… a girl. I should have guessed," said Scotty.

"This is different. Juni's different in a way that's hard to explain. I've never met anybody like her before. It's driving me nuts. I just can't find her. How that's possible in this era of social media confounds me."

"I don't have a Facebook page," said Scotty.

"Mm… neither do I. But still. It's turning me inside out. I'm about to call my father's minions to look for her."

"Aah… the mating habits of *homo erectus*."

"Yes… well, Juni made this *homo* very *erectus*," I said. "I mean that in the Latin sense, of course." I raised an eyebrow.

"That goes without saying. I've known you since college, Sam. Women are definitely your thing."

"And you too," I argued. Scotty might have had his head buried in fossils, but he still liked a pretty girl.

Smirking, he agreed with a nod.

"Speaking of which," said Scotty, watching a couple of girls dressed in short summery dresses crossing our path while giving us the eye. "This may not have been a bad idea after all."

The smell of freshly brewed coffee drifted toward me. Noticing a stall set up as a makeshift café, I said, "Let's go over there and grab a coffee first, hey?"

We headed to the stall and stood in line, which took a while.

"A long black, thanks," I said to the young guy dressed in a brightly striped shirt that played havoc with the hangover I had after spending a mind-numbing dinner with Marie, my potential fiancée. After I'd fought off her advances, I'd dropped into one of those lonely, obscure bars wearing Marie's disappointment on my conscience, given that she'd virtually offered to suck my dick in the car. I'd chosen that bar because the patrons were there to drink and not pick up. I ended up telling an older man with a face that had seen it all, after plying him with shots of bourbon, all about Juni. His eyes animated slightly when I mentioned that I was her first and how that had made me feel, emotionally speaking. Of course, I didn't reveal that she was the hottest fuck I'd ever had. In truth, it was lovemaking of the sort I'd never,

ever experienced, because, before Juni, I'd only ever fucked. A lot. But this was different. Stranger or not, I needed to get that off my chest.

Scotty was a great pal. But when it came to talking about women and sex, he tended to shrug and pat me on the arm while handing me a book written by some celebrated Danish philosopher. I was more a lose-myself-in-a-novel kind of guy, having sat at the back of philosophy lectures, doodling all over expensive textbooks.

"Fair-trade?" the man asked.

"Uh…?" I looked at Scotty, who shrugged and nodded.

"Yeah. Great. Thanks."

As we were leaving, I whispered to Scotty, "We've done our good deed for the day."

He sniffed. "I think it's great. We need to do shitloads more than just buy fair-trade coffee, though."

"That's true, buddy." I nodded.

With coffees in hand, we stood to the side and watched the colorful parade of marketgoers. Normally at that hour on a Saturday, I was asleep or getting up while trying to pep talk myself into sweating out my hangover at the noisy, head-thumping gym, which I'd end up finding any excuse to avoid.

Just soaking in a ton of smiling faces full of pep lifted my energy level as I sipped the strong coffee.

"So, Scotty, a pair of hand-knitted socks. Or…" I craned my neck, trying to read the sign of the stall next to the socks. "Shit, we can have our auras read. What do you think?"

Behind his spectacles, Scotty's dark eyes wrinkled with amusement at my playful tone. "I don't even know what that means, Sam."

"Join the club," I returned.

We stopped at various stalls selling coffee cup holders with famous quotes or interesting loud shirts that the rebel within me itched to step into. There were beanies in a rainbow of colors, along with mysterious purposeless objects.

Noticing a comic stand, we naturally paused to look. Being boys at heart, we had a thing for those. And this dude had created his own, which really impressed me. In my book, creativity merited respect.

As I flicked through one, I encountered strange creatures with misshapen heads leaping through the air like twisted ballet dancers. I was sold immediately, especially when I saw the Chevrolet-like cars with growly faces roaring around. The artwork alone impressed me. I picked up the entire series, which was named Creature from the Slack Cocoon.

"Do you take plastic?" I asked.

Looking like he'd had a bigger night than me, he nodded sheepishly.

After I'd paid him, he placed my purchases in a paper bag and handed them to me. He scratched his head, and asked, "Ah… do you want me to sign them?"

"I don't know. Are you going to be famous?" I asked in jest.

He shrugged. He was one those tons-of-talent-but-no-marketing-drive types.

I laid the comics down. "Go on, then."

A humble smile came and went. I could see it meant a lot to him. And for that alone, I was equally happy to support him.

"I hope you let me have a read," said Scotty as we headed over to the beer stall that I'd spied earlier.

"But of course," I said with a cartoonish voice that always made him laugh.

I might as well have seen a naked beauty. My eyes sparked at the sight of the boutique beer stall. This was my passion after all. Glancing down at my watch, I saw that it was midday. "Good. Beer o'clock."

Scotty laughed.

"Do you want one?" I asked.

"Why not?" he replied, watching me hover over the various little green bottles lying in barrels of ice.

"That's the pale ale," said one of the sales assistants. "And over there we have dark ale."

I nodded pensively, studying their labels and presentation. I wanted in—not at a market stall but in a proper establishment with nice big stainless-steel vats in the back where people could go on tour if they chose.

Opting for a pale ale, Scotty and I grabbed one each.

I took a swig, and like a professional taster, I savored the flavor. Nodding my approval at the assistant, I said, "That's a nice light flavor. Not too complex. Just as I like it."

"Yeah. Me too," he said, looking pleased that at last, he had a customer who was into the holistic approach to beer.

We cruised along, sipping on beer. Feeling revived, at last, I enjoyed the experience of being at a market filled with useful and useless objects. It represented the finer elements of human endeavor.

Scotty stopped at a T-shirt stall. He held his chin and studied an upside-down tree being carried by a big, prehistoric bird. "Hey, I like that."

I reached into my pocket and grabbed my wallet. "Let me buy it for you."

"It's forty bucks," said Scotty. "Even though it's seriously worth it, I can't expect that from you."

I waved my hand flippantly. "It's small change. Pick one. Go on."

Scotty used every dollar he earned from his university position on fossils for his dinosaurs. His thrift was evident from the holes in his jeans, which had been worn out through work and not bought that way, and the faded T-shirts he seemed to always wear when he wasn't in his white lab coat.

"Can I help you?" asked a girl who made Scotty freeze on the spot.

I could see plainly enough he was attracted to the pretty girl, who returned him a smile.

Noticing that Scotty had lost his tongue—for when it came to girls, he missed the lecture on how to come across as smooth and cool—I stepped in to help. "My friend wants to buy a T-shirt." I looked at Scotty. "Go on, pick one."

She studied his torso. "You'll probably need an extra-large."

He nodded silently.

Scotty was a mess. I could see he really liked her.

"Are these your creations?" I asked in an attempt to open up the discussion.

She nodded as she passed a T-shirt to Scotty.

"They're very imaginative," I said, looking at Scotty in a bid to involve him in the discussion.

"They are."

"He's a paleontologist working on a T-Rex at the moment."

Bingo.

Her eyes widened with keen interest. "I love dinosaurs. I'm really into them, big time." Her effusiveness worked magic.

While I hung to the side, sipping my beer and giving Scotty space to chat, someone from behind, called out, "Hey, Jess."

I turned just as she said, "Have you got any…" The final word didn't leave her lips, because her eyes settled on my face, and her jaw dropped.

JUNI

Sam's jaw dropped, and his eyes turned into that alluring shade of what I imagined Satan's eyes looked like. I'd never seen the devil, but I imagined that his eyes were close to Sam's. I hated how Sam looked sexier than ever. That was just plain unfair. I would have preferred him to have a paunch or a face full of pimples or to have lost half a head of hair around the crown area so that he looked like Larry in *The Three Stooges*. Instead, he looked buff, if not a little tired around the eyes, which only added to his sexiness. He wore a blue-colored shirt that those big, taunting biceps threatened to rip a hole into.

Everything went into slow motion.

Snapping out of my daze, I realized that anyone could've walked off with my entire collection when I left my stall to get change for a customer. After forcing my addicted eyes to look away, I continued over to Jess, who, in her own little romantic bubble, was talking to a tall man with glasses. Aware of Jess's attraction to Clark Kent types and noting her rosy-cheeked smile, I sensed a connection.

"Hey, Jess." I cast Clark Kent an apologetic smile. "Do you have change for a fifty?" My cheeks wobbled, an embarrassing tic of mine when I was nervous, while my legs barely held me up.

"Juni, you're here," came from behind.

Jess looked at me and then over my shoulder at Sam. "You know each other?"

I stretched my mouth into a grimace and gave her a wide-eyed don't-say-anything look.

"I have to get back. There's a customer waiting."

"Sure," she said with a crumpled brow while reaching into her waist pouch. "Here." She handed me some cash.

"Thanks," I muttered. Keeping my eyes glued to the ground, I walked straight past Sam, even though I would've loved to slap him on the face. But that was something one did in the dark of night and not at a sun-drenched family market.

As unaffected as I tried to act, my head, led by my heart, went to mush. I placed the dress in a paper bag and handed it to the customer, forgetting to give her the change as my focus went over her shoulder to Sam, who stood behind her.

His earlier smile had smoothed out, and now instead, his dark eyes radiated something deep and needy.

"Excuse me. I gave you a fifty," said the customer.

Snapping out of my haze, I said, "Oh, I am so sorry." I handed her a ten-dollar bill.

Grateful that the rush was over, I took a deep, steadying breath and returned to Jess's store, where I interrupted her conversation with Clark Kent. Knowing her tendency to ramble nervously around guys she liked, I figured it had turned into some multi-tangent rave.

"Jess, can you keep an eye out while I grab a coffee? Do you want one?"

Beaming a smile that seemed indelibly carved on her lips, she responded, "That would be great."

I headed off to the coffee bus, careful not to turn. My heightened senses informed me that a stalker followed. I broke out into a sprint, which had people turning and looking at me. Running was not what one did at a slow-paced market.

"Juni," Sam said. "Please, stop."

I stopped and turned. "Fuck off, Sam."

Now I really had everyone's attention. I asked myself what was wrong with people. Were their lives that dull that mine had suddenly become so damn interesting?

Sam took my hand, and I pulled it away. "Don't touch me!" That missile of rage sent my ears ringing.

"Juni, I was mugged. They took my phone. The day after…" He spoke in hurried words.

Either Sam was more than a brilliant actor, or… he was telling the truth.

With hands on hips, I stood my ground regardless. "Is that the best you can come up with?"

"I was mugged," he said in a loud voice, which made heads turn. Some even stopped to watch. I whipped my head around and glared at them until they shuffled off.

"Sam. You don't have to do this. I'm sure I'm just another notch on that huge bed, which has probably seen more sheet changes than a whorehouse."

His frown melted and his mouth opened, spilling out laughter that, much to my horror, had my own lips twitching sympathetically. I had to admit that it had been an over-the-top comment on my part.

"Juni. That's why I came here today. I've been here every weekend looking for you, but you haven't been here."

That was feasible, I told myself since I hadn't been there for a month.

I didn't move. Our eyes locked again.

"Come, let me buy you and your friend a coffee. And please… give me some time to explain. I've even got the police report."

I moved along silently. It had been an emotional shock just seeing him. And I needed to get back to my stall.

What I really wanted to do was fall into his arms and allow him to crush me with warmth while I cried into that big strong chest. That was what my heart would have done, even though a voice of reason reminded me that this was not the right time or place to tell Sam about my condition.

The barista asking "What can I get you?" distracted me from the crazy voices running in my head.

After I placed the order, Sam jumped in and ordered two more coffees, and that big hand of his slapped down a note. I was too tired and emotional to rant and rave about not needing his dirty money.

Watching him take the tray of coffees, I said, "This doesn't mean you can hang out with me and get into my head with that smooth tongue of yours."

Sam stopped and turned his handsome head to face me squarely. A slow smile grew from the corner of his lips. "I didn't hear you complaining about my smooth tongue last time."

"Now you're being coarse. That was a figure of speech."

"I know that, Juni." He cocked his head, and our eyes once more locked in a battle of sexual tension. I so wanted to berate him, but the chemistry between us was electric, almost palpable, in that I kept losing myself in him.

"Jokes aside, am I that much of a bore?"

"No… But I don't trust you." That came out half-heartedly because I wasn't sure what to think. Sam's mugging story could have been true, in which case my attitude would seem unkind.

I couldn't help but blame him, as flawed and unreasonable as that was, given that I'd been a willing participant. But if Sam hadn't been so fucking hot and sexy, with that deep voice that lulled and massaged my deeper regions into dropping my guard, I would not be pregnant!

When I returned to my stall, there were customers everywhere. Sam's buddy had been watching over it while Jess sold one T-shirt after another.

"Thank you. And I'm sorry for the wait," I said.

He held out his hand. "I'm Scotty, by the way." He leaned in and whispered, "He did get mugged. He's crazy about you. And please do me a favor…"

I responded with a questioning frown.

"Let him explain. Otherwise, he'll drive me nuts." A little twinkle of sincerity shone from behind his spectacles.

I liked him and was excited for Jess, who had one eye on her customers and one on him. The best I could do was return a tight smile and get back to my customers, wearing a warm glow that had been missing for a month.

SAM

"You're in North Beach?" I asked.

"Uh-huh. At my aunt Scarlett's home. She's having a small gathering, and I'm here for the night."

"Hey, that's handy. I'm in Nob Hill."

"That figures," she said so dryly her tongue could have stuck to her palate. It made my lips curl, though. I was just relieved that we were talking. She could have ranted and raved in gibberish, and a smile would have still stretched my face to the limits.

I'd managed to get her number from Jess.

After Juni had turned her back to me at the market, I'd headed over to her friend's stall. After I watched Jess pressing her number into Scotty's phone, I took the initiative and asked for Juni's phone number. Much to my relief, she didn't take much convincing and tapped it into my phone. I then took the unusual step of scribbling the number on my wrist.

"How did you get my number? I thought you'd lost it," Juni asked.

"Your friend gave it to me."

"Mm…"

"I'm thinking of getting it tattooed on my wrist," I said.

"Huh?" A long pause followed.

"Are you there?" I asked.

"Yeah, I am."

Her breathy response was doing things to me that had begun earlier that day after I saw her golden hair blowing in the wind and those beautiful green eyes filled with fiery disdain. As I watched her loose floral dress flapping about, I had unconsciously breathed furiously along with the wind just to catch sight of her soft, milky thighs, the feel of which still tingled on my fingertips.

"Any chance of catching up? Could we meet in Little Italy for a drink before your party?"

"Um… I suppose you can come here."

I punched the air. Even if I would have preferred to see Juni alone, I would take any meeting I could get. "I'd like that. Your aunt won't mind?"

"She's that more-the-merrier type of person."

"Okay then. Text me the address. How should I dress?"

A chuckle tickled my ear. "Just wear clothes."

"Oh… really? I was hoping to arrive naked."

She sniffed. "Around Scarlett, that wouldn't be so weird."

"Now you've got me seriously curious about this aunt of yours."

"My aunt's rather colorful. Compared to her, I'm kind of beige."

A picture formed in my mind of Juni in that purplish-red dress, ankle boots, and short purple lace socks. The whole ensemble would normally have made me cringe, but somehow Juni wore her individuality with style. I couldn't have seen her any other way. If anything, it added to her sexiness.

"Juni, you're anything but beige."

"I'll take that as a compliment."

"And so you should." I paused for a breath. "Okay. I'll be sure to wear my green-and-purple polka-dot shirt then."

"It's not a clown party, you know," she said.

I laughed at her mocking tone. "That's a shame. I was looking forward to wearing a red spongy nose and smothering my mouth with red paint."

She giggled. "Somehow, I think you could pull that one off."

"Mm… I can… but I prefer the milky-white hand of a girl called Juniper."

"Huh?" She paused for a moment, mulling over my cheeky innuendo. "Ooh… You're being crass again."

"Harmless banter, Juni. At least you're talking to me. And I do like the sound of your voice. Especially when it's all breathy and in my ear."

"Sam… stop it," she said with a smile in her voice.

"Okay. I'll promise not to turn up dressed as a clown. I'll wear something simple."

"Something tells me you don't do simple, Sam."

"I'll take that as a compliment, Juni."

Another pause followed. "I'll text you the address," she said.

"I'd like that. And Juni…"

"Mm?"

"I can't wait to see you."

Another pause followed before she said, "Look, Sam, I hope you're not getting any ideas. I am not an easy fuck."

A rush of blood headed down to my groin. "No, you're not. You're what I call a hard fuck. Really hard."

"Sam, stop it." I sensed her stifling a giggle. "Are you always this crude?"

"Sometimes. It depends on the situation. Around my mother, I'm not. I'm all proper grammar and expletive-free, but we've been through a lot, Juni."

"It doesn't mean I'm going to sleep with you again, though."

"I'm really happy to take this slow, Juni. Just hanging out with you and seeing those pretty lips curl slightly at my dirty mouth is priceless. We can do what they did in the fifties and hang out at a soda fountain."

"You've been watching too many silly movies," said Juni.

"Guilty as charged. Not proud of that. But hey, if you promise to hang out with me, I'll have another go at Marcel Proust, a big heavy book I use as a doorstopper."

"Don't read it on my account. I've never even heard of him," she said.

"He's the literary equivalent of me crushing a bear with my bare hands just to impress you."

"How gross. I'd hate you if you did that. I love animals."

"Mm… sorry, that was a sloppy metaphor. Hang on, let me see if I can come up with another superhero analogy that doesn't involve bones being crushed. Ah, I know: diving off a craggy cliff to save a dolphin.

She laughed. "You're crazy, Sam."

Just like my home, the elegant double-story blue Edwardian house boasted bay windows and detailed white scrolled features on the facade.

Taking a moment after the steep hill, I wiped my brow and exhaled a steadying breath. I headed up the steps and arrived at a dark-blue door with a brass knocker in the shape of a Gorgon's head. As I lifted it, the creature's wild eyes stared menacingly into mine as if to warn me of something.

The door opened, and a dark-haired man said, "Hey, man, welcome."

I stepped in, and incense, weed, and hard-to-define aromas wafted up my nose. I became light-headed just standing there.

"I'm Javier," he said.

I stretched my arm out to shake his hand. "I'm Sam, a friend of Juniper's."

"Welcome." He extended his arm. "After you."

I headed toward the sound of voices and ethereal music swirling away in the background.

Stepping into a large room with red walls and an unhindered view of the bay, I joined a crowd of folk dressed in every color known to humankind. The women wore flowing dresses, while the men, who seemed to outnumber the women, were young and softly spoken.

I looked about until my eyes landed on Juni. Everything else faded as though a spotlight shone on her beautiful face. Her eyes looked up and met mine. She resembled a goddess. In a tight-bodiced dress, Juni's cleavage was so considerable, it was enough to make any grown man melt. A rush of testosterone inflamed me.

Snapping out of my trance, I noticed men standing close by and ogling her. Although I didn't own that right, it was time to claim her, so I strode over and hugged Juni. Instead of struggling, she allowed me to linger for a delicious moment.

Juni gently pushed away from my hold and studied me with that curious, semi-amused expression that always made me smile. "And hello to you."

I took her hand. "You look beautiful. Green's your color."

"It's the color of Venus," said someone from behind me.

I turned and saw a woman who looked like Juni, only older.

"You must be Sam," she said, opening her arms and hugging me.

A strong scent of sandalwood flooded my nasal passages as I removed myself from her embrace.

"I'm Scarlett, Juni's aunt. It's lovely to have you here." She cast Juni a flicker of a smile loaded with their own secret language. "We have food and a lovely mulled wine, and a special punch." Her eyebrow lifted at the word "special." I could only assume that the punch contained more than fruit juice and liquor.

"That sounds interesting," I said, shifting my focus back to Juni. "Say, I can see the family resemblance."

The women looked at each other and smiled.

Javier came and whispered into Scarlett's ear. She looked at me and said, "I look forward to having a chat later." Slinking off, she took the younger man's arm.

JUNI

Dressed in a cream-colored linen shirt and Levis, Sam stood out. Although his garb was a departure from the loud shirts, striped draw-stringed pants, or velvet jeans worn by the male guests, it wasn't just his clothes that made Sam stand out. He was breathtakingly handsome, and I'd forgotten how much so, especially with the twinkle in those bedroom eyes of his.

My heart and head went into battle. Was I to hold my ground and play hard to get? Or just fall into his arms? Even though I managed to remain cool, I wasn't sure how long I could keep that masquerade up, given that my resolve weakened considerably after his hot soft lips brushed mine for that little welcoming peck.

The green-eyed monster lurked close too. This was a new sensation for me, which concerned me since I'd thought I was above jealousy and those types of silly emotions.

Slinking about, Melissa, a notorious and self-proclaimed sex goddess, cornered Sam at the punchbowl. I'd forgotten to warn him about the herbal intoxicants that had been mixed with pomegranate juice. As he took a sip of the punch, Melissa touched his big bicep, and I swore I could smell sex oozing from her.

In I marched to claim what was mine. In another out-of-character gesture, I stood between them, allowing Sam to take my hand again. I indulged in the warmth of his grasp, while Melissa, known for her huge sexual appetite dressed up as tantra, kept flirting with Sam.

"I see you've met Melissa," I said coolly.

Sam's smirk made me want to slap him. He could read my jealousy. I hated that. I needed to stand my ground and make him work harder, I kept reminding myself. But as Melissa rubbed herself against him while whispering something in his ear, I had to strike.

"Um, Sam, can I have a word?"

Grabbing his punch, he followed me out.

I led him to the porch, which overlooked a water feature cascading over a statue of Venus standing on a bed of crystals.

"This is an amazing place," said Sam.

As he touched the glass to his lips, I warned, "That's got all sorts of mind-altering substances in it."

He set it down as if it were tainted. "Scarlett implied something to that effect." He paused. "I'm not in the mood to trip. I'm pretty straight when it comes to taking anything other than alcohol. I should have brought some beer along." He studied me. "What about you?"

"I'm not drinking. And to be honest, my family is wilder than me. I'm the straight one." I smiled tightly.

He held my gaze and nodded. "I don't think you're totally straight, though."

His unshifting gaze almost stole my sense of balance. "What do you mean by that?"

"I mean that you're curvy and flexible and…" Sam took my hand.

"You're being frisky, Sam," I said.

He removed his hand. "Sorry. It's just that you're even more beautiful than I remember, and I…" He smoothed back his hair. "I wish I'd brought some beer."

"There's some beer in the fridge. I'll get you one." I started to go, but he took my arm.

"Stay for a minute." His eyes stared deeply into mine. No humor, just deep and meaningful. He reached into his pocket and brought out his phone and touched the screen. "Here."

I took the phone, and an official document gleamed up at me. I handed it back. "I believe you."

"That's a relief." He let out an audible breath. "I've been going crazy this past month looking for you. I tried googling Juniper Berry, but all I kept getting were images and details of the plant on Wikipedia, along with a ton of information relating to gin." I chuckled at Sam's exaggerated grimace. "And how is it that you don't have a website or an online presence? And your father's brewery? I tried everything. I couldn't find anything on any of you. Do you really exist?"

"I think so." I giggled. "I share Jess's website for my range of clothes, which is under her name. And my father's a serious Luddite."

He cocked his head. "Okay. He hates technology. So how does he do business?"

"Dad's old school. That's how he describes himself. His business is word of mouth, just as he likes it. He's seriously suspicious of the internet," I said.

He nodded slowly. "If I hadn't seen you today, I would have sent some of the company's minions to hunt you out."

My head pushed back. "Really?"

"Yeah. Really. I couldn't believe how you could be so invisible."

After learning about how Sam had actually gone to great lengths to find me, I thawed out a little. It was also a fair reminder that I needed to get with the game and set up a Facebook and Instagram account. Jess often chided me for being so behind in that area.

We locked eyes again. Behind that playfulness, Sam had a sensitive side to him, which only made me want to push him against the wall and fuck him.

"Melissa was just hitting on you," I said. "She's a slut."

His head pulled back. "You're very direct, aren't you?" He grinned. "I like it though. You're unpredictable. Now that's sexy." He waited for my response, but I just kept staring at him while basking in his compliments. "In any case, I'm not into that dark witchy look. I'm more into fair-headed fairies." He stroked my cheek, leaving behind a fiery sensation.

What Sam didn't know was that my room was filled with fairies, a little obsession that had followed me into adulthood.

Looking the stylish vixen in a black-velvet, medieval-inspired maxi dress with chiffon tulip-shaped sleeves, Scarlett swanned by and joined us.

"Ah…there you both are." She looked at Sam. "Can I get you a drink?"

"Juni mentioned that you have some beer. I'm sorry, I came empty-handed, I wasn't sure…"

"Hey, it's all good. We're just happy that you came along." She smiled sweetly. "Let me get you a beer."

"You're not drinking?" Sam asked, turning to me.

I shook my head. "No… I'm abstaining for now." I wasn't ready to break the news. And I'd sworn Scarlett to secrecy. In any case, I still hadn't decided which way to go. Scarlett had even offered to create a brew known for bringing on miscarriages, but the thought of that repulsed me, as it had Scarlett, who admitted she was dying to hold a baby, given that she hadn't been able to conceive in her later years when she was ready to embrace motherhood.

Scarlett returned with a bottle of beer. "Here you go. I didn't get you a glass."

Taking the bottle, Sam screwed off the top. "It's all good, thanks."

"So, Sam, when's your birthday?"

True to form, Scarlett, an avid astrologer, could barely wait to get into Sam's star chart.

"March the third," he said, wiping his lips with the back of his hand. Even such a common gesture as that had my hormones pinging.

"Oh… a Pisces," she exclaimed with enthusiasm. She looked at me, brimming with joy. "That's a perfect trine. How great is that?"

A line grew between Sam's dark eyebrows. "Is that good?"

"Juni's birthday's the third of November. She's a Scorpio."

He nodded slowly, scratching his head. "Okay."

"That means that you're extremely compatible," she explained.

"I could have told you that," he said with a hint of humor in his eyes. "Still. That's nice to know."

He took my hand, and I felt a spark of electricity running through me.

How could I stay cool for long when my bones were melting and a thick swelling sensation had stolen any sense of reason or balance?

We went back inside, and Claude sprung out from one of the shadowy corners, taking me by surprise. He leaned in and kissed me on the cheek. I could see from his heavy eyelids that Claude was drugged as usual. He was a very productive drug addict, however, in that his artwork hung on the walls of corporate buildings.

"Juniper, here you are," he said. His languid blue eyes undressed me as always, even though I'd never been attracted to him. Hovering close, Claude ignored Sam. "I've been looking for you. I've brought a painting, which you inspired."

"Oh. Um…" I turned to face Sam and gestured toward the artist. "This is Claude."

Sam held out his hand as any gentleman would, and my feeling for him went up a notch. There was no pissing competition, which would have been justified considering Claude's arrogance.

After a brief nod in response, Claude cast his attention back to me and took my hand. "Come and have a look."

I looked at Sam with a subtle eye roll, my way of telling him that Claude meant nothing to me.

In the hallway, I spied a painting of a figure surrounded by thick brush strokes of purples and blues. The nude, bordering on obese, had very big breasts.

My face puckered in dismay. Did I look like that?

"What do you think?" His eyes opened wide with expectancy.

"Juni doesn't look anything like that," said Sam, standing behind me. "It's impressive, though."

Claude, who resembled a Viking with his wild shock of blond hair, looked up at Sam and noticed him properly for the first time. “Who are you?”

“I’m the boyfriend,” rasped Sam with a cold smile.

I turned and looked at Sam. My eyes widened. But it was convenient nevertheless because Claude would have chased me around the party otherwise.

Claude looked at me. “Do you like it, Juni?”

I nodded slowly. In truth, I was horrified by how big the figure in the painting was. “Um… yeah. The colors are nice. Although I’d like to think I’m not that large.”

“Ah… but it’s sexy. A full figure is sexy. I based it on the earliest sculpture of Venus.”

“That explains it. The Venus of Hohle Fels, I believe, known for its larger proportions.” Sam looked at me first, then Claude.

Not hiding his surprise, Claude nodded. “All the earlier effigies of Venus were voluptuous.”

The fact that Sam supported me while demonstrating he had some brains in that beautiful head made my legs weaken that much more.

“She’s not voluptuous, she’s obese,” I said, almost to myself, taking it personally.

Scarlett came to join us in the hallway. “Hey, what have we here?” She looked at the canvas and then at Claude. “It’s gorgeous. I love it.”

Looking dejected, for his ego had taken a pounding from my tepid reception, Claude replied, “I’m afraid my muse is unamused.”

Scarlett looked at me and then laughed. “Juni’s got this silly idea that she’s overweight. That is a beautiful rendering of the mother. Can I buy it?”

“It’s yours, darling.” Claude cast me a sleazy “I’m going to have you if it kills me” gaze and then slid off with Scarlett by his side.

I turned my attention to Sam, who shrugged. “He’s a dick. A talented one, I’ll admit. But he wants to fuck you. And I want to knock those yellowing teeth out of his stoned head.”

I had to laugh at his alpha display. “Sam, he’s harmless.”

"And you're not overweight, Juni." His eyes shone with sincerity.

I returned a tight smile. "Thanks for supporting me."

Accompanied by a young guitarist, Melissa belted out *Fever*. Her sultry voice, despite being husky, was out of tune and therefore grating, as were those hips swaying shamelessly toward Sam.

I whispered, "I might go now."

Sam's big shoulders relaxed. His obvious relief made me appreciate him more. I was heartened to see that Melissa's overt flirtation hadn't registered.

"You're off to Oakland?"

Biting into a fingernail, I nodded. Despite my plan to stay at Scarlet's, I'd decided I needed to leave. The trouble was I didn't want to leave Sam. I wanted to go somewhere quiet, just us alone. But I couldn't bring myself to say that.

"I'm only up the road a little. Why don't you stop over at my place? I promise not to pounce on you." A slow smile formed at one corner of his mouth. "That is unless you want me to."

I bit into my lip, pondering his offer, which of course I knew I wanted to accept within a breath. "I suppose I can trust you. After all, I think I was the one that pounced on you last time we spent a night together."

His eyes gleamed. "And how sweet it was."

"That doesn't mean we'll have sex this time, though. I'd had a few margaritas," I said.

"And here I was thinking it was my animal charm." He cocked his head.

I rolled my eyes.

His animal charm was on fine display, then and there, I thought, with those big arms crossed and his handsome face gazing back at me with a dimpled half smile.

"I know you might find this weird, but I actually had a great night with you. It wasn't just the mind-blowing lovemaking."

My eyes slid over to his face again. Why did he always manage to say the right thing? "Lovemaking?" I challenged.

"Well, that's what it was for me." I searched for a hint of mirth but fell into dark, serious orbs instead.

I had to take a steadying breath, for my legs nearly buckled. Under that joker's mask, Sam had so much depth, I found him difficult to navigate.

After a long pause, I said, "Okay. We might have to walk, though. My car needs charging."

"You've got an electric car?" he asked.

"Yeah. Trouble is, I keep having to think ahead. Something my spontaneous approach to life is unaccustomed to." I giggled.

"I get it. If that were me, I'd be constantly stranded." He chuckled. "I like the idea of them, though. I'm waiting for the ones that recharge while driven to hit the market." His head tilted slightly. "Why that puzzled look?"

"You just don't strike me as an electric car sort of guy."

"There's a lot about me that might surprise you." I was about to respond when he added, "I do have a fondness for my gas-guzzling Mustang."

I grimaced. "Then for the sake of the planet, you may have to get rid of it."

He hissed behind his teeth as though I'd suggested something painful. "Or simply find a magician who can fit my sexy car with an electric motor."

"You make it sound like a love affair. A car's just a car in my mind."

"In the same way that you love clothes, I love a nicely designed car. I'm very male in that way."

Mm... you're very male. Period.

I took another steadying breath as Sam's eyes smoldered suggestively.

"You'll have to excuse the mess." Sam picked up papers off the sofa.

I shook my head. "It's fine. It's got that lived-in feel." He must have read the surprise in my face.

"What's that look, Juni?"

"I was expecting something white, clean-lined, and modern."

He sniffed. "Do I really give out that kind of vibe?"

I shrugged. "The penthouse had that feel."

"That was the only place available. I normally go for classic hotels. I'm a bit of a retro guy in that I love anything to do with the sixties. Especially cars."

"This place is older. It's Edwardian. Like Scarlett's house."

He nodded. "It belonged to my grandparents. I've always loved it. I liked the blue exterior and detail. Nice curves." He raised a brow as though he was speaking about a woman. "It's a bit noisy, though."

"It's definitely full of charm." My eyes settled on the many books strewn about on the coffee table, one of which was open. The cover read: *Essays by Gore Vidal.*

"Do you read?" asked Sam, standing over my shoulder, while his breath caressed my neck.

I turned and fell into his eyes. "Um... I do from time to time. Novels mainly. I also like to read about clothes, fabrics, and sewing, which as you know is my passion."

"That's the beauty of books. One can learn independent of institutions."

I nodded. "I agree. I was homeschooled, so they were very much a part of my upbringing. I do prefer holding a book to reading on a computer screen."

Wandering about the lamp-lit room, I picked up a model of a red vintage car that was heavier than it looked.

"That's my boy thing," he said, with an apologetic smile. "I've never grown out of my love for cars."

I looked into a glass cabinet filled with model cars—from the very first models ever built to sleek, stylish cars I'd seen in old movies.

"One gets a good insight into a person by visiting their home." I did a quick visual sweep of the walls, upon which hung black-and-white photos of villages in Europe, along with more curious images, one of which I recognized: a woman with markings on her naked back. "I love that. She resembles a cello."

"I bought that in Paris. It's by Man Ray, a surrealist from the twenties. It's wonderful, isn't it? I love black-and-white photos, just in case you haven't noticed." He sniffed "And films, too."

I nodded slowly.

Watching me move from corner to corner, picking up the odd book along the way, Sam asked, "So, Juni, what's your verdict, then?"

"Um… I think you're different from my first impression."

"Let me remember. Ah yes… a devil in a suit." His dark eyes danced with humor again.

I wanted to either slap him or eat him. Probably both.

"You gave me good cause to believe that with the way you strutted about as if you owned the place."

Sam laughed in that infectious way that made my lips twitch. Keeping my cool, however, I remained neutral. "When I didn't hear from you, I reverted to that first impression. I had you roasting over a hot spit." I lowered myself onto the sofa.

Responding to my mock smile, Sam grimaced. "Ouch." He joined me on the sofa. "I'm sorry for putting you through that." His face sobered. "I hated the thought of you thinking of me as some sleaze." He touched my hand. "I meant everything I said that night."

Our eyes locked.

His gaze softened, revealing a flicker of vulnerability I hadn't seen in him before, and within a breath, a magnetic force drew me into his arms. I rested my head on his hard but comfortable chest.

"You could have contacted me." His soft voice massaged me. "I hoped you would."

"I did call Chalmer and Sons a couple of times but I hung up," I admitted.

"You should have, Juni. Gender equality means that women can also do some of the chasing."

"Chasing?" I lifted myself off his comfortable body to study him.

He opened his hands and shrugged.

"Mm… I just needed to know you weren't making it all up, Sam." As much as that sounded weak, I couldn't admit that if I hadn't been pregnant, I probably would have called him. If only to abuse him for turning me into a one-night-stand. But that now seemed pointless, given that Sam was there. I fell into his strong body again.

SAM

After what had been a very strange if not interesting evening, I allowed my body to sink into my old leather sofa and do what I'd been dreaming about all month—holding Juni close.

Life felt complete.

Although removing that pretty green dress would have lifted my spirit to that hard-to-reach summit of bliss, just having her there, quietly in my arms, with her heart beating against mine, seemed perfect enough.

I stroked her silky, thick hair, getting drunk on her rose scent.

After having spent half a night listening to music that I wasn't into, I unwound, soaking in the silence. Creative expression aside, when it came to live singing, I liked knowing I was free to leave without causing offense. Although the unceasing hum of car engines and muffled voices, from the busy street of my home, sounded like a type of ambient soundtrack, I welcomed its simple normality.

"I have to say that you don't strike me as someone who embraces witchcraft. And you don't do drugs, which I appreciate."

She studied me for a moment as though trying to figure me out. A faint smile touched her lips. "I'm close to my aunt Scarlett. She's always been there for me, especially this month." She stared at me, and her eyes sparkled with a hint of emotion.

I held her tight. "Oh, Juni, I tried everything to find you."

"It's all good. We're here now. And you're right, I should've called you."

She pushed out of my hold and stared at me again. From wide and innocent to seductive and sensual within a blink, her green eyes made me go to liquid. Just as my hand slid over her hip, my fingers itching to travel up to her nipples, which provocatively pierced her blouse, the doorbell sounded.

We both jumped at the same time.

"Shit." I raked through my hair. "Ignore it." I took Juni into my arms again.

While my fingers traced the deep indent of her waist again, the bell went off again. I had a grating feeling that the intruder wasn't going to budge, and it was obvious I was in because of the lights.

"Just wait a moment. I'll see who it is and send them away."

Juni sat up and smoothed down her dress. I lingered for a moment, staring at her.

"Why are you staring?" she asked with that impish grin of hers.

"Because I'm enchanted by you."

"Must be the punch," she said, lifting a brow.

I shook my head. "Nope. I didn't swallow." I grinned. "Besides, I don't need any drugs to be aroused by you."

The buzzer snapped me out of my romantic haze. I exhaled a frustrated breath and headed for the door. When I opened it, I discovered Marie teetering on her skyscraper heels and leaning against the wall for support.

"There you are," she said, falling into my arms. "I've been calling you."

"You've been drinking, Marie."

A silent gasp of frustration followed. I couldn't have her ruin my night, especially since I was on such thin ice with Juni.

Taking her hand gently, I led Marie down the steps onto the busy sidewalk just as a cable car rattled past, which was a godsend in that it drowned out her whiny voice.

"Why aren't you inviting me in?" she slurred.

I looked about and saw a cab heading my way, another stroke of luck. I hailed it and, much to my joy, it stopped.

"You're drunk, Marie. You should go home. I've had a big day. I'll call you tomorrow. Okay?"

She fell into my arms, and I prayed that Juni hadn't decided to stand at the window, for she would have seen us for sure.

After a little more groping from Marie while she slobbered incoherently into my ear, I held her up by the waist and helped her lie down on the backseat of the cab, while she insisted that I go home with her.

"I promise to call you tomorrow. We can catch up for lunch," I said.

Rubbing my neck, I stood there and watched the cab go off, grateful that I lived on a main drag. A deep breath untangled the tightness in my chest. As I stepped back into the hallway, I cursed my father and that promise I'd made. That was a crack in my personality. I was that guy who wanted to make everyone happy, which contradicted the side of me that hated being dictated to, namely by the force of nature that was my father. I'd entered unchartered waters. I'd never fought for a tree before. But then, I'd never met anybody like Juni before or fallen so hard.

Juni looked up at me with large, questioning eyes.

"Just a drunken friend wanting to come up for a drink," I said, keeping it as close to the truth as I could.

"You could have asked him up. I wouldn't have minded."

I took a deep breath as I mulled over whether to tell her the truth. Instead, I lowered myself and moved up close to her again. "I just want to be alone with you, Juni."

She responded with a shy smile.

Good.

I didn't mind some sexual tension here and there, but not at that moment. I was famished. Inflamed.

I took Juni into my arms again. She slotted into my frame comfortably. No adjustments needed. No bones digging in. Just a natural fit as if we'd been made for each other.

Her tongue caressed her rosy lips, enticing my mouth onto hers. Hot and ferocious, that ravaging kiss reflected the hours I'd spent fantasizing about tasting her again.

My tongue parted her mouth and entered deeply. She tasted of peppermint and something sweet and pure.

Our bodies fused together. Her breasts pressed against my chest, where my heart thumped hard.

Juni drew away first and looked into my eyes. "I want to take this a bit slower. I need to know I can trust you, Sam."

I exhaled a jagged breath in order to still the charge of blood racing through me.

"Okay… Sure." I slid away from her reluctantly. "We can just hold hands and talk if you like." I smiled.

"I'm too tired to talk," said Juni, stretching her arms. "I've been up since seven."

"I can understand that." I stared into her eyes and noted a serious glint. "Are you okay?"

"Yeah. I'm good." Her wavering response was unconvincing, but I rolled with it.

I'd learned from my mother that when a woman was temperamental and moody, holding her hand and listening, even if she was an incoherent mess, was the best remedy. Over the course of a few girlfriends, I'd found that advice had helped. But Juni was different. I had this feeling that it was going to take more than holding her hand to get into that pretty head of hers.

I removed myself from the sofa, and Juni looked up at me. Her disappointed frown confused me. "Where are you going?"

"I need to make up the bed in the guest room."

"Can't I sleep with you?" Her girlish tone belied the sexy woman I knew existed somewhere beneath those artful folds of fabric.

"Of course." I ruffled my hair. "But I thought you wanted to take this slowly."

She bit her lip and shrugged. "We can still cuddle."

"Okay, then. Great." I clapped my hands together, keeping it all nice and easy while wondering how to get my dick to behave, given that I could barely walk.

"I'll go and make the bed, then."

"You don't have to," said Juni, rising from the sofa. "Unless you're removing evidence of recent fucking."

Now that stopped me in my tracks. I searched for that little smirk of hers, but Juni seemed pretty straight. She was testing me.

"Juni, I haven't been fucking lately. The only fucking, which was lovemaking in my mind"—I raised a brow— "was with a sexy girl named Juniper Berry. In any case, since then, other women haven't even registered."

Holding my gaze, Juni bit her lip. "I haven't had much of an appetite, myself."

I took her into my arms and stroked her long, silky hair.

JUNI

Tears pricked the backs of my eyes. I'd become so sensitive. My emotions were all over the place. When was I going to tell Sam? And would I? I still had to decide what I was going to do.

Our lives would change forever.

For that reason alone, I had to wait and bide my time.

We were very different. But yet when we were alone away from the world it felt natural—and, more significantly, I felt safe in his muscular arms. Flashbacks of Sam holding me up while I had been chained to the tree kept recurring. Despite the near-death experience, it still warmed my spirit. That was the moment it had happened for me. When I looked into his eyes, instead of that playful smile, I encountered the deep pools of a complex man. It was then that my soul spoke to me: this man, a complete stranger, who a moment earlier had been my enemy, was ready to die, needlessly, with me in his arms. It all seemed a tad dramatic, given that we had been rescued before the water reached my shoulders.

Just like the rest of his place, Sam's bedroom surprised me. Grainy photos of black-and-white nudes hung on a pale-yellow wall fringed with florid white cornices. While not sleazy in any way, the images were sensuous and artful. I'd arrived at the conclusion that Sam had great taste and that he was, deep down, a creative soul, despite playing the corporate guy who happened to look sexy in a suit.

Sam smoothed down the unmade bed and then looked at me as if lost. He was out of his comfort zone, which was endearing in many ways. The lothario would have made all the moves by now, but Sam just kind of bumbled about which made me giggle.

"What?" he asked, shaking his head.

"You're moving about doing very little," I said.

"Yeah." He ran his fingers through his hair. "I'm nervous."

"Why?" I asked.

He looked at me with a sexy dark gaze that quickened my pulse.

"Have you got something I can sleep in?" I tilted my head. "How about that cute dinosaur pajama top? Just for old times' sake."

He ambled over to a drawer and removed the pajamas. He kept the bottoms and handed the top to me.

I turned. "Can you unzip me, please?"

After the zipper was released, Sam's fingers lingered. Tingles flushed through me as he stroked my naked back. "Shit, Juni, you're not wearing a bra. You better go and change in the other room. Otherwise…"

As my dress fell to my feet, I asked, "Otherwise what?"

His eyes hooded. "You're teasing me, Juni. I'm going to have to go into the bathroom and do what any hot-blooded male would do if you keep this up."

"I'm sure you'll be able to control yourself." I buttoned up the pajama top slowly.

"That's better," he said, unzipping his jeans. "You've got the sexiest tits I've ever laid eyes on, Juni. And they've grown."

That made me all hot and sticky. Now it was my turn to ogle. My breath hitched. Sam was all muscle. I was unable to stop my eyes from traveling downwards when they landed on his big bulge. His naked, sculpted torso revealed a six-pack and a well-defined chest that I couldn't wait to rest my head against.

As he began to lower his briefs, I had to look away. My heart was beating all the way down to my sex, which was hot and swollen. I too would probably need to do something to douse the fiery ache below.

Jumping into bed, I stretched out my legs, and Sam joined me.

I rolled into his arms and rested my head on his chest. His heart beat against my ear. My own was beating just as fast.

We turned to face each other, and all my earlier resolve to take things slowly evaporated. His mouth found mine, which was just as hot, and I fell into a trance as our lips melted together.

Caressing my thigh, his touch left goose bumps in its wake. Breathless with anticipation, I craved his fingers. I'd thought of little else since meeting him.

His tongue tangled in mine, and while his hands squeezed my butt, a groan vibrated from his chest.

"Juni, this isn't going to be easy. I mean…"

My mouth landed on his again. I couldn't stay away from those hot, sensual lips. Sam's strong body supported mine, holding me close. He caressed my breasts, and my nipples spiked on his rotating palm.

I let out a moan. But then my head got involved, and reality stepped in. I pulled away. The complexity of the situation hit me again.

Sam pushed back an unruly strand of hair that dangled sexily on his forehead, revealing a pinched brow.

"I promised myself I wouldn't have sex with you."

He nodded slowly. "It's not exactly easy with you holding me. You're beautiful and hot, tormentingly so. I'll try to be stronger."

"Tormentingly?" I laughed.

"Having you close…"

I rolled into his arms and with my head on his chest, I inhaled his male scent, which smelled of arousal—or so I guessed it to be, for that same intoxicating scent had emanated from him the last time we'd held each other.

He stroked my hair gently. I'd arrived at the safest place in the universe.

How could a man I hardly knew make me feel so safe?

Our bodies touched again. I could feel his hard cock on my thigh, and our lips met again.

This time, I almost jumped on top of him.

Passion had the winning edge. I'd be sensible tomorrow, I told myself as he clutched my butt, drawing my pelvis close to his.

"I'm getting mixed messages, Juni," said Sam.

In response, my lips landed on his and fused with his fleshy, moist mouth.

SAM

"What are you into, Sam?" she asked. Her eyes were half closed, and my heart raced, pumping blood to my groin.

"I'm into you, Juni." I caressed her breasts, and my mouth landed on her nipple, which hardened on my tongue as I sucked on it.

My fingers smoothed over her curves as a sculptor would to memorize every inch of soft contour.

As I lowered my pajamas, I noticed her eyes widen slightly. "Is this what you want?"

Juni nodded. Her eyes were on my dampened, hard cock.

I lowered myself to the bed and parted her thighs. I lingered there and breathed in her femininity. My fingers walked up her silky thigh and, parting her folds, entered her tight pussy. Her thick creaminess made me hiss behind my teeth.

"You sound like you're in agony," said Juni.

"Yeah… of the sweetest kind," I rasped, sucking on my finger.

I lowered my head between her thighs, which she'd widened to invite me in. Placing the tip of my tongue on her clit, I licked her softly, sucking back her juices, as my hands gripped her writhing ass.

Her moans grew in strength.

I lifted my head and asked. "Are you okay?"

"Please don't stop," she murmured.

Happy to comply, which was far from a chore, given that her taste was so sublime, I buried my face between her thighs and sucked, licked, and rotated my tongue over her swollen clit.

Her pelvis pushed up to my mouth, and gripping my shoulders, she uttered, "Aah…"

My tongue plunged in deeply, followed by my finger, which opened the floodgates to a gushing climax.

"I want you to fuck me," she uttered.

"Are you sure?" I asked.

Her eyes were hooded. A strand of blonde hair curled provocatively over her full breasts, an image that cried out for my camera.

She nodded, and I released a silent sigh of pure contentment. The thought of being inside that angel was so fucking hot, I could honestly say I'd hit a new spiritual high just thinking about it.

I reached over into my drawer and brought out a condom.

Juni touched my arm. "No… no need. I'm… on the pill."

Her stammering made my forehead lower.

Strange or not, who was I to complain? Skin on skin was the ultimate pleasure for a man, especially with a woman as ripe and responsive as Juni. That had pretty much made it to the top of my list of what to do before dying. Only I hoped to be around a long time for many repeat performances.

With Juni.

"I've had a recent blood test," I muttered.

"Just fuck me," she said.

I certainly loved the assertive Juni. And she could boss me around all she liked if it meant us getting naked and dirty.

I parted her legs. A hot flush went through me as I eyed her pink, glistening opening. The promise of entering her made it hard for me to breathe.

Her eyes all the while remained on my hard cock, which by this stage had gone a shade of blue from aching all night long.

Taking my weight on one arm, I guided in the wet head of my dick.

Battling through her tight walls its sensitive nerve endings sent sparks through me. My body shuddered. Her feisty pussy was sure to challenge what little staying power I could muster.

"Are you okay?" I gasped, overwhelmed by a sensation that went beyond pleasure.

"Yes. It feels beautiful. I love the stretch," she purred.

"I love how you feel, too."

I entered as deeply as I could and then withdrew. So as to not bruise her, I took it slowly.

Juni clutched my ass and impelled me on nevertheless.

My eyes flitted between her voluptuous tits and her eyes, which seemed as drunk on lust as I was.

I buried my face in her breasts. Each thrust threatened an eruption.

I knew she was close, because Juni dug her fingernails into my biceps, and the walls of her pussy contracted around my dick.

I had to summon up almost superhuman control to stave off an orgasm.

"I need you to come, Juni," I said.

"Aah…" Her mouth fell open.

My jaw clenched as an orgasm thundered through me.

And then, perfection. Intoxicating euphoria of the type I'd only experienced once before on that first night with Juni.

A shower of stars cascaded over me. I swear I saw rainbows as my mouth fell open and a guttural, primal groan blended with Juni's screech, as we rode that wave together.

I must have emptied a month of fantasies into Juni.

Sweaty, breathless, and sated, we held each other.

JUNI

It was the nicest day I'd ever had. We just lolled about, eating, talking, and laughing. And to be honest, I never wanted to leave Sam's place. There was something relaxing about the atmosphere he'd created in there.

"I can't believe that you work for a conglomerate of assholes."

Sam had just closed off a call, and by the way his face tightened as he spoke quietly into the phone, I sensed it was business related and that he'd been crushed by something.

Rubbing his neck, he looked at me, and the line on his forehead smoothed out as amusement flickered in his dark eyes. "A conglomerate of assholes? Now that's not a very pretty sight."

I giggled again, something I couldn't stop doing around Sam.

"Tell me all about it, then. Your work," I said, sitting up. Noticing the line between his eyebrows return, I sensed that this wasn't Sam's favorite topic. "I just want to know more about you," I added. "And we didn't exactly meet in the most auspicious of circumstances."

A hint of a smile tried to fight through his obvious unease. "No, we didn't." He let out a deep breath. "I'm fighting for Oscar, believe me."

There was something almost desperate in his tone. None of that silliness I'd grown seriously fond of.

"Are you being pressured?" I asked.

A dismissive shrug told me that Sam wasn't in the mood to talk about the subject of my beloved tree. Standing by the bay window, Sam stood between a pair of palms in large terracotta pots. His worn T-shirt with its dinosaur print reminded me that he hadn't quite grown up. I adored his boyishness, despite Sam being a man in the sexiest sense of that word.

I couldn't even look at him without feeling fire between my legs. Or was that a pleasant ache from our endless fucking?

Allowing my dress to ride provocatively up my thighs, I stretched my legs out on the couch.

Sam noticed. Stupid me. Here I was wishing to talk.

When his eyes settled on my naked thighs, a flush of heat colored his neck, and his eyelids lowered. That look of lust I'd become hooked on took hold again.

He came and sat by my side. His hand landed on my thigh. His eyes looked deeply into mine. At first, they were intense before softening with sexy mischief.

His fingers crept under my dress slowly. I didn't move, because I just wanted him to touch me again and again.

"You're not wearing panties," said Sam almost admonishingly while licking his lips.

I opened my thighs a little wider.

"I thought you might like me naked." A shy smile took over even though the vixen within had well and truly made an entrance. I hadn't known that sex could be so addictive until I met Sam, especially with his ravaging tongue and that big, yummy cock. Although it was buried in denim, I indulged in its rock-hardness by stroking it.

My upper palate salivated at the thought of taking him in my mouth. I'd never done that before.

"What's that little grin on your face, Juni?" His focus shifted between my naked pussy and my hand unzipping his jeans.

I helped him pull down his jeans almost impatiently.

Sam's eyes landed on my lips as my tongue whipped around.

Watching his cock throb hard against his briefs, I placed my hand inside and started to stroke him. The veins of his cock pulsed against my palm.

"If you keep doing that, I will have to fuck you again, Juni," he rasped.

"I want to put it in my mouth."

His head pushed back. "You want to blow me?"

"Yeah. I've never done that. And it's such a nice penis. It's given me a lot of pleasure. I've had so many orgasms. I didn't think it was possible to come that often."

"Nor did I," he responded with a serious expression.

"Huh? You've never made a girl come?" I wasn't really sure if I was ready for a conversation about him giving girls other than me pleasure.

He shrugged. "I preferred the conversation about sucking my dick, Juni. Not ex-girlfriends."

"I will want to know at some point," I said, my hand around his cock, which had lost some of its spring.

"I promise to divulge all the sordid details, which I can say are quite dull in comparison to being with you… and this moment." His voice strained as I pulled at his cock.

I lowered myself to my knees, and taking him into my mouth, I opened really wide.

"Mm…" Was all I heard as I explored his velvety hard cock with my tongue. Swallowing it deeply, I squeezed my lips around it, moving my mouth up and down it while holding the base of the shaft.

Although my mouth ached after a while, a gush of heat traveled up my legs.

Sam's breath became rough and jagged. His veins popped around my tongue.

"I'm going to come, Juni. You need to pull out."

Ignoring him, I sucked and moved my lips up and down, swallowing his cock deeply again. An agonizing groan followed as his veins pulsated against my tongue, spewing hot cream to the back of my throat.

As I wiped my lips, Sam shook his head. "Holy fuck. Juni. Juni. Juni." He paraphrased a Cary Grant movie we'd watched earlier, which made me giggle.

"Did I get it right?" I asked.

"You got it more than right. Wow." He ran his thumb around my swollen lips.

"You've got a beautiful mouth." His hand brushed my cheek. "And a beautiful face." And his hand traveled to my breasts. "And tits that just make me go hard thinking about them and…" His fingers walked down to my sex and I opened wide because like Sam, I'd become insatiable. "And a pussy that I just want to devour with my mouth and cock."

I fell back on the couch.

What was a girl to do? With such a gorgeous man pleading to lick me to kingdom come, I could only thank the gods of lust for that!

Sighing deeply, I opened my thighs as I surrendered to his soft, tantalizing tongue.

After a weekend of endless fucking, or lovemaking as Sam kept calling it, I sat with Scarlett at a café in Little Italy.

Sam had dropped me off in his Hollywood car, which was as sexy as its owner, especially with the top down and my hair blowing in the wind. It felt as though I was in a sixty's movie. I even made a mental note to bring a scarf next time so I could do a Grace Kelly and tie it around my head.

When Sam had pulled up in front of Scarlett's, he'd cut the engine and turned to look at me. The air filled with intensity suddenly, which I think was radiating off me. The fun was over for now, and reality had made a very big, serious entrance.

It felt wrong to hold back on telling Sam about my condition, but for some reason I did. I suppose I didn't want to put him in that precarious decision-making position.

He leaned in and stroked my cheek. Sam's eyes had that unmistakable loving glow that mirrored my full heart.

"Juni," he said. I could see him battling for words.

"You don't have to say much," I fibbed. Because I needed to know in the harsh light of morning what he planned to do.

"I'm smitten." A slow curl at the side of his lips reminded me that like most men, Sam found it hard to put his emotions into words. It was something he made up for in body language.

"So am I, Sam." I bit my lip, and then we held each other tight.

Our lips fused for a long, tender kiss. My lips were sore from the endless kisses. But as with every other part of me, it was very pleasant soreness.

"Will you be my girlfriend?" Sam asked, his forehead touching mine.

"Yes. Of course," I said with a smile that would have lit up the whole of San Francisco.

He took a deep breath. "There's my dad. He's got ideas and plans for me. I'm not that man, but I do need to navigate this carefully."

His big chocolate eyes took me in deep again.

After a moment, I replied, "I get it. You're a billionaire's son… you have to behave in a certain way."

"It's not the money, Juni."

I took his hand. "Then I'm sure we can find a way. And to be honest, my dad's quite difficult to navigate, too. He's got ideas about my future."

He sat up. "Really? I thought it would be all peace and love."

"Oh… Sam, that's such a cliché."

He took me into his arms again. "Then we'll work through it together."

We stared into each other's eyes and giggled, which I really needed, considering that my trenchant left-wing father was the least of my worries.

Flirted

Book Two

SAM

I paced about, chomping on my pen, a horrible habit I'd adopted when young and one that I found hard to break especially around my father. He looked up at me from his desk, which was probably as large as the president's.

"Now, listen." He raised his voice. "The Carters are part of my plan. Mike's gone all kind of liquidy in the brain, and I've been after that plot of prime beachfront land in Florida for years. The bastard beat me to it thirty years ago, and I mean to have it. Marie's his sole heir. She's ready to take over the empire. When you marry, Chalmer and Son will grow to stratospheric heights."

"We're billionaires," I said coolly.

Clawing, kicking, and scheming in order to climb up the Forbes top one hundred was not my idea of a great life. It seemed like such a needless waste of time and energy in order to prove that "mine is bigger than yours."

"What's got into you?" He headed over to a shimmering crystal decanter bathing in sunlight, a reminder of a fine day outside and a contrast to that gloomy chamber— a room in which my future had been discussed ad nauseum from the moment I'd stammered the word "Daddy."

It was true to say that I didn't like my father. But hell, what was a man to do when his elder insisted on calling the shots? All I wanted to do was to set up my boutique brewery in Malibu and convince Juni to come with me, which was a little radical, given that we hardly knew each other. But I'd always followed my heart, a tendency that my grizzly father deemed indulgent and foolish.

He poured out half a glass for himself and a smaller portion for me. Strutting back to his desk, he set the glass down in front of me.

I mumbled, "Thanks."

"There's the annual charity gala on Saturday. You'll take Marie."

After the fiery spirit slid down my throat, I said, "I've met a girl."

I might as well have told him I'd joined a satanic cult. His face scrunched with horror. The last time I'd seen that look of condemnation was after I'd told him I wanted to become a journalist, and that did not end nicely. He banged his fist down on the desk and roared like a lion. Instead of giving in, I stood my ground, and the next thing I knew his big fist crunched into my jaw. I stumbled back and then charged forward with fury pumping through me as I went to retaliate. But then reason kicked in. I refused to stoop to that level of violence just to make a point, even though I could fight like the best of them. Lifting weights and boxing classes in senior high had seen to that. Belligerent when drunk, my dad was a force to be reckoned with. He had missed his calling as a prizefighter; instead, he bullied his way in boardrooms and used me as a punching bag with those little play fights that started when I was seven-years-old—games that I didn't initiate. My father, his liquor breath firing close to my cheek, would hit me on the arm or butt, seeking a reaction from me. He'd laugh at my tiny little fisted hits but would retaliate nevertheless with painful blows, which he insisted would turn me into a man. From that point on, I made sure I kept out of his way. In many ways, that had been why I took up boxing: to protect myself from my father. Apart from learning how to land knockout punches, boxing also taught me how to dodge them.

"Fuck her senseless, but marry Marie. Just keep it away from social media this little love affair."

I winced at his coarseness. Instead of matching his fire with fire, I rested my chin on tented fingers while contemplating a diplomatic response. "I'm serious about her."

A frustrated growl thickened the air between us. "The trouble with you, Sam, is that you're an idealist. A romantic. Why can't you be like your sister? She's the one with the balls."

"Then get her to marry Marie Carter." I stood up.

"Don't throw that lesbian shit at me. It fucking disgusts me."

I had to stifle the urge to laugh.

"I don't give a shit where you land your dick, only that I expect you there this Saturday, with Marie by your side. Remember the promise you made? I'm still negotiating on that piece of land—a price that I might add is ridiculously inflated."

Rubbing my neck, which had gone hot and prickly, I responded, "I'll be there Saturday. But I'm serious about Juni."

"I suppose that's short for June?"

My father's mocking tone was not lost on me. "No. Juniper."

Having swallowed a shot, he spluttered out a throaty cough. "She's not a fucking hippie, is she?"

"She's creative."

"Oh…holy shit. You've fallen for a goddamn artist." His eyes narrowed. "Broke, I suppose?"

An image of Juni's busy stall packed with customers came to mind, as did her accidental-billionaire father.

"Not broke. Her father's filthy rich."

His face smoothed out a little. "What's the family name?"

"Berry."

The way his eyes widened made me want to laugh.

"Her name's Juniper Berry?"

I just stared him in the face and remained blank, even though within, a rumble of nerves was doing its damnedest to erupt into laughter.

"Over my dead body will a Chalmer be affiliated with someone named after a berry that makes gin."

"Shit." I nodded, wearing a derisive grin. "I'm impressed. And here I was thinking that money, golf, and money were all that you knew."

"Don't be disrespectful. I'm your father. And you'll do as I say!"

There it was again: that command that opened a floodgate to rage. Rather than yell it out, which is what normally happened when he pulled that "I rule you" bullshit, I stormed out with enough fury pumping through me to power a small city.

Arranging flowers in a crystal vase, my mother looked up and saw me. Having just fired off a few "fucks" under my breath, I couldn't even contrive a smile.

"Sammy, sweetheart," she said, taking my hand. "Come and have a coffee with me. I've got some homemade blueberry pie."

As always, her soft voice and cheeriness softened my mood.

I followed her into the kitchen, where sunny streaks poured in through French doors leading out to a terrace filled with potted flowers. It was by far my favorite room in that house.

"Your father's giving you a hard time again?"

I puffed out an air of frustration. "I'm a disappointment. As usual."

"You know your father," she said with a note of resignation.

"He's got my life figured. Or so he thinks." I watched my mom as the coffee spluttered out noisily from the espresso machine.

"Short or long?" she asked.

"I'll have a short black." I smiled, watching her as she selected the right cup. "You'd make a fine barista, Mom."

She looked at me for a moment and then smiled. "I've never had a job. Is that strange?"

Although she had come from privilege, my mother was pretty down to earth—a quality I admired in people.

"I suppose." I combed back my hair nervously. It wasn't an easy subject for me. I'd only ever worked for the family. "That's not going to be me. I've got plans. And it has nothing to do with property development or dealing in hedge funds."

"Yes, the land's dry," she said, referring to the family's former oil fields.

Resembling something out of *The Beverly Hillbillies,* my great-grandfather, a farmer, had struck oil, which meant money pumped out of his land for years to come. As an astute businesswoman, his daughter, my grandmother, then shifted the company focus to acquiring land while learning all about the stock market. Before long, millions had turned into billions, and if my father had his way, it would be trillions. I didn't even know how many zeroes that signified. That type of obscene wealth sickened me given the growing amount of pain and suffering in the world.

Passing me a demitasse, my mother cut a slice of pie for me. "Do you want some cream?"

I shook my head. "No, I'm watching my waistline." My girlish tone made her laugh.

I swallowed a forkful of crusty pie, and as the sweet, fruity flavor tantalized my taste buds, all that heavy expectation my father had dumped on me melted away.

"Yum," I said, wiping my mouth with a cotton napkin.

"I experimented with this one by adding some coconut cream."

"It's sensational, Mom."

Pride emanated from her smile. That was what I loved about passionate cooks: the need to entice through their cuisine. And a great blueberry pie was almost as good as sex. Definitely better than ordinary sex. But good sex… nothing compared to that. And that was something I knew about, because boy, had I hit the jackpot with Juni.

"I've met a girl," I said.

Another smile animated her face. As an avid romance novel reader, my mother was in love with love.

"Oh really." Her eyebrows drew in slightly. "I take it it's not Marie Carter?"

I shook my head. "You'd really like her. Juni designs clothes that are unique and very much in demand. She's also very beautiful."

My mother's earlier frown ironed out. "She sounds lovely. But what about Marie?"

Dread washed away my smile. "What am I going to do? Even without Juni, I still wouldn't want to marry Marie." I opened my hands. "I just don't feel anything for her. We have nothing in common."

"That's the problem with money, darling. It's an incestuous little trap. Often at the expense of romantic love."

"That's not going to be me." I sighed with frustration. "We're not living in the eighteenth century when kingdoms arranged marriages in return for territorial power."

"No, love. But around rich families, there's still an element of that, I'm afraid. Only instead of gaining a foothold in Spain or France, one inherits a beachfront property in Florida or a Beverly Hills mansion on priceless acreage." She raised a brow. "And what about you, Sam? What do you want from your life?"

"I want to set up a brewery in Malibu. Craft beer, as it's known." I paused for a moment to think. "And I want to be with Juni. And…hopefully, one day, have a family."

"Then, if that's what you want, you get out there and follow that dream."

"You better not let Dad hear you say that."

She waved her hand dismissively. "Don't worry about him. There's Julia. She's killing it out there. And it's only natural. We're closer and closer to a female president. I can't wait for that day."

"Then you really better not let Dad hear you say that," I said with a chuckle.

"In any case, who says it's the son of the family that has to carry on the family business? Look at our family. Cary's mother, your grandmother, was responsible for all of this."

"Don't I know it. Grandma was formidable. She never slept."

"Your father was in awe of her."

"Then Julia takes after her, and Dad should just accept that and move on."

My mother nodded pensively before touching my hand. "Don't worry about Marie."

"But I do. She came over to my place the other night, uninvited and drunk. I need to end it."

"I'm sure you'll find a way." She smiled gently. "And I look forward to meeting Juni."

"Does that mean I don't have to go to the ball on Saturday?"

My mother played with her long fingernails. "Darling, let's do this one step at a time. Do go. Just to make your father happy."

I nodded slowly with resignation.

When I finished off my pie, my mother asked, "Another slice?"

Stretching out my arms, I said, "Yeah, why not."

JUNI

Cameron looked at me through his spectacles as though trying to solve a complex mathematical equation. Had I desired him I would have needed something more than that puzzled expression he always wore whenever our eyes met. He also walked into doors or tripped over things, leading me to wonder if he needed new glasses.

My father, like most humans, was riddled with contradiction. That do-as-your-heart-desires approach to life, the underpinning to my family's freedom-loving lifestyle, no longer rang true the older he got. Although I accepted that stability was the cornerstone to any family, it was his hope that Cameron and I would one day marry that I found to be distasteful, if not hypercritical of my dad. Just like ours, Cameron's family had adopted an alternative lifestyle, which my father often cited during his subtle attempts to matchmake us as being ideal for a compatible relationship. The fact that Cameron, an only child, stood to inherit acreage that adjoined our property helped. For a man who'd spent my formative years ranting on about the evils of the capitalist system, my dad had turned into an astute businessman.

My mom lived in another universe entirely. She spent her days spinning wool, playing the harp, or cooking. She had this inventive streak in the kitchen, where she'd create colorful meals that some days were adequately edible, while others… well, let's just say that kale and lamb's liver burger was never going to make it to a second serving.

Only Jess and Scarlett knew about my predicament. The vomiting was limited to the mornings, enabling me to keep my pregnancy a secret. When I stayed at Sam's, I turned the faucets on full to obscure the heaves that belched out of me.

I'd just returned to the farm after staying with Sam for a whole weekend. As I went about my duties, I fantasized about living with him in thriving downtown and designing clothes, mainly because farming life had become dull and exhausting. My brother had escaped from the farm when he was eighteen. Now a big-shot lawyer, Lingam, or Lee as he preferred to be called, had distanced himself from the family. He hated my parents' hippie lifestyle, and had come to blows with my father when as a fourteen-year-old he refused home schooling by insisting on going to a public school. That had left me from an early age to do everything around the farm.

As I pressed a batch of freshly dyed fabric, my cell went off. Cameron still lingered in my studio, talking about things I pretended to be interested in, like a new strain of kale he'd managed to grow or that he'd created this app that linked home gardeners to vegetable consumers within the community. I turned to him with an apologetic smile and moved away to take the call. It was from Sam. My heart missed a beat as his sexy rasp impaled my ear and sent a gush of heat through me.

"Hey," I said.

"Hey, gorgeous. How's your day?"

"It's okay. About the same as two hours ago." I giggled. This was Sam's second call for the day. I liked it. I'd decided he could pester me all he wanted.

"What's on tonight? Can we catch up? I'm missing you."

"It's only been a day," I responded. A big smile stretched my face to the limit. Cameron continued to hover, so I stepped into my bedroom. "It's my mom's birthday. I have to hang here."

"What about afterward, then?" Sam persisted.

"Why don't you come here?"

"Really? You want to introduce me to your folks?"

I mulled that over for a moment. It did seem a bit soon. But then again, in many ways, it seemed as if we'd known each other for ages.

"Yeah. Sure. Why not? I'm game if you are," I said.

"Right." He sounded worried. "Is there anything I should know beforehand? Or should I just mind my P's and Q's?"

I laughed. "What does that mean?"

"I'm not sure. But I have this thing for vintage English cop shows, and they often say it when asking someone to behave."

"You're so unpredictable, Sam."

"That's good, I hope."

"I think so. In any case, my parents won't bite."

"Ah, that's a relief. I'd hate to be dining with cannibals."

"What?" My voice went up.

"Sorry. Dark sense of humor. I'll make sure to leave that behind."

"No. I like you the way you are. You're just a bit crazy, that's all."

"I'll take that as a compliment."

"You should. Crazy's fun. As long as it's not the type that needs medication."

"Hm… I'll be sure to hide the Prozac."

"Are you serious?" I asked, even though I could hear the jest in his grinning tone.

"My only medication comes from a bottle, preferably brewed locally."

I giggled.

"Text me the address, Juni. I'm actually looking forward to seeing where you live. That way I can stalk you if you don't take my calls."

"As if I wouldn't take your calls."

"Mm… it's just that…"

"Just what, Sam?"

"Nothing. We'll talk later. What kind of wine does your mother drink?"

"Don't bring anything. We have plenty of everything. My mom's partial to mulberry wine, which happens to be made here."

"Text me the details and the time…Um…"

"Yes?" I asked.

"Will we be able to spend the night together?"

"You can crash here if you like. I live in a separate space at the back of the house. I even have my own kitchen and bathroom. But as a word of warning, it's nothing like your place."

"I don't need a warning. I'm rather adventurous."

"Then you won't mind Pablo and Miss Prissy waking you up."

"Huh?"

I giggled. "We have a rooster and chickens. Miss Prissy, the noisiest of them all, cackles loudly."

"Where's Foghorn Leghorn?" Sam asked.

"He died."

"Oh… shame. I liked him. He was kind of domineering in a very bumbling but seriously amusing way. Miss Prissy must've been devastated."

"She's got Pablo. He's equally domineering." I chuckled. "Okay. Tonight, it is."

"And Juni?"

"Yes."

"Don't wear any underwear."

"I never do at home," I responded dryly.

"Yum… now why did you go and do that?"

"What have I done, Sam?"

"You've made me fucking hard, and I'm about to go to a ball-crushing meeting."

"I'm sorry. It sounds like your princely jewels are about to be assaulted."

He laughed. "Princely jewels? They like you. More than like, to be honest."

"That's nice," I said. By this stage, a little throb had started to lay siege down below.

"But thank you for giving me something to fantasize about, not that I needed any new material."

"You're a sex maniac," I said.

"I haven't heard any complaints."

"From me? Or all the others?" That came out unexpectedly, and my mood dampened as our banter spiraled toward the prickly subject of Sam's sexual history.

"While we're on the theme of jewels, they were of the fake, forgettable variety, whereas you're that priceless, indescribable gem that's so rare a man spends his entire life looking for it."

"Oh. God. That's almost too sweet. What's got into you?"

"You have," he responded.

What could I say to that? I was just as smitten. "I suppose I better let you go before this descends into something cheesy."

He laughed. "And here I was thinking I was being poetic."

"Ha ha ha… On that dairy note, I must go and churn the butter for more cheese." I giggled. "Which, I might add, I love… and I don't mind listening to it when it's about me."

"I'll bear that in mind."

There was silence. "Are you still there?" I asked.

"I am. I better go. Until tonight."

"Bye," I responded.

I could hear his breath. "Sam, you go first."

"Ladies first."

"That's old-fashioned," I said.

"Bye, Juniper."

He closed the call, and I lingered, basking in a shower of blissful warmth. I'd even forgotten Cameron was still in the other room.

SAM

As I drove along the dusty track, bumping up and down, I regretted having gotten my car polished earlier. I even wondered if I was at the right place until I finally spotted a charming yellow two-story homestead fringed with a white terrace. I pulled up next to some odd-looking vehicles, which I speculated were custom built, judging by the assortment of mismatching parts.

As soon as I stepped out of my car, a dog came running up to greet me.

I patted him and gave him my hand to sniff. "Hello, handsome boy." A friendly lick later, slobber coated my hand. I began to wipe it on my pants but realizing I'd worn pale chinos I ran my hand over my denim shirt instead. The dog's enthusiastic welcome relaxed me as I inhaled a deep breath. This was a first for me. I'd never met the family of any girl I'd dated before.

The house was lit up with lamps, which enabled me to study the surroundings. In amongst the various sheds and barns scattered about, a bright-pink structure stood out, which I presumed had to be Juni's place.

A pleasant herbal scent clung to the warm night air as I walked along the pathway leading to the house. Lamps along the way helped me to avoid stumbling on the uneven ground.

After climbing some wooden steps, I landed on the patio, where I saw work boots on the ground and a table with an ashtray filled with cigarette butts. A half-finished drink glistened in the moonlight, and I was almost tempted to gulp it down. Instead, I took a deep breath and placed the bunch of flowers and bottle of wine I'd brought on the table.

I knocked on the door with the panting dog by my side. His big, friendly dark eyes shone with that kind of reassurance one needed in situations like meeting a girlfriend's family for the first time. The door opened, and Juni's friendly face greeted me. I fell into her welcoming warmth, and suddenly it was just us. Everything else blurred into insignificance.

"You found it okay?" She stepped away from the entrance.

"Yeah. No problems. The car got a bit of a thumping. It was a rough ride getting in."

Her brow gathered. "Oh, no. I'm sorry. I should have warned you."

"It's all good." I leaned in close and kissed her on the cheek while drawing in her rose scent.

"I see you've met Jeff," she said, patting her dog.

"Jeff?"

"Short for Jefferson."

"After the president?" I asked, a little mystified as to why anyone would name a dog after a seventeenth-century president.

"No." She giggled. "My dad's crazy about *Jefferson Airplane.* They were a sixties rock group."

I nodded. Of course. "That makes sense." I bent down and patted Jeff, who kept eyeballing me with those large, almost startled eyes.

"Anyway, come on in," she said.

The first thing that hit me was the smell of incense. The walls seemed to be soaked in it. An easel stood in the corner, and there were many interesting objects strewn about, including original artworks. It was impossible to absorb everything in one go.

"That's an interesting piece. A sculpture?" I pointed to an embellished wooden spinning wheel.

"No. My mom spins wool."

I nodded. "That's rather quaint. Does she knit too?"

"She does. My mother makes sweaters and beanies for everyone. You better watch out—she'll be eyeing your shoulder proportions. And not in *that* way either." She raised an eyebrow.

Taking her into my arms, I asked, "In what way do you mean?"

"In an ogling way."

"Oh… so you ogle me, do you?" I asked.

"Always. Don't you?" Juni unraveled from my hold.

"Not myself, I don't." I smirked. "But… I'm constantly ogling you. You're my eyes' favorite subject."

"Nice," said Juni, taking my hand. "Come. I'll introduce you to the clan."

Along the way down the hall, I noticed framed album covers from famous sixties and seventies bands.

"Are those four signatures on the Beatles' *Abbey Road*?" My jaw dropped. Something like that would go for a fortune at a Sotheby's auction, as would the Rolling Stones and Led Zeppelin albums that I noticed, all of which had also been autographed.

"Yep. My grandfather hung out behind the scenes. He used to be a roadie and was always invited to the parties."

"You're kidding me. He must have some interesting stories to tell." I paused at a Doors album and studied a scrawled Jim Morrison autograph.

"He's sworn to secrecy. Suffice to say it was sex, drugs, and rock 'n' roll without the glare of social media to spoil the party," said Juni.

"Ah… those were the days," I said with exaggerated wistfulness.

"Which part do you pine for?" Juni challenged.

I shrugged. "I'm not sure. I guess I like the idea of wild abandonment. Maybe I'm more of a voyeur, though."

"Really? You like to watch others having sex?"

My forehead contracted. "Not as such…" I wavered, wondering how we had arrived at that subject. "I think this is one of those discussions we have alone at midnight after a few margaritas. Somewhere away from your family home."

Juni's eyes narrowed as she sized me up in a bid to understand me. She wore that expression often around me, and considering we'd only been seeing each other for a couple of weeks, we were still strangers in many ways.

Laughter and chatter snapped me out of that parallel universe that Juni and I had made a home of together.

As I moved along, I had a feeling I was about to enter yet another dimension. And sure enough, all it took was a few more steps, and boom, I found myself in a room that had so much going on that my eyes battled to grasp everything. I likened it to stepping into a modern art gallery, where there was so much to see one had to take a breath and do it a little at a time.

Juni took me by the hand and led me to the center of the large room. By this stage, everyone stopped what they were doing and made me the subject of interest. It felt as though I'd time-traveled into a seventie's movie set, and found myself regretting that I hadn't chosen the loud floral shirt in my wardrobe that I'd worn to a costume party once.

In the background, Miles Davis's smooth jazz added an air of sophistication. I recognized that tune from the retro-hipster café I frequented downtown.

"This is Sam," Juni said.

A lady with long blonde hair, an older version of Juni, came to me. Wearing a blue velvet dress that had a corseted bodice, she resembled a medieval wench. She hugged me, kissing my cheek and leaving behind a strong sandalwood scent. I was instantly reminded of Juni's Aunt Scarlett, which made sense, given they were sisters.

"Pleased to meet you, Sam. I'm Luna." Her warm, affable eyes studied me for a moment, making me feel welcomed. She sure as hell owned that name. With that ethereal glide, one could almost see a beam of light emanating off her.

A man with long, wavy, graying hair and a beard, wearing a faded T-shirt with "The Grateful Dead" printed on it, held out his hand. "I'm Juni's father, Harry."

I took his hand, which was calloused and hard from labor. "Pleased to meet you."

Unlike Luna, Harry didn't leave behind the kind of friendly smile one needed for such awkward situations. Not that I could blame him. His daughter was a goddess who merited a god for a partner. I felt very ordinary all of a sudden.

I passed the bunch of flowers I'd been carrying to Luna. "Juni mentioned it was your birthday."

She took them and smiled brightly. "Thank you." She buried her nose in the blooms. "Mm…they're sublimely fragrant."

"I also wasn't sure if you liked wine. I believe this is a good year." I set the Merlot down on the table.

"Oh, that's so kind of you. You needn't have." She smiled sweetly.

"This is Cam," said Juni.

I nodded a greeting to the skinny guy with glasses and shook his damp hand.

"And this is my granddad," she said.

Outlandish in purple pants and a floral shirt, the man with long gray hair looked young and healthy. Sashaying over, he hugged me. "Just call me Clint." He spoke with a feminine voice. "That's with an 'n.'" He chuckled.

I searched for a clean rebuttal but settled for a lopsided smile instead.

"And this is Ginsberg, my better half." He pointed to a man dressed in velvet striped pants and a loose pirate shirt. All that was missing was an eyepatch and dreadlocks.

I took his long, soft hand, and he held my eyes as if undressing me.

Juni led me to a chaise lounge, where we finally settled down.

"So, Sam, what's your poison?" asked Harry.

"Um… I normally like beer. But wine's good."

"I've got some homebrew," he said.

Now he was talking my language. "Juni mentioned you brewed beer. I'd love to try some."

"Sam wants to set up a boutique brewery," said Juni.

Harry nodded. No smile, just an earnest, intense stare, which made me uneasy. “Dark or pale?” he asked.

“Pale, thanks,” I said.

JUNI

Holding Sam's hand for support, I felt a twinge of guilt, as though I'd thrown him into the fire of my father's scrutiny. I flashed my dad the occasional "be nice" grimace. A smile would have cracked his face, it seemed.

Sam did a fantastic job of maintaining a dignified but affable air, which only made my fondness for him grow.

My father passed a bottle of beer to Sam.

"This is great," Sam said after savoring the flavor. He looked at my father, who remained stony, and then me with a tight smile.

I resented my father for wearing his judgmental ways on his sleeve.

We sat at the large dining table laden with a colorful array of dishes. My granddad, a keen cook, had helped prepare most of the meal, which we'd all quietly thanked the gods for. Unlike my mom and her culinary experiments, my grandfather possessed a natural flair in the kitchen and always managed to come up with something delicious.

"This sure smells good," said Sam, sitting next to me, while under the table, his hand remained glued to my thigh.

"Eat as much as you like. There's always plenty left over," I said, not feeling too hungry myself. Much to my horror, I'd started to crave fatty, unhealthy foods like fries, hamburgers, and undercooked meat.

There were chickpeas, veggies, a kind of lamb dish that my mom had made that didn't really smell that appetizing, and a quiche made from goose eggs, which was also one of my mom's creations. Battling nausea, I had to work overtime not to vomit. So instead, I toyed with a plate of salad and a slice of cold turkey.

A squawk echoed out of the kitchen. Our cranky parrot resented being caged, which we had to do during dinner so that he didn't fly around while we ate.

Sam's brow shifted slightly. "What's that?"

"That's Timothy, our parrot. I'll introduce you later." I looked up at Sam. "He gets a bit noisy when we're eating."

Casting me that puzzled frown that I'd grown used to seeing, Sam made me want to laugh most of the time. But I had to feel sorry for him. He was really out of his depth.

Meanwhile, my father threw a few scraps for Jeff, who was at his side watching, open-mouthed and slobbering.

"Don't feed Jeff the chickpeas, Harry. They don't agree with him," said my mother.

"He'll be all right," said my father.

"Don't do the brown acid… Don't do the brown acid… You'll be fucked up. All fucked up," Timothy squawked from the kitchen.

As usual, everyone giggled, while Sam's handsome dark eyes slid over to mine questioningly.

"Timothy's been around for a long time. He's now fifty-nine," said my grandfather.

"Brown acid? Timothy?" Sam asked.

"I named him after Timothy Leary. And let's just say that like his namesake, he was rather partial to the odd trip," replied my grandfather.

Everyone else laughed while Sam remained puzzled. "He was given drugs?"

Clint shook his head. "Oh God, no. We'd never do that. Although he's rather partial to a bit of smoke." He gave Sam that knowing look.

Sam nodded slowly. He looked boyish, as though for the first time, he'd experienced something taboo.

"He pecked at a blot of paper on the table back in the late sixties, and he's been coming out with all kinds of trashy shit since," said my granddad with his signature raspy chuckle.

The conflict in Sam's expression was understandable, for I too had often thought it rather cruel to laugh at the expense of the poor bird's unfortunate encounter with psychoactive substances.

"Hey. In the wild they all do it," defended Clint. "Birds eat leaves that make them see all kinds of things. And they won't eat fruit until it's fermented into alcohol. We're not the only beings on this earth that love being off our tree, so to speak."

Sam nodded slowly before casting his attention on a platter with purple, yellow, and red vegetables. "It resembles a work of art," he said, spooning some onto his plate.

Leaning in, I whispered, "Go easy on that. It's one of Mom's dishes. They're a little different." I raised a brow. No one had the heart to tell my mother about her cooking. Instead, often her meals ended up with Mary, our goat.

"I'm a rather adventurous eater," he said quietly, arching a brow as though he were referring to my pussy. Or was that my reading sex into every utterance Sam made? Especially with that mischievous grin he wore so well.

I watched as he took a mouthful of the purple cabbage, a dish my mother had invented purely for its color. Sam regarded me and nodded approvingly.

"You like it?" I whispered.

"It's great," he said with a sincere glint in his eyes.

Sam looked up at my mom and said, "This is a great spread of food. I don't think I've ever had every vegetable known to mankind in one meal before. I can feel cells regenerating with each bite."

Everyone laughed, except my dad, of course.

"You're not just handsome but funny too," said Ginsberg, who'd spent the whole evening checking Sam out.

I couldn't blame him. With that denim shirt that hugged his big shoulders and curvy biceps, I'd fantasized clawing apart those studded buttons in one hungry grasp. Sam's dark hair had grown a little in the time I'd known him and now sat on his collar, and with that healthy tan and chiseled features, Sam looked good enough to devour—something I planned to do later.

"So, Sam, you met Juni chained to the old oak," said my father.

Sam rubbed his neck. "I would have preferred for us to meet in more pleasant circumstances."

"Sam saved my life, Dad," I said, praying that my dad wouldn't jump onto that anti-capitalist bandwagon.

"I take it your development firm has gone on to greener pastures?" asked my father.

Sam looked at me for a moment before replying. "It's my father's firm. Therefore, not my decision to make. However, I did manage to talk him out of felling Oscar."

"Sam wants to set up his own boutique brewery," I said.

"Yes, so you said. Where are you from?" my father asked.

"I grew up in North Beach," Sam answered.

"Ah… near Scarlett," said my mom.

"Where is that hussy?" asked Ginsberg.

Noticing Sam's forehead lowering, I said, "That's an endearment." Turning my attention to Ginsberg, I replied, "Scarlett's gone to Columbia with Javier."

"Oh… she's off to powder her nose," sang Ginsberg.

"So that was rather chivalrous of you to save our darling Juni," said my grandfather. "And now you're together. How romantic."

I noticed Cam, who as usual sat in the background, looking rather defeated. I felt sorry for him. But he was never going to be my guy. He knew that, and so did my dad.

"It *is* romantic," said my mother, who'd welcomed Sam with open arms. I loved her for that.

After dinner, my parents performed a couple of tunes, something they often did after eating my grandfather's chocolate brownies. And before I could stop him, Sam had munched on a few, unaware that they contained marijuana. Not a fan of being stoned, I always abstained. My brother and I had obviously missed out on the stoner gene that ran in the family. My grandfather, who still smoked, much to my chagrin, was the biggest user. But at seventy, he bragged about how his Irish background had equipped him with an iron liver.

Accomplished and smooth was the best way to describe my father's guitar playing, which synergized beautifully with my mom's mellifluous harp plucking. Heavy-lidded, Sam lounged back on the couch with a big Cheshire cat smile that seemed to grow.

"Your parents are really talented. I've never listened to live harp before," he whispered.

"Dad went to Berkeley and studied music. That's where he met Mom, who studied piano."

I studied Sam. His eyes had that unmistakable shine about them. "You're stoned. I warned you."

He laughed. "I'd already eaten two. They were delicious. I didn't know until afterward."

"I'm sorry," I said, taking his hand. "There was so much going on."

"Don't worry. It's actually very pleasant."

SAM

With my perceptions accentuated by the hazy lightness of being stoned, it seemed as though I'd drifted into a strange land. I struggled not to laugh by thinking of a math equation or something mundane like that.

After the excellent musical recital, which I couldn't really describe, I followed Juni into the kitchen. Hanging cast iron pots and mismatched crockery sitting on a wooden sideboard gave the room a rustic feel.

"Scarlett's got a hungry pussy… Scarlett's a slut." An attractive green parrot with a red head flew past me and settled on top of the cupboard as it squawked at me.

In a state of perplexed amusement, I looked over at Juni.

"Stop being crass, Tim," she scolded the bird.

That did it. The potty-mouthed parrot finally broke me. I held onto my belly and laughed until tears streaked my cheeks. And then Luna floated into the kitchen, which didn't help. If anything, her high-pitched giggles made things worse. I could have quite easily been one of those straight-laced visitors in a hippie version of *The Adams Family*. I almost expected a loose hand to scurry past me.

"Tim's saying dirty things again," Juni told her mother.

"I don't know what you must think of us, Sam."

I looked at mother and daughter standing side by side. Both were beautiful, and seeing them together gave me insight into Juni twenty-five years on—beautiful in a dignified, if not slightly eccentric way.

My perfect woman.

"It's been a very entertaining evening," I reassured her. "And as for Tim, he's an attractive bird. I've always had a soft spot for parrots. I'm almost tempted to get one myself."

"They're not terribly clean," she said.

"Scarlett's got a hungry pussy...Scarlett's a slut." Unfortunately, I'd just taken a sip of beer, and I found myself having to go to the sink. The swallow was painful as laughter brewed in my chest.

Watching, the two women giggled in unison.

"Sorry," I said, wiping my lips. "I can't imagine Scarlett likes hearing that."

"She finds it funny," said Juni. "Steve, one of her former boyfriends, trained Tim to say that. Story has it that one night he sat in the kitchen, pissed off after Scarlett flirted with one of the guests, so he decided to get back at her by training Tim to repeat that sentence."

I felt a mixture of admiration and disbelief at the capability of that hedonistic bird.

Juni asked, "Do you want to see my little cottage?" She turned to her mom. "I might turn in." She hugged and kissed her mother on the cheek. "Happy birthday."

Luna looked at me and said, "It was lovely meeting you." She gave me a hug before floating off.

Thanks to the brownies I'd scarfed down earlier, it seemed as though I floated on air. I followed Juni, perving at the sway of her hips. When we stepped outside onto the porch, we found Cam and Harry there. It did feel a bit strange having them observe Juni and me leaving together. Harry was her father, after all. I sympathized. If Juni had been my daughter, I wouldn't have been pleased to see her take a new man into her quarters.

"I'm just showing Sam my space," said Juni, who was the most relaxed of all of us.

Poor Cam looked dejected, as he had all night, while Harry puffed on a cigar, sizing me up again. He was the most earnest of that family. The only time he'd dropped his guard was when he played guitar or looked at his wife. They were in love. That was plain to see. I envied Juni that. I wished my mom and dad still shared that sparkle in their eyes.

I hovered about, unsure of myself. "Um… nice meeting you all." I saluted them and followed Juni along the lit-up path.

When we were out of earshot, I said, "That was a bit of a stony reception. And there's no pun intended."

Juni stopped and turned. Her face in the moonlight glowed, and her eyes had gone a dreamy shade of green. I'd never seen anyone as beautiful before, and suddenly I didn't care what anyone thought, Juni's dad or mine for that matter.

We were all that mattered.

"Why are you looking at me like that?" she asked, taking my hand.

"Because I can't believe how stunningly beautiful you are."

She studied me for a moment. "I'm sorry about my dad. He's a bit of a cynic. He'll come around once he gets to know you and sees that you're not that devil developer he thinks you are."

"Right," I said, thinking about my own father, who in fact was that devil developer. That would make for a fun wedding reception. But then, I was getting ahead of myself. "How many other admirers have you?"

Juni giggled. "I don't know if I have that many."

"There's that sleazy artist, Claude, and Cam, who looked crushed. Poor guy. Can't say I blame him."

She sighed. "Cam knows that I'm not interested. It's as much my dad's fault. He's got this crazy notion that I should marry Cam so that we can expand the farm. Cam's folks own the adjoining land."

"That sounds scheming and capitalist to me," I said.

"My dad's a contradiction like that. Between you and me, I think he loves the color of money. Ever since his marijuana crop turned into a goldmine, he's changed."

"That's understandable. But why judge others for being rich, then?"

"You know, Sam, you're right." She took my hand and added, "I will put that to him one day."

We arrived at a pink building, which looked more like a barn than a cottage.

"Are we sleeping with the animals?" I asked, taking her into my arms. "That's if I'm allowed to stay. Or… I can always sleep on the floor."

Juni laughed. "My bed's big enough for both of us. And no, the animals are over there." She pointed to another barn. "My dad had converted this for me. It was meant to be for Lingam, but he left years ago. I had it painted."

"It's bright. Even at night," I said, acknowledging the hot-pink wood panels. Who's Lingam?"

"He's my brother."

"You mentioned you had a brother. Strange name."

"Yeah, he hates it. It means 'phallus' in Hindi."

That stopped me in my tracks. "Your parents named him after an Indian word for penis?"

Juni turned on the light, and a large room that looked more like an artist's studio announced itself. "Yeah. Strange, isn't it? That's why he changed it to Lee."

"Well, I'm glad they didn't call you pussy, or even the C word."

Mischief reflected from her gaze. "Say it. Go on."

I opened my hands and shook my head. "I meant cat. You know… like pussy."

She fell onto a green couch and laughed. I joined her. With everything I'd experienced and heard that night, the laughter just barreled out of me.

It felt good, especially being there with Juni. Crazy, yes. But exciting, as though I'd stumbled on some kind of magical little village where people were both amiable and odd.

She turned on a lamp, and although her space was cluttered like her family's home, it was Juni that my eyes craved.

"I see you've been on water all night," I said.

"Yeah… Um… I've decided to go off alcohol for a while." She seemed a little fidgety for some reason.

"A health kick?" I asked.

"Sure."

Despite her sudden unease leaving a few unanswered questions in the air, I had other things on my mind, her lips for one. My mouth touched hers, and at last that rosy, expressive mouth was mine to devour as my tongue plunged in deeply.

My hands moved up her soft, warm thighs and squeezed her voluptuous butt. "I love this not wearing underwear, Juni."

Blood drowned my brain of coherence. The intoxication from the brownies had ramped up my arousal beyond belief. An ache overwhelmed me as I unzipped my pants, unleashing a deep throb so intense that if I didn't enter her, I would come all over her pretty sofa.

For someone who normally had staying power, I found myself on new ground with Juni. I could barely make it past a dozen thrusts. And the way she was stroking my dick didn't help matters.

"I need to be inside of you," I urged. "I've had a hard-on all night."

Juni stood up and removed her dress. My mouth watered as I gazed at her naked curves. I ran my tongue over my lips and sucked her nipples, which hardened on my tongue as my hands held onto her small waist and drew her close.

Sliding over her curves, my finger landed between her legs and felt an instant heat. I groaned as thick cream flooded my finger. I removed it and placed it in my mouth.

"Take me to bed," she murmured.

I carried her in my arms, and just as I placed Juni down onto her bed, a loud squeal made me jump. A black and white furry thing dashed past me.

"Edipuss!" Juni yelled. "You know you shouldn't sleep in here."

Scratching my head, I remained standing. My eyes shifted from Juni to the black-and-white cat on the couch glaring back at me.

"Oedipus?" I grinned. "Considering you're its mother, naming your cat that was never going to end well."

"What are you talking about?" Juni asked, her eyes shining with curious amusement.

I settled down on the bed. "The Oedipus complex: the Greek myth about a man who unknowingly has sex with his mother."

"Oh yes, of course." Her forehead creased. "That doesn't mean I'm going to have sex with my pussy."

"Yeah. But I want to have sex with your pussy. I want to eat your pussy. Right now," I growled.

Juni giggled and giggled. She held onto her tummy. She looked over at her cat, who stared up at us in dismay. "She understands, you know? And now she thinks you're going to eat her."

I tilted my head with a grin. "Sorry, I couldn't resist. It was just ripe for a smutty double entendre. Now, who doesn't like those?"

Juni's eyes sparkled with humor. "The brownies have really gotten to you, haven't they?"

"You've gotten to me, Juni. When I'm around you, I feel light and crazy. In a good way. A really good way. I don't need to eat cannabis to feel that way. But it has somewhat heightened my senses."

I held her close to me. It was so comfortable being there with her. As we lay on the silky sheets, an extended sigh left my parted lips as her hands massaged my dick.

"I love how you feel inside of me," she said.

"Keep doing that and I won't make it."

She opened her legs wide. Her wet, swollen pink pussy made my hungry cock dribble pre-cum.

"I haven't got you off yet."

"No need. You'll make me come this way." Her tone was as needy as I felt. That was all the encouragement I needed.

JUNI

A deep, satisfied moan shot out of my mouth. The stretch was so divinely agonizing that my skin prickled and my eyes rolled to the back of my head.

Moving up and down, I rode on top. Sam's favorite position. He had my breasts in his hands, and my nipples were drenched from being sucked.

As Sam filled me, his unshifting gaze bore deeply into me, his hooded stare seemed intoxicated by lust, just as I was.

"I need you to come now," he panted.

The walls of my vagina contracted uncontrollably, making my legs tense and tremble. I rode that wave of pleasure, and just when I thought it was over, another took me even further away, showering me with a warm glow. Moving faster and faster and deeper and deeper, Sam growled in the most primal way. As he shot deeply into me, a tormented "Oh…Juni…" exited from his lips.

I collapsed onto him and rubbed my nose against his hot, sticky neck.

As always, Pablo's crowing woke me. Despite that, it comforted me rather than annoyed. All animal sounds, particularly birds, had that effect on me.

Sam stirred in my arms. The first light of dawn snuck through the curtains and danced on the pale-pink walls.

"Good morning," I whispered.

"What time is it?" he asked, wincing as Pablo's insistent crowing cut through the air.

"Five o'clock."

He snuggled against me. And feeling his erection growing against my thigh, I smiled, knowing where that would lead.

"Is it always this noisy here?" he asked.

"No noisier than your street. Only here, it's nature and not car engines."

"Point taken," he said with a sleepy smile. "I almost thought I was dreaming."

Pablo's "cock-a-doodle-do" pierced through the walls again.

"How long does that last?" he asked.

"Um… all morning."

"And you can sleep through it?"

"I like to get up early when I can," I said, rising.

He touched my arm. "Where are you going?"

"I'll be back in a minute," I said, feeling suddenly nauseous.

I hurried into my bathroom, turned on the faucets, and then knelt down at the toilet bowl. The previous night's dinner spewed out in Technicolor while the faucet blasted its own deluge. Vomiting quietly only added to the strain, I'd quickly discovered. Haunted by my state, I lifted my sad, sorry frame and stood gingerly before the sink, where I expelled a "What the fuck am I going to do?" sigh.

I brushed my teeth and gargled repeatedly.

When I returned, I joined Sam and his warm body again.

"Are you okay?" he asked, stroking my hair.

"I'm fine." My little voice sounded unconvincing, though. Sam turned his face toward me. "I'm good," I reassured him with a tired smile.

We fell into a slumber and woke maybe thirty minutes later to pulsating desire. I couldn't say whether it was pregnancy hormones, but Sam had awakened a hunger in me that seemed insatiable. So that when he ate my pussy, I writhed, panted, and gave in to a toe-squeezing orgasm that only made me want more.

Five orgasms later, we lifted our sated bodies from the sticky sheets and welcomed the day. It was nine o'clock, and since it was Friday, I had to get my stock together for the following day's market.

"This is such an amazing space you've created here," said Sam, checking out my work table, which had fabric laid out ready to cut. He studied my latest drawings sitting up on my easel. "These are great. You're not just beautiful but seriously talented."

"Thanks," I said, looking over his shoulder at my latest wrap skirts with ruffles in complementary shades.

"I have to start work soon, Sam," I said, tying my hair back into a ponytail.

"I'll leave you to it, then," he replied, stroking my cheek affectionately. "I've got a few things to sort out myself. And I've got to meet up with Scotty later this morning."

"Oh, your friend the paleontologist. Jess is smitten."

"And he's into her," said Sam with a big fetching smile. "Love's contagious."

Love? Had Sam just admitted something?

"We'll have to get together for dinner. Jess has told me a lot about him."

"Really? But they only met two weeks ago."

"But we only met *properly* two weeks ago," I responded, arching an eyebrow.

"I suppose we did. One wasted month." Sam rubbed his neck. "Although that first night was seriously special."

I studied him for a moment. "You've been with other girls. Maybe it's the thrill of something new."

He shook his head. There was none of his typical humor. This wasn't the light and breezy Sam, whose chocolate eyes would twinkle away as a joke brewed. I read arousal and affection in his unwavering gaze, but I also perceived something deeper, harder to define.

I gulped back a lump. Tears and raw emotion were another side effect of pregnancy, I'd quickly discovered.

"Juni, believe me when I tell you, that I've never felt like this about a woman before. And the fact that I was your first. That really does something to me." Sam searched for words. I waited patiently with bated breath. I needed to hear every syllable that exited that sensual mouth. He took my hand and kissed it. "I think I'm in love."

Within, my heart cartwheeled; outside, my forehead crumpled tightly. "Maybe it's just attraction. Lust."

He nodded slowly. "Mm… lust, for sure. I'm constantly hard around you." Wearing his sexy smirk, Sam tilted his head toward his dick. "But you also always put a smile on my face."

"We've only spent two weeks together," I challenged.

"Every night, bar one, and I missed you." Searching for the joker, I saw Sam maintaining a straight face.

A nervous giggle left my lips. I couldn't find a response. Or was it that I wasn't as courageous as Sam in opening up about my feelings? And boy, did I have a lot to talk about. But I just couldn't do it. Not after two weeks. I needed time to figure things out.

Changing the subject, I reverted to our previous discussion. "Is that how you became interested in dinosaurs—through Scotty?" I thought of Sam's pajamas.

"I liked them before I met Scotty. But it was something that connected us for sure. I couldn't get enough of them as a boy, especially after seeing *Jurassic Park*. Instead of Disneyland, I was always begging to visit dinosaur parks."

I grimaced. "They kind of freak me out."

He smiled sympathetically. "That's okay. I don't expect you to like them. I'll promise not to drag you along. I still go on the odd occasion, mainly when I'm in Malibu. There's a park not too far away."

I remained quiet, despite thinking of how nice it would be to visit Sam's private beach.

"Scotty's building a T-Rex. Marc Bolan." His growing smile made me giggle.

"And you thought we were nuts for having a goat named Mary Jane."

"I never said that you were nuts," he defended. His brow lowered. "Mary Jane?"

"We have to keep her away from dad's crop of weed. She loves it."

Sam laughed. "A stoned goat. A parrot who's dropped acid. A randy Spanish rooster… what a menagerie of weird creatures you keep."

I studied Sam for a moment. "Is all this too strange for you? I mean…" Had I not been pregnant, I would have bounced along in that let's-see-what-happens kind of way. Instead, I needed to get into Sam's head. Quickly.

Marriage due to my pregnant state seemed too soon, even if the thought of spending my life with him swept me off my feet, flushing my spirit with excitement. Sam inspired me. And he had uttered that big L word. But that was after he'd orgasmed. Maybe it was only lust.

Sam rubbed his neck and looked at me. "I wouldn't change a thing about you or your way of life, Juni."

I studied him for a moment. Gone was that grin that made me want to slap his sexy face and fuck him at the same time. Falling into his arms, I allowed Sam to crush me with affection as I swallowed back another lump.

SAM

I stared at the plastic-covered tux hanging in my wardrobe. The thought of attending that goddamn ball jarred, especially after the great day I'd had at the artisans' market hanging out with Juni. I did the coffee runs and helped her sell her popular clothes, not that she needed much help there. The clothes seemed to do their own selling.

Although she understood why I had to attend that ball, Juni seemed a little sad knowing we wouldn't see each other that night. I wanted to suggest we meet up later, but that seemed a little grubby for some reason. The last thing I wanted was for Juni to think she was just a booty call. That was the old me. I would've done that without giving it a thought.

Picking up my phone, I pressed on her beautiful face, which had that "challenge me" expression I loved about her. After it had rung for a while, I was ready to hang up when she picked up.

"Hey." Juni sounded breathless.

"Were you running?" I asked.

"Yeah… I had to milk Moonie."

"Oh… a cow?"

"Uh-huh. Sometimes it's Mary."

I nodded. "You lead a colorful life, Juni."

"It's exhausting." She sighed.

"Then don't do it. Why doesn't your dad bring in a farmhand?"

"There's Cam."

"Oh, him. Google-eyed lover boy," I said dryly.

Juni laughed. "You sound jealous."

"Pathetic, I know. I've never been jealous in my life."

"I'm not into him, Sam."

"I know. It's just the way he looks at you with those undressing eyes."

"Undressing eyes?" She laughed. "Cam's as sexy as a turnip."

"Ha… Nothing wrong with the odd turnip. And it's kind of phallic, isn't it?"

"It's not just about penises, Sam."

"I suppose not, but I haven't heard you complaining. And you are *very* hands on."

"Mm… how did we get on to the subject of your penis? Which, I might add, is very nice."

The smile I sensed mixing in her words made my lips curl. "Always aim to please."

She laughed. "Anyway, so, to what do I owe the pleasure of this call? Considering you only saw me two hours ago. Hey, by the way, thanks for helping today. You were great. I think you were a girly magnet."

"From where I stood, your customers seemed only to have eyes for your classy clothes."

"Thanks, Sam. You're so supportive."

"I am that, but only if I think the talent's there. And you've got plenty of it, Juni. Which brings me to why I called. How would you like to visit Malibu? We could stay for a few days. And while there, we could visit some shops and have a look around to see what the competition's up to. I'm also interested in checking out some land for my boutique brewery."

"Malibu? When?"

"Whenever you can fit it in. You seem the busiest," I said, pinched by a sense of guilt for having so much free time, despite the contracts that my father needed me to chase up lying idle in my study.

"Can I get back to you on that? I have a dozen orders to fulfill." She sounded stressed.

"Juni, you need to scale up. I'll help you if you like. Why don't you bring someone in to do the sewing?"

"I think I will. Jess's offered, but she's got her screen prints that are growing in popularity too."

"I love her T-shirts." I stared at the one on my bed—a dinosaur with a building between its teeth. Having always had a thing for the absurd, I just couldn't resist buying it.

"Jess's been inspired by Scotty's dinosaur obsession. Not that it took much. She's also into them. They're so well suited. She keeps thanking me."

"And I keep thanking Oscar. If it weren't for that handsome oak, we would never have met," I said.

"Yeah. Life's strange like that."

"It's strange but beautiful, Juni," I said with a sigh.

"Are we going to get philosophical?"

"No time. Sadly. There's nothing I'd like more than to contemplate my navel."

Juni giggled. "Is it that interesting?"

"My navel? Mm… haven't really noticed it much lately; too busy staring into the prettiest green eyes I've ever seen."

"Oh…Sam… you're quite the charmer."

"That's the name."

Juni paused. "That's right, Chalmer's your last name. How fitting. I've got to go, Sammy."

"Sammy?"

"I like that. It makes you boyish. Makes me want to squeeze your cheek."

"Which cheek is that, Juni?"

"Both. Facial and butt. You've got a nice ass. In fact, you've got nice everything."

"As do you, Juni… Do you want me to go on and on about your delicious curves and how hard I am thinking about your tits?"

She giggled. “Oh God, you make it sound painful.”

“That it is,” I said. “Enjoyably so.” My face ached from grinning. “Can we do breakfast?”

“Yeah. Why not,” she said. “I’d like that.”

“I’ll call you. I might even call you later if I’m coherent.”

“Are you planning to wipe yourself out?” asked Juni.

“The only time I drink to excess is around my dad.”

“I’m sure it will be fine, Sam. And yes, do call me later if you like.”

“Bye, gorgeous girl.”

“Bye.”

I tugged on my cuffs. The gold cufflinks that I’d inherited from my grandfather bearing an MG logo twinkled in the moonlight. Apart from his house in Malibu, those cufflinks were a fine reminder of a man who I bore a striking resemblance to, mentally speaking. While my grandma ran the business and added a few extra zeroes to the Chalmer fortune, my grandfather buried his head in books and under car hoods. Throw in a discussion about the constitution or Kantian philosophy, and the man was all ears. But confronted with anything to do with business and profit his eyes glazed over as he ambled over to the crystal decanter and pour himself a large shot of Glenfiddich.

I loved that man and wished he’d been my father instead. When he died of throat cancer, my heart broke. I was only fifteen at the time. My grandfather was responsible for giving me an almost normal childhood. He gave me my first picture book of dinosaurs, and his love of botanical science motivated many camping trips to Prairie Creek over the summer holidays. They were memories that I would always cherish. My father, who hated anything to do with dirt and nature, preferred the bump and grind of city living.

I took a deep breath and ambled into the entrance of the grand ballroom. I had to hand it to those charity events for their choice of setting. As always, the room sported enough jaw-dropping ornamentation to keep one interested all night. The adorned walls boasted the type of gilt-framed paintings that the guys at Christie's would have teetered on a tightrope over a lagoon full of salivating alligators to possess.

My mother and father chatted among a group of people that they'd socialized with for as far back as I could recall. Funny how when it came to acquaintances, it was always the same faces, the same voices, and the same topics.

Julia sashayed toward me. Dressed in a gown that seemed glued on, she had the kind of dark features that drew men in like bees to honey, and she knew it. My sister was what one would describe as beautiful in the most manicured of ways. Competitive to a fault, she seemed to take delight in telling me all about her conquests even though I showed very little interest. Even as a kid, she had been the one who instigated the wrestling matches or spent hours in front of violent video games. I often wondered if she hid a set of testicles in that gym-fit body of hers.

"If it isn't my dear brother, Carrington Junior," she crooned, annoying the shit out of me in one breath.

My birth name had always been a serious bone of contention. It came with great relief to have my middle name to use—Samuel having been my grandfather's name.

"So where have you been hiding?" Julia stood next to Steve, who shadowed her as always.

"I've been around. Hey, Steve." I cast my attention to her man.

He nodded a greeting and then continued to gaze lovingly at Julia, who seemed to have forgotten the poor guy was even there.

"So, I hear you've become a greenie." She smirked.

"Was that what Dad said?"

"Pretty much. He told me that you're hell-bent on saving some tree, and to do so you've agreed to marry Marie Carter." She glanced at Steve and rolled her eyes. "As if one would need an inducement to marry her. She's sex on legs."

There it was again, Julia showing interest in women. I'd seen it over the years: the furtive glances at girls that I knocked around with.

"So you keep saying," I said, raising a brow.

"I'll ignore that smutty innuendo," she said.

"There was no smut intended. It's just your mind reading into it." I looked over her shoulder, and sure enough, speak of the devil, Marie Carter appeared, wearing a dress that squeezed the life out of her gravity-defying chest. Her blonde hair, looking more like dank silk, slithered over her tanned, sculpted shoulders.

"Sam, there you are." She kissed me on the cheek. A sneeze formed, and in a bid to stifle it, I sucked it back in.

Then it started one after another.

"Oh…" she exclaimed. "I see you haven't cured that allergy yet." Her annoyed tone grated on me, especially that irrational quirk of the rich that anything could be cured with money.

"I know the cure. Stay away from Chanel No. 5." I tilted my head with a mock smile.

"Then you're in for a rough night. The room's awash with it," said Julia with a sarcastic chuckle.

"I'll be fine after a few drinks. Excuse me for a moment."

"I'm expecting that dance," she said.

"Sure. Just give me fifteen." I sneezed again. I left Marie to chat with my sister, who seemed more than eager to entertain her.

Standing at the bar, I spied my father and his bunch of mogul buddies out on the terrace, sucking on cigars big enough to use as assault weapons. I lifted the bottle of Corona, tossed away the lemon, and then drained it as someone who'd lost his camel in the desert would have done.

Ambling back into the room, I waited for a moment before joining Marie again. The charade needed to take place in my father's presence. That way he could observe my effort in courting her.

I noticed Marie's mouth pinned to my sister's ear, with Julia looking more animated than usual as the women shared a joke or two, while poor Steve just stood around. I headed over to join him.

"So Steve," I said, settling by his side. "You're not drinking, I see."

He shrugged. "No. I'm on a health kick at the moment."

"You look like you could use a few pounds, if you don't mind me saying."

Steve shifted his skinny frame. "I'm trying. I'm just not one of those that can put on weight." He smiled tightly.

I nodded. "How's the legal business treating you?"

He nodded slowly. "I'm working at making partner, hopefully within a few years."

Marie turned and flashed her gleaming white teeth at me. "Oh, there you are. How about that dance?"

I took a deep breath, mainly to stifle the sneeze about to erupt. "Sure." I looked at Steve. "Excuse me."

Taking my hand, Marie led me to the dance floor. Along the way, I managed to gulp down the beer in one big swig before setting it down.

The live band played classic jazz hits, which I loved, as the male singer crooned, "I've got you under my skin."

Marie knitted her fingers around the back of my neck. Her heels were high enough that her face met mine. I placed my hands around her waist, and we moved around the dance floor while Marie rubbed her body against mine.

"You seem tense, Sam. Is something wrong?"

I noticed my father enter the ballroom and hoped he could see us.

"No. I'm good."

"I'm hoping we'll catch up afterward." She smiled suggestively.

As her lips tickled my ear, her perfume was turning me inside out as I tried to stifle another sneeze. "Maybe not tonight."

She lifted her chin and studied me. "You're not gay, are you?"

"No. Are you?"

Her eyes lit up in bewilderment. "Why would you ask that?"

I shrugged.

"I'm meant to be your fiancée, Sam," she said.

"Strange, I don't remember asking you," I replied coolly.

"Oh, Sam. Drop all this formality crap. We're marrying the families. You know that." Her cold chuckle made me cringe.

"If that's the case, we don't need to fuck then. Do we?"

"Then you *are* gay," she insisted.

"I'm not, Marie."

She studied me as we swirled about the dancefloor. "You're in love with some girl?"

My mouth tipped up at one end.

"Ah… You are. And let me guess: she's broke, and your daddio doesn't approve."

"Look, Marie, this will be a lot less painful if we just play the game. Okay?"

Turning down her lips with a simpering girly voice, Marie said, "Oh… but I was looking forward to fucking you."

"There are plenty of men around here that would love to return the favor, I'm sure."

"But I've already fucked most of them." She arched her drawn-on eyebrow.

A mock smile was the best I could return. Noticing Julia and Steve dancing next to us, I caught Marie rolling her eyes at Julia in what seemed like their own little private conversation.

After we stopped dancing, I headed for another drink, which soon turned into ten as I spent the rest of the night by Marie's side. She was just as thirsty, it seemed, sinking into champagne as if it was soda.

JUNI

The sewing machine revved as my foot pushed down on the pedal. I hadn't heard from Sam, and it was Sunday morning. By now, he should've called. Apart from an earlier text the night before, Sam hadn't called later as he'd promised. I'd even lain awake waiting for it. By morning, I was beside myself.

I hated myself for being so needy. What happened to that independent spirit I'd prided myself on?

Nausea had me over the toilet bowl half of the morning. I made sure I stayed away from my mom, who I sensed was psychic. She'd already noticed something had changed in me, and my boobs had grown.

"Damn." I'd made a mess of the seam. Sam and sewing did not mix.

One hour later, I was at his door. Radical. Stupid. I hated myself. I waited with leg muscles clenching and fingernails half eaten. It took a couple of bell rings before I heard footsteps, which were short, light steps, unlike Sam's heavier tread.

When the door opened, I'd already curled my lips into an apologetic smile that quickly ironed out when a woman appeared.

"Who are you?" Her eyes narrowed as she studied me.

"Is Sam in?" My voice trembled.

"He's taking a shower. Who are you?"

"I'm Juni," I said.

"Well, he's indisposed." She slammed the door in my face. And that was that.

Frozen, I stood there in shock. My heart hadn't even had a chance to beat.

I moved away and stood against the wall as I tried to gather my senses. The woman, who was beautiful in that heavily made-up way, wore nothing but a towel. Tears pooled in my eyes. Light-headed and feeling out of body, as though I was drugged on sorrow, I leaned up against a wall. Pedestrians happily yapping about their Saturday night blurred past me, oblivious to the pain in my heart.

Not knowing what to do, I jumped in my car and headed over to Scarlett's.

When she opened the door, I fell into her arms and cried and cried.

"Oh, darling," she said, leading me into the kitchen. "I'll brew some damiana."

I told Scarlett everything that had just happened in hurried words. "She was so beautiful and with a bath towel around her. Fuck, Scarlett, he obviously took her home."

"Where was he going?"

"To a charity gala."

She nodded.

Claude came shuffling in, rubbing his head. "Hey, sexy," he rasped.

Oh, God. The last thing I needed was horny Claude around. I gave him one of those tight smiles that said, "Stay away from me."

"Claude, leave us," Scarlett said with a smile.

After he ambled off, I whispered, "You're not back together again?"

She shrugged. "After my fight with Javier, who decided to stay in Columbia"—she took a deep, mournful breath—"Claude came over and succored me."

"Yeah. I bet he did," I said with a note of irony.

My phone went off, making me jump.

It was Sam.

My finger hovered over it, unsure. I wanted to pick up so that I could scream at him, but I chose to ignore him instead.

Thirty minutes later, after numerous calls, Scarlett implored me to give Sam a chance to explain, so I took his call.

I stepped out into the overgrown garden, which calmed my jaded state. "Hey," I answered coldly.

"Juni. There you are. I've been trying to call you." He sounded like he'd been running.

"Why?"

"Why?" he asked.

"The woman who answered the door obviously forgot to mention that I dropped in an hour ago."

"What?" There was a pause. "You're fucking kidding me. Marie didn't say anything about that."

"You're one hell of a good fucking actor."

"Marie stole my cell and refused to give it to me unless I took her back to my place. It's crazy shit, I know. But I still haven't written your number down. I should've tattooed it." He paused. "Can we meet? I'd prefer to speak to you face to face. That way you can see I'm not lying."

Meeting him face to face would've forced me to capitulate. One look at those bedroom eyes shining for forgiveness, and I would have fallen into his muscular arms within a gasp. When did I become so fucking weak?

"Mm… I've heard this story before, and it always centers around losing your cell phone. And there is a cloud, you know? For backing up numbers. You could have found it that way. You do have a computer, don't you?"

"I haven't got your number on my cloud. I've been seriously all over the place lately, what with us spending so much time and me getting my business plan together."

"I don't know what to believe. She only had a bath towel on."

He released a jagged breath. "Marie did try to seduce me. Although it was half-hearted. I don't think she's into me. It's a fucking game. All about money and status. Our parents want us to marry. I don't want her. I don't even think she really wants me, to be honest. Just let me explain. Face to face."

"I don't know what to do…" I said. "I feel like telling you to fuck off."

"I'm not going to let you."

My brows squeezed. "What? You don't own me."

"No, I don't." He paused. "I wish I did."

He sounded exhausted, and instead of being annoyed at him, I wanted to fall into his arms and give myself heart and soul. My inner strength weakened the more his voice massaged my senses. I should've been stronger. I'd always been one to stand my ground.

"I'm at Scarlett's." My heart was too invested. I just caved in.

Ten minutes later, Scarlett led Sam into the garden, where I sat with Claude staring into my eyes and telling me I could do better than be entangled with a cheating cad. I hadn't told him what had happened, but he'd somehow guessed. He took my hand, and leaning in close, he brushed my cheek when Sam strode in. I'd known Claude for a while, and although he'd tried to seduce me in the past, he was more into my polyamorous aunt.

Before I knew what was happening, Sam charged in and pushed Claude away from me. "Take your hands off her," he blustered. The tendons in his forearm popped out as his fist clenched.

Claude lifted up his hands in self-defense. "Hey, it's cool, man. I was just offering some support." A grin touched his face. "And I'm not the one cheating here."

That explanation did little to appease Sam, who lunged forward with his big fist heading for Claude's face. I stepped forward to stop him, lost my footing, and tumbled over.

Scarlett rushed over to me, and as Sam bent down to help me up, I yelled, "Don't touch me."

Scarlett had a look of concern on her face. "Oh my God, in your condition…"

A deep line appeared between Sam's eyebrows. "What condition?"

I slid my eyes over to Scarlett as furtively as possible, to which she returned a subtle nod of understanding.

Avoiding his large hand that hovered above, I got up off the ground and smoothed down my skirt. Apart from a sore butt, I felt okay, while Sam continued to wear a questioning frown.

"It's nothing. I'm premenstrual, that's all." Despite that lame-sounding excuse, I wasn't ready to reveal my condition. Besides, I still hadn't decided what to do. While floating in a romantic bubble, I'd almost gone into denial and pushed it to the back of my mind, even though it hung around like grit in one's shoe. And so, once again, I found myself paddling in those murky waters of single motherhood. I'd always believed in marriage before breeding, therefore the thought of going it alone scared the crap out of me.

Scarlett returned with a glass of water and, satisfied that I wasn't hurt, left me alone with Sam. That primitive alpha display of chest-beating had only made Sam sexier. Messy dark hair that would have looked ridiculous on anyone else made him look as though he'd been fucking, which really pissed me off. But I felt weak. Really weak. After copping a whiff of him earlier, my hormones had gone into a state of erotic meltdown.

Prompted by Scarlett, Claude ambled off reluctantly. I sensed that his natural rebelliousness had been roused by Sam's tirade, and had he remained, there would have been a fight between them for certain.

"That was so unnecessary, Sam. You came bursting in here as if you owned me." I flicked back a strand of hair.

Looking contrite, Sam said, "I don't know what came over me. I saw his eyes all over you." He waited for my response, but I bit my lip instead. "I'd do it again. If any man comes near you, Juni."

"How can you say that?" I pointed at him. "And after what's happened, we're not even"—my voice cracked—"together."

He shook his head vehemently. "I'm not into Marie at all. She somehow got my phone, which I'd stupidly left lying on the table just after I sent you *that* text…" He tilted his head, seeking acknowledgment for the sexy little message he'd sent me the night before.

I reflected on his sweet text, which had made me giggle and glow at the same time—the same way I reacted to all his cute, smutty texts.

"Marie grabbed it. And told me that she'd only return it if I took her home with me."

"She sounds pretty determined." I knitted my fingers. "If that's what really happened."

"Even if it's the last thing I do, I'm going to make it my mission to get Marie to tell you that I slept on the sofa."

"But she was naked under that bath towel," I persisted.

He shrugged. "She'd had a shower. And when you called, I must've been in the shower, because I didn't hear the door." He leaned in and took my hand. I allowed it to remain this time. The fire from his palm sent sparks through me. It was impossible not to fall under his spell again, especially with those dark bedroom eyes glistening with sincerity.

"She's beautiful. Seriously rude, though."

He sniffed. "She's not beautiful. She's fake. I'm crazy about you, Juni. Only you."

I bit my lip. I wanted to hate him. I wanted to throw him out and huff and puff and be all sulky, but I just couldn't. A tear slid down my cheek instead. I'd never been this emotional before. I was always the tough one, like my dad in many ways. But then I met Sam, and overnight, I became an emotional wreck.

SAM

I sipped on a cup of bitter-tasting tea that Scarlett had brewed up. I wasn't sure what was in it, but it not only helped me smile again, but it had gotten rid of a throbbing hangover. As Scarlet brushed her niece's hair, Juni's eyes softened with each stroke, making my heart melt. Claude hung around like a bad smell, and the best I could manage was a mumbled apology. I didn't trust him, with those roaming eyes zeroing in on Juni's chest, which was hard to miss in that tight tank-top. The girl was exploding. Just like my desire for her and its ugly sister, jealousy was.

We sat in silence for a while, which suited me, for that was another thing I loved about Juni: we could do silence with ease. She allowed me to kiss her lips, and as I savored the sweetest, softest mouth I'd ever tasted, stormy clouds of frustration dispersed, leaving behind a sun-drenched sky filled with possibilities.

What a fucking night it had been, though.

Marie had followed me back to my place. I'd told her I wasn't interested, but she persisted. She had my phone, so I had to let her in. As soon as she entered my living room, Marie unzipped her dress, let it pool to the floor, and stood naked before me. Then she paraded about, showing off a toned body, gravity-defying tits that resembled balls, and a hairless pussy.

I remained cold and unmoved, just like my dick.

Leaving her alone, I returned with a bathrobe and tossed it to her. “This is never going to happen, Marie. I’m with someone else.”

She ran her tongue over her plumped lips. “We can still marry. This is for the family. Our families. It’s a tradition.”

“It might be tradition, but I’m not into this Marie. And you don’t strike me as being into it either. Why the fuck carry on like this?”

“Because of your daddy.” She raised an eyebrow.

“What, he put you up to this? To steal my phone?”

“Not exactly. But when he noticed you giving me the cold shoulder earlier at the ball, he reminded me that you were stubborn and that with a little encouragement”—she raised an eyebrow— “you’d agree to it.”

I shook my head. “There are other rich bachelors out there that would love to marry you, I’m sure.”

Her mouth turned down childishly. “But I want to be part of this family. Julia and I are really close. Like sisters. And I am a little… you know?” She raised that eyebrow again as though I was meant to get that. “And if you want your pretty little girls on the side, I won’t mind.” Showing me what crooked morality looked like, her face hardened. “And I’m certainly no angel, Sam.”

She lowered herself onto the sofa, parted her legs, and started stroking her clit.

“I’ll leave you to it, then,” I said, heading off to bed.

Driven by a delusional sense of entitlement, Marie entered my room and, lifting the comforter, slid into the bed, where she rubbed herself against me and grabbed my cock. “You’re a big boy, Sammy, even when it’s droopy.”

I pulled away, mumbled some filthy words under my breath, and left her to sleep alone in my bed. Fortunately, she left me alone after that, while I spent an uncomfortable night on the couch.

Of course, I left out the grubby details of Marie’s attempted seduction as I stammered through a recounting of the night to Juni. I didn’t do a good job of it, because Juni wore that same suspicion I’d seen the first day we met. At that time, it had been cute, but now it frustrated the crap out of me.

"Can I buy you lunch?" I asked, holding her hand.

She studied me again for a moment. Taking a deep breath, she shrugged. "I suppose."

Scarlett's earlier comment about Juni's condition came to mind. "Are you feeling okay?"

She brightened quickly, almost jarringly. "No. I'm good."

I studied her for a moment. Something didn't gel. But I left it. We'd already battled enough monsters for one day.

After descending the steps, we landed on the sidewalk where the hot afternoon sun burned into my face.

"How about a swim?"

"I haven't got anything to swim in," Juni replied.

"We could go to the nudist beach." My eyebrows rose.

"You wouldn't mind others seeing me naked?" Juni asked, tilting her head.

My eyes wandered over her voluptuous tits and landed back on her face. "I would. That was a joke. I hated the way sleazy Claude leered at you back there with those stoned bedroom eyes of his."

Juni's smile thawed me out. It was the lightest she'd been so far that day. "You certainly went all alpha. That's for sure."

"Not one of my finer moments." I shook my head. "But fuck, Juni, you're bursting out of that top. You need to dress in less revealing clothes."

"What? Are you kidding me? This is the twenty-first century. Hello, you had a naked woman prancing about in your house this morning."

"Marie does nothing for me, Juni." I placed my arm around her waist. "Your little finger is sexier than the whole of Marie."

Her lips curled at one end.

"That's better." I smiled back at her.

As we continued walking, I added, "Do you know what you do to men?"

"No." She turned to face me. "I'm not going out of my way to be seductive. I just like this top. It's one of Jess's."

I studied the bird carrying a building as a stork would a baby, and I had to smile. It was a great piece of art. "It's a great image." Taking her hand, I added, "Hey, why don't we go and buy some swimmers and towels and go to the beach? We can grab a cheeseburger or whatever you desire for lunch. What do you think? I'd love a swim."

She studied me for a moment and nodded slowly. "Yeah. Sure. I'd like that. I haven't been to the beach for a long time."

We sat on towels and munched on hamburgers. It surprised me that Juni consumed more meat than me. She virtually ate it raw, dripping in blood. I'd even joked about her being a vampire in a former life. Instead of giggling, which was her customary reaction to my silly comments, Juni went quiet. I shrugged it off, despite noticing her increasing introspection.

Since the day was a scorcher, I lavished sunscreen on Juni, which was not a chore but a labor of lust as I stroked her soft skin. Swamped by a rush of arousal, I was glad that I'd opted for baggy shorts as Juni kept pulling at the tiny triangles that barely covered her tits—a choice, of course, prompted by me, or more accurately, by my dick.

"These are a bit small, Sam," said Juni, adjusting her bottoms. "I'm looking a bit cavewoman, I'm afraid." She giggled as she covered an escaped pubic hair. "I know I should probably wax. It just frightens the hell out of me."

I hissed in sympathy, thinking of the few hairs on my chest, which weren't going anywhere. "You're perfect." A grin formed at one corner of my mouth. "Besides, I like a bit of hair down there."

Her eyes fell into mine, and mesmerized, I took Juni into my arms and devoured her warm lips. My frisky fingers itched to hook inside those tiny bottoms as her tits rubbed provocatively against my naked chest. But noticing an older couple seated close by, I doused that temptation.

"I wish we were at my beach in Malibu," I said

Juni squinted in the sunlight. "You're obscenely rich, aren't you?"

I answered with a shrug. "From what I've heard, your father's not exactly scraping around for crumbs."

Juni laughed, but within a breath she grew serious again, casting me that vulnerable glazy-eyed stare I'd seen earlier.

I stroked her hair. "I'm sorry about this morning. I'm going to prove that nothing happened with Marie if it's the last thing I do."

She fell into my arms again, leaving a damp stain on my shoulder. I lowered my chin to look at her and noticed tears welling up. "Oh, Juni."

"I've become a bit emotional lately. It's just…"

"It's just what, Juni?"

Those big green eyes made me lose myself again. Her sensitivity reached in deep and plunged me into unchartered depths. "I've changed a lot since meeting you, too, Juni."

She smiled back sadly.

There was something going on in that pretty head. I could only put it down to Juni grappling with whether to invest her trust in me. I couldn't blame her. After everything that had happened, I also would've been a little wary.

I took her hand. "Come on, let's have a swim."

With the sun burning away it didn't take much coaxing to submerge ourselves up to our stomachs.

Clutching her arms, Juni shivered. "I haven't been in the sea since last summer."

I was the first to dive in, while Juni bounced about, and I mean literally, Phew… that girl was tormentingly top heavy. And the water did little to dull the ache in my groin, especially with her nipples piercing that stretchy fabric.

"Juni, I think you should have opted for that one-piece."

She laughed. "I can feel you on my leg, Sam."

"Feel what, Juni?" I asked, cocking my head.

"Your big throbbing dick," she said with a challenging smirk.

"You're being seductively ribald, Juni."

"Seductively ribald?"

"Dirty. Your mouth is deliciously dirty." I ran my thumb around her wet, salty lips. "Why don't we go to Malibu today?"

Juni stared at me as though I'd suggested something crazy, like diving off the Golden Gate Bridge.

I cocked my head. "You can always write to your customers and tell them that your sewing machine's broken down."

Juni's smile faded. "Sam?"

"Hmm…"

"Can I really trust you?" she asked.

JUNI

Balls flew in the air. Jet Skis sprayed water in the distance while solitary figures stood on boards, stroking the water with paddles. The deep blue sky was cloudless, and the air was still. The sun left a burning but pleasant sting against my puckering flesh.

We remained lost in each other. The sea could heal many things, but a fragile heart needed more, like reassuring words. Gestures. And what an intimate moment we found ourselves in, as we stood in the water, discussing something better left to quiet little shadowy corners and not the middle of a sun-drenched beach amid boisterous children and grownups splashing about.

Waiting patiently, I took a deep breath as Sam looked at me as though I'd asked him to explain $E=mc^2$.

I'd let him back in, almost without a fight. But then, lust was such a mind-fucker. Droplets of water clung to that hard, toned chest. I salivated at the thought of rubbing myself naked against it as Sam entered me with his enormous dick. I sighed. Lust had taken a grip on my senses, all right. I just couldn't think straight with him looking like that.

Sam's tanned face softened as we looked into each other's eyes. It was the longest gaze I'd ever experienced. And not once did he flinch. I, however, struggled not to smile. He had the type of face that made me want to laugh, not because he looked like a clown or anything but because he was so damn hot.

"Juni." Sam's deep drawl snapped me out of my daze. "I don't know what I can do and say to clear this with you. I will, though." He lowered his head, and his forehead touched mine. "Thank you for being here. I missed you last night. You got that text. You told me so."

I nodded slowly, reflecting on the message that had pinged while I sewed. It read: "I'm having a horrible time, Juni. I miss you. If I see another fake pout, I think I'll take up smoking again."

"Did you end up smoking?" I asked.

Sam chuckled. "No… I controlled that urge. Since meeting you, I've decided to become healthy."

"I'm not that much of a health freak. I don't even go to yoga." A pang of guilt hit me at my lack of discipline when it came to fitness. "Jess dragged me to hot yoga last month, and I nearly fainted. I'm not that masochistic."

Sam laughed. "I'm there with you. I'm not big on pumping iron, but I do like tennis. And I swim laps when I can fit it in. In any case, we're getting enough exercise." He caressed my arm. "Speaking of which…" Sam's eyebrow arched.

I laughed. "You've got a one-track mind."

"Seeing you in this bikini is sending me crazy," he said. "I don't even think I'll be able to walk properly to our towels. I might get arrested for indecency."

After that, we ran to our towels, laughing like teenagers. What a roller coaster ride it had been that day—from gut-wrenching despair in the morning to soaring elation by afternoon.

In the distance, a white mansion glowed in sharp contrast to the deep blue sky. "What a gorgeous house," I said. Having always been a sucker for classical architecture, detailed with columns and ornamental appendages, I sighed with appreciation at Sam's stunning Malibu home.

"I'm glad you like it." Sam smiled. "It was my grandparents' home. I had to have it. My sister drove a tough bargain. But that's Julia."

"She sounds formidable."

"She is that. Along with my father, Julia wears the pants in the family."

Sam pressed a remote control, and a garage housing six cars opened.

"So many cars," I said.

"Yes. Apart from the SUV, they're all vintage. They've even been featured in a few movies."

"Really? You hire them out to Hollywood?"

He nodded. "Yeah. A friend works there, and whenever they're shooting anything set in the fifties or sixties, they contact me."

"I love old cars. And I'm very fond of Sally." I stepped out as Sam held the car door open.

"She's stylish, all right. I hope it wasn't too uncomfortable getting here?"

I shook my head. "No. I loved it. The wind in my hair. I felt like Grace Kelly. Only I'm not as beautiful."

"Bullshit. Don't undersell yourself, Juni." Sam leaned in and kissed me.

The six-hour journey had seemed more like an hour. It was a pretty drive. And I needed to get out. Expecting my help as always, my father wasn't too pleased, given that he was harvesting his weed crop. But when Sam arrived in his Mustang, my dad, who had a love for that model, dropped his guard. Sam lifted the hood at my father's request, and I left them to discuss the minute details of car engines. Despite not sharing that same passion for the inner workings of cars, I was heartened to see my dad being friendly for a change.

After I stopped admiring the mosaiced ground at the entrance of Sam's mansion, I stepped through the door. The warm-colored interior had that comfortable, lived-in feel about it and was cluttered with gorgeous objects.

Studying a ruby-glassed vase that glowed in the sunlight, I said, "Your grandfather had amazing taste."

"He certainly did." Sam dropped our bags on the Persian rug. "There's a fantastic collection of trains upstairs."

"An electric train set, you mean?"

"Yep. One big one." That boyish flicker in his eyes made me want to ruffle his hair. "I'll show you later. It's really cool." He smiled. "That was one of the many reasons why I bought Julia out. She wanted to clear everything out." Sam pointed to the art on the wall.

After he showed me around the ground floor, we headed upstairs. Once we reached the landing, I gasped in wonder at a display of Art Deco figurines.

"I love these." I touched a silver woman in a flared gown.

"I'm sure you can now understand why I fought to keep this place." Sam placed his arm around my waist and, drawing me close, kissed my neck. As his scent wafted through me, my knees weakened from the warmth of his strong body against mine.

We had three days together, which both excited and frightened me. I didn't really know Sam that well. We'd only been together for ten days, nine of which we'd spent in each other's beds, fucking our brains out. And boy, the thought of another three days of that made me swollen and hazy-headed. It also meant time together. And I needed to get to know Sam. Fast.

When I wasn't trying to establish whether he was for real by dealing with my trust issues, I felt comfortable around him. I even learned more about myself. It was like he'd held up a mirror before me. But more importantly, Sam instilled me with the confidence to follow my dreams. His staunch belief in my work was like fuel, inspiring me to master my craft by becoming the best I could be.

I just wished I wasn't pregnant.

"I could use a little siesta," he said with that raspy bedroom voice, which traveled all the way down to my groin.

"You wish to sleep?" I asked, grinning.

A twinkle of mischief in his eyes told me otherwise, and taking me by the hand, he led me upstairs to the bedroom.

Along the way, I nearly got whiplash. There were so many paintings and photos that caught my eye, all fighting for space. I stopped at an abstract with splotches of color and rough brush strokes nearly leaping off the canvas.

Sam held his chin. "I love that piece."

"It's wild, to be sure. It's different from all the others, though."

"My grandfather had eclectic taste. I like to think I take after him. He was definitely an inspiration."

"You looked sad then," I said, noting Sam's sober tone.

He shrugged. "I'm not sad. The opposite." He drew me in close.

Although unconvinced, I decided to leave the psychoanalysis for some other time.

"What did he do?" I asked.

"He restored cars, and, as you can see"—he stretched out his arm—"collected beautiful things."

As we continued down the long hallway, I kept becoming distracted in the jaw-dropping artwork. Sam led me on. He seemed hungry, and not for food.

He opened the door to a large bedroom. The first thing I noticed was a balcony with a curved balustrade jutting out over the lush garden.

Sam opened the beveled-glass doors, and we stepped out onto the terrace. Behind trees of varying greens, the turquoise sea rippled gently under the beam of the sun. I took a deep breath. An intoxicating blend of sea and earth entered my lungs as I sucked it in as one would a healthy drug.

"Oh my… this is amazing. The trees are so big. And there are statues and fountains. What a paradise," I uttered, instantly falling in love with the place.

Sam's desire to live there permanently suddenly became all too clear. I wouldn't have been able to stay away from the place. It was dreamy and romantic.

"Now you can see why I had to have Manderley."

"Manderley? Where have I heard that?" I asked.

"It's from *Rebecca.* My grandfather was a huge Hitchcock fan, which I must admit I'm also rather fond of." I noticed the same awkward smile as earlier.

"There it is again," I said, my eyes narrowed as though studying an object a little more closely. Only Sam was flesh and blood. And boy, didn't I know it.

Opening his hands, Sam shook his head. "What?"

"That look of guilt. Do you feel bad because you're like your granddad, who, from what I've heard, may have raised a few eyebrows for being a Renaissance man and not some kick-ass businessman?"

Sam had been staring at the calming blue expanse when he turned and stroked my cheek, wearing a rueful smile. "Am I that transparent?"

"You've got nothing to be ashamed of. In any case, I wouldn't be here had you been that guy I thought you were."

"I'm meant to be him. That's the problem." His mouth tipped up at one end.

"Why is it a problem? You have all of this." My arms stretched out to the breathtaking view before us. In the late afternoon, the sky resembled a watercolor, with pinks and oranges weeping through the aquamarine sky.

"True."

"Your father has expectations?"

"You could say that." He exhaled an uneasy breath. "He's not an easy man to be around."

"That's like my dad. I'm sure you've noticed."

"I have. He's got plans. And I mean to mess with them." He cocked his head in that delightful way that always made me giggle.

I'd never been much of a giggler before Sam. In fact, I was always the earnest one: the one that rolled my eyes whenever family and friends carried on in their silly air-headed ways, especially after munching on weed-infused chocolate brownies.

He took my hand and said, "Now, let's get you out of that pretty dress and forget about our ball-crushing dads for a while."

Taking me by the hand, he led me to bed.

Sam pulled back the embossed silk bedspread and then gently pushed me onto the bed and tickled my belly, making me laugh and protest at the same time.

SAM

I'd discovered the biggest buzz ever, and that was Juni with her thick golden hair hanging over her breasts, a moan escaping her parted lips, and her eyelids heavy with arousal. Moving slowly on top of me, Juni took control. I loved it that way. She would rub her clit against my cock in that special way that would make her come. Her tits in my face, and her nipples piercing my tongue. Erotica personified. Juni didn't have to try, she just gave in to her desires, taking me somewhere I'd never been with a woman before. The sensual and at times agonizing undulations of her curvy body on mine teased me to kingdom come. I was constantly teetering over the edge.

I entered her deeply. Her fingernails dug into my arms.

"Yes!" she cried out.

After exercising the control of a saint—well, maybe not a saint—I let go, and my head fell back, shuddering through a release that seemed like my first in months. Colors exploded before me, and a deep, satisfied groan bounced off the walls.

Juni fell into my arms. Our bodies were hot and sticky, while her panting breath caressed my neck.

"There's definitely something magical about making love in the afternoon," I said.

"It's early evening," she said, sitting up and combing back her hair with her hands. Her cheeks had that post-orgasmic pink glow, and her eyes were bright and playful. "Sex always makes me hungry," she said, touching her belly.

"Me too," I replied, stretching my arms. "How about a quick shower and then we hit the town? What do you think?"

"Town?" she asked.

"Not downtown. I'm speaking locally. I know of a great Italian restaurant not too far away. Would you like that?" I asked.

She nodded slowly.

"If not, there are plenty of options," I said. "Perhaps afterward, we can walk along the main drag and check out some of the boutiques."

Juni looked at me for a moment. I wasn't sure what to make of her frown. "Italian food's great. Shops? You're serious about this?"

"About this? About us, you mean?" I headed to the bathroom to run the shower.

Juni followed me in.

I tested the water. "I know we're only just getting to know each other. It's just that I thought you could expand your blossoming business. Your designs are great. And what better way to get them out there than to establish a market among the rich and powerful?" I lowered my chin. "I'd be happy to back you."

Checking the water temperature, I stepped in then led Juni in by the hand.

I pumped out some body wash and lathered it over her body, massaging her shoulders and neck.

"That's so sweet, your offer to back me, Sam. But I'd prefer to use my own money. I'm sure Dad would help."

"Would he agree to it, though?" I asked.

She bit her lip. "It's not that. He would just hate me to move away from the farm."

"You're a grown-up, Juni, I'm sure you can make your own decisions."

And there it was again, that wistful, wide-eyed stare. I'd never been great at reading women's changeable emotions, and Juni's moods flipped from elation to reflection within a breath. I'd had my share of crazy girlfriends, and compared to them, Juni was the epitome of sanity. If anything, her quirkiness made her perfect. As an art expert had once told me, it was those little idiosyncrasies that made something special. I believed that of humans, too. Although I would've liked to ask her about those furtive glances, intuitively I figured that with time she'd open up.

In any case, I had my own little secrets. A shadow dampened my spirit at the thought of that impossible promise I'd made my father, even if it had been made out of desperation. What could I do? Juni would never have forgiven me had Oscar been felled. But then, I would have preferred to have joined the armed forces fighting in Syria to marrying Marie. The more I churned over my dilemma, the more I knew I was well and truly sunk. So instead, I did what I did best: embrace denial and give into pleasure, which was a skill that I'd honed in well at boarding school.

When he had sent me to the most prestigious school known to mankind, my father expected me to become the success story that he'd always seen himself as. But instead of learning how to win, I'd adopted the fine art of avoiding anything that involved developing brain cells. Most of the rich kids were experts at it. As I quickly discovered, we all shared that delusional belief that one day we'd inherit the earth not through hard work but by sheer luck of our genes. So we adopted that couldn't-give-a-shit attitude, which allowed us to party hard and fuck everything that wore a skirt or pants… depending on gender preference, or clothing choice, of course. For me, it was the curvier, the more female, the better.

As an adult, I regretted that I hadn't paid attention in Latin classes and that we'd objectified our English lit teacher by ogling her tits. With the benefit of hindsight, I speculated that it was probably our hormones reacting to something missing in our lives. Because at the end of the day, all we ever wanted was to hang out with our time-poor, money-hungry fathers and shoot some hoops, or go fishing, camping—that kind of underrated but normal activity that bonded a father and child, activities of which, when I became a father, I was determined not to overlook.

The waiter managed to fit us into a corner table.

Once we were seated, Gino came over to say hello.

He opened his hands. "Ah… Sam… it's been some time."

I shook his hand. "Yeah. Too long. I forgot how much I missed the place and your cooking."

"*Ciao, bella.*" He nodded a greeting at Juni.

She smiled back.

"Juni, this is Gino, a friend of my grandparents," I said.

"Pleased to meet you," she said.

"And you, *signorina*." He smiled brightly and then looked over to me again. "So, what can I get you?"

I looked at Juni, who'd been studying the menu for a while. "I might go for the lasagna."

"Make that two. A salad. And your finest Chianti."

"Not for me. Water's fine," said Juni.

"Then I'll just go for a beer, I think," I said, studying Juni and recalling all those margaritas she'd enjoyed our first night together.

"*Una birra Italiana*?"

"Yeah. Good. I'm always eager to try different regions," I said.

After we'd eaten with the healthy appetite that only a delicious meal and lots of lovemaking can bring, we decided on a walk along the promenade. It was a still and balmy night as we walked along arm in arm, pausing occasionally to look through the windows of women's boutiques.

"It's stunning here. I didn't think it would appeal to me. I was expecting lots of glitz. But there's also plenty of style and individuality," said Juni, stopping in front of a dress shop and scrutinizing the clothes on the mannequins.

"I thought you'd like it. I'm crazy about the place. And tomorrow, that's if you want to, we can go for a swim at our own little private beach," I said, raising an eyebrow.

"Are you always like this, Sam?" Juni cocked her head.

"Like what, Juni?"

"Smutty."

I laughed. "Smutty? Now, what's given you that impression?"

"Those bedroom eyes of yours."

"I haven't heard any complaints. And when it comes to bedroom eyes, yours are abundantly suggestive."

"Oh really?" Juni knocked me playfully with her shoulder, and we locked eyes and smiled.

I leaned in and kissed her on the neck. "Home?"

"Uh-huh." She gave me that knowing look.

As we sauntered along in our own happy bubble, I noticed heading toward me my neighbor, Aidan Thornhill. After fighting for the Special Forces, he'd become wealthy through playing the stock market. My grandfather had known him well.

"Aidan." I stopped walking.

"Ah… Sam… good to see you back," said Aidan. "You've met my wife, Clarissa?"

I leaned in and kissed Clarissa on the cheek.

"This is Juni." I gestured toward her and said, "And these are my neighbors, Clarissa, and Aidan Thornhill."

Juni returned Clarissa's smile.

"How long are you staying?" asked Aidan.

"Just a few days. A quick visit," I said.

"Then you must come over for dinner." He looked at Clarissa, and she nodded in agreement. "How's tomorrow night sound?"

I looked at Juni, and she responded with a nod.

"Clarissa and Aidan's house resembles a gallery. It's enchanting," I said, shifting my focus from Juni to the Thornhills.

"That sounds lovely. It's beautiful here."

"It is. The beach is stunning. As is the climate," said Clarissa with a gentle smile.

"Then tomorrow it is. Say, seven?" asked Aidan.

"I look forward to it." We shook hands, and I saluted Clarissa.

As we made our way to the car, Juni said, "They seem nice."

"Aidan's a great guy. A self-made billionaire. Really down to earth. Clarissa's into art, and he's into buying it. They live in an amazing place. I can't wait for you to see it. My grandfather was rather close to Clarissa's father, who lives there too. He used to lecture in English literature and my grandfather used to love hanging out with him in the library they have set up there. After each visit, I always walked away with a spurt of synaptic growth." I chuckled.

"Synaptic growth?" Juni asked.

"They're pathways that link neurons. The more we have, the brainier we are. We need to be challenged to build them. Like playing music, doing crosswords, or learning new words, amongst other things."

Her eyes twinkled with affection. "I love learning new things."

"So do I. I'm a little intellectually restless, you might say."

"I don't think I could continue seeing you otherwise," she said quietly.

"Well then, I better start reading like mad. Can't have you getting bored with me," I said.

Juni sniffed. "There's no way I could ever get bored with you, Sam. You're surprisingly bent."

"Then we're very well suited, aren't we?" I tapped her nose.

She shrugged. "I'm straighter than you think."

"I kinda know that. It's your creativity I love, amongst other things." I couldn't resist: with that inviting cleavage pouting at me, I walked my fingers over her soft tits, palming her hardened nipple. "You're one very impressive young lady."

"You sound old," said Juni, her eyes softening from my caresses.

"Well, I am a little older."

"Only by a few years." Juni fell into my arms and let me rub myself against her as I groped her peachy ass.

JUNI

Sam turned to look at me with that curious half smile he wore when wishing to delve deeper into one of my comments.

"What if I had turned out to be that man you originally thought I was?"

Considering I'd slept with Sam while assuming he was a demon developer, I chose my words carefully. "Then I don't think I would've continued seeing you."

"But you still slept with me?" he challenged.

I studied him for a moment, searching for the playful glint that Sam often got whenever he spoke about our sex life—one of his favorite topics and mine, it seemed, because just talking about it made me horny.

Sam looked serious this time, which struck me as odd.

"You were hard to resist, Sam. And by then, I'd gotten to know you a little. You made me laugh, and…"

A grin came to his lips. "And?"

"You were hot," I replied.

"Were?"

I giggled at his exaggerated grimace, which would have made an ordinary face ugly, but no matter what faces Sam expressed, he always looked gorgeous.

"You're still hot, Sam," I said, rolling my eyes.

"You think I'm vain asking that?"

I shook my head. "No. I hate vain people. That would be a deal-breaker."

"A deal-breaker?" Sam drove up the steep ascent to his driveway. "You make us sound like a business transaction."

"You know what I mean," I said.

He pulled up the driveway, and then, springing out of the car, he ran around and opened my door just as I rested my hand on the handle. Sam took my hand and helped me out. The independent woman in me would normally have protested, but I would have had to freeze my heart because I loved Sam's dashing gestures.

I stood in the garden and took a deep breath. My skin tingled from that healthy sense of well-being that came from being around nature and the sea.

Sam stood by my side and looked up at the stars. "It's a beautiful night."

"It is. I love it here."

Sam held me. "That's music to my ears. If I promise not to wear a suit, will you come here with me?"

I expected his customary playful smirk, but instead, his eyes shone with sincerity.

Should I tell him?

If there was ever a time to utter those life-changing words, this was it. But as I fell into his addictive dark eyes, sparkling with expectation, the best I could say was, "I'd love that… Only..."

"Only?" He tilted his head.

"We've only known each other for such a short time, Sam."

He held my gaze for a moment. And I thought he wanted to say something more, but he replied, "It's nice to know you love it here. Wait until we go to the beach tomorrow. In the daylight, this place has a whole different feel. The bird life is phenomenal. And the trees…"

"I did notice the trees and the birds, earlier. Sam, you don't have to sell it to me. I'm sold. I love it. And seeing those boutiques inspired me. Thanks for taking the time to show interest in what I do."

"Everything about you interests me. And that's not just a line," he said, pulling that serious face again.

"I think we've got past the pick-up line stage," I said, raising a brow.

A half smile grew at the side of Sam's mouth. "I don't recall ever using one." His eyebrows gathered. "Why are you smirking at me like that?"

"Because you were full of pick-up lines when we met."

"Really? I was just being myself."

"There…" I pointed. "It's probably become a natural part of your patter."

"Patter?" He laughed. "I don't babble, do I?"

I laughed. "All the time."

He held me again, and his breath gusted over me as he pecked at my neck. "I like your patter. I also like you all sexy and adventurous, like earlier."

Sam, of course, alluded to our hot and steamy leave of senses, eventuating in our DNA staining the ground of an alleyway. The memory of that encounter sparked a pleasant ache in my sex.

After we'd turned a corner on the busy thoroughfare, we came across a dimly lit alleyway. Sam leaned me up against a wall for a spontaneous kiss, which quickly descended into heart-pounding debauchery. Before I knew it, he turned me around and, with his tongue in my ear, made me see stars.

He rasped, "I want to fuck you now. Right here."

I was too inflamed to protest. He lifted my skirt and ran his hands up my thighs. The only thing hiding us was a shadow. In the background, street chatter reminded me just how public we were, which, instead of freaking me out, flushed me with excitement. Sam leaned against me. I could feel his hard cock, naked and impatient, against my butt while his heartbeat echoed in my ear. He hooked his finger in my panties and ripped them off, entering me in one quick, sharp thrust, so deeply his balls rubbed against my ass.

I panted quietly, which was a feat in itself, given my tendency to groan when fucking.

Sam's thick length pounded me with the kind of desperate thrusts of someone starved of sex.

"You're so hot and fucking wet," murmured Sam. "I love how your little pussy grips tightly around my dick."

Forgetting that we were only a few feet away from the main sidewalk, he pounded harder and harder, sucking on my neck, until his breathing became rough. He groaned in my ear as he shot hot cream deeply into me.

Sam laid his head on my shoulder while steadying his breath.

I turned around and nearly fell over; my legs had gone to jelly after coming. I'd also forgotten my panties were around my ankles. I stepped out of them while giggling at how sordidly exhilarating that had been.

Sam picked up my torn panties and placed them in his pocket.

"They're ripped. Maybe we should toss them out," I said, feeling a little strange about my panties being in his pocket.

"Are you kidding?" he said.

I frowned. "They're a little, you know…smelly?"

"Yeah. Nice."

I rolled my eyes. "That's sick."

"There's nothing sick about having a thing for your panties."

"What are you going to do with them?" I was not sure why, but a little throb took place where Sam had just ridden me hard.

"I'll take them to bed with me on those nights when you're not there."

"Really?"

Sam laughed at my shocked grimace.

I suddenly had an image of Sam masturbating while sniffing them, which repulsed and aroused me simultaneously.

"Don't you want to know what I do with them?" He asked as we walked back to his car.

"I can imagine."

He had that little smirk he wore whenever smut entered our conversation.

"You're enjoying this," I said.

"Juni… I can't tell you how much."

We'd only just stepped through the door when Sam said, "You're a fascinating woman. And that's not just my dick talking." He arched a brow. "I can see you achieving great things in your life."

My eyes pooled with tears. Even my dad had never supported me like that before. If anything, he wanted me to remain at the farm to run his marijuana empire when he no longer could, which was the last thing I wanted.

Sam took one look at me and said, “Come here, you angel.” He opened his big arms.

I felt so safe and complete resting my head on his chest that my tears became the substance of happiness.

“You’re a sensitive girl.” Sam passed me a tissue.

I blew my nose and sat down on the velvet couch. “Sorry about that. It was what you said. My dad’s always viewed my passion for making clothes as a hobby and not a profession.”

“He’s set in his ways I suppose like most fathers. Only he’s not meant to be conservative, at least according to his beliefs, so there’s a contradiction there.” Sam unscrewed the top from a bottle of water, which he handed to me. “Do you need a glass?”

I shook my head. “Like most people, I suppose, Dad’s riddled with contradictions.” I sniffed. “He’s harmless, though.”

“He doesn’t like me much.” Sam sipped from a crystal tumbler that shimmered in the warm lamplight.

“He’ll come around,” I said.

Sam nodded. “Our lives are quite similar.”

“In what way?” I asked.

“In that our fathers have our futures mapped out for us. Futures that we both don’t really see ourselves in.”

I nodded pensively. “Yeah… so true when you put it like that.” I looked up at Sam and felt that flush of warmth that only togetherness could bring. He’d not only become my lover, but Sam had become my ally. My best friend.

With that thought spurring me on, anticipation flushed hope and possibilities through me. Wiping tears away, I felt my spirit surge.

Stretching out my legs on that comfortable burgundy sofa, I felt as though I'd arrived home. It felt so natural being there in Malibu, following my dreams.

Sam's description of the Thornhills' home resembling a gallery was not an exaggeration, as I soon discovered while pausing at one of the many astounding works of art. I studied the large painting of the sea, shaking my head in disbelief. It was as though the artist had captured the howl of the wind through his depiction of choppy waves.

Clarissa and Aidan held hands as they showed us around. Following at their heels were their gorgeous children—a boy named Orlando, who resembled his mother with big brown eyes and dark curls, and an angelic golden-haired girl named Allegra, who shared her father's big blue eyes.

My heart grew that day. When beauty had been handed out, I think the Thornhills took the lion's share. And the love in that room was contagious and uplifting.

Dressed in fitted cream-colored chinos and pale-blue linen shirt, Sam looked so god damn delicious my mouth kept watering, especially as I conjured up memories of our passionate lovemaking. By morning, we were eating each other for breakfast in a kind of carnal cannibalism, only it was sucking and gentle little delightful bites here and there. My neck bore the marks, and I had to wear a silk scarf to hide them.

Aidan lifted his daughter into his arms. She resembled a doll, especially in a floral pinafore, which made her look very retro, just like her stunning mother.

A young cattle dog charged up, and Orlando ran to it, aiming to play with the creature's ears.

"Be gentle," asserted Aidan.

"He's like a younger version of Jeff," I exclaimed, patting the dog, which was black with a white chest.

Aidan looked at Sam. "Jeff?"

Sam chuckled at Aidan's grin. "Short for Jefferson." Noticing Aidan's brow crease deepen, he added, "Not after the president but a sixties rock band."

"Ah… Jefferson Airplane," said Aidan.

There was so much to see as the Thornhills took us on a tour of their home.

Studying Clarissa's floral dress, I said, "I love that dress."

"Thanks." She smiled almost apologetically. "I'm a bit of a sixties tragic."

"Do you mind if I feel it? I've got this thing for textured cotton."

"Sure." Clarissa looked at my wrap dress. "I love your dress, too. It's a classic cut."

"It's a recent design. I make most of my clothes. I just wish I could get my hands on more textured cotton just like this." I kept stroking the fabric as if trying to learn something new.

Having joined us after discussing something about a model car, Sam said, "Juni's a designer. She makes great clothes. Uses natural dyes and sells them online and at the artisans' market."

Clarissa looked impressed. "I love it. I'm not normally into modern clothes. But that's such a flattering shape, and it looks so comfortable."

"Thanks. I try to design for comfort while maintaining a shapely line. Mostly wraparounds or slip-over styles. I hate sewing in zippers." I chuckled.

Little Allegra clung to Clarissa's legs. She was like a cherub, quiet and well behaved, unlike Orlando, who chased the dog around the room. He was so adorable, though, that one could only smile.

We ended up sitting on the terrace overlooking a swimming pool that was more like a pond with a rockery from which water cascaded. On the horizon, behind the pool, in complimenting blue was the ocean. It was tasteful wealth. The home was not obscene and garish or soullessly minimal but filled with beautiful, fascinating pieces that left one awestruck by the magic of human ingenuity.

Drinks and snacks were served up, and we chatted about all kinds of subjects, mainly about clothes and art with Clarissa and music and books with Aidan.

After lunch, Aidan took us upstairs. On the way up, we came across an abstract painting.

"This looks similar in style to the paintings upstairs," I said to Sam, referring to the abstracts from his grandfather's vast collection.

He nodded in agreement and then, looking at Aidan, he asked, "Say, do you think you could pop over some time and check them out for me? You have a good eye for art."

Aidan gestured to his wife. "Clarissa's the expert. She majored in art history and is my advisor where buying art's concerned. I've met a few, and no one has her eye for art."

Clarissa smiled shyly. "I'm not that much of an expert."

"For one so talented, my beautiful wife is extremely humble."

"A gracious and, in my opinion, underrated quality," added Sam, stroking my arm as though suggesting that I too possessed that trait.

As we continued down the long passageway, we passed a music room, where guitars hung on the walls and cluttered the floor.

The children remained downstairs with their nanny, from where I heard a piano.

"That's Allegra," said Clarissa. "She's taking lessons. Our nanny's also a piano teacher."

"That's so good," I said, wondering whether my child would take piano lessons.

After we entered Aidan's music room, Sam headed straight to the electric piano, sat down, and started tinkling away.

"Twelve-bar blues," said Aidan, picking up a guitar.

As the men jammed away, my eyes nearly popped out of my head. I hadn't even known Sam could play. And he was accomplished. I had to wipe my brow as I watched him bobbing his head gently to the rhythm.

Clarissa whispered, “We may have lost our men for a while. This room will do that. Can I offer you a drink?”

“No, I’m good, thanks.”

SAM

"Why didn't you tell me you could play the piano?" asked Juni as we made our way back home.

We'd been at the Thornhills' for a few hours and decided to exit after Tabitha, Clarissa's very young mother-in-law, turned up with Aidan's father and shamelessly flirted with me.

"I'm not that good," I answered. "When I was young, I practiced scales and theory, but I didn't have the desire to play Mozart or Debussy. I've always loved jazz and blues. My dad hated that 'black' music as he called it, and so it became something I did at friends' homes."

She followed me into the house. "There's so much I don't know about you. I didn't notice a piano in your house when I stayed."

"That's because I don't have one," said Sam.

"But you sound really well practiced."

"There's a bar up the road that I head to occasionally. They host jam nights, and I play with whoever's there."

"Really?" Juni looked at me as if I'd just confessed to an affair. I shook my head. "What?"

"Just that you're so sexy when you play. Are there lots of women there?"

I drew her into me and squeezed her butt—a habit that I couldn't shake. "Are you jealous?"

Her chin lifted toward me. Her soft green eyes glistened. "I am a bit."

"Jealousy I can do, given that I'm seriously possessive of you. We're even on that score. I don't even notice other women."

"Not even Tabitha?" She bit her lip.

I headed to the kitchen for water. "I'm not into Tabitha. I've already met her a few times. She's married anyway."

"If she wasn't married, then?"

I shrugged. "Look, she's a shocking flirt. I could never fall for someone like Tabitha because to be honest, I wouldn't be able to trust her."

Juni looked down at her feet and nodded.

I lifted her chin. "Hey, sweetheart, where's this coming from?"

She looked away again. "I just hated the way she kept bending over, and not wearing a bra…"

"Hey…" I took Juni into my arms again. "I'm with you, baby. I'm really with you. Okay?" I stroked her hair. "I'm not into cheating. It's not my thing. It sickens me, actually. In any case, she's not even a patch on you. You're so gorgeous, Juni, that men's eyes are glued to you. Grant couldn't stop staring at you."

"I thought that was out of pity and seeking sympathy, given that his wife wasn't hiding her slutty ways."

I sniffed. "She hasn't got a killer body like yours." I stroked her thighs and headed up to her ass, where I hooked into her panties and felt her warm nakedness burn desire through me. "And Juni." My fingers traveled up her belly to her breasts. "I like my women really curvy. Even if you were not here and she was available, I wouldn't go for Tabitha. She's not my type. And I'm not really into her conversation."

"Conversation?" A smile washed away her moodiness.

"We talk all the time, Juni," I defended.

"I guess so."

"Although… to be honest." I untied her dress. "I'm not in the mood for talking right now."

Juni's hands snuck into my shirt and slid over my chest. "I'm not either."

We floated off into the bedroom, where we fell onto the unmade bed and gorged on each other.

After a few days in paradise, I fell back down to earth with a thud. My gruff father had earlier that morning insisted I drop in for a talk. And with a heavy, reluctant tread, I entered my parents' home.

The door was unlocked, so I walked in.

"There you are, darling," said my mother, wearing her hair in a bun and all dressed up.

"Are you off somewhere?" I asked.

"Yes. I'm having lunch with Gretchen."

I hugged her. "Is his lordship in a good or bad mood today?"

She opened her hands. "You know your father."

"Oh well, better get in there." I was about to move off when I said, "Mom… I'm in love."

She turned and studied me. Her eyes misted over. I thought she might even cry. "I'm happy for you, Sam. You'll have to introduce her to us."

I sighed loudly. "I'm not sure how Dad will take it, considering this obsession of his with Marie."

"As long as you're happy. In good time, he'll come around."

I scratched my arm. "It's just that goddamn tree. He's got me over a barrel. I promised Juni that it wouldn't come down. It would break her heart. And I hate breaking promises."

"I'm sure she'd understand if you explained it to her."

Nodding slowly, I kissed her on the cheek. "Bye, Mom."

I strode upstairs and straight into my father's office.

He peered up at me over his reading glasses. "At last. The prodigal son returns."

I plunked down in the leather armchair. "And hello to you too, Father." An ironic smile brushed my lips. "So… what's the emergency?"

Removing his glasses, he studied me with bloodshot, sleep-deprived eyes. I reminded myself that I would never deprive myself of sleep or fun just for the sake of adding a few extra zeroes to my already adequate wealth.

"How was Malibu?"

I sat forward. "How did you know I was there?"

"You were spotted."

"By who?" I asked.

"The Carters."

"I didn't see them." My neck heated up, hoping they hadn't caught sight of us in that alleyway.

"They saw you with your hippie girlfriend."

"Juni's not a hippie. And it's nobody's business."

"You're with Marie. It *is* their goddamn business."

"I'm *not* interested in Marie. You know that." I stood up. "Is that why you summoned me?"

He stabbed his finger toward me. "Sit."

Blowing a resentful breath, I lowered myself down again.

"We're developing that land. A deal's a deal. You haven't honored your end, Sam." He paused for a reaction, but I remained deadpan. "I'm about to order the lumberjacks again. I just thought I'd give you the heads-up so that your girlfriend doesn't chain herself to that tree again." He swung around to look out the window.

I rose, and placing my hands on his desk, I leaned over toward him. "I told you I'd buy that land."

"Have you got a spare fifty mil?"

My brow scrunched. "What? That's ridiculous. It's only worth about five."

"That's what the seller wants. He stands to make a hell of a lot more from the condo development. A third of which we'll profit from."

My stomach clenched.

"There is one way to save that tree," he said.

I held his stare, stone-faced.

He shook his head. “What are you doing with your life, Sam?”

“I’ve got plans.” There was no point in telling him about my boutique brewery. He’d only have viewed that as fluffy nonsense.

“You’re just going to drift around and live off your inheritance. You better watch out, boy, because I’m not going to leave all of this to you. You’ve done nothing but take from this family. You haven’t contributed. And what about a grandson? A boy that I could at least have a second go with.”

“A second go?” I said. “One you can manipulate, you mean?” I lowered my voice. “You know your problem, Father?”

“I’m not interested in your bullshit views. I’m the one that has created all of this.” He waved his hand.

“Your father was a boy once,” I said, thinking about my grandfather and his creatively carefree ways.

“Yes. Yes. I know. My mother had more kick-ass in her than that whole family combined.”

“And Julia’s that other kick-ass woman. Let her hold up that trophy. I don’t mind. And with regard to this fortune, she can have it. Love is more important than all of this put together.”

“Goddamn it.” He thumped the table. “You and your fucking idealism. That tree’s coming down this week.”

“Let me talk to Marie.” I thought if I stalled him a little longer, it would at least give me time to explain my predicament to Juni.

“I give you one more week. There’s a dinner party at the Carters’ on Saturday. Be there.”

I walked to the door. “Whatever.”

He headed to his crystal decanter and turned toward me. “Be there!”

Another dinner party.I’d lost count of how many dinner parties I’d been to at the Carters’. Dullsville. Even as a boy, I’d hated going there. The only fun I’d extracted was from running down the marble hallway in my socks and sliding along, mimicking a surfer.

JUNI

Sam sat at the piano playing some delightful little melody that my mom hummed along to as she knitted. Basking in the warmth of domestic harmony, I doodled in my sketchpad.

I felt good about things. And my nausea had subsided.

Sam wore a sweater that my mother had knitted for him. I'd mistaken his wide-eyed surprise for shock, given that it was the last thing I'd ever expected him to wear. He was actually moved by my mother's generosity, Sam had admitted, while staring at the sweater as though it was something mystical. No one had ever made him anything before. For me, there was an element of sadness to that admission, but that quickly faded after Sam tried it on. And despite the weather being too warm for the thick mohair sweater, Sam wore it as he sat at the piano. Looking more Salvation Mountain than downtown San Fran, Sam looked almost comical in it. I'd only ever seen him in either sports jackets or stylish shirts. Even in his boyish dinosaur T-shirts, Sam carried himself with unassuming sophistication.

He gazed up at me from the piano, and I returned a smile that was in fact a stifled giggle. Oblivious to my humor at his expense, Sam returned a big, contented grin.

Our connection had deepened, especially after Malibu. Although we couldn't take our hands off each other, finding it difficult to remain clothed for long, we'd also bonded. Our outlooks on life were very similar. I had changed too. I wasn't as pent up about things as I had been before Sam. And Sam went out of his way to buy products that he knew would please me by fulfilling my philosophy of clean living. He'd even asked a bemused waiter where the chicken on the menu had been farmed without my prompting him.

I was now two months pregnant, and after a lengthy conversation with Scarlett about it, I'd decided the time had come to tell Sam, despite my nerves being frail. I trembled at how Sam might react once he knew. Perhaps he might even think I'd contrived it to force his hand. The thought of that alone sickened me to the core. Always the voice of reason, Scarlett insisted Sam wasn't the type to think like that. I nodded sheepishly, biting every fingernail, even eying my toenails.

My dad came in. He was grumpy because I was no longer his slave.

"I need those designs for the labels, Juni," he said.

"I'm sorry. I haven't had time."

Sam stopped playing and looked up at me. "Can I help?"

My father shrugged. "That's up to Juni. She's the expert when it comes to computer art."

"I normally design Dad's labels for his bottles of gin."

"You've got a gin still?" Sam asked.

"I told you that when I met you," I said. "Juniper's Nectar."

Sam smiled. "Great name. I remember now. I'll help with some of your orders, and you can work on the label."

I nodded. "If that's okay with you."

He rose from the piano. "If I can help in any way, then it's more than okay." His positivity and energy inspired me and shook away the growing resentment I'd felt toward my dad, who stood there studying Sam as if trying to find something wrong with him.

Sam headed back to his car to get his phone. When he returned, he entered my studio while I sat at the computer playing with fonts. I looked up and observed a line between his eyebrows.

"What's up?"

"There was a bone. A dinosaur bone in my car. A present for Scotty's birthday."

My eyes widened and my mouth fell open. "Oh… Shit…" I rushed out the door.

Sam followed me. "What did you do with it?"

"I thought you might have brought it here for Jeff. I gave it to him."

His jaw dropped. "You gave it to the dog? It's not even a real bone."

"But it looked like a bone," I said, confused suddenly.

"It is part fossil but has been rebuilt. It's for Marc Bolan. The arm bone." He held his arm in a T-Rex pose and pointed to his lower arm.

Too stunned to speak, I ran outside and headed for the field, where a familiar pungent aroma entered my airwaves. In the distance, a large crop of marijuana waved about in the wind, emitting a heady scent guaranteed to drug anyone who breathed it in deeply enough.

I spied Jeff at my dad's heels.

"Have you seen a big bone?" I panted.

My father shook his head. "No. Why?"

"It's a dinosaur bone that Sam bought for his friend."

"What?" His forehead creased.

Sam explained, "My friend's a paleontologist. He's been searching for this bone for over a year. And when I found one online, I bought it for him."

"You can buy dinosaur bones online?" my dad asked.

"One can buy anything online," Sam responded.

"I'm so sorry, Sam," I said.

"Did it cost a lot?" My father looked bewildered.

"$5,000. But it's not the money. My friend's building a T-Rex."

"He's building a dinosaur?"

"Marc Bolan," I said matter-of-factly, which only made my father's perplexed smirk deepen.

I looked at Sam. "Why didn't you tell me?"

Sam rubbed his neck. "I don't know. I just plain forgot."

I looked at Jeff. "Where's the bone?" His big brown eyes shone back with a hint of guilt. "Show me the bone, Jeff."

A rare laugh escaped my father. "He's probably buried it somewhere. That's what he normally does with all his bones."

Sam took a deep breath and shrugged. "Oh well, these things happen."

"I'll pay you back, Sam."

He took me by the hand and said, "No need. Come on. We've got some work to do."

My dad nodded. "Yes. Those labels, Juni."

I gave him a military salute and scurried off.

I pressed save on the label I'd created and looked up at Sam, who was trying to unstick a roll of tape. His earlier attempt at wrapping could've been better, but I loved him for doing his best.

Noticing my little smirk, Sam asked, "What?"

I removed the roll of tape from his hands and managed to free a strip with my nail before passing it back. "This is so nice of you, Sam. You're so giving. And look, I'm seriously sorry about that bone. I've finished. Let's go for a wander and see if Jeff might have left it lying about."

Sam rose. "What about the orders?"

"They can wait a few hours. I'll send them off in the morning. Will you stay with me?"

He held me close. Kissing me on the lips, leaving warm, moist arousal behind, he nodded. "Sure. I'd like that."

"I think we've become inseparable." I studied Sam intently.

He drew me close and pressed himself hard against me. "I think I'm addicted to you, Juni."

"You make it sound like an affliction." My breath hitched. Sam's fluttery strokes were provokingly close to my cleft. I reluctantly removed his hand. "We should go and look for that bone before it gets dark."

He nodded and pointed. "Lead the way. That way I can gawk at that sexy, swaying ass."

As I moved forward, swinging my hips, I flicked my hair back coquettishly, laughing at Sam's playful hissing sounds. I loved the clown in him.

We met Mary along the way, munching on something. "What are you eating?" I went up close and saw a cannabis leaf poking out of her mouth. "Oh, shit, she's eating the weed again. Dad must have forgotten to close the fence."

Sam looked at the goat and then at me and laughed.

Mary's glassy-eyed stare confirmed that she'd been hard at it as she wobbled along on her spindly legs.

"She certainly looks wasted," said Sam, scratching his head.

In the distance, I saw Cam carrying pails of milk. I called out, and he turned and stopped.

I went up to him. "Hey, Cam, Mary's been into the crop again."

He nodded slowly and then looked over my shoulder at Sam. "Okay. I'll go and check the gate." Cam lingered, as he tended to. He was never in a hurry for anything.

"Also, if you see a bone about this big"—Sam used his hands to describe the length— "be sure to grab it. It's an important relic."

His mouth moved up at one end, which was Cam being expressive.

"Is that yes?" I asked.

He nodded.

"You were a little rough on him, Juni," said Sam as we entered the field.

"He just stares at me as if he's been blinded by light or something."

Sam chuckled. "He's blinded by your beauty. You have that effect on men."

"I don't mean to do anything. I'm not a flirt. Not like Scarlett."

"No… But you don't have to do anything. You're so sexy in your natural skin. Men love natural women."

"Do they?" My eyebrows gathered as I studied him. "Then why do women go out of their way to look like porn stars? With those pumped lips and boobs."

"That, Juni, is a great question. And one that me and my pals have often asked each other. Anyway, you should be nicer to Cam, that's all. The poor guy's seeing you, the love of his life, in the arms of another man. That must be breaking him."

With that mess of dark hair that he'd been fingering all morning, ever since that damn bone went missing, Sam looked ready for bed, and not for sleeping. I melted into his arms. "I love that you're so considerate, Sam. I couldn't be with you otherwise."

Sam smiled and took me by the hand. "Come on, let's do some bone hunting. At least it will give me a chance to see this place properly. I must say it's a huge plot of land."

Just as we traipsed down the path that took us to a little stream at the bottom of the garden, a black-and-white creature scurried past. Sam stopped in an instant, while I bolted toward it.

"Harmonious, there you are." I bent down to pat it.

Sam looked horrified. "What the fuck? Juni… That's a frigging skunk."

"He's been de-scented." I stroked his white, furry stripe. "We thought you'd gone for good."

"Harmonious?" asked Sam.

"Yes. Harmonious Skunk."

Sam bent over and laughed. "Does he play jazz piano, too? Especially 'round midnight?"

"No…" Now it was my turn to look baffled. "Why around midnight?"

"That's Thelonious Monk's famous tune."

I nodded. "My granddad named him that."

Harmonious, who didn't like strangers, ran away and left Sam scratching his head. I was just relieved that he hadn't been run over by a car.

"Why a skunk as a pet?" asked Sam as we stepped through the scrub.

"We had a rat problem, and Granddad suggested we get a skunk."

"What about Edipuss or any other cat?"

"That's a question for my weird family."

Sam shook his head.

"You're giving me that look again," I said.

"I'm not meaning to, but to be honest, I've never encountered a de-scented skunk. Let alone one named after a jazz luminary before." He chuckled.

I smiled and took his hand. "Come on, then."

SAM

While in Malibu, I'd found that piece of land I'd been dreaming of. The one-acre lot was perfectly appointed near the beach, ticking all the boxes for where I wanted to set up my new business. I quickly made the call and met the owners and scribbled out a check with the full amount for ten million dollars while Juni watched. I'd actually become twenty million dollars richer in the space of one day, not from any kind of wheeling and dealing at my end, I wasn't that type of guy, but due to more good luck. I even started to wonder if someone from above was sending me down good vibes because I'd gotten into the habit of pinching myself in the hope that it wasn't a dream.

Aidan and Clarissa, as promised, had dropped in to check out the paintings my grandfather had bought in his later years. As it turned out, Clarissa's eyes widened upon seeing one of the pieces that I'd always been fond of. I'd thought nothing of it at the time, assuming that my granddad had bought it from some hungry art student, since the small, odd but interesting painting was a far cry from the traditional art he usually picked up.

Clarissa uttered, "Paul Klee. You have a Paul Klee. Oh my God." Aidan held his chin and switched his focus from the art to his wife. His eyes glowed with the kind of admiration one gives an expert plus that little bit more, which I could only describe as love.

"Paul Klee?" I repeated. "I think there might be another here then." Clarissa's contagious enthusiasm fueled my steps. I dashed over to the spare room and turned on the light.

The multicolored spherical and linear shapes with eyes and other strange floaty objects suddenly looked more striking than I'd ever noticed.

"Oh, it is. Look," she said, pointing to the signature.

"It's not a fake?" I asked.

Clarissa shook her head. "No. The brush strokes are really consistent with his, and the pigments have that same special dangerous quality."

"Dangerous?" asked Juni.

"Paints used in the past were made of poisonous elements like mercury and cadmium, which made for striking color." She pointed at the red sphere that seemed to jump off the canvas. "Sadly, modern pigment just doesn't quite match. It's one of the first things to look out for when trying to establish an original."

"You've studied this period of art?" asked Juni, staring closely at the painting.

"Clarissa could give the guys at Christie's and Sotheby's a lesson when it comes to modern twentieth-century art," said Aidan, taking his wife's hand lovingly.

"Aidan, you exaggerate. James is a master when it comes to detecting fraud. Remember that Schiele?"

He nodded. "I missed a bullet there. Fakes are becoming increasingly sophisticated, thus harder to spot."

Clarissa studied the painting closely. "This doesn't appear to be one, though."

"Do you have the provenance for these?" asked Aidan.

I thought about the mess of paperwork in my grandfather's old study that I had yet to sort through. "I'm sure he would have kept that somewhere."

"I'd say he would have," said Aidan. "I used to run into your grandfather at auctions. And if anyone knew about buying art, it was him."

"Really?" I frowned. "I had no idea. He never really spoke to me about it. His go-to subject was either philosophy or politics."

Aidan chuckled. "Yes, I remember his long and impassioned conversations with Julian."

Clarissa smiled wistfully.

"Where are Julian and Greta?" I asked.

"They're in Venice," said Aidan.

"We should go, Aidan," said Clarissa. She cast her attention to me. "If you can locate the provenance documents, we can get these valued for you." Clarissa took one final look at the painting, which seemed to show new elements of wonder each time I looked. Almost like magic. "I love it."

"Do you want to sell them?" asked Aidan, who seemed to take his cues from Clarissa where art was concerned.

"Let's just see what it's worth and if it's real," I said, following my cultured neighbors out.

As it turned, out the pair was worth twenty million dollars. And although I never liked doing business with friends, when the Thornhills turned up with a checkbook offering just that, Juni and I spent the next day going through every piece of paper in my grandfather's study. We finally landed on that magic letterhead with "Christie's" stamped on it. Attached were the provenance documents to the set of Klee paintings. I learned that my grandfather had purchased them back in the eighties and paid fifty thousand dollars for the pair. He'd kept that one quiet. I couldn't imagine my grandmother being too keen on the purchase. Unlike my grandfather, she didn't follow art.

I'd become busy—in a good way for a change. Instead of sleeping until ten or eleven, I was up at seven, which was easy to do at Juni's, given that Pablo had an annoying tendency of waking me up at four. Whenever I ran into him strutting about with the kind of cockiness that came naturally to his breed, I'd scowl at him for being so goddamn noisy. He'd bob his head and pause, staring straight into my eyes with a "Fuck you" response.

At night, it was a battle with Juni's pussy, by which I meant Edipuss. That cat had its territory well and truly staked out. The bed was his, and he was not shifting. So apart from sleeping with Juni, I now slept with her pussy, too, who was a shifty little beast. He'd slink to the bottom of the bed and lie at our feet, which was harmless enough and great for warmth. But then, in the middle of the night, I'd wake, spooning Juni while a lump of warm fur spooned me. In the mornings, Jeff would join us for breakfast, drooling while eyeing my breakfast. As I dangled the crusts from my toast before him, I pleaded with the canine to take me to the bone, which I'd accepted by now as being lost forever.

After dropping Juni off at Scarlett's, I returned home to do some work. As I stretched my legs out on a seat in my makeshift study at home, I studied profiles of local architects. I wanted to build ASAP, and I needed to find someone who'd never worked with my father or sister, which was not going to be easy, considering they knew that scene inside out.

My phone buzzed. It was Scotty.

"Hey, there, stranger," I said.

"I'm just up the road, thought I'd drop in. If you're up for a visit. We haven't seen each other for a while."

"Great. Come on up. Good excuse for a beer break." I looked at the wooden Art Deco clock on the mantel. It was five in the afternoon.

I favorited the webpage of an architect known for his work with restorations. Knowing my father's dislike of anything antique, unless of course it was valuable, I had a feeling this was my guy.

The buzzer alerted me to Scotty's arrival. I ran down and opened the door, and his smiling face greeted me.

"Hey, man," I said. "It's been a while."

"Yeah…Girlfriends, hey?" He followed me to my living room.

"Yep… It's sure been an eventful month. I haven't forgotten about your birthday, though."

He nodded. "Hope you can make it. And please bring Juni. Jess's all excited. And being at my mom's house, it's kind of a special occasion, I suppose."

"Ah… you're introducing Jess to your folks."

He followed me into the kitchen, where I grabbed a bottle from the fridge and handed it to him.

"It's serious, all right." He looked a little perplexed.

"Are you worried that it's too soon?" I asked.

He shook his head. "No. I'm in love."

"But that's amazing." I nodded, taking a swig of beer. "Can you believe it? We're dating besties."

"Yeah, it's cool. I didn't think it would ever happen."

"Ever happen? Jess's not your first, though?"

I suddenly realized that despite being good friends, we'd never really done that typical male thing and discussed sex in all its alluring anatomical detail. We'd only ever commented on how pretty certain girls were—innocent observations, almost juvenile. I didn't mind. When it came to talking dirty, I had a bunch of dudes I'd often chat to at my favorite late-night bar, where it was so dark, I only recognized fellow drinkers by their voices. They'd lean at the bar, sharing a few drinks, and then launch into their deepest, darkest urges. Some were a bit fucking weird, like the guy who insisted that being pissed on presented the pinnacle of pleasure. Never one to judge those who liked their sex kinky, I was, in many ways, pretty straight. I just loved eating pussy. I suppose that was as kinky as it got for me. I didn't even go for anal. In any case, Juni's pussy, a magnet for my overactive dick, was responsive in that addictive way, so I was one very fucking satisfied man.

"Kind of," he said, looking down at his feet.

"No way," I said, taking a sip.

He nodded sheepishly. "I just never fessed up."

"I get it. You were more into peering down microscopes than girls' blouses." I laughed, recalling my own stint at science in my first year at college, which was where I'd met Scotty. I had been *that* guy peering down girls' tops.

We moved back into the living room.

"Make yourself at home," I said, sat down onto the sofa. "So, does Jess know she was the first?"

He nodded. "Uh-huh… She was shocked." He smiled meekly. "A twenty-eight-year-old virgin's pretty rare these days, I suppose."

"Is it good? The relationship, I mean."

"It's amazing. And Jess's crazy about dinosaurs. I mean, every girl I've ever spoken to about them always freaked out. But not Jess. She's right into them." He sat forward. "How's this for bad luck. I found a radius online the other day. I was thinking of mortgaging my home, but then the damn thing sold. Fucking heartbreaking."

I shifted in my seat. How could I tell Scotty that I was that jerk that had bought it? Only to lose it.

I decided it was best to keep it a secret. And made a mental note to tell Juni not to tell Jess. What good would it have done?

"Marriage then?" I raised a brow.

"For me, yeah. I'm crazy about her." Scotty took a sip of his beer. "So have your folks met Juni?"

"Nope." My chest tightened, and my breathing suddenly became uneven. "I'm in the shit, there. My dad's making these demands that I marry Marie Carter."

Having met her at my last birthday party, held at my parents' house, Scotty winced. "She's really not your type."

"You're not kidding."

"She's kinda scary."

I sniffed. "Yep… she's a self-entitled rich princess, all right."

"Juni's the complete opposite," he said, rising and heading to the mantel to pick up a miniature model of a red MG.

"I've met her parents." I rose and opened the balcony doors to let in some air. "That's a strange scene. She lives on a farm. Her father's worth more than mine."

Scotty whistled. "Shit… that rich?"

I nodded. "Marijuana. According to Juni, he's got some magic genus that's been in the family since the sixties."

"No shit." Scotty shook his head. "Juni seems to have her head together though."

"She sure does. But, hey, so does her old man… too much so. He's definitely not one of those stoners that laze around all day. It's one hell of a busy farm. Trouble is he expects the world from Juni. The brother ran away years ago, and now he's expecting Juni to carry on his little empire."

"Hey, that's kind of like your dad. Isn't Julia the one running his empire now?"

I scratched my neck. There were certainly parallels: We both had controlling fathers, only Harry, unlike my grouchy old man, kept things close to his chest in an intense, unsettling way.

"Anyway, I have to find a way out. My father's threatening to fell that old oak, which I promised Juni wouldn't come down. She's really attached to it. She even knows the fucking birds."

"Birds migrate."

Scotty's matter-of-fact remark acted as a reminder of just how silly the whole thing was. "Mm… they do. Anyway, Juni's got it into her head that the land's still in her family and that they donated it so that it would be recognized as federal land and therefore untouchable."

"Then it can't be if it's being developed."

"I know. I looked into it and discovered that it isn't federal land. My father doesn't even know the source. Only that it's some lawyer. The deal's being brokered by a third party."

"Then she should understand your dilemma. Explain it to her."

I sighed. "I promised her that I would move mountains to make sure Oscar wasn't murdered."

"Ha? Oscar? Murdered?" Scotty's baffled expression made me laugh.

"That's the tree's name."

"Shit. She sounds kind of kooky. But then Jess's sort of kooky too. I like that about her."

"And I love that about Juni, too."

We drank our beers with smiles, even though deep down inside, a little twist in the gut reminded me that I had to deal with this issue.

JUNI

"So, have you told him yet?" asked Jess as we lounged about at a café close to her studio.

"I'm getting there." I sipped my decaffeinated cappuccino pensively. The place was abuzz with young and free people, mostly our age. I thought about how that had been me two months ago. Not that I missed being single or anything. But my current condition certainly dampened my spirit.

"We had such a great time in Malibu. It felt like home. And a wonderful place to bring up a family." I smiled tightly as I recalled Sam and how playful he'd been with the Thornhills' gorgeous children. All the ballgames he played with them, and his patient fascination as they showed him their drawings and toys. He pulled silly faces, which made them giggle. There was no doubt that Sam was a natural around kids.

"Then you're going to move," she said, turning her lips down. "I'll miss you."

"I'm not going yet. There's a lot to think about. And then there's my dad." I shrank at the thought of my father's reaction upon learning of my pregnancy.

"But he's open-minded in that free and easy-going way, surely."

"My mom is. But Dad's a businessman. He's become really serious. Or maybe he always was."

"You don't think he'll be supportive of your relationship with Sam?"

"Mm… not really. He's been trying to get me with Cam, who you've met." I winced. "He's definitely not my type."

"Hell… your dad sounds old-fashioned."

"Isn't that ironic? Here they were embracing that free-love, hippy-trippy shit. And now he's trying to control me."

Jess smiled sadly. "I'm sure you'll talk him around."

I shrugged. "I will because Sam feels right. And then there's junior." I patted my belly.

"I think you need to tell him. What are you waiting for?"

"I just haven't had the courage. And I wanted to get to know Sam, obligation free. You know? The real him. And not him behaving in that responsible way a father-to-be needed to behave."

"You don't think he'd be honest enough to express his feelings about starting a family so soon?" Jessie asked.

"Mm… good question. Sam's one of those easy-going, nice guys that try to be all things to all people. He'd probably act as if it was fine, but deep down, he'd probably bury his true feelings. A bit like I'm doing, I suppose."

"I don't know. Sam strikes me as a man in love. He's crazy about you, Juni."

I sighed. "Shit. We've only been dating for four weeks. It feels like six months. We've nearly spent every single night together."

"That's intense." Jess knitted her fingers. "But that's the same as me and Scotty. I've virtually moved in with him."

"You're such a great pair. It's really awesome that you're dating."

"What would you do, if you weren't with Sam? Hypothetically speaking, of course."

"I would still have the baby." I took a breath. "There's no way I'm going to have a termination. I wouldn't be able to live with myself. Not that I judge other women for doing it. Scarlett's had a few. But that was in the seventies when she was really young. And she now regrets it."

"Oh…" Jess frowned. "That's sad."

A lady walked by, and a magazine she had under her arm slid to the ground. I bent down to pick it up, and a page fell open. Inside it read: *Carrington Chalmer Junior, San Francisco's hottest bachelor, is finally getting hitched.*

The name Chalmer piqued my interest, and as my eyes settled on the picture, I saw Sam and the woman who'd answered the door that morning wearing a bath towel. I read on, gripping the magazine with trembling hands: *Marie Carter, daughter of Michael Carter, Forbes Top 100, is about to fly to Paris to have a specially designed Dior wedding gown fitted.*

My emotions went into overdrive. Thoughts crashed into one another, and a storm swallowed me up. I'd forgotten that the magazine's owner stood before me.

"Excuse me," she said, cocking her head.

I looked up at her. My sight blurred from a welling of tears. "I'm sorry." I handed it back to her.

While this played out, Jess, who'd also seen the article, took my hand. "Hey, Juni… I'm sure there's an explanation. Is it a current issue?"

I stared at her. There was a smidgeon of hope. Maybe it *was* an old issue. Sam had, after all, admitted that his family intended for him to marry Marie Carter.

I rose and went over to the woman, who owned the *Hello* magazine.

"Umm… Excuse me. Is that the current issue?" I pointed at the magazine that had turned my hopes into dust.

She nodded.

I moved off in a trance.

"Jess, I need to go and buy a copy.

"Oh, sweetie, don't put yourself through this. Maybe there's an explanation."

The masochist within impelled me, regardless of Jess's sensible pleas. I picked up a copy of *Hello* and flicked through the pages. And there, in a big spread, were images of Sam and his bride-to-be, looking all loved up. They were at a function and seemed to have eyes only for each other.

My legs buckled. The nausea returned with a vengeance. I just made it to the toilet in time. Falling to my knees, I spewed bitter anguish.

Although I was meant to meet Sam, I stood him up. I couldn't face him or anybody. I needed to be alone to think about my future as a single mother.

Overlocking hems, I pedaled away. Having fallen behind in my orders again, I was actually grateful for the distraction. My phone buzzed again, making me jump.

After the fifth call from Sam, I decided to talk to him. We needed to talk about this like adults.

"Hey," I said with the coldest tone I could muster, even though my voice quivered.

"What's up, Juni? I waited for you here."

"Hello, Carrington." I exaggerated his name, which felt foreign to my tongue.

"Why are you calling me that? I hate that name."

"It kinda suits you," I snapped.

"What's happened, Juni?"

"Have you seen the latest copy of Hello?"

"It's not my go-to read. And I would have thought not yours either." He paused. "I'm more into *Brewers' Weekly* or *Classic Cars for Gentlemen*."

If he was trying to lighten me up, it didn't work. "Then grab a copy. That will explain everything to you." I didn't wait for a comment. Instead, I closed the call and turned my cell off.

An hour later, Sam arrived at my door. "Juni, I know you're in there."

I heard Mary bleating, and Pablo clucking, who had a fascination for Sam, maybe because they both shared that jutted-chest-swagger typical of the cocky male.

When I opened the door, I almost laughed. There was Pablo glaring at Sam with his beady eyes, as though to say, "Don't fuck with Juni." Harmonious was stretched out in a sunny patch by my door. He lifted his lazy eyes to see what the fuss was about and then closed them again.

Sam looked at me imploringly to be let in while Mary and Pablo remained close, acting like my bodyguards. I shooed the animals away and stepped out of the door for Sam to enter.

Wearing a white polo that showed off his big shoulders and a tanned complexion, Sam looked every bit the hot, sexy bachelor the magazine had described. All that was missing was the gold chain and a sparkle in his teeth.

Tears threatened to erupt again. I bit my lip and took a deep breath.

He began to sit down, but Edipuss, hidden under clumps of fabric on the couch, jumped out screeching, startling Sam. The look on his face made my lips curl into an uninvited grin.

"Juni..." He looked at me earnestly with those big, gleaming eyes. "It's all bullshit. I'm going to sue them. They photoshopped us together. Marie knows the fucking editor."

"It just keeps happening, Sam. I don't know what to believe anymore."

I fell onto the chair, determined to ignore his handsome head, those bedroom eyes, and sensuous mouth. Rubbing his shadowed jaw, Sam looked good enough to devour. It was as though pheromones had wafted through every pore of my body, enslaving me to desire. My mind wandered to thoughts of him bending me over like he had that morning in the kitchen, ripping my panties, fingering me, and then fucking me senseless.

But it wasn't just lust. I'd fallen deeply, madly in love with him.

Taking a steadying breath, I held my ground. "I know that magazine's notorious for cooking up stories about marriages and divorces. But this is not going away, Sam. Before I can let you back into my life, I need proof."

He nodded slowly. He sat by my side and took my hand. "Can't you see how much I'm into you? We've been inseparable. When would I have had the time to sleep with Marie?"

I removed my hand roughly. He had a point. But we'd only been seeing each other for one month. Tears spiked my eyes. I didn't want him to see me like this.

"I can't handle you at the moment, Sam. Please…"

Frustration was written all over his brow. Sam rose. “I’ll get that proof, Juni. Even if I have to drag Marie here screaming.” His anger gave me hope. Either that, or he was a brilliant actor.

SAM

I jumped out of a cab and stood before the black wrought-iron gate that was taller than me. I hit the buzzer, and the gate opened with a yawn. Driven by nerves and frustration, I strode with purpose up the long driveway to the Carters' grand Victorian mansion. For once, I didn't linger at the numerous embellishments that ornamented that imposing structure. Instead, I went straight to the stained-glass door, and before I had a chance to knock, it opened.

I'd had a few shots at my favorite bar and was suitably tipsy. I needed it that way because I planned to get a lot off my chest that night.

Nancy Carter came toward me and kissed me. "Sam, you're looking handsome as always." She spoke with a Southern twang, which I suspected was an affectation or maybe it was just something passed down in her DNA, given that oil had pumped through the veins of that family.

"Hey, Nancy. They're all here, I take it. And why are you answering the door, anyway?"

She chuckled. "I happened to be walking by and saw you on the security screen."

Nancy was an older version of her daughter Marie. Although Nancy wore a perennial smile, her skin was so doll-like smooth it never moved.

I followed her into a dining room the size of a normal family home. Around the table were a ton of faces I recognized from the many dinners over the years. Their names were interchangeable, in that half of the guys were named Mike, and the women were either Nancy or Mary.

I saluted them all with a smile and then headed over to the bar, where a waiter poured ice into a bucket.

"What can I get you, sir?"

Having already hit it harder than usual, I pointed to a bottle of beer. He twisted the top off and was about to pour it into a glass when I lifted my hand.

"Just like that's fine, thanks."

Clasping the chilled bottle, I headed back to the guests. I noticed my father wasn't around, which was always a relief. I sat down at the oval dinner table and opted for a handful of nuts rather than the floral-shaped items sitting on a plate. I couldn't decide whether they were there as decoration or snacks.

"Sam… long time no see," said Mike Carter.

"Hey, Mike." I shook his hand.

Mike did what he always did: smile and nod his head. He had very little to say. We'd probably only ever shared about ten words in the time I'd known that family, which had been most of my life.

After a few more nods and smiles, he tapped my shoulder and moved to the next person, who I imagined Mike would treat similarly.

Most of the conversations centered around someone either making a killing on their latest condo development or someone losing a bucketload after leaving his wife for a younger woman. It was always the same old stories. My grandfather had always hated attending these dinners. In the end, he'd refused to grace them, much to my enterprising grandmother's chagrin.

"Darling," I heard over my shoulder and discovered my mom's smiling face.

I rose from the table and kissed her on both cheeks. "Just the person I need to see. Can we have a word?"

With champagne in hand, wearing a sparkly dress that emulated her natural effervescence, my mother led me to a quiet corner in the living room. With its moody lighting and classy, antique curios, this was more my sort of room.

She sat on a floral divan and tapped it. "Sit here, love."

I exhaled a breath in order to find the right words.

"You're looking very tired. Are you eating?" she asked.

Ignoring her question, I launched straight in. "Have you seen the latest Hello?"

Her dark eyes reflected that uneasy resignation I'd often witnessed when broaching a subject that she found difficult.

"I'll take that as a yes."

She nodded, crossing her hands on her lap. "I was going to tell you." She touched my hand.

"Don't I get a say in any of this? I mean, it's bullshit. I'm not going to marry her."

My mother smiled sadly. "Darling, those magazines are always making false claims and embellishing the truth. Everyone knows that."

"Juni doesn't know that."

"Oh…" Her eyebrows contracted. "She saw it?"

"She sure did. Not that she buys that stupid magazine. But just my luck, she stumbled on it in a café." I paused for a breath. "I'm seriously pissed off. And tonight, I'm going to have it out with Marie. No more charades. And father can go and…"

"Oh, darling, don't say that."

"I just wanted to give you the heads-up. I promise to wait until after dinner." I rose.

She nodded. "I'll make sure I'm somewhere else."

Her fragile response filled me with guilt for dragging her through a situation that was my selfish father's doing. "I hope you realize that I'll always be here for you."

My mother nodded, wearing a sad smile.

"Can I ask you something?"

She looked up at me.

"Why do you stay with him?"

She studied me for a moment. "Because I love your father." She shrugged. "He has his sweet moments. And when one's been married as long as we have, it's no longer about romance. It's about family unity. That's what matters."

I nodded with a frown. I wondered how my father's notorious philandering fit in with our so-called family unity.

After dinner, the fun began in the most unexpected way. If anything, it made what I needed to do a whole lot easier. As expected, Marie sat next to me at dinner. And while I was dying to rip into her over that bullshit article, I remained courteous and even smiled at a couple of her silly jokes, which were not silly in an interesting way but in that a-five-year-old-could-have-told-it-better way.

I tried hard to see the good in Marie, but then this piece of gold came out of those plumped lips. "The homeless have only themselves to blame. I mean, this is America. Everyone can make a go of their lives if they get up early enough."

"What time do you rise, Marie?" I asked, dryly.

"Depends on what I've got planned for the day," she responded, looking about her.

"So, what did you major in at college, again?" I asked, knowing that Marie had left school early after it was established that she couldn't apply herself. The story had it that she'd paid someone to write her papers in boarding school and got caught. Her dad ended up donating a pile of cash to hush it all up and quietly withdrew his daughter.

Tilting her head, Marie said, "Life."

She giggled and looked over at Julia, who was by her side. My sister, who'd been an exemplary student, having achieved the highest of honors in business, politics, and law, shared a momentary sympathetic smile.

The lobster mornay squelched away in my gut. I hated hearing that bullshit about the downtrodden in society having the same opportunities as "silver spoons" like me and all the others at that dinner party.

"It's not that black and white, Marie. Some people fall on bad times through no fault of their own," I said.

She tapped my arm. "You're still preaching those left-wing views, I see."

"That's not left-wing. They're just realistic and compassionate views."

Taking a sip of her wine, she turned and faced me with that blank look she got whenever a subject had landed somewhere too complicated for her simple mind. "Let's not argue about this, Sam."

I switched my attention to Daniel, who was the most interesting person there. A neurological scientist, he spoke about brain plasticity and how we can train ourselves to do almost anything by adopting certain regimes.

Apart from a grunted hello, my dad hadn't uttered one word to me. And as I sat there playing with my food, his guttural utterances intruded on my thoughts. As always, my father dominated the conversation with his loud opinions.

I needed to take this one step at a time because I had Oscar to consider. And when it came to stonewalling, my dad was a master. If he'd been brighter, in that erudite, could-talk-himself-out-of-a-paper-bag way, he could have even run for president.

JUNI

I'd decided to visit Oscar for some quality contemplation. While some visited churches and temples to reflect on life's big issues, I had Oscar and the many colorful birds that frequented that field. Just being there always lifted my spirit. And boy, did my spirit need lifting. I walked with my head down, eyes on my feet, more of a downcast shuffle, which is how my grandfather described it a day earlier when he popped over and witnessed my sad state. After I told my family that Sam and I were having a break, they returned a "What a pity" head tilt—except my dad, who seemed quite upbeat for a change.

I looked up, and "What the fuck?" blasted out of my mouth.

The land had been cleared. Oscar was gone.

There was nothing but a vacant lot of land. My heart started to beat wildly.

"How could Sam do this to me?" I said loudly, sounding more like a mad woman by the minute. Nobody was around, so my "fucks and shits" and foot stomps were for my own benefit only. And just to add insult to injury, a wire fence had been erected, incarcerating what had been a public space.

Such was my fury that I tapped a fiery text to Sam. It read, "Not only are you a cheating asshole, but you're also a murderer. You promised not to touch Oscar. I hate you!!!!" The exclamation marks did little to express the anger that I felt as I ran all the way home in a bid to shake off the fury pumping through my veins.

Walking out with one of his weed customers, my father witnessed me storming through the yard. After saying his goodbyes, he followed me back into the house and asked, "What's up?"

"Oscar's been chopped down. That land that was once ours is now going to be a tower."

"That's capitalism for you—unfettered disregard for nature."

I sighed angrily. Was that the best he could do? I needed infuriated indignation, not some cliched platitude.

"How the hell did our land end up in the hands of another?" I asked.

"It's a long story, Juni," said my father, evasive as always when it came to that plot of land.

"I've got some spare time," I said, stepping inside my mother's studio.

"Juni, it's best we don't go there for now. It's very complicated."

"What is, darling?" asked my mother, who'd entered the room.

"They've chopped down Oscar, and Dad won't explain why we no longer own that land."

My mother peered up at my father. I swore I caught a glimmer of confusion in her expression.

"Come here, sweetheart," she said, noticing my eyes drowning in tears.

I fell onto the sofa and allowed her to rock me as I cried and cried.

My father looked down at his feet. Guilt was written all over that normally inscrutable expression.

"We have a few nice oaks here, love." My mother held my hand.

"It's not the same. I spent my childhood there. That tree was magical. I wanted it there for my children." I choked on sobs. And with my face down on my mother's shoulder, I drenched her blouse.

"There, there." She stroked my head. "Has Sam got back to you?"

"Yes… But I won't speak to him."

"But you should let him explain. Those magazines are full of fantasy."

I stared at her for a moment, and her soft green eyes transmitted such a comfortable, safe place that I wanted to tell her. But I didn't want my dad to know, and in any case, after what had just happened to Oscar, I was even entertaining a termination. I hated the idea of my child sharing the DNA of a liar.

"Mom, do you think a father's morals are passed on in the womb?

My mother frowned, studying me for a moment. "Um… I'm not sure. I think it's more nurture than nature. If the child's reared by dysfunctional parents or exposed to evil when young, there are chances that the child may become a bad person. But then, it's not always that black and white."

I let out a long, ragged breath.

"Oh, darling, don't go worrying your pretty head over all of these deeper issues. Just enjoy being young. You're so talented and successful. I'm proud of you," she said with an encouraging smile. "And you're so much tougher than me. I've always been a bit of a pushover."

I blew my nose and looked at her. "What do you mean? Do you have regrets?"

She shook her head slowly, which was somewhat unconvincing. "No. We've built a good life here."

"What are you not telling me? Dad was all coy about that land. Now you are."

"Let's put it this way. I got pregnant, and then I married your father. Not the other way around."

"Does that mean had you not been pregnant with Lee, you wouldn't have married? I wouldn't have existed?" I asked.

"I'm not sure," she said.

"What would you have become?" I asked.

"A musician, I suppose. But I lacked drive. Scarlett was always the one with enough drive for both of us." She smiled.

"Then I must take after Scarlett, I suppose," I said.

"You do, darling. But not in that wild way, of course."

"I'm still young. And…" I bit my lip. "Sam was my first. That's why this is so hard." My voice cracked up. Tears again splashed down my cheek.

"Sam's besotted. And you both seemed so happy."

That didn't help. My mouth wobbled. I needed to go somewhere alone and howl my heart out.

"Mom, I love you. Thanks." I kissed her. And with a heavy tread, I headed back to my space.

When I entered, Edipuss looked up at me from his position on the sofa and gave me that "I told you so" expression that possessive creatures radiate when they don't like sharing their owner.

I joined him on the couch, where he climbed onto my thighs, purring as I stroked him.

SAM

I'd nearly pulled my hair out by its roots from frustration. What I really wanted to do was punch a hole in a wall somewhere. I stormed into my father's study and stood before him. It was evening, and normally I'd be somewhere other than that stifling, smoky room.

"You had that fucking land cleared," I growled.

He sucked on his after-dinner cigar and took a swig of cognac from the balloon that balanced between his thick fingers.

"We discussed the deal. You went against it. And this client got really impatient." He drained his glass. "Besides, his figure doubled overnight. No one in their right mind would have paid one hundred big ones for that land."

Juni hadn't answered my calls. I'd texted her, pleading ignorance, which was the truth—even though I'd intuited that after the party, at which I pretty much told everyone I had no intention of marrying Marie, my father would move forward with his plans.

"You're the one that got drunk and acted like a first-class ass at the dinner party. All that commie bullshit and left-wing drivel. Whose son are you anyway?"

"That's a question that I've often asked myself."

We locked eyeballs. I returned his unwavering cold smugness with icy blankness. If he hadn't been my father, I would have punched that smarmy look off his face. Instead, mustering the self-control of someone at a banquet while fasting, I dug my fingernails deep into my palm. After brandishing silent resentment as my weapon, I left without uttering another word.

I headed to my temple of worship. Miles Davis's smooth, mellow notes welcomed me as I stepped into Hearts of Jazz, a bar not too far from home, and one that I could crawl back from if I needed to: something I didn't do that often. But hell, this wasn't the week for moderation.

Dark and moody, which was just as I felt that moment, the venue had almost been created with me in mind. There were pictures of vintage cars on the walls between images of famous jazz musicians. I peered up at Louis Armstrong, cheeks puffed out, horn balancing against his fleshy lips, before shifting my attention to a framed image of a sexy red Corvette Stingray. A wistful sigh followed. I wished I could time travel back to that era when there were no vitriolic text messages to read.

The barman set down a double shot of bourbon along with a beer. The extraordinary events of the past forty-eight hours played out in my mind. What kept revolving around and around was the dinner party. If I wanted to be a real jerk, there would be much to milk from that little juicy encounter.

By the time I'd ordered my sixth shot, I'd summoned that jerk within. Desperate times called for desperate measures, which spelled sending my inner Mr. Nice Guy off on a holiday somewhere.

I'd always sensed that Julia had a predilection for women. But Marie? I couldn't get that image out of my head. If it hadn't been a dramatic couple of days with Juni, I would have been gloating. In many ways, it was entertaining to know that my sis was not the model, upstanding conservative my dad believed her to be. The fact that Julia didn't own up to it rankled me. Now that took guts. And for all her grandstanding, platitudes, and ball crushing, Julia had demonstrated that she was just as human as any of us.

Marie was no better. I'd spoken to her at length about that *Hello* article, and she'd responded, "I'm not sure who leaked that story." Marie was not a good liar; she didn't even try to put a hand over her mouth or widen her eyes in disbelief.

"And that bit about you having your dress fitted in Paris?"

"Well, I often go there to shop. Who doesn't?" she asked, raising a brow and painting on a fake smile.

"Um… about three hundred and thirty million Americans," I said.

She leaned in and whispered, "You know you can still fuck your little hippie when we're married. You can fuck whoever you like. This is what the rich and powerful do. You should know that by now." She cocked her head and tottered off.

Yes… I did know that. I'd seen enough fucked-up marriages and heartbreaks to know that that was not for me. Open marriages were for those governed by their genitals and not their hearts. And as much as I couldn't control a rampaging libido where Juni was concerned, I was sure as hell not going to marry someone just as a front.

After gulping down a fiery shot, I grabbed my cell and pressed on Marie's number. It went to voicemail. I sent her text, and a few minutes later, she replied with: "Can't make it, babe, I'm kind of busy. Tomorrow, though."

Then an idea came to me, I called my sister. A voicemail came up, so I texted her. She replied, "Not now. We'll catch up tomorrow."

I texted, "Are you home?"

She answered, "Yes. But it's not a good time."

I'd always followed hunches. Sometimes they ended badly, like at the horse track or the roulette wheel, but when it came to human shenanigans, I was always pretty much on the money.

The main things that separated upper-class suburban homes from normal peoples' homes were big fences and impenetrable gates. Behind those barricades, all kinds of things took place, just like at my sister's that night. She wasn't up in bed reading Danielle Steel or Nora Roberts, she was entertaining. I knew that because her two-meter wooden gate was unlatched, and when I stepped into the garden, I heard females giggling in the distance.

Having made my way down the garden path, I unlatched another gate and headed to the porch, to the side of which I discovered, sitting in a Jacuzzi, my sister, and Marie.

That hunch of mine had delivered.

They must have sensed my approach because they both stopped chatting and turned.

"Who's there?" asked my sister, covering her naked chest.

"I'll give you a hint. It's not Steve," I answered dryly.

"Is that you, Sam?" she asked.

I stepped into the light. "None other." I saluted them with a smirk larger than the Golden Gate Bridge.

"What the fuck!" Julia grabbed her robe. "Turn around, will you."

I'd already turned. "Are you decent?" I asked. "No… maybe not the right question, because we all know the answer to that."

Marie had escaped by the time I turned to face them again.

"Come out from wherever you are," I sang. "I know you're here, Marie." I shifted my focus to my sister. "I saw you both at the party with Marie's spikes up around your ears. You really need to get into the habit of locking doors, Julia. I mean, what happened to that scrupulous eye for detail?"

"What do you want, Sam?" she asked.

"Not much. Just the truth. And for Marie to make a public statement through one of those trashy mags that I am not her fiancé. And for her to tell our father that she's met someone else." I looked around. "Did you hear that, Marie?"

JUNI

Claude sat there with his sleazy smile. One didn't need to be clairvoyant to read his thoughts. His pants were so tight that a roll of fat hung over the edge. Yuck.

Scarlett, who'd reconnected with Javier, was floating around being everything to everyone. Her friend Jane, who'd just had a cancer scare, was Scarlett's primary focus. She handed Jane a vial of her 'miracle cure' after performing a healing ceremony in the backyard.

Needing a distraction, I just couldn't remain at home.

"You're not looking yourself, Juni," said Claude, inching closer to me.

"I'm okay, I guess." I shifted my butt to the edge of the bench.

"Where's Mr. Big Bucks?"

"Umm… he's gone away."

"Last time he was here, he couldn't take his hands off you." Claude's eyes crept down to my ballooning chest. "Not that I can blame him."

While I admired Claude's considerable artistic talent, I was not in the mood for his philandering. Without meaning to, I noticed a boner and felt the vegetarian curry I'd had for dinner making its way back up my esophagus.

I managed to slip away to join Scarlett. I was just about to tell her I was leaving when a familiar voice floated through the air.

The next moment went in slow motion. Sam arrived looking as though he'd been in a wind storm. His hair was sticking up and ruffled. Dressed in flip flops, ripped Levi's, and a very faded T-shirt with a dinosaur head, he nearly made me laugh. But more significantly, I wanted to fall into his arms, despite everything.

"What are you doing here?" I asked.

He looked at me and then Scarlett. "Sorry for bursting in like this. I just need to talk to Juni."

I didn't want to cause a scene and couldn't help noticing the guests were keenly watching, as their eyes shifted from me to Sam.

"Let's go to the back," I said.

Sam followed me and took my hand.

I pulled it away. "Don't."

"Sorry." Sam lifted his hands. I could see he'd been hitting it hard because he looked tired.

We entered the garden, and a cauldron from the earlier ritual sent up a puff of steam, issuing a heady but pleasant fragrance.

"I hope you haven't thrown in a lock of my hair and the tongue of toad in there. I'm suddenly feeling itchy and a little stabbing pain." Sam scratched his arms.

Playfulness lit his face, making my lips twitch as I fought off a chuckle.

"There aren't any effigies of me in there, are there?" He continued with his jokes, hoping to draw me closer with that seductive twinkle in his eyes.

In order to remain cool, I had to look away. "Why are you here?"

"Because I've got this to show you." He reached into his pocket and handed me a shiny page that had been ripped out of a magazine. The headline read, "Good news, girls: Carrington Chalmer Junior is single again."

The article explained how the pair had parted and that they had never been an item, "as expressed emphatically by Chalmer."

I stared up at Sam. And just as I was about to speak, Claude joined us. He'd been drinking and drew me in tight to his waist, stroking my arm. His fingers were inches from my breast.

Before I had a chance to snatch my arm out of his grip, Sam collected Claude by the scruff of the neck. His face had gone a deep shade of fierceness and his big arm muscles flexed so hard sinews popped out.

A punch landed on Claude's face, causing him to stumble. He rose with fists clenched ready to smash away, but Sam crunched down on his face again.

I yelled for them to stop.

"Sam… Please… Don't."

Sam picked up Claude as though he were a rag doll. And staring into Claude's sweaty face, foreheads close to colliding, he said, "You lay another finger on Juni, and I won't be so nice next time. Get it?"

Scarlett and Javier ran out to see what the commotion was about. And instead of being shocked, Scarlett grinned. "Mm… Mars conjunct Pluto in Scorpio. How apt." She turned to me. "Was Claude misbehaving again?"

I nodded. Glowering at Sam, I replied, "But it was an over-reaction."

His mouth turned up at one end. Reluctantly contrite, Sam wiped his brow with the back of his hand. His eyes trapped mine.

"Are you okay?" Scarlett asked Claude.

Sporting a cut lip, Claude nodded gingerly. "I'm fine. My ego isn't though." He shuffled back inside.

That night, I encountered a different Sam. It was as though he'd aged—not withered but matured. I was used to the flippant, playful version of Sam. His eyes were so dark and intense I had to look away to avoid losing myself in them; otherwise, I wouldn't have made it out in one piece. Not that I was threatened. It was more that I wanted Sam to fuck me hard against a wall somewhere dark and dangerous, which was weird. As a pacifist, I no longer recognized myself. Maybe I too had changed.

SAM

I stretched out my throbbing hand. Carrying a bag of frozen peas, which looked out of place in her pentagram-tattooed hands, Scarlett passed it to me for my aching knuckles.

"Here, I think you may need this."

I rubbed my hand. "It's okay. Claude might have more need for them."

"He's being seen to," she responded.

"Hey, I'm sorry. But he was hitting on Juni, and I…" What could I say? I had no right to her. Juni wasn't my property.

"She's fragile at the moment. You've deeply affected her." Her stare lingered as if she was trying to say more.

"That makes two of us. I'm totally smitten. But then, I'm sure you know that." I raised an eyebrow.

"Go to her and hold her hand. I'm sure she'll forgive you," she said. "And look, Claude had it coming. He's had a thing for Juni for a long time. I've even had a word with him over the years."

"Over the years? Juni's only twenty-four."

Scarlet remained blank-faced.

"I hope he didn't try to lay a hand on her when she was a teenager."

Scarlett shook her head. "No. I guarded her against that."

"Can I ask you something?"

"What's that?"

"Would you cast a spell to bring Juni back to me?"

Her head pushed back in one sharp move. "Ah…"

I grimaced. "Have I crossed a line?"

A slow smile grew on her face. "I didn't think you went for this kind of thing."

Juni joined us. She looked at me and then her aunt. "What kind of thing would that be?"

"Sam wants me to create a spell to draw you back together."

I frowned at Scarlett. "That was meant to be confidential."

She laughed. "You don't need a spell. Look at her." She pointed at Juni, who rolled her eyes, putting a smile on my face for the first time that week.

"Scarlett," Juni protested.

Her aunt held her hands up. "All right. You two need to talk. I will leave you. Can I get you a beer?"

I nodded. "Please. I can come in and get it."

"No… Stay here and sort out your issues." She cast Juni a long, serious stare as if they knew something I didn't.

After she floated off, I tapped the wooden bench where I sat. "Let's talk."

As she sat down, a whiff of rose scent wafted through my senses and lifted my spirit. There was nothing I wouldn't give to bury my nose in her golden hair. It was soft and fragrant and magically seemed to take me places that only people like Scarlett believed in.

Juni turned and stared me straight in the eyes. "That was so unnecessary."

"I'm not sure what came over me. He's a sleaze, though. And I don't regret hitting him."

"Mmm…" Her green eyes burrowed into mine as though trying to learn something about me.

Scarlett came back out with a bottle of beer and handed it to me.

"Thanks." I smiled and took the bottle from her. Untwisting the top, I took a thirsty gulp.

"You're not having anything?" I asked.

She shook her head.

"Juni," I said turning to face her square on, "I'm sorry about what happened. But none of this was my fault."

"What about Oscar? You promised not to remove him."

I sighed. "I know. But that mysterious client refused my twenty-million-dollar offer."

Her forehead lowered. "You offered that much?"

"Uh-huh." Gathering my thoughts, I took a sip of beer. "My father arranged it behind my back. He's a force. It was out of my control. We had a deal, and I broke it."

"What kind of deal?"

"That I marry Marie in return for Oscar and the land to remain untouched."

She studied me for a moment, shaking her head. "That was a big promise to make. Unless…"

"If you're implying that I want to be with Marie, you're seriously mistaken. She's not my type, Juni." I touched her hand, and this time she allowed it to remain. "Anyway, I'm not her type, either, it seems."

Juni studied me for a moment. "Why wouldn't you be? You're everyone's type, aren't you?"

"I'm not sure whether you're complimenting or insulting me." I returned her smirk. "What I meant to say was that Marie prefers my sister's company to mine."

"Oh…" A line formed between Juni's eyebrows. "You mean like that?"

"Yeah… They're gay."

Her head pushed back sharply. "You're kidding me. Then why did she go to such great lengths, like stealing your phone, and that seduction act? Why not own up to it? It's legal."

I nodded. "Yeah. It's pretty fucked up. I asked her the same thing. She just explained that she wanted to join our family any which way. She assumed that if we slept together even once it would be enough to seal the deal." I raised an eyebrow. "She also reminded me that she'd suggested having an open marriage and that our conservative families would never ever condone a gay relationship." I looked up at Juni to read her response. She just remained wide-eyed and expectant. "I told Marie that my future wife would be my one and only partner in life and in bed and that I wouldn't be sharing her with anybody, woman or man."

Her lips twitched into the making of a smile but quickly reverted to a tight line. "Marie sounds fucked up. Does your father know about them?"

Shaking my head, I smiled faintly at the thought of my father's explosive response once he learned that Marie would be joining the family but not in the way he expected.

"God. It's like some kind of twisted soap opera," she said. "And I thought my family was weird."

"Yeah, every family has something hidden. Even though being gay shouldn't be viewed as weird. It's legal. And rightfully so. Although my father will see things differently, seeing that he's still stuck in the Dark Ages."

"He sounds scary."

"Formidable is the word that comes to mind," I said.

"And so you promised to marry Marie for Oscar?"

Nodding, I sighed. "I had to stall him somehow." I placed my hand on hers. "You never would've stayed."

"So you stalled in order to charm the pants off me?"

My shoulders slumped. This was not going to be an easy argument. "Juni, trust me, I did everything."

"Trust you?" She tilted her head as if I'd asked for something unreasonable.

"I'm not sure what more I can say. It's all out in the open now. The games the wealthy play to have their own ways. Not pretty. But welcome to the world of 'divide and conquer.'"

"Divide and conquer?" Juni laughed.

"When it comes to power games, not much has changed since the time of the Medicis. If my father read books, I'm sure *The Prince* would be his book of worship."

"What's that?"

"A book written in the sixteenth century by Machiavelli. His political views have been adopted by the rich and powerful throughout the ages and are still in favor, sadly for those less ruthless of us."

A smile touched those lips I wanted to make a meal of. "You're not just a pretty face, are you?" she murmured.

I chuckled. "Pretty?"

"You know what I mean."

I leaned in close and took her into my arms. "At least it brought a smile to your pretty face."

Her body relaxed in my arms. Juni let me kiss her. Even though gentle and affectionate, her lips sent a rush of burning desire between my thighs.

She pulled away gently. "I suppose the fact that you were willing to pay that much," she muttered quietly. "But how can I believe that?"

I shook my head. "God, Juni, do I really strike you as being that dishonest?"

"I'm not sure what I believe anymore. That article really freaked me out."

"Will you come with me to visit Marie?"

"Huh?" Her eyebrows squeezed. "I'm not sure I wish to meet her. She was very rude the last time I saw her. And if she was into all that free-loving shit, why slam the door in my face?"

"Great question, and one for her." I sniffed. "At least if I introduce you, she can tell you herself that I'm no more going to marry her than build the pyramids."

Juni laughed. "I can't imagine you carrying heavy rocks around."

Now it was my turn to frown. "I'm not as lazy as you think, Juni. I've been working around the clock with a designer for the new brewery, which now comes with a bar and dining area."

"You've done that in a week?" Juni asked.

I nodded.

"What are you going to call it?"

"Oscar's Place?"

"That's kind of random. But nice, too, I suppose," she said, with a little smile.

"If it weren't for Oscar, I would never have met you."

Looking tearful, she nodded. "It broke me up seeing that land cleared. I cried. That was my childhood."

"I get it." I brushed her cheek and then walked my fingers up her arm.

"Will you have dinner with me?" I asked. "Or we can visit Marie. She's expecting it. I told her that this needed to be addressed and put to rest forever."

"Dinner sounds good. I'm not sure if I feel like visiting Marie, though."

"Anything and everything for you," I said, smiling so brightly my face hurt after not smiling for a week.

JUNI

The air was crisp and refreshing as we stood outside Scarlet's house trying to decide where to go. I really didn't feel like being around people, so when Sam suggested takeout, my chest collapsed with relief. I had this hankering for Chinese food, and Sam, always eager to please, arranged it.

After a week's absence, I felt a sense of relief as though I'd come home. Despite our having been together for such a short time, there was something about Sam's space that made me feel complete, perhaps due to the fun we'd had there, which wasn't just all the hot sex we'd had in every room of that house, but also the long chats, watching movies or quiet moments reading.

I followed Sam into the kitchen, where he placed the cartons on the island. He went to the fridge and brought out a bottle of wine. "Can I get you anything other than water?"

I shook my head. "Water's good." He poured me a glass, and I followed him back into the living room.

Noticing a mess of paperwork, empty food cartons, and bottles, I said, "This place looks like a wild bachelor's pad."

Sam laughed. "I've had a big week. But not in that fun way you were just alluding to." An eyebrow arched. "I've been working on the plans for the brewery." He paused. "Hey, how about 'Here's to Oscar'?"

My brow creased. "Huh? What happened to Oscar's Place?"

"That's for the café. But 'Here's to Oscar' is for the beer label."

"Oh..." I mulled over it for a moment. "It's kind of quirky. And suggests we're drinking to someone... in this case, my beautiful tree."

Sam took me into his big arms. "I am so sorry, Juni. I promised you, and I fought hard. It was a promise that was impossible to keep."

I removed myself from his arms.

"It's kind of strange," I said. "Because my dad recently told me that it was federal land." I pictured my dad's evasive, almost stuttering response. "It originally belonged to my grandmother."

"That doesn't add up," said Sam. "Unless..."

"Unless what?" I asked.

"He sold it. Plain and simple. Your father must have sold it."

I nodded slowly. Something sat uncomfortably in my belly, and that wasn't the little life growing, even though that was another issue needing to be faced.

I looked up at Sam. "So you promised to marry Marie in order to keep Oscar alive?"

He exhaled a frustrated breath. "It wasn't one of my finer moments. But shit, Juni..." He stared deeply into my eyes. "I'd made a promise to you."

"Then you're forgiven." I placed my hand in his. "I can see the pain it's caused you."

Our faces neared and our lips fused in a sweet, warm, almost innocent kiss. But then my rumbling tummy got in the way of passion as an appetizing aroma wafted up to my nasal passages. "I'm starving, Sam." I unfolded out of his embrace.

He went back into the kitchen and returned with plates, which he set down on the dining table covered in paperwork.

I noticed a drawing of a building. "Is this the architect's impression of Oscar's Place?"

"Yep." Sam smiled, looking pleased. He moved the pile of files onto an armchair to make room for the food and then poured the contents of the cartons onto two large plates. "I'm thinking of having a mural of an oak tree painted on one of the inside walls."

Although it seemed over the top, the idea grew on me the more I thought about it. "That would give it a colorful, creative vibe."

"And there'll also be an oak tree planted outside."

Sam's enthusiasm was contagious. A bubble of excitement took hold of me. Did he mean for me to be part of it? I thought of the little life growing inside. Was I ready to start a family, move to Malibu, and help run a business while continuing with my clothing designs?

"And you can design the curtains, tablecloths, and menus," he said. "Only if you'd like to."

"That's a tad old-fashioned, isn't it? Curtains and tablecloths."

He nodded thoughtfully. "I do love retro."

I thought of Sam's charming car and his eclectic taste in furniture and bric-a-brac. "I've noticed," I said with a gentle smile.

"Is that a look of approval, then?" he asked, tilting his handsome head.

"Mm… I like your tastes, Sam. I'm not into empty space and minimalism either."

He nodded. "Too right. It stresses me out."

I laughed. "It's meant to be calming."

"Bullshit. That's my sister's idea of stylish living. Not mine."

"I could never live in an environment devoid of objects and color," I replied.

An aroma floated up to my nose, reminding me that I needed to eat. Lifting the fork, I looked at Sam. "Do you mind if I dig in?"

"Of course not. Let's eat."

I helped myself to both dishes, tofu and vegetables and beef and vegetables, until my plate nearly overflowed.

"You are hungry," said Sam, pouring the rest of the contents onto his plate.

I swallowed a forkful of noodles and nearly collapsed from the bliss of fine-tasting food. I hadn't eaten much that week.

"This is yummy," I said, wiping my mouth with a paper napkin.

"I'm glad you like it. I must eat this meal at least twice a week," said Sam, pausing for a sip of wine. "I've got the number on speed dial." He lifted the Chardonnay. "Are you sure you don't want some?"

I shook my head.

Once more his puzzled look caused that little knot of guilt to tighten. I had to tell him soon. I just needed to find the right time and place. And given that we were only making it back onto firm ground, I wasn't quite ready yet.

SAM

For some reason, I loved seeing a woman who ate with gusto. Most of the women I'd hung out with before Juni picked at their food as though it was something to be feared. Not Juni. She polished off her entire meal, which was almost twice the size of mine.

Blessed was how I felt. I almost wished to embrace that god, or more accurately that goddess that Scarlett preached poetically of. Having always held an interest in Greek mythology, I found Scarlett's colorful references to Gaia and Aphrodite illuminating at times. Not that I believed in their existence, but the mind was powerful in that it could conjure up meaning from anything.

Scarlett had even talked me into placing a ribbon around an oak tree, which brought to mind that sugary seventies pop song. I still did it anyway. Lost for options after Juni wouldn't take my calls, I'd visited Scarlett. Scrutinizing me with the intensity of a clairvoyant detective, she'd asked, "Do you really like Juni?"

I gulped. "Like" was way too tame. "I think I love her," I replied, which surprised me. The only other time I'd ever used that "L" word was to do with my mom or my childhood dog, Jasper.

Scarlett clasped her hands. "Right then. Follow me."

Somewhat hesitantly, I sauntered into her backyard, where she instructed me to stand inside a pentagram mosaic.

Scarlet clutched a jewel-handled dagger that could have belonged to the evil witch in *Snow White*. Wearing a hooded cape, she moved from one corner to another, reciting an ode to each element. For a moment there, I thought that perhaps she'd placed a drug in the glass of water I'd gulped down earlier because I couldn't believe I'd somehow allowed myself to be part of this strange ritual.

Scarlet kept uttering, "So mote it be." I remembered that because she made me repeat those words too.

Of all the crazy things I'd done in my life, I'd never resorted to witchcraft before, and out of respect for Scarlett, given that she had that serious remote glint one gets when entering a spiritual zone, I maintained a respectful silence even though a little voice within screamed for me to run.

After that was over, Scarlett insisted on reading the tarot cards. The reading, according to her, spoke of great tidings. Speaking in symbols and using language that best belonged to *The Lord of the Rings*, I managed to decipher something about a birth. Sitting up, I asked her to elaborate. Scarlett muttered something vague about it symbolizing growth.

I asked, "What about Juni?"

She picked up a pretty card illustrating a couple embracing, followed by another bearing two cups. "There you have it. Soulmates. Love… Marriage."

Marriage? Was I ready for that?

I did leave with a lighter step. So that was probably my subconscious punching the air. My rational self, however, judged it as mumbo-jumbo. But then, I believed in the Big Bang, which to many was considered just as implausible.

After leaving Scarlett's, never one to go against my word, even if it was a bit flaky, I tied a pink ribbon around Oscar as instructed, and then one week later, the tree came down. That really hit me hard.

After dinner, we stretched out on the couch. "I'm so glad you're here, Juni," I said, stroking her soft arm. I regarded her wrap-around dress with shapes of flowers sewn on. "This is new." I touched the fabric.

"Yeah. I'm using the applique method. It's time consuming, but I like the crafty effect."

"Crafty?" I laughed.

"As in arts and crafts," she said.

"Speaking of craft," I said, moving a little closer to her. "Did Scarlett tell you that she wove a spell around us?"

Juni sat up straight and looked at me. "Huh?"

"I visited Scarlett a couple of days ago. I was so frustrated. You weren't taking my calls."

"She didn't tell me."

"That's kind of decent of her. I did ask her to keep it a secret."

"Why?" asked Juni.

"Because it seemed weird and a little desperate." I turned to stare at her in the eyes. "It seemed hypocritical of me."

"I can imagine." She cast me a teasing smile. "Who's your god again?"

"I don't have a god. But if I had to choose someone whom I admire, it would have to be Noam Chomsky."

"My dad speaks about him a lot. But he looks up to Gandhi," she said.

"Your dad isn't that chilled, though, is he?" I asked. "There's something bubbling away under the surface."

"He's just a little pissed off with the world," A slow smile formed on her face. "So, Scarlett cast a circle?"

I nodded. "Uh-huh… I thought she was going to get me to chant and stand on one leg. But it was nothing like that."

"That's so funny. I can just see your face," said Juni, giggling.

"It worked. You're here now." My sober response wiped the smile from her face.

"I'd still be here, Sam, with or without witchcraft." Her voice was tiny, almost as if it was a difficult admission.

I took her into my arms and held her, soaking in her soft warmth against my beating heart. Her thick, soft hair radiated that intoxicating rose scent.

I turned her face toward me.

Her tongue swept over her lips, drawing mine in like a magnet.

Sweet and soft, the taste of her lips sent a surge of blood to my dick. All of life's hassles disappeared with that kiss.

I ate at her lips with the ferocity of someone who hadn't kissed before. Her plump, hot lips acted as a portal into a world that promised to seduce and comfort at the same time. Our tongues tangled, and I devoured her as if I'd been starved of passion.

I slid my hand into the flap of her dress, which opened and revealed her curvy, milky thighs.

My fingers crept up her leg and reached into her silky panties. She moaned in my mouth.

I untied her dress, and it fell open, revealing a sensual wonderland of femininity that left me breathless.

"These dresses are designed well for these moments. I'm not a fan of zippers unless they're placed in the front."

"I'll bear that in mind with my next designs."

I smiled and then continued to caress her warm, smooth skin. I unclasped her bra, and her breasts tumbled out.

"I need to be inside of you, Juni," I said, pulling down my zipper.

I removed her panties, and she lay back provocatively on the sofa.

"I'd love a photo of you like this."

"Would you just?"

"So is that a yes?" I asked.

Having removed my T-shirt, I lowered my jeans and stood before her in my briefs. My throbbing shaft stretched the cotton fabric impatiently.

She lifted her chin. "Only if you let me take of photo of you like that."

"Deal."

"They have to come off, though," said Juni, pointing to my briefs.

Lowering them, I indulged in Juni's sexy naked ass as she sashayed over to her bag.

She held her phone and aimed it toward my dick.

"You must promise me that you won't send this off to *Homo Erectus Monthly.*"

Juni giggled. "Is there such a magazine? Or are we talking Neanderthal?"

"I heard they were all well hung," I said, arching an eyebrow.

She stared into her phone. "Then you would have fit in very well."

I cocked my head and studied her for a moment. "Are you poking fun at me?"

"No, I meant it as a compliment. We were talking about down below and not above." She tapped her head.

I laughed. "Have you taken it?"

She nodded.

"Let me see," I said.

Biting her lip, she passed her phone to me. My mouth stretched into a line. "Wow. You really captured it. What about the rest of me? It's only my dick."

She lowered onto her knees and took my cock into her little hand. My chest collapsed with pleasure.

"I'll take a photo of your face another time," she said, licking her lips.

"Oh God, Juni… No," I said, pulling away. "I'll blow straight away. I need to be inside you first. You can suck my dick later." A grin grabbed my lips. "Only if you want to, of course."

I took her into my arms and squeezed her ass before traveling up to her heavy breasts. My lips planted kisses all over them before settling on her nipples, teasing them with my tongue and sucking on them.

"You've got the sexiest tits, Juni." I stepped back and stared into her eyes. I bent down, and reaching into my jeans pocket, brought out my phone.

"You're serious?" she said.

"I let you take a photo," I protested.

"Yeah. I suppose." She bit her lip and appeared so bashful suddenly, it made me even harder. "What will you do with it?"

"I'll look at it."

"Will you jerk off to it?" she asked.

"When you put it like that, I might have to."

Our eyes locked. Her smile turned sultry.

"I'll take that as a yes, then, will I?" I pointed. "There, on the sofa."

She laid down and placed long blonde locks over her breasts.

"Don't hide the nipples, Juni," I said, studying her image in my phone.

I noticed her eyes had that heavy arousal about them and snapped an image of her face. Those hooded green eyes when she was about to come had been stamped into my soul, and I would've paid thousands for that shot.

I walked my fingers up to her pussy. She opened her legs, willing me in.

Her little moan of anticipation encouraged my touch.

As my finger entered between her folds, her heat and slickness told me that Juni was as turned on by our little photo shoot as I was.

"You're getting off on this," I said.

"And so are you," she said, pointing to my steel-hard erection.

I parted her legs. Her glistening pink pussy made my tongue flood with saliva.

Lowering to my knees, I placed my head between her thighs. My tongue settled on her swollen clit. Grasping her voluptuous ass, I devoured her. Her groans melded with the rattling noise of a passing cable car in the street below.

She squirted cream onto my tongue while pulling at my hair, which made for pleasant pain.

I undid myself and grabbed my phone.

Her legs remained wide apart. That delicate opening engorged with blood was bright pink and dripping with her creamy cum and my saliva.

"Can I take a photo of your wet pussy?"

Her breathy "Yes" traveled straight to my groin.

After I snapped the perfect shot, I set my phone down. Taking her into my arms, I murmured, "Thanks."

JUNI

Drugged with lust, I wasn't sure how I'd feel in the cool light of day, but at that moment, the swell of desire was so great that I wanted him to photograph me in the dirtiest way possible.

"Do you like me photographing you?" He sounded so aroused his words had a sticky quality to them.

"Yeah," I responded. "It's nice dirty."

"Speaking of nice dirty." He lifted me up into his arms. "I need you in my bed."

"I'm heavy," I protested.

"No, you're not. You're light as a feather," he said, carrying me in his arms and making me laugh as he jiggled me along.

We entered his room, where neon signs and streetlights bounced off the walls, making for a moody ambience.

Sam set me down. "I'm sorry I haven't had a chance to make the bed."

"It's okay. I can smell you," I said.

Rubbing his neck, Sam studied me. "Should I change the sheets?"

"I like it." I held out my hand. "And I like you."

He joined me and held me close. "That's good. Because I'm crazy about you."

His lips found mine, and again, I floated in a sensual cloud. Sam's caresses made my body come alive as his hands fondled my breasts.

Opening my legs wide, I held his dick, which dwarfed my hand, and placed it between my folds. He entered slowly. The stretch set off a divine ache. His eyes plowed deep into mine. Sam hissed behind his teeth at the sheer pleasure of the tight fit.

His sensuous mouth opened slightly. A gasp escaped.

The extreme burning stretch hit nerve endings already sensitive from when he'd tongued me.

"I need you on top," he said. He held me tight so that he remained inside of me as he turned me over.

He looked into my eyes again, his dark eyes burning with that need to surrender everything.

I moved up and down, his hands clutching my ass, his mouth devouring my nipples, and his hungry cock driving hard, building and building, causing my eyelids to flutter.

"I need you to come." He struggled to speak.

As he pumped hard, it was so hot, I cried out something ridiculous as I rode a wave that just kept me climbing higher and higher. Sam's jaw tightened, and his head fell back as he shuddered through his release. The veins of his cock throbbed inside me, and a growl exited his parted lips.

I lay in his arms, waiting for my heart to still and for my senses to return.

"Holy shit… Juni…"

"Are you okay?" I asked.

"I sure am. That was intense. You're so fuckable," he said, slapping my ass gently.

"And so are you," I replied. "I like the way you feel."

"And I like the way you feel. You've got an expressive little pussy." He stroked my breasts tenderly. "I think I'm going to have to fuck you all night, Juni. Do you mind?"

I pulled away and looked at him. His eyes twinkled playfully.

"What do you think, big boy?" I said, squeezing his big bicep.

He laughed.

"I thought you were going to really hurt Claude earlier," I said.

"If that greasy hand of his had brushed your breast, it wouldn't have ended well."

I drew away and looked at Sam. His eyes had gone so dark they were almost black.

"You're serious," I said.

"I am." He gazed at me with such intensity that my breath hitched.

"There'll be no need. Claude's harmless."

"Bullshit. I know a sexual predator when I see one. I don't give a damn that he's a successful artist. The guy's a sleaze. And wasn't he with your aunt?"

"Scarlett's into polyamory."

"I could never do that," he said, pushing back a stray hair.

"Neither could I. In many ways I'm pretty conservative," I said, surprising myself, for I'd never thought of myself like that before. But then, I'd never fallen hard for anyone before.

"Good. Because when it comes to love, I fly the flag for monogamy."

He took me into his arms again as if to emphasize that fact, claiming me with a tender kiss.

A whiff of him after sex wafted through my pores.

Sam looked at me earnestly. "You will have to meet my family at some point. I'm into this, Juni."

I stared into his face again. "So am I, Sam."

"Have you thought about Malibu?" he asked, stroking my arm.

"I have," I said.

"And?"

"Let's see how we go for the next month," I said, tilting my head and smiling.

Sam's chocolate eyes had that warm glow that made me want to eat him. He opened his arms and invited my head onto his bulging bicep.

For the first time in ages, I felt content and peaceful.

And although I hadn't committed to anything, my heart already knew the answer to that question.

Flourished

Book Three

SAM

Juni shook her head in disbelief. “Holy crap, this thing’s huge.” She referred to Marc Bolan, the skeletal T-Rex that Scotty had spent his whole professional career building. I responded with the same jaw-dropping awe as always while staring at the imposing creature’s shadow clinging eerily to the walls. Juni clutched my arm and shivered. I had to sympathize. For someone not into dinosaurs, it gave off that late-night-horror-movie vibe. Monstrous in that typical bent-arm pose, the bipedal creature seemed ready to pounce.

Jess, who was besotted with the creature, had photographed the cinematic skeleton in every which way and printed it on T-shirts, one of which I’d become the proud owner of.

“All the bones appear to be intact,” said Juni. “Did Scotty find another arm bone?”

“No,” I said ruefully, thinking of the radius that was buried somewhere on Juni’s property. “The bones are made from casts.”

“But they look so authentic,” said Juni.

Scotty joined us. “Nothing beats the real thing, though.”

I nodded. “I’m sure we’ll find it, buddy.”

Juni looked at me and then Scotty. “Do you know about Jeff and the bone?”

"Who's Jeff?" Scotty turned to me.

"That's Juni's dog."

"Oh." Scotty's lip curled up at one end.

Having been understandably shattered upon hearing about that ill-fated bone, Scotty now saw the funny side to its disappearance.

"I'm sure it will turn up," said Juni with a sweet, reassuring smile.

He shrugged. "It's been buried for seventy-odd million years. An extra year or two shouldn't matter."

The cries of a baby bellowed through the space, which was like an echo chamber.

"I better go and see if I can help," said Juni. She paused for a moment and looked at me. "No, you should, Sam. Every time you hold Johnny, he seems to settle."

Scotty nodded. "Sam's got that special touch, all right. No one else can get that baby to calm down." He sighed with a hint of frustration.

We went back into the living area, where Jess held a ten-month-old baby in her arms, rocking while the baby screamed.

I stepped in and said, "Here, give him to me."

Jess passed the chubby, cute little boy into my arms and I went all silly again. Out of my mouth came a stupid baby voice—cartoonish and weird. But more significantly, in the space of thirty minutes, I'd grown attached to that little being.

Juni and Jess looked at each other, sharing that same odd exchange that I'd noticed earlier.

"I'm sorry about this," said Jess for the umpteenth time.

"It's okay. Your sister needed the work. And after what's happened to her, it's important you give her your full support," said Juni, turning her attention to Scotty. "I'm sure you won't mind for one night."

"More like three nights," he replied. I could see he was exhausted by the thought of babysitting the unsettled infant.

Looking apologetic, Jess said, "I promise this will be the last time. Penny's going to arrange childcare for the weeknights." She looked at me and explained, "My sister's husband did a runner, and now she's a single mom. She works as a nurse, and working nights pays double. I promised to take him, and now that I'm living here, it's all become a bit crazy."

Her eyes held a tinge of moisture. I could see she was torn between her duty to her unfortunate sister and her desire to spend time alone with Scotty. As she spoke, Johnny settled in my arms and started to laugh at the kooky expression I didn't even know I possessed until that moment. I looked up, and I swear it seemed as if Juni was about to cry. Her eyes shone. Then Jess hit her arm. And there was that mysterious exchange again. My eyes slid from Juni to Jess and back again.

"You're such a natural, Sam," said Jess, taking the baby from my arms and placing him in his bassinet.

"That's good to know," I said, gazing at Juni, who returned an unsteady smile.

After we left Scotty's, I turned to Juni and asked, "So what was going on in there between you and Jess?"

"Nothing." Her eyes shifted away. "She was just impressed by your natural parenting skills, as I was."

My brow contracted at Juni's slight stutter. "Right." I nodded slowly and studied her face in the shadow of the night. "Well, at least we get to go home without the baby."

She stopped walking and turned. I might as well have told her I'd joined a satanic cult by the way she glowered back at me. "That's not a nice thing to say."

"I was kinda joking, Juni. Please, don't take it to heart," I said, drawing her close.

Feeling her sweet breath on my face, I devoured her lips, something I'd been dying to do all night, especially after watching her biting at them. Apart from stimulating curiosity, it also brought back memories of that morning, when she'd taken my whole length in one smooth swallow, making my eyes roll to the back of my head.

Lowering my head, I studied her long face. "What's wrong, Juni?"

"I just feel pity for the mother."

I stroked her cheek. "You're a compassionate, beautiful soul. I love that about you."

She smiled sadly.

I couldn't help but feel she was taking the whole Jess-becoming-a-surrogate-mother situation a bit too seriously, however. "Hey, how about if I pay for her childcare for a year? Just until she gets on her feet."

Juni frowned. "You would do that? You haven't even met Penny."

I shrugged. "So? She obviously needs support. And that asshole husband of hers, who should be strung up and quartered, can't be relied on."

"Strung up and quartered?" Juni giggled.

"It's an old English punishment. Pretty fucking awful. But they were cruel bastards back then—always seeking to inflict the most pain possible."

'I know. I watch old movies, too."

"You do. With me." I stopped moving.

We looked at each other, and the twinkle of a smile in her eyes changed into desire within a breath, registering straight to my dick.

Holding onto her, I walked Juni to the wall of the alleyway.

Within a breath, our tender kiss turned fiery. My tongue parted her lips and entered deeply. Opening the flap of her dress, I touched her pussy through her moistened silky panties and felt her heart race against my chest as my finger hooked in and tore her panties off.

I fluttered over her clit. Her creamy response drenched my finger. Parting her folds, I entered her deeply with my finger. Pushing impatiently against my zipper, my dick ached to be inside her.

Turning her around, I bit gently into her neck. Unzipping my pants, I released my dick and in one sharp thrust entered deeply into her.

I growled, "You feel so hot." My hands caressed her breasts as I rubbed against her voluptuous ass.

It was deliciously sordid. The dark alleyway was a perfect setting for a hard, hot fuck. We'd fucked there before, and the flood of arousal sweeping through every cell was heightened by the threat of being discovered.

Breathing heavily as my hardened balls rubbed against her hot butt, I didn't hear the couple coming toward us. They must've heard my groans, and like stunned creatures of the night, our heads turned toward the silhouetted couple.

"That's disgusting" I heard a woman saying to her partner as they moved away in the opposite direction.

It should have put us off, but I was too aroused. When they were out of sight, it took just two more deep plunges, and as her tight, wet pussy contracted around my cock, I blew so hard it nearly took my head off.

After I'd regained my senses, I turned Juni to face me.

"That was a close call," I said.

"It made you harder," she said, matter-of-factly.

"You seemed a little creamier, too," I said, raising a brow.

We stared at each other and laughed. I bent down and, picking up her panties, placed them in my pocket.

"I hope you throw those out," she said.

"Are you kidding? I've got a drawer full of them."

Her mouth stretched into a grimace. "That's kind of gross."

"No, it's not. It's hot."

"All mine, I hope," she said with a playful smirk.

"Indubitably."

She laughed at my exaggerated English accent.

I took her hand and kissed it. "I'm so glad I met you, Juni."

She smiled sweetly, which was a vast improvement to the perplexed expression she normally wore whenever I opened up about my feelings.

Hand in hand, giggling at nothing in particular, we floated back to the car.

JUNI

I pedaled slowly past our old block of land. Resting my bike between my legs, I paused to study the aftermath of the carnage leveled at that former green oasis. It was unrecognizable. There were no delicate leaves and flowers shining in the sun, breathing beauty and goodness into the air. The birdlife that had become my friends, along with the myriad of insects that I loved to study, were all gone. Smoothed out dirt was all that remained. Gripping my handlebars, I thought about Oscar, the tree I used to climb as a child. Inspired by *The Magic Faraway Tree* and its enchanting world that I wanted so to inhabit, I used to entertain imaginary friends there. As a grown-up, it had been my sanctuary when I needed alone time to contemplate. It was where my mind wandered through a field of possibilities, stumbling on some new idea along the way. The magic that I'd discovered there as a young girl had never gone away. And now all those memories were to be buried under an ugly rectangular structure.

I sighed. If it weren't for that land being developed, however, I would never have met Sam. A bitter pill, yes, but one I would've swallowed over and over, because I couldn't imagine my life without him. Sacrificing my childhood wonderland, although devastatingly sad, was a small price for having Sam in my life. I thought of the child growing inside of me and what kind of world she would grow up in. And although I fancied myself a firm believer in progress, I despised this endless need to destroy nature for the sake of profit.

My emotions were on edge. It was time to tell Sam about my condition. And after seeing how he was with Jess's nephew, Johnny, I breathed a little easier. At least Sam had a natural paternal side. A baby whisperer, Jess had called him.

I just had to find the right time and place.

Sam was in Malibu to work on his new venture, and although he'd invited me along, I'd decided to stay home to finish off orders. I'd fallen behind again. I just needed to spend more time at the machine and the cutting table. Sam was right: expansion was necessary. Sitting at the top of my to-do list was to find someone who could cut and sew. That way I could focus on designing, which was the fun part. My orders were going through the roof. I couldn't believe how popular my reversible wraparound skirt had become. I'd also created a top for breastfeeding that tied at the shoulder. Made of organic cotton and a flattering shape, the blouse had proved very popular.

While I continued to gape gravely at the dead land, in the distance, I saw a familiar figure dressed in a suit, and in discussion with a couple of men. When I realized who it was, blood drained from my face.

I sped off, pedaling as fast as I could. When I arrived back at the farm, out of breath, I nearly ran over Harmonious, who had this annoying habit of snoozing on the path. Leaning my bike against the wall, I ran inside, where my mother sat spinning wool. My legs started to shake, and the next thing I knew, I was on the ground with my head on my mother's lap. Her concerned eyes stared into mine. My head hurt, and my legs and arms were too weak for me to rise off the ground. My mom placed a pillow under my head and then hurried off.

When she returned, she passed me a glass of water. "Don't move, Juni. Drink some water. You might be dehydrated."

After swallowing a few mouthfuls of water and feeling stronger, I sat up. My mother lowered herself to my level and rested my body against hers.

"I'm going to take you in for some tests," she said, touching my forehead. "You're looking a little pale. You could be anemic."

I did feel weak. The first thing I thought of was my baby. Gripped with fear, I massaged my belly as tears streamed down my cheeks. She held me and rocked me in that caring way that only my mother could. I cracked up, and the tension of having carried that secret while being unsure of what to do just flooded out of me.

"It's okay. You can move your arms and legs now. You were probably in need of water. I'll drive you in for some tests, though, just to be on the safe side." She reached for a tissue and passed it to me. "It's probably the shock of fainting." She stroked my face.

"I'm pregnant," I murmured.

"I thought so," she replied soberly.

I looked up at her. "Did Scarlett tell you?"

"No, sweetheart. I could just tell. Your craving for undercooked meat, bordering on raw, raised my suspicion. When I was pregnant, I virtually drank blood," she said with a chuckle.

Sitting up, I nodded. "Me too. Sam…" I bit my lip, and tears splashed down my cheeks again.

"He doesn't know, I take it?"

I shook my head, sniffling. "It's so soon. I conceived the first night I met him." I winced at the thought of telling my mom, despite her being open-minded, the details of that impulsive dalliance with Sam. "How unlucky was that? And he used protection."

"Oh, darling, it happens all the time." She smiled. "Sam's a great man."

"He is. And I'm crazy about him. And he's got plans for us. Plans that I'm more than excited about. But I'm just frightened he'll think I've done this on purpose to tie him down."

"Sam doesn't strike me as being that cynical, surely." My mother held onto my arm to help steady me as I rose.

Although my legs were a little wobbly, I managed to move freely.

"We're off to the hospital. Now."

"I'm feeling a bit better," I said weakly. There was little resistance however, because deep down I needed to know that my baby was doing well.

Looking as though he'd been in a tornado, Sam came rushing down the corridor of the hospital just as my mom, the doctor, and I stood there chatting. Sam had called me earlier, right after I'd been examined. After he'd heard what had happened, he'd insisted on being there, despite my protests. I then made my mother promise not to tell Sam, given that I'd planned to tell him later that day, privately.

Having followed us out, the doctor reassured me that the baby was alive and well. He'd also revealed the child's sex, which I'd asked him to do.

Sam took my hand. "Are you okay?" Before I could answer, Sam turned to the doctor. "Is she okay?"

The doctor smiled. "Both mother and child are doing very well."

Not for long, because my legs buckled, and I nearly fainted again as I leaned against my mom. The look of horror, or so I'd interpreted, on Sam's face revved my palpitations. Like an afterburn, his unblinking bewilderment blinded me. I pushed past him. Sam's response upset me. Jumping to conclusions, which was something I did well, I ran out of the hospital without looking back, muttering something like, "He doesn't want it."

My mother caught up to me. "Are you okay?"

"Please take me home, Mom," I said.

Pausing so that Sam could catch up with us, my mother said, "Juni, perhaps you should give Sam a chance to process this. Talk to him, at least. It's come as a shock."

"I don't want to talk. You saw his face. He looked like the sky had fallen," I said glumly. "Please take me home."

Sam joined us, breathing unsteadily. "Why didn't you tell me?"

I didn't answer him, because a thick lump in my throat had stolen my voice.

"It's mine?" he asked.

If there was ever a time I wanted to scream, it was then. I turned to face him. My eyes widened. "What do you fucking think? It's either yours or an immaculate conception."

He combed back his hair and his eyes softened. His lips twitched slightly into a curl before straightening into a tight line again. "It's a shock, that's all. I wasn't expecting it."

"Of course, it is," said my mother, who wasn't sure where she needed to be. "Look, how about I leave you two to discuss this. You can drive Juni back home, can't you?" She looked at Sam.

"Of course." He cast his attention back to me and took my hand. I couldn't say what had come over me, but all I saw playing out in my overwrought mind was Sam's initial shocked horror.

"No… I need to be alone." I turned to my mother. "Can we go?"

We left Sam standing there rubbing his neck and frowning. I'd never seen him look so dark and serious before.

SAM

I nearly wore a hole in the floor of my living room. My hair was sticking up, looking like Mary's hair in *that* movie, only I didn't need a product or bodily fluid to make it that way. The productive week I'd just experienced had turned into a distant memory as impending fatherhood invaded my thoughts.

I'd tried calling Juni, but she'd refused to talk. If only I could've re-enacted that scene just as the doctor told me that I was going to be a father. I wanted to explain to Juni that it wasn't that I hated the idea of procreating with her. If anything, that bit was easy, given that I'd decided that she was the *one.* But it had come as a shock, pure and simple. And why keep it from me for so long? That needed answering. If anything, I should have been the one pissed off for being kept in the dark.

And then that same question revolved around and around, pounding away in the background, screaming the loudest—What kind of a father would I make? My head spun, robbing me of the focus I needed to manage the brewery. After a night of tossing and turning, I was not in a state to return the builder's calls and discuss costs. Instead, I paced backward and forward. I saw myself holding a screaming baby, bouncing it on my knees, just as I'd done with Johnny. But then, he wasn't mine. What about that trip to Europe that Juni and I'd spent hours fantasizing about? And all the other dreams we'd made together? Those priceless moments after experiencing the orgasm to beat all orgasms, I would hold her and we'd talk about our aspirations, dreams, and ambitions we wished to share. Together.

As I drove along the dusty driveway, I tried to avoid running over the nosy creatures that always ran out whenever I arrived.

I stepped out of my car, and there was Miss Prissy, her head bobbing back and forth. Suspicion reflected off her beady eyes, as though she knew that I'd been a douche. A few feet away, Pablo, with that proud jutting chest, strutted about, acting every bit the head cock. Jeff barked at me. It was as though the animals were in on it. I was that jerk that had come and conquered their beautiful mistress's heart only to behave like an insensitive prick.

After knocking on the pink door to Juni's studio and getting no answer, I decided to head to the main house. Clucking loudly, as though nagging at me, Pablo bobbed along, while Jeff ambled by my side. Given that I had a literal bone to pick with him if anyone should have harbored resentment, it was me.

Luna answered the door. "Hello, Sam." Her genuine smile helped thaw my veins.

"Hey… Um…" I rubbed my neck. "I just came over to see Juni. I tried calling…"

Luna stepped out of the way to allow me to pass. "She's here. Come in, and I'll make you a nice cup of tea."

Needing more than herbal tea, I returned a grateful smile.

Following along, I drew in a steadying breath as a pleasant floral scent filled my nostrils, and with each step, I became calmer.

"Scarlet's got a hungry pussy. Scarlett's a slut" rang through the air. Tim the parrot was perched on a cupboard, poking fun at me, or at least trying to make me laugh, which he was good at doing because I felt my lips curve.

"Is that all he knows?" I asked.

"No. He's been taught other filthy things too. It's too late. I've tried to unteach him, but my father-in-law has gone to great lengths to get that bird to shock visitors." She stopped walking and looked at me. "Juni's very sensitive." She studied me for a moment. "And at times very young. I'm sure you've noticed that."

I nodded pensively. "I probably could have handled it better by not appearing so shocked."

She touched my arm. "Hey, you had every right to be. It's huge. And hearing it second hand would have made anyone react that way. You're not in the wrong, Sam. She should have told you."

Who doesn't love an ally? I leaned in and hugged Luna. "Thanks."

Juni's parents' home, although heavily cluttered with furniture, musical instruments, and books, was huge. In fact, I could have sworn it had grown since the last visit. Or was that the marijuana-laced brownies I'd consumed at the time warping my memory? As I walked from one room to another, it seemed as though more rooms had been added, impossible as that would seem. One door would open and then another and another, each room as distracting as the last. There were so many colors, shapes, and weird objects I almost forgot where I was.

We finally arrived at the dining area that adjoined the kitchen.

I heard Juni's father saying, "What did you expect from a capitalist with a penchant for knocking down old trees?"

I stopped in my tracks. Luna looked at me with an apologetic tight smile. "I'm sorry you had to hear that." She gestured. "Come on. Don't worry about Harry. He's actually a softy."

"That's bullshit, Dad!" Juni yelled.

She turned around. The fire in her gaze mellowed slightly when she saw me.

"I'd have to agree with your daughter," I said, stepping into the fray. "I actually love trees. I've never overseen the clearing of any tree before. In fact, I've just had an old oak transplanted to the new site of my brewery."

"Oaks don't like being moved," stammered Harry, who looked a little taken aback by my sudden appearance.

"I've employed one of the best arborists around, and he assures me that the tree should survive."

Juni's searching gaze fired up again as she returned her attention to her father. That girl had spunk, I thought, feeling hot and bothered in that inappropriate way, considering I was in the kitchen surrounded by her family.

"Speaking of capitalist developers, what was Lee doing on our old block?" she asked her father.

"Your brother might have been visiting it for old time's sake."

"Lingam was in the area and he didn't visit?" asked Luna, looking upset suddenly.

Tim got in on the act, flying over our heads and cackling, "Lingam's a big dick. Lingam's a big dick."

I had to bite my lip again. That damn bird's timing was always impeccable in the worst way possible.

"He was there talking to a land surveyor," Juni continued without as much as flinching at her feathered pet's interruption. "He was dressed in a suit. Lee's got something to do with that land, hasn't he?"

In a bid to remain inconspicuous, I lowered myself down onto a stool despite deep curiosity. If the brother, as I now suspected, was that mysterious client, at least I would no longer be an evil developer in Harry's eyes. Despite that being the case, I probably had more hope of landing on Mars than of Harry liking me. Ironically, the man he thought me to be was the man my father wished I'd become. What a tangled web I suddenly found myself in. Nothing but expectations and misconceptions.

"Sweetheart, you need to tell Juni. And to be fair to Sam," Luna implored her husband.

Luna had become my champion, and just when I thought Harry had it in for me, he went and removed two bottles of beer from the fridge and handed me one.

I was so parched I felt like hugging him.

"Scarlett's got a hungry pussy. Scarlett's got a hungry pussy."

"Shut the fuck up, Tim," snapped Harry.

Luckily, I hadn't taken a gulp, because this time, I did laugh as silently as possible.

Harry pointed to the empty stool next to mine. "Sit down, Juni."

She lowered herself onto it, and rather brazenly, I took her hand. To my delight, her soft, warm hand remained in mine, igniting that spark that somehow always magically charged through my veins.

Harry swallowed some of his beer and then began to pace. "Lee owns that land."

"But that land belonged to Granddad's father. He passed it on to the family," said Juni.

Harry stared solemnly at his beer.

"Juniper, your father had to sell it to Lee because he was in debt," said Luna.

"What happened to the accidental billionaire?" asked Juni.

"That's now." Harry looked at me for some reason and then Juni. The side of his mouth curved up slightly. He was one of those for whom smiling didn't come naturally. The only other person I'd ever known with that affliction was my own father.

"How long ago did this happen?" asked Juni.

"Four years ago." He took a swig from his bottle. "I invested in some bad stocks."

"Bad stocks?" Juni's brow furrowed. "You played the stock market?"

The irony wasn't lost on me either. Knowing all about Harry's views on Wall Street, I couldn't believe it.

"It wasn't my finest hour. Cannabis stocks."

"But that's the one investment that's been flying high," I interjected, turning to Juni with a wry grin. "No pun intended."

She rolled her eyes, but then a little grin followed, and my heart expanded. I squeezed her hand, and she looked up at me with a tight smile. Was I forgiven?

I hoped this family thing would be resolved quickly so that I could rip that pretty dress off her, the thought of which, had my dick springing to attention. I crossed my legs and started counting in Roman numerals.

"True," responded Harry. "But just my luck, the company I invested in was run by a bunch of crooked hippies, and the whole thing fell to pieces. I lost a bundle."

"Without that experience, sweetheart, you wouldn't have set up your own plantation," said Luna.

"Have you floated it on the stock market?" I asked.

"No way. That was the only time. I think I was dazzled by the idea of marijuana, that much-maligned drug, having made its way into the mainstream. That made the whole transaction irresistible."

Luna looked at her husband with sympathy. I could see that she supported this complex man in every way possible.

"So let me get this straight: four years ago, the family was broke so you went to Lee for help?" Juni asked.

Harry nodded.

JUNI

Questions kept coming thick and fast. I couldn't think straight. The heat radiating off Sam's hand had plenty to do with that. Sam was impossible to hate, let alone walk away from. Yet his wide-eyed shock on learning about my condition kept replaying itself in my head, despite a voice of reason reminding me that considering we'd only just met, it was a natural reaction.

I left my hand there because I needed to feel Sam's energy. I'd become addicted to the electricity that smoldered through me whenever Sam's fingers came in contact with my body. From the first moment our lips had touched, something deep within me had bloomed like a bud bathed in sunlight. It felt as though my soul had been impregnated with his essence. And from then on, I'd become possessed by his spirit. When I described it as such to Scarlet, she insisted that Sam and I had lived a past life together. She went on to explain that our type of deep connection and the insatiable desire we shared only affected twin flames and that we were soul mates. Although I didn't believe in past lives, my heart broke into a happy tune.

"I didn't realize Lee had that kind of money," I said, turning to my father.

"Lee's filthy rich. When it comes to the stock market, he's got that Midas touch. God knows where he gets that from."

My dad looked at my mother, who pointed out, "He looks exactly like you, Harry."

I nodded in agreement. "You're also very talented in business, Dad."

He grunted, which was his typical response when caught out contradicting his stringent dislike for the free market.

My mother said, "Your father had little choice. We were about to lose everything."

I nodded pensively and then looked at Sam. "Did you know any of this? Considering your father's company is in partnership with Lee."

He shook his head. "I asked my father repeatedly. I wanted to know, because I made an offer to buy that land in order to keep my promise to you. But in the end, this mystery owner refused, and the price was so ridiculously inflated, it was an insult."

"So all this time, you knew?" I looked at my father. "And you pointed the finger at Sam, making out that he was the bad guy when it was Lee."

"He's still part of the machine that's behind the development, though," he argued.

"I'm not." Sam turned his attention to my father. "I've left the family company. I was never into it. My dad, who you'll probably meet one of these days soon"—Sam's eyes caught mine— "wanted me to run the family business. But it's not my thing."

"Sam's building a boutique brewery and café in Malibu," I said with pride because if there was ever a time that Sam needed my support, it was then. He'd been treated poorly, and I wasn't exactly blameless.

Learning that my brother had been behind the clearing had left a horrible taste in my mouth. Lee had taken advantage of the family. The fact that he'd resorted to such a radical low act by destroying the place he'd played in left me gob-smacked. He knew its significance. That land had belonged to my mother's family. All the picnics and memories. Lee obviously didn't have a sentimental bone in his body. Or was that his final act of cutting the umbilical cord to a family he'd divorced long ago?

I turned and faced Sam. "I'm sorry for blaming you."

He opened his hands. "It's all good. I would have blamed me, too, had I been in your situation. My father always got me to do his dirty work." A gentle smile grew. "Not anymore."

My father asked, "So what's this about meeting the parents? You've only known each other for a few months. That's a little too soon, isn't it?"

I had to pull my eyes away from Sam, which was not easy to do with those smiling eyes casting their spell on me again. Looking over at my mother, who gave me a little nod of support, I said, "I'm pregnant."

A deep lined formed between my father's brows. "How the hell did that happen?"

I winced at his gruff tone. "Well…"

My mother jumped into the rescue. "Oh, Harry, you've got a bad memory, haven't you?" She tilted her head.

Sam, all the while, moved his attention from one person to another, like a spectator at a tennis match.

To answer Sam's quizzical frown, I said, "My mom was pregnant with Lee three months after meeting Dad."

He nodded slowly. "Oh… history repeating itself, then."

Ignoring that comment, my father turned to Sam. "And what about you, Sam? What are your plans?"

"I…" His eyes never left mine while he chose his words carefully. My heart beat wildly. Now that he'd had time to process things, I was dying to know his thoughts. "I was initially shocked, to be honest. But having thought of little else, I've arrived at one conclusion." Sam's eyes remained on mine.

"And what's that, if I may ask?" my father pressed.

"That…" Sam's stammering made my palpitations increase. "I want to spend my whole life with your daughter." He took my hand. His eyes shone with bone-melting sincerity. "That's if she'll have me."

The next few sentences that exited my father's mouth were a blur, because all I heard was that Sam wished to marry me. My heart grew like a flower in springtime.

He turned to face me. Suddenly it was just the two of us. My mother had led my father away, leaving us alone.

We'd barely made it through the door of my studio when Sam had me pinned against the wall, eating at my lips as though it was our first kiss. My lips parted willingly and my tongue tangled with his. Enough talking. Enough reassuring.

His hand slid under my blouse and fondled my breasts. He groaned against my mouth, which emulated my own crushing urgency for him, especially with that hard, thick erection pressing against my thigh.

"You're so fucking hot," he rasped.

My head fell back as he sucked on my nipples.

I turned my face toward the wall.

"No… I want to ravage your pussy first," he said.

We stumbled along to my bed and both fell onto it, laughing. Edipuss jumped out and meowed with deep displeasure that we'd again crashed in on his slumber.

"Go away, Edipuss," I said. The thought of my pussy watching my pussy being devoured felt strange for some illogical reason.

Sam ripped my panties off. And as impractical as that was, given that my underwear expenditure had doubled since meeting Sam, it was a small price to pay for the thrill and gush of heat that it delivered. He parted my legs wide and placed his head between my thighs. His tongue landed on my clit, which winced from sensitivity. His tongue ravished me to the point of a screaming orgasm that burst out as though it had been trapped like a hungry beast needing to be unleashed.

After regaining my senses, I returned the favor. Licking my lips, I took his veiny, thick shaft into my hand. It was velvet smooth and steel hard. I guided it in, stretching my mouth wide. I swallowed him deeply.

Moving it in and out of my pursed lips, I tasted his salty arousal, while sucking and licking until his inflamed veins contracted on my tongue.

"I want to come inside you," he rasped.

I got on all fours.

He entered me in one deep, delicious thrust.

Cupping my breasts, he growled as he impaled me. It was animalistic and primal—raw sex that I had grown addicted to. The friction from his pumping dick sparked a blaze of indescribable bliss that left me gasping for air. Increasing in strength, his ravishing thrusts made me see stars. After climbing and climbing to even higher realms, it all ended in one big primal scream. The intensity of the release was heightened by earlier tension.

"I love you" left Sam's mouth as he shot deeply into me. His breath gusting over my ear.

After a few moments of stillness, I heard the words "Will you marry me?" Sam's heartbeat vibrated against my rib cage.

"Yes," I replied.

We turned around and embraced.

"Are we really going to do this?" I whispered.

"You bet." Sam pulled away to look at me. His smile turned into a chuckle.

"What?" I opened out my hands.

"You look like someone's shining a searchlight on your face."

"You're making fun of me." I hit his big arm.

"In the nicest way possible." He stroked my hair.

We snuggled into each other.

"I hope I can keep you excited," I said.

"I know you will."

I looked at him. "How do you know?"

"Because my cock's addicted to you. You've got a very sexy pussy."

"But is that all it is?"

"No..." His brows pinched slightly. "I love hanging out with you. But I'd be lying if I didn't admit that you make me hard all of the time."

"What about when I'm fatter and uglier?"

"That will never happen. And what about me? I'm might go bald and grow man boobs."

"Man boobs?" I laughed. Stroking his hard, rippling chest, which I couldn't imagine going flabby, I added, "You'll still be sexy." I tilted my head. "Besides, I'll make you work out."

"Will you?" He grinned. "I'll be sure to carry heavy logs around, then."

"Shirtless," I added, imagining him chopping wood.

"Only if you promise to ditch the underwear around the house."

I giggled as he tickled my belly.

He stared at me earnestly. "You'll always be sexy, Juni."

We snuggled tight, and after enduring a couple of sleepless nights, I surrendered to deep and contented sleep.

SAM

"I'm sorry for calling you a murderer," said Juni as she lounged back, dressed in my dinosaur pajama top and sipping coffee. Her shapely naked thighs stretched out, and her dainty feet were poised on the coffee table.

I sat opposite her and couldn't help feasting my eyes on her beauty. She always looked best in the mornings with her messy hair and sparkling green eyes smiling up at me.

"As long as you keep walking around like that, you can call me whatever you like."

"You're a sex maniac." She giggled, throwing a small cushion at me.

I caught it with one hand as it headed over my shoulder. "I haven't heard any complaints, Juni." I arched an eyebrow.

Juni remained quiet for a moment as she studied me. "Were you serious last night?" She shifted her legs and revealed her naked pussy, and by that I didn't mean Edipuss, who lay at her feet looking up at me with those mean, possessive eyes. I wondered if that cat was in cahoots with Harry.

"Why are you looking like that?" she asked.

I pointed. "You might want to reposition yourself, Juni because at the moment, I'm finding it hard to concentrate."

She laughed and then crossed her legs. "It's nothing you haven't seen."

"Yes. I know. But haven't you heard about us men and our tendency to think of sex every seven seconds?"

"With the same woman?" Juni asked with a smirk that was more challenging than playful.

"In my case, yes. You. I've thought of little else since meeting you."

"That must be exhausting. It must leave you no time to think of other things."

"There are those idle six seconds… that makes room for the more mundane matters." I grinned.

Juni thought about that and laughed. "Then you won't get much done, should that be the case."

I went and joined her on the sofa and took her hand.

"I'm very serious about you, Juni. And yes, I do want to marry you."

She touched her belly. "Because of the baby?"

I exhaled a slow breath, searching for the right words. "Not entirely… I just love you." I brushed her cheek. "It's been three months, and sure, I would've waited a little longer to pop that question. But now that you're having our child, it's only right we do this properly."

"Are you sure?" She wore a searching frown. "If it's only because of the baby, I can do this alone, you know."

I took her into my arms and stroked her hair. A little moisture fell on my arm.

"Hey." My chin touched my neck as I brushed a tear from her cheek while gazing into her limpid eyes. "I've never felt this way about any woman. It was love at first sight."

I got up and grabbed the box of tissues, passing them to Juni.

After she blew her nose, Juni studied me. "Love at first sight?"

"Uh-huh." I nodded slowly.

"You thought I was some tree hugger who hadn't washed for days," she protested.

"I did not." A sly grin grew. "Although I do like you dirty and unwashed."

She rolled her eyes. "Then why did you suggest I have a shower as soon as we entered that penthouse suite, where you later seduced me?"

My jaw dropped. "What are you talking about? You were drenched. And it was you who seduced me."

Her eyes glistened with mischief.

"In any case, you hated me. Remember? I was the devil in a suit." I tilted my head.

"I couldn't help it. The way you swaggered around as if you owned the place." Juni paused. "So what was the first thing that attracted you to me?"

I conjured up an image of Juni drenched, crossing her arms over her big chest. "Soon as you started verbally abusing me. Your big fiery green eyes made me hard as hell."

"I didn't really abuse you, did I?" Juni asked.

"You didn't like me. And I don't swagger, by the way," I said. "And getting back to what we were talking about earlier, the fact you hadn't showered and that little bit of mud on your cheek was actually a serious turn-on."

Her lips squeezed stifling a smile. "You're perverted."

"I haven't heard any complaints. And I must admit you give as good as you get." I arched a brow. I'd never been with a woman as sexually responsive as Juni before. But then, I probably hadn't devoured other pussies in the way I devoured hers.

"I thought you were sexy, too," she said with a faint grin. "You looked yummy in a suit."

"Did I?" I cocked my head. "And here I was thinking it was my dinosaur pajamas that sealed the deal."

She pulled at the elastic of my pajamas and reached in for my dick, which was already hard from seeing the buttons of her pajama top half undone. Stroking my cock, she swallowed my length slowly while looking up at me with those big, provocative eyes. Her luscious full lips wrapped around my dick, tormenting and possessing me at the same time. I exhaled a contented sigh as my head fell back, surrendering to bliss.

The architect had found me a builder he trusted and things were moving quickly in that the foundations were already in place. I couldn't believe how smoothly things flowed, especially with the permit arriving so quickly. The fact that this would be the only boutique brewery for miles had probably worked in my favor. It had been a busy week meeting with builders, designing labels, and reading all I could on brewing beer. The person I should have consulted was Harry, even if he still regarded me at times as being solely responsible for rapacious greed and the demise of social equity. HaightAshBerry Ale was the best I'd tasted. After all, I'd invested years in savoring beer, which had been a labor of love, and something that would probably have been viewed as wasteful by many, especially my father. At least now I was putting my so-called questionable talents to practical use.

Although I had to drive to Malibu for a lightning visit, I needed to see my folks first. They were yet to learn of my intention to marry Juni, and although I was filled with dread, it was incumbent on me to inform them.

I took a deep breath and entered my parents' home wearing shades. It had been a big night. Harry had invited me to try a few different ales he'd brewed. I appreciated the gesture. It gave me the chance to show my future father-in-law that we shared a few things in common. Although Harry was not the type to express enthusiasm for much, I got the vibe he approved of my plans to open a boutique brewery. In any case, for Juni, I would have tolerated a father-in-law who howled at the moon and changed into a flesh-eating monster.

"Darling, there you are," said my mother, carrying a bunch of roses.

"From your lover?" I asked with a wry smile.

She giggled. "I wish."

I bit my lip. Although my dad was a cheating cad, I hated the idea of my mom taking a lover. I would have understood her walking out of the marriage, but to cheat was another thing. Infidelity represented the pinnacle of immorality in my book.

"Why have you got your shades on, sweetie?" she asked, shaking her head. "You haven't been drinking heavily I hope?"

Sliding my shades to the top of my head, I replied, "Me? Never."

"Come into the kitchen," she said.

I followed her in, and the smell of freshly cooked bacon made my tummy rumble. "Mm… that smells good."

"I whipped up an omelet. Knowing you were coming at midday, I figured you hadn't had breakfast yet."

"I've been up for ages, Mom. I've had a very eventful few days." I sighed. "To say the least."

She studied me for a moment. "You look tired, son."

"Of course, he's tired. He parties hard and does a scrap of work," grumbled my father as he joined us.

My appetite suddenly vanished as I regarded my father clad in brightly colored plaid trousers, suggesting that he'd had a round of golf.

"Now Cary, don't be like that. Sam's got something important to talk to us about. I've whipped up a little omelet."

"You shouldn't be cooking. What about Olympia? We employed her for that."

"I know… But I like it."

My father's eyes slid to me for that "I'm willing if you're game" look. Cooking was never one of my mother's strong points.

My mother, oblivious to my father's dig, spooned some food onto a plate and set it before me.

"Smells great," I said, taking a forkful. The bacon was slightly undercooked, but I wasn't going to give my father the ammunition to poke fun at my sweet mother. That had happened one time too often, and the result wasn't pretty. It was me that ended up having to hold a bag of ice against my eye. When it came to fighting, my father had learned from the best. One didn't need a boxing ring, just boarding school with a bunch of self-entitled, hormonally charged brats for that.

"Can I get you a coffee?" my mother asked.

"Yes, please."

My father headed to the cupboard and brought out a bottle of bourbon.

After he'd poured some into his cup, he passed it to me. "Here. You look like you can use something strong."

Pushing my cup toward him, I nodded. "Thanks."

JUNI

"I'll have to introduce you to Demeter," said Scarlett, excited about Sam's proposal.

Sipping the bitter herbal tea that she'd insisted I drink to remove the toxins of anxiety from my liver, I scrunched my nose.

"Bitter?"

I nodded. "So who's Demeter?"

"She's a doula."

"What's that?" I asked.

"A birthing enabler."

"A midwife, you mean?" I asked.

She moved her head from side to side. "Sort of. Better. She advocates the natural approach, thereby removing the need for drugs. She'll teach you to open up your base chakra in order to stimulate the right flow of chi."

Her enthusiasm did little to lift me. I was just plain scared.

"Look, Scarlett, I'm not sure…"

"Hey… don't worry about it. It's early days. I'll introduce you. You can attend one of her workshops. I saw her in action when Eurydice, Athena's daughter, gave birth. It was so inspiring. In that natural way the goddess intended."

Drawing in a deep breath, I could only think of the horror stories throughout history of women giving birth naturally and how only half ever made it out alive.

I smiled meekly. "Let's play it by ear. As much as I love the idea of a natural birth, I'd like to make sure my body's up for it."

She pressed my hand. "You'll be a star. And a great mother, too."

My lips wobbled as I tried to stop the flow of tears. I'd become such a teary mess since becoming pregnant.

It had been an eventful few days now that my parents were aware of my condition and had accepted the marriage. At least, my mom had. My dad, on the other hand, had mentioned quietly that I didn't have to marry and that they'd gladly look after me and my child. I'm sure that's what he would have loved, for me never to leave the farm and continue to slave away with a new helper in tow.

Claude shuffled in naked, rubbing his scruffy yellow-haired head. I didn't quite know where to look.

"Babe, put my robe on."

"Ha..." He squinted. "It's cool. Juni's a grown woman."

I averted my eyes, staring up at the ceiling, as Scarlett shooed him away.

"Hey, I just need a coffee," he protested with a smoker's rasp.

"Go and cover up, and I'll bring you one," she said.

He removed his sagging ass from my view, and for that I was grateful.

"He creeps me out," I whispered.

"He's okay. We're together, you know."

I just could not understand what a beautiful woman like Scarlett saw in him, and although Claude had ridiculous talent that made him stand out among his peers, he was seedy. I recalled as a teenager his eyes wandering all over my body and how that had made me break into a cold sweat.

"What happened to Javier?"

She brushed aside a long blonde wave with an artful streak of purple. "He's gone away. Claude's amazing in bed. He's a very giving lover." She held her hands apart to demonstrate a big penis.

I had to smile. Sighing silently, I knew what she meant. That constant little ache between my thighs reminded me of the joys of having a well-endowed man with staying power and a desire to please.

"Why that little smile?" she asked, tilting her head.

"Nothing."

"You're glowing, Juni. You look like you're in the throes of ecstasy."

"Oh, Scarlett. Surely not. I'm just happy." I knitted my fingers. It was the truth. I'd conquered that mountain that was my dad, and with my pregnancy out in the open, I was just plain relieved, although Sam had looked pale when I left him that morning. He was off to see his family and tell them the news. I'd offered to accompany him, but he'd said needed to calm the beast that was his father first and that he'd arrange a dinner. From what I'd heard about his father, I was sympathetic.

"So, it's a he," said Scarlett. She rested her elbow on the wooden table carved with pentagrams and astrology signs that doubled as a séance table.

"Yes. I'm having a boy," I said, a little disappointed that it wasn't a girl, but I kept that to myself.

"Does Sam know?" Scarlett asked.

I shook my head. "Nope. He did intimate he'd love a little girl. A small version of me."

"Mm… how Freudian," said Scarlett.

"Do you think that's a sick thing to say?" I asked.

She shook her head. "No. It's natural. Men are very protective of their daughters to the point that they would kill for them."

I nodded. That sounded a tad dramatic to me, but that was Scarlett all over.

I waited for Sam at his favorite café. It was late afternoon, and we'd planned to catch up before heading out for dinner. I wasn't exactly dressed for it in my ruffled skirt and loose floral blouse. As I stared down at my magenta skirt, I watched a few women pass the window wearing fitted jeans and tight tank tops, which was standard wear if you had that great bod you could brag about. I didn't see myself that way at all. I'd always been awkward about my abundance of curves, despite the fact Sam couldn't take his hands off me. His admiration should have instilled some confidence in me, but I just hated how I looked in body-hugging outfits.

With that easy stride, making him hard to miss, Sam walked ahead of a crowd of women, who all turned to check him out. He paused in front of a saxophone busker and tossed a note into the musician's case, which was typical of him. He always gave buskers and beggars cash.

Sam entered the café and looked about until his eyes landed on mine. His face lit up. That bone-melting smile that made my heart sing took everyone with it. He was so ruggedly handsome with that unruly dark hair that never seemed to remain in place. His sensual mouth with that relaxed half-curl made him irresistible. The women in the café thought so, too, as they stopped what they were doing to ogle him. Dressed in cream-colored Lees and a green western shirt, Sam strode toward me, and for a minute there I thought I was watching an advertisement for men's casual wear. His muscular thighs flexed with each step. Running his tongue over his lips, Sam bent down and kissed me on the mouth. Although it was only a peck, it still left behind a fiery mark.

Would my heart ever stop beating wildly around him? We'd been together only that morning, and flushed with endorphins after he'd devoured me for breakfast, I'd left Sam's place floating.

"You're glowing," he said, taking my hand.

"And you look rather dashing yourself," I said, stroking his cotton western shirt.

"You like it?" he asked. "I just bought it. My other one was a little sweat stained." He raised a brow.

"From visiting your folks?" I asked.

He nodded. "Yeah. My father insists on meeting your folks." He paused to absorb my reaction. "Like asap."

"Right. Does he know about my condition?"

Sam nodded.

"That should be fun then," I said.

He returned my sarcasm with a mock smile. "You're not wrong."

I cringed at the thought of his well-heeled parents meeting mine.

"Perhaps it might be better if my parents go to yours," I said.

Sam nodded. "Whatever you think."

I placed my hand over his. "Sam, do you really want this?"

His eyes narrowed slightly before relaxing. I could see he was trying to read me. "Do you?"

"Hey. I asked first." I cocked my head.

"Of course, I want this. I'm just trying to get used to the idea of being a father and all that comes with that."

"Do you think you'll get bored with me?"

His brow shifted dramatically. "This again?" He shook his head, and a tinge of self-loathing hit me for being so insecure. "Are you kidding? I think it will be the reverse and that you'll get bored with me."

"Now, why would I?" I asked.

"I'm not that interesting, I suppose," he said, rubbing his neck, which had reddened, revealing his stress.

"You don't have to lecture me on the virtues of fifteenth-century Florentine architecture, you know," I said.

He laughed. "That's exactly what I was thinking of doing tonight, discussing Romantic classicism versus clean and unfussy modernism."

"That book exists, you know," I said.

"Oh, I bet it does." He laughed and went serious in a blink. He held my hand. "You're exciting, Juni."

"In bed, you mean?"

He shook his head.

"I'm not?" I asked, unreasonably hurt.

"Of course, you are. You're fucking hot. Like really hot." He ran his hand up my arm, making my skin pucker. "But I love your quirky, mercurial nature, too." He paused before adding, "And I love that you're open to trying new things."

"By that you mean rough-and-ready, against-the-wall, anyone-might-see-us-any-minute sex?"

He laughed. "That's exciting to be sure, but I'm just as excited by Florentine architecture, or at least learning about it. With you. In Florence." His finger crept under the fold of my skirt. And even though he'd tried to drift away from sex patter, it had fired me up, as it had Sam, for an unmistakable bulge appeared. His hand touched my panties. Sitting close to one another, we assumed nobody could see.

"You're showing, Sam," I murmured.

"And you're fucking wet," he whispered.

"Should we go back to your place before dinner? Or do you want to stay here and order a drink?" I asked.

"Let's have a drink. Is there any way you can take your panties off?"

I rolled my eyes even though I could barely move. "Sam, we'll be arrested one of these days."

"So?" His cheeky smile made me giggle. I'd forgotten all about the frightening prospect of our parents meeting.

SAM

My father's expression of horror sat at the forefront of my mind. After I'd relayed that I was about to become a father and that I loved Juni, he'd responded, "Not that fucking greenie?"

I regarded my mother with a roll of the eyes. If ever I needed support, that was the time.

"Now Cary, she sounds like a lovely girl. And she's having Sam's baby. Our first grandchild."

He switched his focus from me to my mother while muttering gruffly under his breath.

"She's a talented designer," I defended.

"What about Marie Carter?" he asked.

If there were ever a time to be a nasty prick, that was it. And considering Marie's underhanded antics, spilling the truth about Julia and Marie sleeping together was justified. But I didn't have it in me. It would have killed my seriously conservative father.

"You know that I'm not into Marie Carter. I'm about to be a father. I have to do the right thing."

"This is the twenty-first century, Sam. You don't have to do anything. Why don't you pay her off, or monthly payments?"

"What?" I snapped. My forehead scrunched from disbelief. "I love Juni. Even if she wasn't pregnant, I'd probably still marry her."

My mom held my hand and nodded with a supportive smile. Thank God she was there.

He exhaled a frustrated sigh. After toying with his drink for a minute or two, my father said, "There's nothing to be done then. Bring her here with her folks. They're not vegetarian, are they?"

I nearly laughed at his abrasively mocking tone. Visualizing Juni and her almost shocking penchant for eating virtually raw meat, I shook my head. "No, they're not. They're actually quite normal in that alternative sense. I mean Luna…"

"Luna? Who's Luna?" asked my father.

"She's Juni's mom," I said, losing my train of thought.

"And I suppose the father's named Sky."

My lips twitched into an involuntary smile.

"That's a girl's name, Cary," said my mother, who had an indelible smile. I could see that at least she was happy about becoming a grandmother.

"Ah… you know what I mean," he growled.

"His name's Harry," I said soberly.

He studied me for a minute. Dissatisfaction radiated out of every crevice in his face. "Why couldn't you take after Julia?" he grumbled.

I bit my tongue again. The bad boy within itched to wipe the halo from my revered sister's head.

I'd offered to drive the Berrys to my parents' home but they'd insisted on making their own way. I only hoped that the strange vehicle that ran on vegetable scraps would either be replaced by the more conventional SUV I'd seen parked at the farm or that at least they'd park it somewhere away from my parents' home.

Earlier that day, Scotty had been downtown and met me for a drink at my favorite café. Soothing jazz floated through the air, drowning out some of the dread stalking me. Bringing our fathers together would be like experimenting with two combustible, potentially noxious substances for the first time. I was uncertain if they would blow the roof off.

"You're going to be a dad, you old rat." Scotty shook his head. "I didn't even think you wanted children."

"Yeah, life's kinda strange like that. When we're young it's all idealism and bravado. That's not going to be me.... Yada yada. But now that I've gotten used to the idea, it's exciting and frightening all at the same time."

He sipped his beer thoughtfully. "Right."

"Juni was always going to be the one. Baby or not. I was her first, you know?"

He swallowed his beer and looked up at me. "Wow. That's kind of Old World, isn't it?"

I nodded pensively. "They're almost an endangered species."

He laughed. "As impossible as that is. It's still funny." His face changed. "What's it like?"

Unlike most male friends, we never spoke about sex. With Scotty, it was always those big subjects like science, philosophy, or politics.

Knitting my fingers, I searched for an answer. "I take it you've never been with a virgin?"

He shook his head. "Nope. I was the inexperienced one. In reverse to you, Jess was my first time."

My brow furrowed. "Shit... Really?"

He shrugged. "It's been an eventful few months for both of us."

"Great, isn't it?"

"It's incredible. I think I've made up for lost time," he said with a little grin.

"Now who's the old rat?" I laughed.

I sipped my beer, thinking about my first time, which had been with an older woman. She'd certainly taught me a thing or two and couldn't stop blowing me. Recalling Scotty's earlier question, I said, "When I discovered Juni's inexperience, I wanted to run, to be honest."

"Really?"

"Well, that lasted ten seconds." I chuckled. "Juni's a very beautiful woman, and well, I'm weak like that."

"I think we all are, Sam." He wore a tight smile. "And she's now carrying your child."

"Yep. And I want you to be my best man."

"That would be an honor," he said. "When's the wedding?"

Great question.

"To be announced." I clinked my bottle against his and laughed.

Just as Juni and I climbed the stairs to the entrance of my parents' home, Julia arrived with Steve straggling behind.

I introduced my sister to Juni. "This is Julia and Steve."

Juni jumped in and took Julia's hand and introduced herself. From the corner of my eye, I caught my sister's customary pompous smile.

"You're looking buff," I said to Steve.

He nodded, looking pleased with himself. "I figured it was the only way to win your sister over. She's hard to please," he said quietly.

I'd never felt sorry for him before, but knowing what I now knew, I felt for the guy. Julia was leading him on. Or perhaps she liked it both ways. The thought of which made me squirm as that image of Marie and Julia locking lips in the Jacuzzi came to mind.

We hovered at the entrance. Julia's eyes landed on Juni's dress, which was one of her own creations. The green dress with sewn-on flowers accented her eyes and gave her that girlish look, even though beneath that dress, Juni was a curvy seductress.

Rocio, our maid, who'd been with the family longer than me, opened the door and hugged me. Just as I was introducing her to Juni, my mother arrived.

She held out her hand. "You must be Juniper. I'm Sam's mother, Sylvia."

"Hi…Pleased to meet you." Juni leaned in and kissed her cheek.

Just as that was happening, I whispered into my sister's ear, "Let's make a deal. I won't mention that little matter of you and Marie swallowing tongues and god knows what else." I paused to soak in her embarrassed glower, which, coming from my normally unflappable sis, was priceless. "As long as you play nice and drop that holier-than-thou-bullshit. Okay?"

Her lip twitched at one end into what was trying to be a smile streaked with resentment.

"Come and make yourself at home," instructed my mother just as the doorbell rang. She jumped a little, revealing that she too was nervous.

Noticing my jaw stiffen, my mom whispered, "Don't worry, sweetheart. Juni's gorgeous." She had that genuine look of support that helped me breathe calmly again.

Rocio led Juni's parents into the hallway. Dressed in a purple crushed-velvet dress, Luna wore her hair up in a bun. Her essential-oil scent filled the room, and I felt languid just being near her. In contrast, Harry wore a scowl. I could imagine a smile cracking his face. As the pair stood under the chandelier in the white entrance, they seemed as though they'd landed on another planet. The incongruity wasn't lost on my sister, who wore a this-is-going-to-be-fun smirk.

I pulled down the cuff of my new mauve shirt that Juni had begged me to buy after we'd passed it in a shop window. Harry wore a blue western shirt and Levi's. That's all I'd ever seen him wear, and I wondered if that's how he'd dress at our wedding. That led me to think of Juni's outlandish grandfather, and a smile peeked through at the thought of him and his flamboyant husband making cheeky comments to all the guests. It was sure to be a circus. But then, I wouldn't have missed it for the world. I would've entered a lion's den without a chair to marry Juni. I clutched her hand, and my lips curled as that ridiculous thought lingered in my mind.

Her brow moved slightly. "What?"

"I'm happy."

Her smile turned into a giggle, which was probably more nervous laughter, which helped ease my nerves.

When we entered the living room, my dad was on his cell, gesticulating and growling.

JUNI

Sam's father's stare almost burned a hole through to the back of my head, explaining Sam's earlier unease about us meeting. I also noticed a sharp contrast between his parents, just like my parents, in that Sam's mom was as supportive and gentle as mine, while our outspoken fathers were quick to judge.

Dinner went well enough, with just the regular small talk, which was nothing too outrageous, or stomach-tightening. My father, who wasn't into chit chat had hardly spoken, and instead drank wine and ate as though he hadn't eaten for a while. Being the driver, my mom stuck to mineral water, and in her amiably mercurial style carried the conversation on behalf of the family. Not that she talked too much. With that gentle lilt, my mother conducted herself politely but as always exuded intelligence and worldliness. I noticed Cary stealing glances here and there. She did look beautiful with her hair up, showing off a long neck and elegant bearing.

"I believe you're a musician, Luna," said Sylvia.

"I play the harp, and Harry plays jazz guitar. We both studied music at Berkeley. That's how we met."

"Oh, how interesting," Sylvia exclaimed. "Isn't that?" She looked at Cary and he grunted something back.

"I'm told you're running a successful business," Cary said, directing his attention to my dad.

"Depends on how one measures success," responded my father.

"I generally measure it by the number of zeros following a number."

"Mm… yes, that's the capitalist way."

I swallowed tightly, hoping that my dad wouldn't launch into one of his anti-capitalist rants.

"And you're not one?" Cary asked.

"Harry believes in self-sufficiency," said Sam in a bid to ward off any political discourse that might swallow up the night. He'd already been involved in a few of those exchanges with my father, and while Sam seemed to enjoy them, we both knew this was not the right time and place for such raves.

"Right," Cary nodded. "So what does that mean exactly?"

"We grow and produce nearly all our needs," said my mother.

"I hope the food tonight is to your liking," said Sylvia.

"It's very nice, thank you," answered my mother.

I gave Sylvia a big smile at her attempt to change the subject.

"So, Harry, I've heard you're making a killing on marijuana," Cary persisted.

My father nodded. "It was an accident."

"Harry's a self-proclaimed accidental billionaire," said Sam with a chuckle.

Cary looked at him almost with disdain. I didn't like the way he made his disappointment with Sam so obvious.

"In my eyes, that's pretty goddamn fortunate." He studied Harry for a moment. "So tell me, why an accident? Didn't you plant the crop with the sole intention of selling it?"

"I didn't plant it while it was illegal, if that's what you mean," he said. "I wouldn't put my family at risk." My dad cast his attention to me for a moment. "The truth is that as soon as it was decriminalized and what with the growing market for medical marijuana in California, my father turned up with some seeds he'd procured back in the sixties. Those seeds have delivered an impressive strain that one of my clients refers to as being the marijuana equivalent of Penfolds Grange."

Cary's head pushed back. "That sounds successful. Tell me, have you tried that wine?"

My father nodded. "That same client brought over a bottle after I'd shown complete ignorance. And it's quite a drop. We polished off the whole bottle, which I might add cost forty thousand dollars."

I could see Cary looking impressed suddenly. "A few of my contacts have made a killing with marijuana stocks. Have you made an initial public offering on the stock market?"

"I don't believe in the stock market. It's criminal."

Cary sniffed. "It's America."

"It actually began in Venice during the thirteenth century," said Sam. In response to my amused grin, he murmured, "I was once a trivia junkie."

"Mm…" grunted Cary in his natural dismissive way.

At least Sam had found some love in that family through his sweet and doting mother, who had gone out of her way to make me and my family feel welcomed.

"So, Harry," continued Cary. "Can I be so bold and ask how much that crop's worth?"

"Last time I looked it brought in about three or is that four?" my father said, scratching his head as he looked at my mother. "Luna's the accountant in the family."

Cary's head did a sharp turn toward my mother. "I thought you played the harp?"

She giggled. "I do more than that."

"Luna knits and makes her own wool," said Sam, with a glow of admiration.

I had to stop myself from laughing because only a few days earlier, my mother had gifted Sam another sweater. He'd sauntered about looking as though he should sit by a fire and smoke a pipe. After I'd stopped laughing,

I pleaded for him to change back into those body-hugging shirts or sexy ripped T-shirts that he wore so well. The sweet look of gratitude on his face was priceless, though.

"So was that three or four million?" persisted Cary.

"Do we really need to do this?" asked Sam.

"Billion," corrected Harry.

Were our fathers having a pissing competition? I raised a brow at Sam, who I'm sure had the same thought judging by his subtle grimace.

"Well then… you're doing well. Very well," muttered Cary almost to himself. I got the vibe that my father's status had gone up a notch in Sam's father's eyes.

The blueberry pie and coconut cream were so delicious I had two servings. Sam watched with a smile. I never thought anyone could get off on watching me eat as much as Sam did. It bordered on strange. But then, there were a few little behaviors of his that fell into that spectrum of oddity. For a man who looked as though he spent his weekdays staring at a screen of colored stats and weekends pumping fists at ballgames, which had been my first impression, Sam had turned out to be attractively eccentric.

"So, let's discuss this marriage," said Cary, looking straight at me and making my blood freeze, as though I was somehow responsible for getting pregnant. "You've only just met."

"What are your thoughts on it?" Cary asked my father.

Interestingly, both men seemed to consult each other and didn't even think to involve their wives in the discussion.

"I'm not happy about it. Juni's young. Her business is growing, and what with the farm producing so much money…"

I turned to face Sam and rolled my eyes. He smiled tightly, taking my hand as a comrade would in the face of opposition.

"Dad, I'm not your de facto son or your worker."

Cary looked at Julia, who'd remained quiet throughout the dinner, making just the odd bit of small talk with my mother and Steve, who hardly spoke. Knowing what I knew about Julia and Marie, I felt sorry for him.

"You don't have a son?" asked Cary.

"I have." My father shifted in his seat. "Lingam. He's known as Lee. You're working with him, I believe."

After taking a sip of bourbon, Cary coughed. He cleared his throat and asked, "Lee Berry's your son?"

My dad nodded mournfully. My brother was an uncomfortable subject.

"He's a mover and a shaker. For a lawyer who specializes in mergers and acquisitions, he knows his game."

"You know more about him than I do," my father replied.

"You've had a falling out?" asked Cary.

My father nodded.

"You should be proud. He's a very successful man." Cary looked at Julia when he said that, which made me wonder if he'd considered trying to pair them off, considering they were of the same age.

My dad took a deep breath and chose to remain silent on that uncomfortable subject.

"Do you kids really know what you're doing?" Cary asked, redirecting his attention back to our impending nuptials.

"Juni's pregnant," said Sam. "And even if she wasn't, I'd still want to be with her."

He squeezed my hand.

"But there are ways. We can pay for nannies and when the child's born…"

"I'm not having my daughter brought up by nannies, and I want Juni to be my wife," Sam insisted.

After hearing the word "daughter," I glanced over at my mom, who returned a sympathetic smile. Only Scarlett and my mom knew that I was carrying a boy.

"What do you say to that, Harry?"

"I'm with you on this. I don't think they need to marry. I'm happy to bring up the girl on the farm."

"It's a boy," I blurted.

And suddenly the table went quiet. By the way they looked, I might have said that I'd actually slept with an alien and that the child would have an oblong head with an antenna.

SAM

The blueberry pie squished about in my churning gut. Here I'd been visualizing a little angel on my knee, giggling and pulling at my hair. A small version of Juni. But a boy? What kind of role model was I going to be? With a girl, it would be stories and ballet and pretty things. But with a boy, I'd have to teach him to do what?

The background rumblings brought me back to reality. I noticed my father's perplexed frown had ironed out into a look of relief almost. He'd always been an easy man to read. From the sudden twinkle in his eyes, I read: There was going to be a boy in the family. A second chance. A game-changer. A boy, he could mold into himself.

I looked at Juni. "Why didn't you tell me?"

"Because you didn't ask." She paused before adding in a small voice, "And I wasn't sure until a few days ago if I was even going to keep it."

Her soft tone still managed to penetrate. The table went silent. Blood drained from my face. What Juni had just admitted was highly controversial, especially to my father, whose face had almost gone green.

"Well then, I'm glad you've seen the light by deciding not to murder my grandson."

I glanced at my father coldly. "That's a bit melodramatic, wouldn't you say?" After he grunted something unintelligible, I added, "It would have been Juni's right to do that. Only, I would have stopped it, because I want this child. And I also want to marry Juni. Something I would have wished for whether she was pregnant or not."

Juni looked up at me. She appeared young and frightened. A film of moisture pooled in her eyes. I took her hand and reassured her with a nod.

Harry looked at Juni and then his wife. "Were you to change your mind, you could rest assured that your mother and I would welcome a little boy with open arms."

"As would we," said my father with a competitive air.

I stood up. "There'll be no need for any of that. I'm marrying Juni, and our son will be born into a happy, loving house with his mom and dad by his side. Grandparents are welcome, but they have no say. I repeat you'll have no say in how my son is raised. That will be up to Juni and me."

I helped Juni up. "We're off now. Juni's tired, and so am I."

"We should be leaving too," said Luna.

We said our goodbyes quickly and left.

I helped Juni into the car. It was a relief to be out of there.

Relaxing into her seat, Juni said, "My God, did you see their faces when I mentioned that it was a boy?"

"Sure did," I said, driving off. "A clear display of sexism if you ask me. And your father was just as complicit."

"Yeah... He's never gotten over Lee leaving the family. He treats Cam as a de facto son."

"Is that why he wanted you to marry him?" I asked, not hiding my resentment.

"Probably. But, hey..." Juni touched my arm. "I'm with you. You're more my type."

I tilted my head and smiled. "Glad to hear it. Here I was thinking you'd expect me to live on a bowl of mung beans and tofu every day, grow a beard, and drive a car fueled by veggie scraps."

Juni giggled. "I like you the way you are. All big-shouldered, alpha-ish and sexy."

"Alpha-ish?"

"Well, sometimes you are. Claude?" She raised a brow, reminding me of that little scuffle.

"I was defending what was mine," I said.

"You make me sound like I'm your property," she said.

"I'm yours…" I gazed into her deep eyes. "If you want me."

She smiled sweetly and squeezed my leg.

"I hope you're not pissed off that I didn't tell you about our child being a boy?" Juni asked.

"I didn't ask, did I?" I paused for a moment. "And for some reason, I assumed it was a girl."

"Why do I sense disappointment?" Juni asked, tilting her head.

"I'm not. Really. Just the thought of a little you running about kind of melted my heart."

"And the thought of a boy doesn't?"

I searched for the right words. "I'm terrified."

She smiled gently. "Don't be. You'll do great. And you're so amusing when you want to be. You and your silly faces. You make me laugh. And remember how you were with Jess's sister's baby?"

I shrugged. "Maybe."

Juni sighed and slumped back on the seat.

"Are you tired?"

"A little," she said, turning to look at me.

I glanced over at her. "What is it, Juni?"

"Do you think we're jumping into this?"

"Do you?" I asked.

Juni shrugged. "I'm not sure what I think, to be honest."

"You're not sure about us?" I asked. Slowing down, I pulled up at the curb.

"Why are we stopping?" Juni asked.

I slid over and held her. Kissing her neck, I whispered, "You looked so beautiful, and the more vulnerable you are, the more I want to hold you."

"I'm not that vulnerable, you know," she said, pulling away to stare at me.

"I'm sorry. Am I being too alpha?"

A little smile grew. "No… I don't mind you being a little alpha here and there."

"Okay…" I pushed back my hair. "I'll bear that in mind and do my caveman act occasionally."

Juni giggled. "No… Well… maybe… without a shirt."

I traced her waist with my finger, and as it crept up to her breasts, her nipples pushed against the cotton blouse, and my palms rubbed against them.

"Juni…"

"Yes, Sam?"

"I need to fuck you."

"That I figured," she said with a breathy voice.

My fingers crept under her panties. "You're very wet."

Her little hand released my zipper and burrowed in. "And you're very hard."

I moved away and opened the car door.

"Where are you going?" Juni asked.

I walked to her side of the car and opened the door. I bent down and helped her out. "Come and sit on my lap for a minute."

Juni stepped out and then after I was seated, I patted my thigh. She straddled me, which had become my favorite position.

Our lips met, and we ate at each other's lips as if we'd only just met. My tongue entered deeply as my fingers rotated over her slick, swollen clit.

"Oh God, Juni…" I unclasped her bra, and her full breasts fell onto my hands.

The street was dimly lit by Victorian streetlamps, giving us privacy. Or so I believed. Flushed with a raging libido inflamed by a voluptuous beauty sitting on my lap, my brain drained of blood, flooding my dick instead. We were parked one street up from my family's home. All one could see were large trees and their squiggly shadows on the walled fences that hid the palatial homes of the rich.

Juni lowered herself slowly over my throbbing cock, which slid deeply inside of her. Her wet and tight inner muscles resisted in that gaspingly eyes-rolling-to-the-back-of-one's head way. My groan merged with the sigh that escaped her lips.

With my hands around her small waist, I guided her up and down, while I stared into her eyes. Although we were obscured by shadows, I could still see the glint of arousal in her eyes.

"Oh, God… You feel so good," I rasped.

We found that magic rhythm, Juni bobbing up and down, provoking the hell out of my dick. Just as I was about to blow, a person walking their dog came by, and although we were in the dark, I imagined that the car rocking about would have given us away.

Juni turned first and saw him. Her tits were in my face, and she quickly covered up. "Shit," she uttered.

I turned, and he remained there eyeballing me. I wound down the window. "Fuck off," flew out of my mouth before I'd had a chance to see the jerk. As my sight adjusted to the dark, it occurred to me that I was gaping at my parents' neighbor—a man I'd met at a few of the family barbeques.

Words crashed about in my brain. "Oh… Bob…. Um…"

Meanwhile, Juni slid down the seat, trying to make herself invisible.

"Sam… You could get arrested doing that."

A nervous chuckle escaped my lips. "This is my wife-to-be and…"

"It's okay… I won't tell anyone," he said raising a brow.

After the old man sauntered off, I said, "Shit… caught."

"Will he tell your parents?" Juni asked.

I shrugged. Stamped in my mind was Bob's lingering presence. A decent person would have walked on, pretending not to have noticed.

"He's a fucking dirty old man. That much I do know," I said, stepping out the door.

"We have to stop fucking in public," Juni said after we'd driven off.

"Mm… maybe…" I turned to face her. "Are you okay?"

She combed back a stray blonde lock. "I guess so. I only hope that doesn't cause issues."

It did.

The following day, first thing in the morning, I got a call. It was my mother. "Bob dropped in earlier. He told us that he discovered you and Juni together in your car."

"Oh, God…" My body slumped. The frustrated thought "Why are people so goddamn predictable?" entered my tired brain.

"Your father's very angry."

I could hear him yelling in the background.

"Yeah… I bet he is." I sighed. "It was what? Ten o'clock at night. The streets were empty and…" The last thing I wanted to do was talk about my sex life with my mother.

"You're a disgrace to the family," said my father, who'd joined us on the phone.

"And good morning to you, too," I replied.

"I am ashamed to call you my son. Why didn't you turn out like your sister?"

Despite hearing that lament one time too often, I remained silent.

"What have you got to say for yourself?" His tone scraped at me. Since it was morning, I hadn't even had a coffee and regretted picking up the phone.

"Nothing. Juni and I'll soon be married. I'm sure I'm not the only one caught out sharing a moment of passion with his wife-to-be."

"You could've chosen another neighborhood. Instead, you decided to shit on our good reputation. Julia would never do…"

A fireball of fury swept through me. "She's not exactly a paragon of virtue."

"Compared to you, your sister's a saint. You disgust me."

I hung up on him. I couldn't take it any longer. If I had remained on the phone, I would have snitched on my sister's predilection for pussy, which would have turned my father upside down.

JUNI

Amused surprise flickered in Sam's eyes. "Her name's Demeter Moon?"

I nodded meekly.

"Are we still going to be at a hospital, at least?"

"Scarlett suggests a deep bath, candlelit, with a full circle of witches chanting."

The horror on Sam's face made me laugh, which was probably how I'd looked when Scarlett had made that suggestion to me. I quickly explained to her that my giving birth in the presence of witches was never going to happen.

"You're fucking joking, aren't you?" he asked.

I bit my lip. I loved seeing him look crazy, with his hair sticking up and that wide-eyed-just-seen-a-monster expression. Sam made for a very comical figure when his emotions were slightly frayed.

"Having a bunch of Morticias chanting in a circle will scare the shit out of the baby. He'll be the first kid ever to need counseling before he can walk."

The absurdity of that suggestion had me holding my belly from the pain of laughter. After I settled, I put him out of his misery and explained that I was only joking. I wiped my eyes. "But, hey, let's just go and meet Demeter and see what she has to say. Okay?"

Even though he remained neutral, I could almost hear Sam's misgivings. This discussion took place a few steps away from Demeter's bayside home. It had taken a lot of convincing just to get Sam to agree to accompany me, and as he stood there with that suspicious frown etched on his handsome face, I had to fight back the urge to giggle again. It was more from nervousness because like Sam, I had my own doubts about the holistic birthing of my child.

We opened the iron gate with a sun and moon etched on it and walked along a charming cobbled pathway. The garden reminded me of an English garden, with an overgrowth of floral bushes and a languid old willow. A sea breeze kissed my face, making my skin tingle.

Hidden behind all that nature was a white wooden house. Sam held my hand, and up the stairs we climbed to the door with a stained-glass image of a goddess with a moon for a headpiece.

As soon as the door opened, a strong aroma of incense oil hit us, while standing at the entrance to greet us was Demeter. She was a middle-aged woman who would've effortlessly blended with normality. Sam instantly relaxed. I think he expected someone in a flowing gown with a broom parked at the doorway.

"Please enter." She extended her arm.

Sam and I stepped into a sunny room that boasted bay views.

"Can I offer you a tea or homemade lemonade?"

"Homemade lemonade sounds good," said Sam, looking boyish suddenly and making me want to ruffle his hair.

"For you too?" asked Demeter, who really looked more like a suburban grandmother.

I nodded. "Yes, thanks."

Once the drinks had been delivered, Demeter directed her attention to Sam. "I'm sensing hesitation and reluctance."

Sam looked at me and swallowed the lemonade before replying. "To be honest, I'd prefer that we went about this in the traditional way."

"I see it all the time. The men are always very traditional. Hospitals, epidurals, and the like. But it doesn't have to be like that. Most women can have very healthy, natural births."

"I get that. But what about if a doctor is needed?" He persisted.

Demeter crossed her hands and, with a relaxed tone replied, "If the preparation is done well, there will be no need."

"I read a journal of a man's life in a village in Sicily…" said Sam.

I sat up. As always Sam surprised me by his eclectic reading choices.

"It was a biographical account of life in that village, post Second World War. He relayed how when a woman was about to give birth, they would call not only the midwife but a priest, because half of the time either the mother, the child, or both would perish."

Demeter nodded with a gentle smile. "Yes. That's rather alarming and very sad. Our practices are more sanitary. And look, if for some reason the mother requires a cesarean, the bed would have been booked. I am basically here as a birthing enabler.

Sam nodded slowly. "Meaning?"

"I will help with breathing exercises and simple meditation techniques to deal with labor pains. Sometimes that's all that's required to avoid numbing the lower half with an epidural, which is a cocktail of strong drugs." Her raised eyebrows made my spine stiffen.

"But not all births require anesthetic, do they?" I asked, suddenly realizing that I had no idea what to expect.

Demeter shook her head decisively. "None of my women have needed it. One hundred percent track record. With the right exercises, meditation, and breathing techniques, and the mother immersed in a bath, I've delivered many healthy, rosy-cheeked babies."

"In a bath?" asked Sam.

"That's a great place. It mimics the watery environment of the mother's womb."

I looked at Sam, noticing his forehead remained creased.

"If anything"— I looked at Demeter— "you seem to know your subject." Shifting my focus to Sam, I added, "I could try a few sessions. The breathing exercises are meant to be beneficial. Jess mentioned that."

He nodded slowly.

After leaving Demeter's house, Sam said, "You will also be consulting a doctor during the pregnancy, I hope?"

"Of course. He's already given me a list of midwives."

"That's good. Maybe you need to use that as your primary care."

"You're being really pessimistic, Sam." My palms had dampened. I was just plain terrified, whichever way—traditional or alternative. "And to be honest, I don't want an epidural."

"What about if you need it?"

"It could harm the baby. You heard Demeter. It's full of harmful chemicals. Imagine what that will do to the baby's health. Don't we want what's best for Adonis?"

Sam's head turned sharply toward me, as though I'd just admitted to inviting Satan for dinner. "Adonis?"

That name had been Scarlett's suggestions. It didn't connect with me either, but I felt like playing, and Sam's wide-eyed response worked a treat, making me laugh and relax in the process.

"Or Phoenix?" I added.

"What's wrong with Max or Robert? Something normal like that?"

"What about Otis?" I persisted.

"I'd prefer Miles if I had to choose a famous musician's name," said Sam.

"Miles Chalmer," I uttered. "Mm… that's not bad."

Sam nodded. "Yeah. It's got a nice ring to it."

I took a deep breath and uttered "Adonis Chalmer" only because I wanted to stir Sam so that he would pull that silly grimace again.

SAM

I turned to face Juni and was met by a cheeky grin. "I know you're trying to provoke me," I said.

"You look so sexy when you're outraged." She continued to smirk.

"And you look sexy with that little tight blouse that I'm dying to tear off."

"No, you won't. I made this. Which reminds me, I have to go home and finish orders."

"Okay, I'll drop you off there." I looked at her. "Can I pop in for a coffee?"

"Mm… Are you propositioning me?" asked Juni.

"I sure am." I peeked at her exposed thigh.

When I drove up her driveway, Jeff ran up to the car and barked, while Pablo with that proud chest strutted about, looking indignant as always.

Cameron and Harry were standing close by.

I jumped out and opened Juni's door.

Harry touched the hood of my car. "How's it running?"

"Great," I replied, reminded that my car was one interest, other than brewing beer, that both Harry and I shared.

"Take it for a spin if you like," I said.

Harry looked at Cam, who nodded in his usual sheepish way.

"We just have to make a delivery downtown."

I handed him the keys.

"How are you feeling?" Harry asked Juni.

"I'm good. We've just visited a doula."

"A what?" Harry asked.

"She's a birthing enabler," said Juni.

"Are you expecting?" asked Cameron, looking shocked.

"Yep. Sure am. Hey, Dad, what do you think of the name Miles?"

He nodded pensively. "Only the best trumpet player known to mankind. It sounds all right to me. So, this doula... was one of Scarlett's suggestions?"

"How did you guess?" I chimed in.

"Speak to your mother," said Harry. "She had one of those, who had us all standing by while Luna floated in a bath."

"All?" I asked. I turned to Juni. "There's no way this is going to be a performance piece. It will just be me, a doctor… or a midwife."

Harry switched his attention from me to his daughter. "Anyway, I was trying to say that it wasn't pretty. Speak to your mother."

As we left them behind, I said, "There you go. If your mom had issues, it's possible that the same thing will happen to you. You're very alike physically."

Juni turned, and I swear to god the look on her face could have frozen water on a hot day. "It's my body. My baby. And I will do what I like. Now stop going on about it."

She ran off and left me standing there with Pablo looking at me as if I'd murdered Miss Prissy, who pranced about in the distance bobbing her head. As his beady eyes pierced mine, I said, "Fuck off." Combing back my hair with my fingers, I asked myself, "Did I just tell a rooster to fuck off?"

I ran up to Juni and took her hand. "I'm sorry. Let's not talk about this anymore. Okay?"

She stared at her feet and nodded.

I followed her in and nearly tripped over Edipuss, who was lying in a pool of sunlight by the door.

It had been a crazy day. All I needed was to take Juni into my arms and forget about the future. But it wasn't going to be that easy, I soon discovered. Juni's mood darkened. She looked at her sewing table, where fabric, paper, and sewing paraphernalia were scattered about, muttering, "Fuck." She swept her arm over the mess and pushed it onto the ground and remained there frozen as she looked down at her unfinished clothes.

I bent over and picked everything up in silence, while Juni moved about as if she was looking for something.

"Is there anything I can do?" I asked quietly.

"No," she snapped.

I hadn't seen her like this before. "It seems as if you need to be alone."

"There you go again." She pointed at me.

Opening my hands, I asked, "What?"

"You keep telling me what I need and what I should do." She fell into a chair.

Out of my depth, I was unsure of how to navigate the situation. I got a moment's reprieve when a knock came at the door. I opened the door, and Harry stood before me.

I stepped outside. "That was quick."

He handed me the keys to my car. "We ended up driving it up the track and back. I forgot I had to meet a client here soon. It's got this little roaring hum I always remembered. I learned to drive in the same model."

"Feel free to take it for a spin whenever I'm here." I rubbed my neck which was burning from tension.

"Don't worry about Juni," he said. "When it all gets to be too much, she tends to blow up. It doesn't last long. She takes after me. Irish blood."

"Thanks. I'll bear that in mind." I saluted him and returned to Juni.

When I stepped in, I found her picking up pieces of fabric and rearranging them on the table.

"That was your dad returning the keys," I said. When she didn't respond, I asked, "Do you want me to leave?"

A remote, glazed stare followed. "Do you want to leave?"

I took her hand. "No, I don't."

She kept her hand in mine this time and stared at me like a frightened child. Her eyes pooled with tears. Juni's fragility made her even more beautiful, like a flower after rain.

I led her to the couch. "Let's just sit for a moment. It's been a big week."

She followed along silently. And when she lowered herself next to me, she fell into my arms and bawled her eyes out. Her tears splashed over my neck. I waited for a moment and then reached out for the tissues which were on the table close by.

"I don't know if I can do this." She blew her nose so loudly, my lips curled slightly at one end.

"Having a child, you mean?" I asked.

Resting her chin on her fist, she nodded. "There's so much I wanted to do. Plans. Europe. My clothes. Open a shop somewhere…"

"But we can do all of that," I said.

"With a child? Do you know how much work is involved in bringing up a child?"

"No… but I'm willing to learn," I said with a gentle smile.

JUNI

Sam's big eyes shone with the type of heart-melting sincerity that one couldn't fake. I bit my lip to stop it from wobbling. Unshaven and looking as though he'd been through a trial or two, Sam looked so fucking sexy with those deep dark eyes and stubbled jaw, my emotions bordered between wanting to ravage him and wanting to punch him in the chest for placing me in this life-changing position. I'd had outbursts before, mainly before my periods, when I wanted to throw everything out the window and scream, but they would pass pretty quickly. This time, however, there was a deep sinking feeling and a cloud hanging over me. I just wanted to go and hide from the world.

"Juni… We're rich, which means we can do all of that, and more. We can do whatever we like."

"But what about responsibilities? If I'm to run a shop and you a brewery and bring up our boy so that he's a happy, healthy child, isn't that going to require a massive amount of work?"

"I'm up for it," said Sam, whose resonant, mellow tone soothed my frayed nerves.

We remained still and quiet. Comfortably so. The afternoon light sat on the furniture, highlighting the dusty neglect that had become my life. I averted my attention to avoid the frustration that bubbled not far from the surface.

"I'm not having an epidural," I blurted out of nowhere, surprising myself for it arrived without thought.

Sam turned and faced me. "Juni, I'll do what you want. If you want me to stand on one leg or wave my arms about chanting "Kum ba yay" while Demeter or Aphrodite or any other person named after a Greek goddess rubs your belly, I'll do it."

Sam's comment was so ridiculous I couldn't control the smile growing on my face.

"Although I'm not sure if I could do both at the same time," he added with that cute grin that beat any anti-depressant known to humankind.

I burst out laughing and then fell into his arms, and instead of working on my orders, we made long, slow, painfully exquisite love.

Oscar's Place was coming along nicely, it seemed. The speed of its construction left me speechless. Sam explained that was one of the many advantages of being wealthy—one could move mountains. It was almost like magic. But then, everything about our lives had that touch of unreality to it. Time, for instance. It felt as if one year had passed since chaining myself to Oscar, despite it only being four months. As I walked around the new establishment, Sam showed me the drawings for the interior to the café. It was to be surrounded by wall-to-ceiling windows so one could enjoy unhindered views of the sea. I suggested salmon-colored walls for warmth, and natural wood fittings.

Sam nodded. "My thoughts exactly. Keep it natural. No plastic furnishings or white, clean lines and surfaces."

"Minimal isn't that bad, though." Sam's grimace made me smile. "Don't worry. I don't mean that kind of empty stainless-steel finish. But it's important not to distract from the beauty of the natural surroundings."

He nodded in agreement. "I've got a great idea for the foyer of the brewery."

"Tell me."

"I've sourced images of old breweries in England from the nineteenth century and earlier."

"Oh wow. I love old factories and machinery," I said, visualizing big sepia-toned photos on the walls.

He nodded reflectively. "Me too." He took me into his arms, and his hand went up my blouse.

"I need your tits naked," he rasped.

"Aren't we meant to be meeting the Thornhills for lunch?" I asked.

"Uh-huh. But we have ten minutes. And they're not too far away."

We'd just made love earlier on the beach. Our beach, as Sam called it. Wearing low-slung shorts that provocatively sat on his hips, revealing that veiny V-shape trail that led somewhere mouthwateringly delicious, Sam was difficult to resist. I'd worn the skimpy bikini Sam had picked for me after I'd discovered that mine didn't fit. I'd put on weight—in all the right places, according to Sam, which was reassuring. The one thing that did reassure me more than anything was his dick, which seemed permanently hard.

"Are you always going to be this horny?" I asked, as his finger slid inside of me and made me sigh.

"Are you always this creamy and hot?" he returned.

He danced me to the wall and turned me around. His racing breath gusted over my neck. He went to rip my panties off, and I stopped him. "I have to go out after this."

Sam continued anyway. "So?" His breathing grew heavier. "The thought of your pussy being naked in public excites me."

He unclasped my bra. Running his hands up and down my breasts, he entered me in one thrust. The stretch sent a fiery hit through my veins. His balls rubbed against my ass—hard and deep sex in only the way it could be up against a wall, as we moved in a fast, hungry rhythm. The intense friction pushed me over the edge, and an orgasm ripped through me. I clasped his sinewy forearm. Sam's thrusts built in momentum before my name sighed out of his lips. His seed gushed deeply into me.

With his mouth close to my ear, leaving a damp print, he whispered, "I love you."

I turned and looked into his eyes. "I love you too."

And then I chuckled. It was difficult to remain serious around Sam, who, even when serious, made my lips curl.

He pushed a dark strand away from his forehead. "What?"

"I don't know. You just always make me laugh," I said, giggling at his puzzled grin.

Visiting the Thornhills was like taking a walk through a pretty forest in the afternoon—literally, in that the garden boasted a treasure trove of blooms in amongst old willows, and the beautiful, fragrant rose garden always took my breath away. Clarissa and I sat on a bench, watching her two children running around with joyful abandon. It was at that moment that I realized I wanted to move to Malibu more than anything if only to give Miles a happy childhood by the sea surrounded by nature. Although Sam's mansion wasn't as opulent as the Thornhills', his garden boasted an abundance of flowers that entertained a myriad of birdlife and insects. I was certain Miles would be in his element, just as I'd been growing up around nature. I preferred the thought of him peering down at the simple beauty of a beetle rather than at a screen that offered everything by robbing the imagination of its own creations.

I drew in the intoxicating rose scent humming through the air. "That is so stunning," I said, pointing to a statue of Venus with roses creeping over her body.

"Isn't it? I never tire of coming here. And the children are filled with so many stories. There's nothing better than a beautiful garden to enable children's imaginations to roam free."

"I couldn't agree with you more," I said, taking a little flower that Orlando gave me. I leaned down and kissed him on the cheek. His big dark eyes, just like his beautiful mother's, twinkled away.

"He's so gorgeous, and Allegra looks like a princess," I said, smiling at the little girl dressed in a pink tutu. She'd created a chain of flowers and placed them on top of her head. Her long golden waves glistened in the afternoon sun. It was as though I'd found myself in the middle of a fairy tale. Clarissa, as always, looked stunning, with her long dark hair cascading over a floral cotton shift I couldn't stop admiring. It certainly made for an idyllic scene: Clarissa sitting by the Venus fountain with her stunning children frolicking about.

"They're not always sweet," said Clarissa. "In fact, both Aidan and I are constantly having to remind ourselves not to indulge them, which isn't easy to do. They know how to turn it on and melt our hearts with those big, innocent eyes." She laughed. "Aidan's worse than me. He always crumbles, especially around candy."

I thought about that and did wonder if I'd become one of those worried mothers that one read about—in constant control of her child's actions.

"You're doing a great job. They're really well behaved and are so healthy and happy," I reassured her. "I recall wanting to pour sugar down my throat as a kid." I thought of Scarlett, who had given me chocolate bars when my mother wasn't looking.

"It's not easy. But they're healthy. That's all that counts. And Allegra's showing musical ability."

"Really? At two?"

"I know." Clarissa smiled at my surprised response. "Aidan sits her on his lap, and she tinkles away on the piano. She could just keep going all day. Whereas Orlando loves to paint."

"Creative children, I've read, develop into intelligent adults."

"And mixed up if their creativity's unable to reach its full potential." She sighed.

"Was that you?" I asked.

"It was me before I met Aidan. I could barely afford to eat, and although I wanted to study art, I opted for a more practical art history degree."

"But you paint now, don't you?"

She nodded. "Yes… when I have the time. I'm very lucky. Luckier than most."

"You met Aidan while working for him, I recall you telling me?"

"I did and it happened so quickly. All of this." Her hands swept about the property. "Almost too quickly. But I just couldn't think straight around him. It was one of those fairytale love stories that, at the time, I kept questioning."

I had to smile at that. "I know exactly what you mean. Sam and I got together quickly. I hated him at first. I thought he was an evil land-clearer-slash-developer, but we got caught up as you already know in that flood, and we bantered. And what with that cheeky humor of Sam's, and he's so damn good looking." I sighed. "I just succumbed to his charms, one might say."

"You make a great couple."

"Thanks." I paused in order to bask in the warmth of Clarissa's lovely compliment. "He was my first, you know?"

Clarissa's eyes widened slightly. "Really? You too?"

"Aidan was your first too?" My tone matched her surprise.

She nodded.

"And he was your boss. Nice," I said.

"It felt wrong at the time. But I just went to putty around him. I still do."

I had to laugh. "Join the club. That's exactly how I feel." I paused for a moment. "I'm pregnant."

Her mouth opened. "Oh really? Gee…"

"Yeah… The first night, I conceived. What are the chances of that?"

She nodded thoughtfully. "It's more common than you think."

"And so, you've been with Aidan for four years and he still makes your legs weak?" I asked.

"He does. We're seriously connected, and our chemistry is still just as potent as when we first got together."

"Oh my… I hope that happens for us. It's such a hurried thing. We're to be married."

"Congratulations." She touched my hand and smiled. "We were married within six months of meeting."

"Really?" I asked.

"Yeah… I thought it was too soon, but yet I just knew that he was the only man I ever wanted to be with."

Her pretty face expressed such sincerity that my heart expanded.

"Thank you, Clarissa. You've just made me realize that love at first sight is real."

"But you said you hated him?" Clarissa challenged.

"I know. But Sam made my heart race from the moment we locked eyes. I wasn't immune to his considerable masculine charms, as much as I tried."

Clarissa giggled. "I know what you mean. Sam's crazy about you, Juni… And how couldn't he be? You're so beautiful."

In the distance, Sam and Aidan were laughing as they came toward us. About the same height, and with their muscular physiques, they might have been confused for ruggedly handsome action heroes.

Allegra, who'd been sitting on the ground gathering little flowers, ran to her dad. Aidan lifted her up and swung her as if she was a ballerina. Her ripples of laughter filled the air, while Orlando wrapped his arms around his father's leg.

It certainly was a heart-melting moment. Flushed with joy, my spirit leaped high at the thought of Sam and our new baby boy.

SAM

Juni and Clarissa sitting among the roses made for a pretty sight.

Orlando threw the ball toward me, and I stretched outwardly to catch it.

"Daddy, can we play tennis?" the little boy pleaded.

"Maybe after lunch," said Aidan, who was carrying a tiny golden-haired angel in his arms.

Juni looked up at us and smiled. "How was it?"

I looked at Aidan with a satisfied grin. "It was brilliant. Sally let it rip."

"Sally?" asked Clarissa.

Aidan chuckled. "That Sam's name for his Mustang."

Clarissa looked a little mystified.

"You know, "Mustang Sally," that blues song?"

She shook her head.

"Juni wondered why I'd named her that, too." I looked at Juni, who grinned back.

"It's an amazing car," said Aidan. "We took her down to the track, and she roared."

Juni looked at Clarissa. "Boys and their toys."

It had been a great afternoon. When Aidan had caught sight of my car and fallen in love, he'd suggested we take it to a racetrack he had access to. We'd hit it hard. The geo-forces alone had me seeing stars. Aidan, who'd been in the Special Forces, and had undergone rigorous training, was in his element.

"I want one," said Aidan. "Ever since that movie with Steve McQueen."

"*Bullitt*. One of the best car chases ever," I responded, matching his enthusiasm. "Although this is an earlier model."

Clarissa rose from the seat and said, "Let's go in and have something to drink and eat."

Aidan put his arm around his wife and kissed her. "Great idea. I'm starving."

After lunch, we headed into the living room, where a black shiny piano caught my eye. "What a magnificent instrument. A Steinway, no less," I said, stroking the satiny wood.

"That's right, you play," said Aidan.

I nodded. "I try."

"He's being modest. Sam's great on the piano," said Juni.

"He is. I remember we had that little jam. Feel free to have a play if you like," said Aidan.

"I will when no one's about," I said gingerly. That imposing room demanded concert pianist standard, no less.

"We've always got the Rhodes upstairs," said Aidan. "We could have a bit of a jam if you're up to it, and the fridge is overflowing with different types of beer. What do you say?"

"I'm there." I touched Juni's arm. "Do you mind?"

"No, of course not. Clarissa's promised to show me her collection of vintage dresses."

As I stared at my wife-to-be, I couldn't have been happier. Life was great. And Malibu had our name on it. I visualized my life there with my beautiful, creative wife and our son. For the first time in my life, I had a dream that I could carve into reality.

The real Sam Chalmer had finally arrived.

It had been one hell of a jam session. I stretched out my legs and savored a beer.

"How's that one?" asked Aidan, who I'd discovered had a taste for quality beer.

"It's okay. A bit too complex. I prefer a simpler flavor, like English ale. I spent a couple of months in Britain, traveling from pub to pub."

"Hey, that sounds like fun. I could see myself doing that one day. Maybe when the kids are a bit older. We're planning on a European trip to expose the children to culture."

"Europe's one big museum, for sure," I said.

My fingers ached. I stretched them out after a frenzied session of blues playing. "Freaking hell, Aidan, you've got some great chops. I didn't realize you were that good a musician."

"Misspent youth." He sniffed. "My father's the professional in the family. I saw how tough that was on his family life, or should I say lack thereof. I was brought up by my mom." He brushed back his hair with his hand. "That's when she could be bothered."

"You've come good," I said.

"Clarissa." He had that starry look one got when reflecting on a special period in their lives. "If it weren't for Clarissa, I'm not sure if I would've come good. I was teetering on the edge. PTSD." His mouth tightened into a mock smile. "I still have the odd nightmare. But to be honest, I'm fucking blessed."

"The power of a good woman, hey?"

He nodded slowly. "Behind every successful man's a great woman. They got that right." He smiled. "I was her first, you know? And she was my last."

I sat up. "That's something else we share then."

His brow shifted slightly. "Really?"

There was a profound understanding between us; no words were needed to describe how deep and powerful that experience was for us.

"Then it all makes sense," said Aidan.

"What does?" I asked.

"That glint in your eyes whenever Juni's around. I recognize it. 'Cause I'm sure that's how I look whenever Clarissa's around. It just gets better too." He cocked his head with a little smile.

"The more I'm with Juni, the more I want her. I've never been like that around a woman before."

"Then it *is* love, man. No question."

"I know that." I rubbed my neck. "She's pregnant."

"That was quick," said Aidan.

"We conceived the first night, which doesn't surprise me."

"You didn't use contraception?" asked Aidan.

"Yeah, we did. But…" I bit my lip.

Aidan frowned. "Oh shit… the condom burst."

I nodded slowly. Assuming Juni would have suspected, I didn't discuss it with her at the time.

"They're not much fun. And when a man's hot, it can sometimes come to a disaster," he said, raising a brow.

I wasn't about to brag by admitting that I found them hard to fit most of the time.

"And she didn't know?" Aidan asked.

I shrugged. "I'm not sure. Is that bad? Should we have talked about it? I mean, she could have taken the morning-after pill, and then there'd be no Miles."

"Miles?" asked Aidan, looking puzzled.

"Our son."

"Oh, you know the baby's sex. Miles? Ah… after the greatest trumpet player ever born."

My faint smile vanished quickly. Like a submerged corpse, that little mishap came floating back to haunt me.

If I had told her, where would we be now?

I wanted Juni.

I wanted my son.

Aidan contemplated my moral conundrum. "But wouldn't she have known?"

"I thought she might. It was pretty messy." I looked up at him, and he nodded.

I sighed. "Should I bring it up with her?"

He puffed out his cheeks and blew out slowly. "Mm… shit… I don't know, man. It's a big question. It's happened now, hasn't it? It can't be undone."

"I feel like we're starting this journey sullied."

He nodded thoughtfully. "Do what you think is right. You're both very much in love. I can see it a mile away."

I nodded slowly. "We've also got this woman, a doula, who's going to assist with the birthing process."

"You don't seem too enthused," said Aidan.

"You could say that. I'd prefer modern medicine."

"I know that when Clarissa was pregnant with Orlando, she went for that holistic approach. She had a birth enabler, who I didn't like much. But I went along with it. We'd set up the bath and everything else—incense and whale sounds." His mouth curled up at one end. "And then when she went into labor, it was the most frightening experience I'd ever had. And this is coming from someone who'd been caught in an ambush by the Taliban." He paused for a sip of beer.

My neck muscles tensed as I waited to hear the rest of his story.

"Anyway, to cut a long story short, it was a fucking nightmare. We called the ambulance, and Clarissa ended up having a cesarean. My knuckles were white. It was then that I realized that if I ever lost Clarissa, I don't know what I'd do. I felt so fucking weak." He sighed. "But they're great, mother and children. At least with Allegra, it was a no-brainer. No arguments from Clarissa either. Hell, women sure got the rough end of the stick. The pain she was in transferred to me. I couldn't even breathe."

I couldn't breathe just listening to Aidan's story. I might as well have been watching the *Exorcist* as a teenager because the cold dread I felt was like waiting for each scary scene to unfold.

"Juni's talking about a natural birth, also in a bath, with her aunt, who's into witchcraft, present."

Aidan's grimace matched my own feelings, stirring unease about the birthing process again, especially after hearing about Clarissa's experience.

It's fair to say that I left the Thornhills heavily weighed down.

As we stepped into the car, Juni asked, "What's the matter, Sam? You seem a little pale. Are you not feeling well?"

JUNI

Sam refrained from his usual information gathering and sharing on odd but interesting subjects that ended up fascinating me. He'd show me images of strange sea creatures dwelling miles deep in the ocean from a book out of his grandfather's library or from a book he'd picked up at some bookshop that he'd talked me into entering, even when pressed for time. Or he'd play the piano, making me play two notes, while he swept over the keyboard like a virtuoso. Or he'd whip up a meal from the most incompatible ingredients.

Another surprising discovery I'd made about Sam was that he enjoyed cooking. When it came to knowing what to do with odd ingredients, he had this impressive knack for whipping up something very tasty. I would shake my head in wonder, and in response, wearing that heart-melting grin, he divulged that he had once been a Jamie Oliver and Gordon Ramsay fan.

It had been a quiet drive back to Sam's city home. He dropped our bags on the floor of his living room and turned on his airplane lamp, which I'd always considered cute. Behind that hot manly body was the heart of a child.

He picked up his phone. "What do you feel like eating? I might order some delivery." Sam looked tired. He'd tossed and turned all night after our big night with the Thornhills.

"Um… I don't mind, whatever," I said.

"Pizza? Noodles? We can go vegan if you like," he said jokingly, referring to the fact that I'd become a vampire where food was concerned.

"Pizza sounds cool," I said. "Make sure there's salami or ham."

"Will do." Wearing a denim shirt half opened with a white T-shirt exposed, and shades on top of his head, Sam gave off that sexy cool vibe as he strutted about clearing things away while shrugging the phone to his ear.

After we finished our meal, which we spent in silence, Sam wiped his lips with a cotton napkin, wearing the same remote expression he'd left Malibu with.

Unable to ignore it any longer, I said, "Okay, enough…" I rose from my chair and lifted the plates from the table. "You need to tell me what's got into you. You've been weird since yesterday."

He touched my wrist. "Leave them."

Taking a swig of beer, Sam rose. "Let's get a bit more comfortable."

I followed him to the sofa and sat down. "Speak to me, Sam. I've never seen you look so introspective before."

"I'm often introspective. It's just that around you, I'm kinda different." He shrugged.

My eyebrows gathered. "Am I stifling you?"

He took my hand. "No fucking way." After exhaling a breath, he said, "Look, there's something I didn't tell you. That first time…um…" He bit into his lip.

"What is it, Sam?"

He turned to face me square on. "Were you aware that the condom broke?"

Now that I didn't expect. "Ah… no."

"It was pretty messy. If you know what I mean?" He scraped away at the label on his beer bottle. "I just assumed you would have known, and with us being so, you know, unfamiliar with each other, you just decided to remain quiet about it."

"Huh?" My forehead wrinkled. "I mean, I did notice I was pretty drippy down there." I drew a mock smile at that silly description.

"Drippy?" He raised a brow.

"You know what I mean. I just assumed it was me." For some reason, talking about bodily fluids unsettled me. That was strange, given that Sam was always going on and on about how wet and juicy I was, which I liked hearing for some reason.

His eyes softened, and a hint of arousal flickered there too. "I'm more than aware that you are very wet and responsive."

We locked eyes for a moment, and I swore if I hadn't been so agitated, I would have given in to those glistening lips of his, which were heading my way.

I pushed him away. "No… Sam… Don't try and seduce me. What the fuck?" The realization of his admission finally hit me. Rising from the sofa, I paced about. "You didn't tell me?"

"I was in the moment. You know?" He cocked his handsome head. "I thought you would have known."

I went over to the window and studied the people on the sidewalk walking dogs, chatting on their cells, or walking alone, faces to the ground. As they drifted past, I found myself yearning for their uncomplicated lives.

"In the moment?" I turned to face him.

"I fucked up." He looked up at me with a crumpled, penitent expression. "Since discovering you were pregnant, guilt has been churning away."

"You should have told me," I said, standing firm, even though deep down inside, it did present me with that big question that Sam uttered with his next breath.

"Wouldn't you have taken the morning-after pill? In which case, there'd be no Miles."

Sam's question hammered away at my conscience. Knowing me, I would have taken that pill. I sighed deeply. That really big question forced its way before me: Would I have preferred not to be a mother yet?

"I guess I would've," I said with resignation. I bit into my inner cheek. "But at least I would have been given that option."

"What option?" Sam asked. "I mean, you hardly knew me. I'm more than certain you wouldn't have wanted to get pregnant. I sure as hell didn't want a baby."

"Oh, right." I stood there with my fists on my hips, shaking my head with indignation. I didn't know which way to take this argument. I was pissed off for sure. But yet there was my little boy, who I grew more and more attached to each day. I'd become maternal, which I would never have predicted.

Sam came and stood really close, so close his scent wafted into every pore of my addicted body. I stepped away in a bid to fight off that primal attraction I had for him. The man could have been covered in mud and I'd still want to roll around with him. I hated him for making me want him so much.

"Leave me alone," I yelled.

Lifting his hands, Sam said, "I'll give you space, Juni." And left it at that.

SAM

I promised myself as I rolled over for the thousandth time to invest in a sofa-bed. Although I was very fond of my yellow Art Deco sofa, it was not designed for sleeping on, with those impaling springs threatening to leave an imprint on my spine. When Juni insisted we sleep apart, I naturally gave her my bed. It was an impasse. There was no logical way to claw back time and change it. In any case, I wouldn't have changed it for the world if I could.

I wanted our son as much as I wanted us.

I even got on my knees and asked her to marry me again. Although I noticed the brewing of a smile trying to escape that stubborn tight mouth, my simpering, schmaltzy gesture didn't get through.

Juni had a point. I should have confessed at the time. Taking a breath, after tangling my thoughts around that, I stared up at the geometric patterns on the ceiling rosette as neon signs flashed on and off my wall, reminding me of a scene in a Hitchcock movie.

I fell asleep at last, only to wake from a dream that involved me running through a field, chasing Juni, when a tree came crashing down in front of us. Was that an omen, or just my troubled state of mind?

As though on purpose to terrorize me, Juni pranced about wearing only a towel while making coffee. I rose, and so did my dick. As I searched for my pants, Juni was greeted with a throbbing erection.

She looked away, and I headed over to the fridge for some water. "Good morning, Princess," I said with a sweet smile.

"Hey," she said, biting her lip. Her mouth wobbled, and I knew Juni well enough to predict an eruption of emotion.

I took her into my arms, and much to my relief, she remained there.

"As much as it was wrong. I'm glad you didn't tell me," she said, looking up at me with those big green eyes.

Lifting Juni in my arms, I carried her back to bed, and as my body relaxed into the spongy comfort of my bed, it groaned with relief. I drew in her signature rose perfume, and life was good again.

My hands swept over her warm, soft flesh, and our lips touched, sending a charge of blood through me.

Sliding down between her thighs, I visited my favorite place.

"I haven't showered," she said.

"That's never stopped me before," I said, looking up at her with a smile.

She didn't take much convincing, because her milky, smooth thighs parted. Fluttering and licking, my tongue danced over her bud as a butterfly would a flower until she flooded my mouth like the spring rains.

"I love your taste," I said, moving up to hold her again.

She got up on all fours, a favorite position, which meant animalistic, deep and hot sex. Positioning her so that I could see her in the mirror, in one hungry thrust, I entered balls deep.

Unable to read from her moan whether she was in pleasure or pain, I asked, "Are you okay?"

"It feels amazing."

We were of the same mind there, as hot, intense pleasure rippled through me with each thrust. A blonde lock wound around my hand, and I tugged on it gently. Juni's head fell back. Her lips parted, and her groans grew in strength.

"I need you to come, Juni."

All it took was my finger on her swollen clit for her pussy to go into spasm. Her tightening walls worked their magic, intensifying the friction. A profound charge of heat overwhelmed me, and growling like a beast, I gushed forth an orgasm.

As we lay there caressing each other, Juni asked, "Do you think Miles reacts to our fucking?"

That came down like a ton of bricks. Indulging in the afterglow of a mind-blowing climax, I winced. "I'd prefer not to think of that."

"It's rich in vitamins, you know?"

"What is?"

"Sperm."

"Juni, must we talk about this?"

She giggled at my grimace.

"At least he'll have nice skin and soft hair," I said.

"Since being with you, my hair and skin are so healthy." She smirked, wearing that unmistakable look she got when wanting to suck my dick.

Now, who was I to complain?

"Then it's time we added to that gorgeous shine and body. Let's have a shower, shall we?" I asked, lifting her off the bed.

She giggled and slapped my arm. "I'm too heavy."

"No way. In any case, it beats going to the gym."

Her brow puckered.

"You're not heavy, Juni," I sang.

Holding my cell against my ear, I headed down the hallway and opened the door.

My sister Julia stood before me. Noticing my puzzled stare, she said, "Nice to see you, too."

The builder was on the other end with an urgent issue that required my attention. "One minute, Mike."

"Hey, sis… Make yourself at home."

After I finished discussing cladding with Mike, I closed off the call and joined Julia, who stood by the balcony, peering down at the busy street.

"It's so noisy around here," she said. "I don't know how you stand it."

"I love it. I'll miss it."

She turned and cast me one of her penetrating stares. "You're moving?"

"I'm setting up a business in Malibu. Near Granddad's old house."

"Mm… that crumbling old place. It's haunted."

My head pushed back. "What? It's not."

"It always creeped me out. So dusty. And everything's so old."

I chuckled. "It's very different from your home, which reminds me of the Jetsons' house."

"Hmm… all that clutter stresses me out," she said.

"And white cleanliness stresses me out," I returned. "Can I get you something?"

She stared down at her silver watch. "Have you got any gin?"

"No, I'm afraid. I like it, but it hates me. It makes me maudlin."

"Well, it makes me happy," she said.

I grinned at my sister's typical contrarian response. "I've got whiskey, tequila, bourbon. Or there's white wine or beer."

She turned her nose up at the mention of beer.

"Tequila, then," she said.

"You're starting early, sis." I headed for the bottle of tequila. As I lifted it memories of that first night with Juni flashed back. For some people, it was scents; for me, strangely, it was liquor. And that particular brand of tequila symbolized how that one night had changed the course of my life.

I poured some into a crystal glass and handed it to Julia.

She clasped it. "Thanks."

When it came to drinking, Julia had my father's genes, in that she could outdrink anybody. Julia and my father were always the last ones standing.

Sensing that I would probably need a drink or two, I grabbed a beer from the fridge.

Juni had hurried off that morning to work on her orders. A few hours later, I texted her and was both happy and surprised to learn that she'd completed most of them. My heart grew even bigger thinking of her creative flair and drive.

"So, what do I owe this pleasure to?" I asked.

Julia fell into an armchair and looked down at her fingers. Her long, pointy red nails clinked on the crystal glass, setting off a musical note.

"Have you taken up avant-garde crystal glass playing?" I asked, laughing at how silly that sounded.

Julia looked up at me, and her stunned frown made me laugh even more. "What? Are you on drugs?"

"No… I don't need drugs to poke fun at you, Jules," I said.

"Are you really going to be a father?" she asked.

I nodded. "I am. Which means you will be an aunt." I grinned. "And what's more, I'm looking forward to it."

"Really?" She studied me for a moment. "Shit… you're the last person I expected to become a father."

"What, at the tender age of twenty-eight?"

She shrugged. "Dad's pretty freaked out about it, you know."

"That was always going to be the case."

"Not really. If you'd gotten with Marie…" Her face went red. My sister never blushed. That was a first.

"If Marie and I had hooked up, I would've ended up sharing her with my sister. Now, how fucked up would that have been?" I said, raising an eyebrow.

Watching Julia drain her glass, I pointed to the bottle on the bench. "Help yourself."

She lifted herself off the chair and clip-clopped over to the bottle.

"Have you come straight from the office?" I asked.

Nodding, Julia sat down and kicked off her skyscraper shoes.

"So, have you dropped in to indulge in this very fine drop of tequila or to talk me out of marrying Juni?" Julia remained quiet as she sipped her drink solemnly. "Let's just cut the crap… Are you here at the behest of our father?"

"No fucking way. God, Sam, you're so cynical. You always have been."

"And you've always been Daddy's number one," I said.

"Is that why you resent me?" she said.

"Nope. To be honest, Jules, I'm glad you are the way you are. At least one of us pleases his lordship."

She rolled her eyes and then looked down at her fidgeting fingers again.

"Come on, spit it out."

"I've been caught," she said.

It was hard not to smile a little. My sister Julia, the follower of rules. The snitch. The one that used to always tell my dad whenever I went off the rails. I'd never quite forgiven her after I'd turned my parents' palatial home into a weekend party with all kinds of strangers coming and going. That was the weekend I lost my virginity and had my first blowjob, only to have Julia, who at the time was living away at boarding school, arrive unannounced, yelling threats to tell Dad. She did.

As a sixteen-year-old, walking around with a black eye had been quite normal. What wasn't normal, however, was that it was my father who'd whacked me and not some schoolyard bully. I could give as good as I got on the school fields, but at home, my father always had the last punch—and the first for that matter, because as a boy, I cowered before him like a vampire in the sunlight. I suspected that inflamed his fury. He would have preferred my fists up and ready for a proper fight. "Like a real man," he would bluster.

"Caught doing what, Julia?"

"With Marie."

As I studied her, I witnessed vulnerability in her dark eyes, which glistened with what looked like the makings of tears. That would have been a first, given that I'd never seen Julia cry. She was tough and stoical, almost to a fault. My sister could've outlasted me in any form of torture. Luckily, coming from a privileged background, I'd never been subjected to anything remotely severe, only my father's cold threatening stare and his occasional fist.

"Where? And by whom?" I asked.

"At my place. Steve walked in."

"Holy shit." I hissed. "Steve's got a key?"

"Yep. Stupid me. I gave him one a while back after we got engaged."

"That's kind of normal practice for a couple about to marry."

She bit her painted lips, leaving behind a red stain on her teeth.

"So you were discovered?" I grinned.

"Don't be a fucking dick, Sam. I can see you're enjoying this," she said, about to rise.

I lifted both hands. "No. Stay."

"Hmm…" She remained on the couch, wringing her hands.

"Tell me what happened," I said gently.

"There's not much to tell, only that Marie and I were in bed and he walked in and…" She gritted her teeth in frustration. "We've been outed."

I couldn't believe it. My sister was a lesbian. And there was Marie Carter also, especially after all those over-the-top charades at seducing me.

"Right…" My forehead lowered. This was suddenly awkward, given that my sister and I had never embarked on any conversations regarding sex. "You and Steve, I mean, you were intimate? Or I should say are."

Biting into her lip again, Julia shook her head. "No. I gave him that half-baked bullshit that I didn't want to have sex until we married."

"But you were always going to have to do it, Julia," I said.

She sighed. "I know. I just kept putting it off."

I reflected on how Julia had never had a long-term boyfriend until Steve. For an attractive, confident thirty-year-old, that screamed odd.

"Have you ever been with a guy?"

Her eyes opened wide, and for once she looked more like the child I'd never known. To me, Julia had always been the sensible one. She'd swapped tutus for toy guns, and climbed trees quicker than I could when we were young. She'd kicked ass then as she did as an adult.

"So you're gay? Not bisexual?"

She nodded meekly. "I've been trying to hide it. I've had a few, you know, girlfriends. I fell in love once. Big time. Had my heart broken."

"Really?" I shook my head. "Why didn't you tell me? I wouldn't have told anyone. You always provoked me and made me out to be a loser and treated me like shit, Jules. I mean, I'm the most open-minded person in this family. Mom would be pretty accepting too."

"I know all that." She gulped down her tequila.

I rose. "Another?"

She nodded. "Thanks."

"Okay. So Steve's pissed off. But if anyone's not going to punch a hole in the wall with anger, it's him. I mean, Steve's a pretty timid dude."

"He's pissed off. And he's threatening to sue me," she said with a matter-of-fact tone that belied the gravity of the situation.

"What?" I asked, holding the crystal bottle of tequila. I didn't pour one just for Julia but for myself this time. I suddenly felt my sister's stress.

"Holy fuck. That means everyone will find out. It will become a fucking soap opera," I said.

"Yep."

"Pay him for his silence."

"I tried that. Steve's hurt that I have kept him dangling for a year. He's gone without sex. It was selfish of me to string him along."

I sat down again. "True. It was pretty heartless." I paused to think. "Okay… Let me talk to him. I'll see what I can do. I'll take him out for a boys' night. Get him drunk and get him laid."

"You can do that?" she asked. Her face had brightened a little.

I shrugged. "Well, we'll call it a bachelor party, considering that I'm to be married soon."

"When?"

"When will I have a party?" I asked.

"No… When's the wedding?"

"I'm not sure. But I'd like it to be soon before Juni starts to really show."

"You don't want it to look like a shotgun marriage?" asked Julia.

"Something like that, I suppose. More for the wedding photos."

"Shit, brother, I would never have picked you for the conservative one in the family."

I brushed back my hair with my hand. It was a nervous tic, given that my sister had touched on something there. "I'm not sure who I am anymore, Jules. I mean, if you had asked me four months ago, I would have described myself as a hedonist, lacking direction, who wished to avoid fatherhood and wanted to fuck at least another fifty women before tying the knot, if ever at all."

She whistled. "Hell… Then you're not ready, in my estimation."

"Oh, but I am. I met Juni, and I haven't even noticed another beautiful woman since. No one compares to her."

"But that's lust, isn't it?" Julia asked.

"I've had enough sex in my life to recognize the difference. It is lust, but it's also love."

"Sounds rushed to me," she said.

"What about Marie?" I asked, thinking of how she'd tried to fuck me all those times. "She's definitely bisexual. How are you going to handle that?"

"She's not."

My eyebrows gathered tightly. "Not from what I've seen, Julia. She's tried to seduce me on many occasions."

"That was her ruse. We've been together for two years. We're in love."

"Holy fuck. She's a great actress then."

"Look, she's been with men. But she prefers women. She was overdoing it to make a point. We're both ashamed."

"Are you? But it's acceptable now. You can even marry," I said.

She sniffed. "Sure. Can you imagine Dad's response?"

My mouth stretched into a grimace. "Ick. Yeah, well, you'd have to probably elope, I'd say." A little smile grew. I tried not to extract some pleasure from this prickly situation, but the bad guy in me, call it schadenfreude, couldn't help but find some comfort in knowing that I was no longer the disappointment in that family.

"Do you realize you've now joined that hallowed but much-maligned group of black sheep?"

"You're fucking gloating, aren't you?" she said.

"Too fucking right I am. After all those years of being thought of as the huge monumental fuck-up of the family."

She studied me for a moment, and her mouth turned down. "I guess I too would extract some pleasure. Don't you see? I've had to do it this way to hide it."

"Yeah, sure. I can see that you've had a hard time of it." I gulped down my tequila and rose for another. It was hardly the time for being moderate. "What's Marie's take on all of this?"

"She wants us to come out."

I nodded. "We could always make it a double wedding." I grinned.

Julia wore a perplexed if not horrified frown, but after she downed her third tequila it ironed out, and her smile grew into a contagious laugh that swept me along.

A few hours later, we'd polished off the bottle. And for the first time in my life, I'd bonded with my one and only sibling.

JUNI

I hadn't stopped all day. The orders were finally complete. I'd even managed to cut out a design for a maternity dress. I'd also come up with a great range of dresses, skirts, and blouses for summer. And with Sam's enthusiasm and belief in my work, I was looking forward to opening up a shop. Jess knew about my new shop. I'd offered to stock her range of T-shirts. She didn't even have to think about it, responding with a big, enthusiastic hug. I'd also doodled some ideas to do with a baby's range of organic, naturally dyed leggings, bonnets, and sleepwear, which included prototypes ready for Miles so that I could use him as a model, the thought of which made my heart swell.

My dad had finally hired a farmhand, Jason, who milked Moonie and Mary, collected eggs, and performed all those sundry tasks that used to take up half of my day. He walked around in a shirt that hugged his big chest, giving the impression he'd burst out of it any moment. Scarlett, on one of her rare daytime visits, given that she normally popped in at night, didn't hide her attraction to our new, well-built employee. She lingered for what seemed an inappropriate time, watching a shirtless Jason chopping wood. And as Scarlett ogled, I heard the odd groan exiting her parted lips. Playing up to her flirtatious attention, Jason returned a teasing smile. I could see he loved the attention as his eyes switched from my aunt to me. I had to drag her away, as she mumbled something about needing to calm her base chakra. In normal speak, I imagined that had something to do with relieving herself. Scarlett had always been very forthcoming about her sexual needs. As a teenager, without my asking, she'd told me all about the clitoris and its supposed magical powers. But it wasn't until I'd been with Sam that I truly understood what Scarlett had meant by that.

The Chalmers were expected for dinner that night so that we could discuss our impending marriage. Were we being rash? I kept asking myself about our marrying so quickly. The answer was always the same: I couldn't imagine my life without Sam. He'd become a part of me. He believed in me and made me laugh. And of course, his bone-melting sexiness, and the crazy but interesting stuff he'd talk about always managed to fascinate me. If Sam weren't so sexy, we would have been best friends, only he *was* the whole package. It felt as though I'd won a lottery, where one's soul mate was the prize.

My mom fiddled about in the kitchen as she prepared one of her colorful dishes for that evening's dinner. I'd been so on edge all morning about it that I'd nearly sewed over my finger.

A strange aroma hit me as she removed a tray from the oven.

"Is Granddad coming over soon?" I asked, hoping that he'd cook.

"He is, darling." My mother looked at me and smiled. "Don't worry. We'll have both my and Clint's dishes. How does that sound?"

"Great. Thanks. You're a star." My voice wavered.

"What's wrong?" she asked.

"We're all so different. You've seen how the Chalmers live and what they're like."

"It will be fine. Don't worry. I've kept it simple."

I stared down at the cheese-laden dish before me, which looked anything but simple.

My mother pointed to it. "I've made lasagna."

"Oh… I see." Although it didn't smell like lasagna, I couldn't see how anything could go wrong there.

"And I've got a nice vegetable soup," she said, stirring the pot.

I joined her and peered into the pot. "Is that a flower floating around in there?"

"They're zucchini flowers, love," she said, smiling at my puzzled frown. "Clint's coming over soon to lend a hand. He's bringing over fresh fish he caught on his recent fishing expedition."

My stomach rumbled at the thought of that.

Setting down a wooden spoon, my mother asked, "What's wrong, Juni?"

"Did you have a difficult birth?"

She stared at me for a moment. "Lingam wasn't easy. He was a big baby."

"What do you mean by not easy?"

"I had a long labor." She sighed. "It was a mad dash to the hospital, even though we'd planned for a home birth."

"Did you have an epidural?"

"I did. The pain and the labor…" Noticing me wince, she patted my hand. "I'm sure it will be different now."

"I've got a doula."

"Scarlett mentioned that she'd introduced you to Demeter."

"We had our first session yesterday," I said.

Even after I'd assured him that I could go alone, Sam had insisted on coming along. I liked having him there. And he was very hands on literally, in that he massaged my back. He even participated in the breathing techniques and stretches, which I found amusing at my poor future husband's expense. Sam proved rather inflexible as he struggled to stretch his upper body to one side with his legs wide apart, which proved to be a position that I'd found easy enough to manage. Demeter even suggested my natural flexibility would be a great advantage, only to have Sam wink at me, wearing the hint of a salacious grin. He had sex on the brain. All in all, it had been a pleasant enough session, and after all those deep breathing exercises and meditating, I floated out.

While driving me back to the farm, Sam had said, "I'm not sure if I agree with Demeter about ultrasounds."

"What about harmful radiation to the child?"

"There's no radiation to speak of. It's very safe. I looked it up," said Sam.

I bit into my cheek, something I did whenever thinking about hospitals.

"Juni, I'd like Miles to be monitored. If that means one or two ultrasounds along the way, so be it."

"Mm… maybe." Demeter's constant reminders that I wouldn't need a hospital at all if I stretched and meditated percolated within.

My mother spooned out a small serving of her creation onto a plate and passed it over to me. "Have a taste, and tell me what you think."

Despite a lack of appetite, I was curious to know how it would taste for that night's dinner party. Forking through the soft layers, I discovered pasta mixed with what looked like eggplant swimming in a red sauce, along with carrots and yams. I took a mouthful, and although I expected it to be melty in that characteristic lasagna way, I ended up crunching into it. The vegetables were firm, bordering on undercooked, while the carrot had gone mushy. The whole dish was drowning in cheese and something milky. I swallowed warily.

When it finally went down, I said, "It's nice." My mother had that expectation one wore after creating a work of art. I didn't have the heart to tell her the truth. I was relieved that my granddad was going to contribute to the dinner, even though I hoped he wouldn't arrive wearing a kilt. He'd become rather partial to wearing skirts. During one summer heat wave, he'd swanned around in women's skirts. At least the nights were cooling, I reassured myself with a tight breath.

"Juni, with regard to your earlier question, I think you need both. Go for your regular visits to your doctor. Only don't tell Demeter."

"But that seems a little underhanded," I said.

"Mm… it's all for the baby's well-being. I believe one should adopt the best of both worlds."

"Wise words," said Sam, entering with a big bunch of roses.

"They're beautiful," I said, burying my nose in the flowers, indulging in that intoxicating hit that only roses delivered.

Sam looked delicious in a western shirt that hugged his big shoulders, and as his smile warmed my face, the tightness in my chest unwound.

"I brought them for tonight. I thought a big vase of roses would mark the occasion nicely."

"Lovely thought, Sam," said my mother. "Should I find a vase?"

He nodded. "Sure."

After the flowers were arranged, Sam followed me out to my studio. I knew what he had in mind because of that glint in his eyes. On our way, we ran into a shirtless Jason, whose sweaty, muscular chest and biceps shone in the sun. He looked like he was in a deodorant commercial as he cleaned the chicken coop. Even Miss Prissy looked besotted, and with Pablo strutting about staking out his territory, it made for a testosterone-charged moment. Sam looked at the younger man and then at me. Instead of that customary grin, he usually wore when surrounded by our animals, his mouth tightened.

"Sam, this is Jason," I said.

Jason looked up and gave me that lingering, bordering-on-inappropriate stare he'd gotten into the habit of. He nodded to Sam and then returned his attention to me.

As soon as he entered my studio, Sam said, "I don't like him. He wants to fuck you. I prefer Cam. At least there's no competition there." He mumbled the last bit.

I laughed. "Oh, Sam… I'm with you." I fell into his arms and let him ravage my lips.

He looked at me. "You look so alluring. And that little dress is a bit see-through, you know. I can see your pink panties through it."

"You're jealous," I said with a teasing smile.

"Too right I am. He's built."

"I think Scarlett's more his type," I said.

"She's old enough to be his mother," said Sam.

"That's never stopped her before. Javier's only my age."

"She's a boy-eater, that aunt of yours."

"True. In any case, she's doing what men have been doing forever, and that's enjoying youthful flesh," I countered.

"Then what about that creep Claude? He hasn't exactly got youthful flesh with that leathery droopy skin of his."

"Scarlett's a self-proclaimed omnivore."

Sam laughed and drew me near. His hands walked under my dress and landed in my panties. He tugged at them, and I heard a tear. "And I'm a self-proclaimed pussyvore."

Giggling, I opened my legs a little to indulge in his delightful tickling. "You're a sex maniac."

"I haven't heard any complaints," he said, running his hands over my breasts. "You're not wearing a bra. Fuck, Juni, that dick Jason would've noticed."

"No, he wouldn't." A little smile was dying to burst into a giggle.

"Bullshit. Men notice braless women in the same way that women notice designer bags."

"But I don't notice designer bags," I protested.

"You're not most women." His hands caressed my breasts, making me melt. "That's why I'm crazy about you."

He sat me on his lap. His hard length throbbed beneath my thigh and made me go to liquid as always. Sam may have had a huge sex drive, but as I'd only just discovered since meeting him, so did I.

Jeff looked up at me with his big friendly eyes as if to reassure me that everything would be okay. In gratitude, I patted him. "Hey, cute boy."

Sam stumbled to avoid crushing Harmonious. "Shit, he's got a bad habit of sleeping on the path," he grumbled.

I tilted my head at how cute Sam looked with Pablo ambling by his side and Mary Jane to the other side, munching on an old boot.

On the horizon, a glorious shimmering sunset cast a pinkish golden glow over the meadow, infusing me with optimism, as only a breathtaking twilight could.

Mary Jane sauntered over to me and bleated, and just as I was thinking of locking up the animals, I noticed an SUV driving up toward us.

“My parents are here.” Sam’s clasp tightened around my hand.

“Are they early?” I asked. I’d expected them later.

Sam glanced down at his watch. “No. It’s 8 o’clock.”

My jaw tightened. Jason was meant to have swept the pathway, which was littered with hay and bird droppings.

Sam headed over to meet them with his relaxed stride, while I remained wearing a forced if not jittery smile.

SAM

Harmonious slumbered, oblivious to our existence. I tried to shoo him away, but the creature remained inert, so I stepped around him as always. Sucking in a deep breath, I headed over to meet my parents. I opened the door for my mom and helped her out by holding her arm.

"Thanks, Sam." She smiled.

After kissing her cheek, I steadied myself and asked, "Are you ready for the show?"

"Mm…" My father's gruff response told me two things: he was dying for a drink, and he hated the idea of this visit.

"Try to be nice," I said.

He fluttered his hand for me to show the way.

I held onto my mother's arm along the way, as she'd worn heels that posed a hazard along that uneven path.

"Oh, it's so lovely out here. There are so many trees and flowers."

"It's a big parcel of land. That's for sure. Must be worth millions," said my dad, typically judging everything by its financial worth.

"It's so nice to be around nature. And the air feels so clean," said my mother, taking little steps. "I probably should've worn more sensible shoes, though."

Pablo crowed away in the distance.

"Chickens," said my father with the kind of tone one would use to describe something threatening.

"That's Pablo."

My mother chuckled. "Oh… Pablo, a Spanish rooster."

"What's that?" asked my father pointing downward at Harmonious.

"That's Harmonious the skunk," I said casually.

"What?" He jumped back.

"Don't worry, it's de-scented. He's been in the family for over a decade, I'm told."

My father scratched his head. "Why?"

"Oh, how humorous, I'll have to tell Jan. Harmonious Skunk."

"No, you won't," berated my father, who hated the idea of being seen amongst people like Juni's parents.

"Why have that as a pet?" he asked.

I shrugged. I'd often wondered that myself.

We arrived at the door, where we were met by Jeff, welcoming us with a slobbering tongue. My mother, who'd always loved dogs, patted him. But Jeff it seemed, only had eyes for my dad, jumping all over him.

"Yes. Yes," said my father impatiently. "Down."

"Jeff, down," I commanded.

"The dog's called Jeff?" my father asked.

"Short for Jefferson," I said.

I could see a perplexed line forming between his brows as he pondered that for a moment. "After the president?"

I had to laugh. "Nope. After a sixties rock band."

He grunted something under his breath and continued to the entrance, where Juni waited for us.

"Welcome," she said.

My father maintained his signature disgruntlement. Although his arrogance wasn't anything new, my father's attitude still grated on me.

"What a colorful room," said my mother. "Is that a spinning wheel? My… how rustic. And a harp."

Juni wore a tight, almost embarrassed smile. "My mother plays."

"She's very good," I added.

As we hovered about as if we'd only just met, Harry casually strolled in. Like my father, he remained stony, but at least he shook my dad's hand. Luna joined us, appearing as though she'd stepped out of an Arthurian legend in a long, flowing burgundy dress. With her waist-length golden hair loose, she looked radiant. Her resemblance to her beautiful daughter remarkable.

"Oh, how nice to see you again." Her soft voice soothed as always.

The more I became acquainted with Juni's folks, the more I noticed how different their natures were. While Harry was introspective, bordering on anti-social, Luna was convivial and all-inclusive. In many ways, the dynamic between the pair was similar to that between my parents.

My mother said, "It's such an interesting room. I see you spin your own wool."

"I love to knit," she said.

"Luna has just recently knitted me a couple of sweaters," I said.

My father's lowered-brow response was predictable. I could imagine him thinking that only commoners and the poor made things.

"Let's go into the living room," said Harry. "Can I offer you a beer, or something a little stronger?" he asked my father.

"I could do with a bourbon," he said. "Sylvia's driving back."

My father's obvious agitation didn't surprise me. He was totally out of his comfort zone. More accustomed to rubbing against fine, expensive Italian suits in grand palatial homes, he'd been thrown into a situation that I'm sure he would never have agreed to were it not for his grandson-to-be. I'd even conjectured that had it been a girl, he might not have made the effort, probably disowning me completely in the process. My mom, on the other hand, was dying for a grandchild, and I sensed that she genuinely liked Juni, which warmed my spirit. One supportive parent, after all, was better than none.

With my arm around Juni's waist, we followed our families into the living room, where in the background, jazz filtered through the air. Just what I needed—some soothing guitar to mellow my mood. I couldn't help but sense that a crazy night was on its way.

From the kitchen came a crash, followed by, "Fucking hell!"

Our heads turned in that direction.

Looking apologetic, Luna said, "Excuse me, I'll have to go and see what's happening. Clint, my father-in-law, has taken over the kitchen."

Harry handed my father a crystal tumbler half filled with bourbon and then looked over at me. "Sam?"

"I'd love one of your home-brewed beers. If you've got some to spare."

"Oh, he's got plenty to spare," said Juni, stepping in to help. "I'll go and get it for you."

After I settled into a comfortable armchair, I looked at my father and said, "Harry brews his own beer. It's excellent."

He nodded and took to his bourbon as if it was his first drink in ages.

Juni returned with my drink and handed it to me. She turned to my mother, who had made herself comfortable on the sofa. "And what can I offer you, Mrs. Chalmer?"

"Oh, please do call me Sylvia." She smiled. "I'm okay for now."

"Just let me know," replied Juni. "We have some spring water in that glass decanter." She pointed to the bar in the corner, which had all manner of colored liqueurs in crystal bottles.

"Thank you," my mother replied, adjusting one of the many brightly-colored cushions against her back.

I sat by her side. "You seem quite at home, Mom. I wish I could say the same for him." I cocked my head toward my dad, who sipped his liquor as if he were at a funeral.

"Well, you know your father," she whispered. "He's a snob." She laughed. "I haven't forgotten my roots. My family were hillbillies."

"Who are hillbillies?" my father asked.

"My family were," said my mother, accentuating her Southern twang.

"That was way back in the forties, Sylvia."

"So?" She winked at me. My mom loved to rib my father on his high-and-mighty ways by reminding him that her family had been farmers once.

I loved my mother's down-to-earth manner, and had it not been for her, I probably would have severed ties with my father completely.

Clint came waddling in with his husband Ginsberg by his side, carrying a tray of snacks.

"Welcome, welcome." He waved his limp wrist about.

Wearing floral pants and a loose silky shirt, Clint dressed as though he was off to a folk music gig that people a third of his age frequented. Ginsberg set down a tray of canapés, the aroma of which hit a hungry nerve as it wafted my way.

"Hello, everyone," said Ginsberg in his bigger-than-life voice. "You must be Sam's parents. And oh my, I can see where he gets his ruggedly handsome good looks from." He cast a cheeky grin at my dad, who seemed to sink into the cushions of the armchair.

My mother held out her hand. "I'm Sylvia. Pleased to meet you."

"I'm the grandfather, and so is he."

"Oh?"

Chuckling at my mom's quizzing stare, he said, "Not by blood. Clint, Harry's father, is my husband."

My eyes slid over to my dad, who finished his drink in one gulp. He looked over to Harry, who had remained his natural somber self. "Do you mind if I help myself."

"Sure. I've got a crate of the stuff."

He nodded approvingly. "It's a nice drop. Can't say I've tried this before. What's it called?"

"Hasn't actually got a name. A man I do business with makes it. He's from Kentucky."

Pouring himself nearly a glass full, my father drained a third of it. "It's smooth and pretty darn good."

"That's all my father drinks. So that's a compliment to your colleague," I told Harry, as I headed over to the decanter to try some myself.

"These are delicious," said my mother. "I'm Sylvia, by the way."

"Pleased to meet you. I'm glad you like them," said Clint. "I made the pastry myself, and I used prosciutto, cherry tomatoes, with a hint of pecorino cheese and basil. The basil gives it that special flavor."

"Mm… so simple but delicious," she replied.

"The best dishes are," Clint agreed.

Juni sat down by my side. "Dinner shouldn't be too long now." She looked about at both my father and mother and then back to me.

I took her hand. "Are you okay?" I whispered.

She nodded with a tight smile, which told me she was doing her utmost to keep things normal and ease the tension that naturally occurs when people of different backgrounds socialize.

The bourbon helped ease my jitters as it had done for my father, who was staring incredulously at a box of cigars that Harry had just handed over to him.

"Holy cow… King of Denmark. Where the hell did you get these?"

Harry shrugged nonchalantly. "A client. He can't get enough of my weed. It's the only thing that's helped his wife's appetite while on chemo. And now that she's in remission, he gifted me a crate of them."

"A crate?" My father's voice rang through the air. "By God, each cigar's worth at least $150."

Clint chimed in. "Mr. Chalmer, haven't you heard? Harry's rolling in money."

He studied Clint, who, although older than my fifty-year-old father, looked younger. "Call me Cary."

"Oh, after Cary Grant?"

"No."

My father's decisive response amused me. He would have been the last person to be compared to that dashing actor.

My mother said, "Short for Carrington, which is also Sam's name."

"Carrington?" Ginsberg looked at me for what I deemed an inappropriate time with those undressing eyes. "Nice. It suits you, Sam."

I cast a quick glance at Juni, who seemed to be extracting humor at my expense.

"I prefer Sam," she said.

"Scarlett's got a hungry pussy. Scarlett's a slut," rang through the air. That quieted everyone down. And now it was my turn to sink into the armchair.

My mother looked at me with the making of a shocked smile. "Is that a parrot?"

"You'll have to excuse Tim. He's a foul-mouthed creature," said Harry. "My father went to great pains to train him." He glared at Clint, who returned a giggle.

"Scarlett's got a hungry pussy. Scarlett's a slut. Lingam's got a big dick."

I lost all control and burst out laughing, mainly from the look on my father's face, which read: "Are you really going to marry into this crazy family?"

JUNI

As far as dinners go, it was a much more conservative affair than we were used to. Even my mother's lasagna went down well. Or was that just everyone being nice? My grandfather had surpassed himself with the baked fish, which had everyone, including my gruff father-in-law-to-be, going for seconds. The only little hiccough came when a fetid odor hit our airwaves. Everyone tried to remain stoically gracious by pretending it wasn't there.

Everyone but my father, however, who said, "Now, whoever that was, all will be forgiven, if you leave before the next one arrives."

Everyone looked at each other and smiled shyly, apart from Sam, who, predictably, laughed at my father's droll comment. Then another blast came through, and everyone scrunched their faces at the stomach-churning noxious gas attack.

I felt something shift under the table, and after I poked my head under, I exclaimed, "Jeff!"

"Get that canine out of here," my father said.

My grandfather grabbed a scrap of food and led our poor unsuspecting dog away.

"Sorry about that," I said, looking about at the guests, while my mom, God bless her, sprayed essential oil in the air.

After dinner, my father took Cary out for a cigar. When they returned, I noticed that Sam's father wore a rare smile. Sam's mother, meanwhile, was doubled over with laughter at something silly Ginsberg had said, and just to add to the hilarity, Tim blurted out, "Lingam's a ballbreaker. Lingam's got a big dick."

Against a backdrop of raucous laughter coming from his father, Sam leaned over and said, "That's a new one."

"It is," I said. "I haven't heard Tim cackle that one before." We looked at each other and giggled. "Hey, your mom's been on the water all night. But she seems to be having a ball over there."

We both watched Ginsberg showing her how to jive. She didn't need a lesson, though, because she was doing just fine.

"Freaking hell, how bizarre," said Sam.

I looked over at Sam's dad and noticed him holding his belly, killing himself laughing at some joke—dirty I guessed—that my grandfather had told him.

"Hey, what's happening?" Sam asked me.

I shrugged.

My parents decided to have a jam, which was something they often did at social gatherings. While my dad sorted through his guitars, my mother brought out a box of percussion instruments for anyone interested in joining in.

Sam, after much coaxing, sat at the piano with my mom at his side, and they played four-handed piano in harmony with my father's guitar playing.

The next thing I knew, Cary had found himself a set of bongos and, resting them between his legs, slapped his big hands all over them. Sam's eyebrows hit his hairline. And then, just to add to the crazy scene playing out before us, Sylvia joined in by tinkling a triangle.

I went into the kitchen and noticed a tray of brownies, half of which had been eaten. These were not just any brownies but my granddad's famous marijuana brownies. It all suddenly added up. The Chalmers must have munched on them.

Sam took a break from the piano and joined me on the sofa. He wore the same stunned expression as earlier.

I leaned in and whispered, "I think they're stoned."

"You don't say," said Sam, glancing over at his father, who was dancing with Luna. "I've never seen my father dance before in his life. Let alone laugh. Unless it was at the expense of someone." He rubbed his neck. "Shit." Shaking his head, he opened his hands. "But how? There's been no weed smoked. I haven't smelled it."

"The brownies," I said, raising an eyebrow.

"The brownies?"

Sam's voice traveled, and Sylvia responded, "They were delicious."

"How many did you have, Mom?"

She shrugged. "Maybe two or three, I can't recall."

"How do you feel?"

"I feel great." Her smile melted away into a frown. "What was in them? Because I do feel a little high."

"Marijuana." Sam pointed at his father, who was whispering something into my mother's ear and making her giggle. "How many did he have?"

"The same, I think." She bit her lip. "Oh my…" She laughed.

I patted Sam's arm. "It's okay. I haven't been drinking, so I can drive them home."

His frown melted away into a smile. It was impossible not to see the funny side. We were meant to discuss our impending marriage, instead, the night had descended into a circus, just as Sam had imagined.

I entered the kitchen and found Cary training Tim. "Cary's a stud…" He kept saying to the parrot, who just sat on his perch, disinterested.

"He needs crackers. And he prefers something controversial, I'm afraid," I said.

He turned to look at me and lingered as if trying to understand me. "Do you really love my son?"

I was not expecting that. "Yes. I do."

He shrugged. "Oh well, at least the baby will be good-looking, and there's always Julia."

Sam entered and, obviously having heard that comment, blurted, "Julia's in love with Marie."

The sound of creaking bones had me concerned that Cary might have dislocated his neck, such was his whiplash-inducing turn of the head. "What was that?"

"Maybe I should let Julia tell you," Sam said, looking a little sheepish suddenly.

Sam had told me about Julia and Marie being an item, and while I was open-minded about people's choices, a part of me delighted in knowing that Sam's smug sister was anything but the straitlaced model daughter that his father always bragged about.

Against a backdrop of painful silence, I remained blank-faced, switching my focus from Sam to his father.

"It's true. But I think Julia should tell you. I'm marrying Juni, blessings or not, and we're going to have the ceremony here."

"Huh?" I asked, looking at Sam. We hadn't even discussed that as yet. "Do you mean that?"

He nodded slowly. "Sure. Why not? I'd marry you in an alleyway."

My father scrunched his nose.

"Who'd marry who in an alleyway?" asked Sylvia.

Sam took my hand. "I just announced to Father that the ceremony, if the Berrys are okay with it, will take place here, as soon as possible."

My face relaxed into a smile, and I fell into Sam's arms. "I'd love it to be here. That's so sweet, Sam."

Sylvia nodded slowly. "Yes, why not? It's nice out there amongst the trees."

As we left the kitchen, I heard Sam's dad whisper to his wife, "Our Julia's a lesbian."

She stopped in her tracks and studied him with an even expression, which surprised me. I was expecting raised eyebrows at the least. "She was always a tomboy, Cary."

"You all look so serious. Oh my," said Ginsberg.

"We were just discussing our wedding," I said. "Sam's suggested we have the ceremony here. On the grounds."

My mother's face brightened, and my father nodded slowly. I think he liked the idea.

Clint clapped his hands. "Oh, goody. A wedding. Here. I can design a nice archway of roses."

I smiled at Sam, who drew me close and kissed me on the cheek, leaving behind a fiery stain.

SAM

After what had been a frenetic day, I dropped onto the sofa and was about to sink my teeth into a well-earned drink when my cell vibrated nearly off the table. My sister's name lit up. The phone hopped about as though Julia's fury had taken possession of it. I picked up the phone and took the call. She'd been trying to reach me all day.

"You're a fucking asshole. You promised. I trusted you," she screamed.

Holding the phone away from my ear, I replied, "Sorry. I'd been drinking, and then Dad carried on about how you would be the one to deliver the perfect marriage, and it just came out. I couldn't help myself."

"He's not talking to me now. I hope you're happy. It's a fucking nightmare. He's even had a word with the Carters about it."

"That's not like him to reveal ugly family secrets."

"Don't refer to it as ugly, Sam."

"Sorry. I didn't mean it to sound that way."

Julia sighed heavily. "I agree, it's not like him. Maybe he was bluffing to upset me. I don't know."

"And Marie?" I asked.

"Oh, you know Marie. She's tougher than all of us put together."

"Then maybe it's a good thing. At least you can be yourself at last," I said.

"Mm…"

"Hey, you can come to my bachelor party if you like," I said, with a chuckle.

"What? And watch scantily clad girls with fake butts and tits sliding up and down a pole, while balancing precariously on cheap slutty heels? No fucking way."

I had to chuckle at her rant. "There's no way I'm doing that. Those places depress me. To be honest, I haven't thought it out. The last thing I want is a *Hangover* scenario."

"You're not even going to drink?"

I laughed at her incredulous tone. "The movie. You know, drinking to excess and ending up in some shithole, or chained up in a Third World prison."

She sniffed. "You know, brother, I'm kinda warming to the idea of it now. What about your friends?"

"My friends are more into discussing the dark matter of the universe than ogling silicone-stuffed girls. Rather than obliterate brain cells, whenever I hang with those guys, I leave a little bit brainier."

"God. How fucking dull. Count me out."

"Pity. I liked the idea of having you along."

"I suppose it's for the better," she said, reverting to her predicament. "And Dad can't stay mad at me for long. He needs me to run things."

"You're brilliant, Julia. And hey, it's nice to bond with you at last."

"Who says I've forgiven you, Sam?"

"Oh, come on. Be nice. I hope you're at least coming to the wedding."

"At the Addams family house? I wouldn't miss it for the world." She sniffed.

"I suppose Mom filled you in on the dinner."

"She sure did. Every last detail. She even asked me if I could buy her marijuana chocolates."

"You're fucking kidding me?"

"Nope," said Julia.

"Our sweet, straitlaced mom… who would have thought." I paused. "I'm sorry, Julia. I shouldn't have outed you like that, but I'd been drinking and I was kinda sick of hearing about how great you are and how much of a loser I am. I just broke."

"Hm… I'm sure I'll find some way to repay you," she said.

"Should I be worried?" I asked.

"Wipe that smirk off your face," she said.

"Clairvoyant, too."

"Got to go."

I set my phone down and walked out onto my balcony, where I contemplated my crazy world while streams of humanity ambled along. Although I liked the idea of living in Malibu, I would always love my place right in the heart of that buzzing city.

The same question gathered in my thoughts: Were we really about to do this?

Was I really going to be a father?

Cold sweat slithered down my spine, causing a shiver. I hoped I could be a better father, man, and husband than my father had ever been. With that overpowering thought bubbling away, I headed to the fridge, grabbed a beer, and kicked off my shoes as I waited for Juni. We'd planned to do what most couples did: dine in, watch a movie, and have hard sex, followed by slow, sensual lovemaking of the kind that only those in love ever experienced.

Feeling numb and light-headed, I'd started to hyperventilate. Demeter had suggested—no, more demanded—that I practice the breathing exercises. Already on thin ice where Juni's doula was concerned, I cooperated without as much as an eye roll, even though I couldn't quite understand why I should pretend that I was the one giving birth. According to Demeter, it would help me empathize. I could have sworn I already felt that without doing deep breathing exercises.

The stretches were difficult but fun, in that they made Juni laugh at my strained scowls. Tossing aside that affected gentle tone of hers, Demeter had gone all militant by pushing me into opening my legs wide, which, being a bit a muscle-bound I found difficult to do. Juni giggled madly, while Demeter, I sensed, took delight at my obvious lack of agility.

The fun part began after Demeter made us herbal tea and suggested— no, insisted—that we watch a video of a mother giving birth in a bath.

"Isn't that a bit personal?" I asked, wincing. "I wouldn't want anybody watching Juni delivering our baby on a video."

I looked at Juni, who was a little red in the face from the exercises and had that drifty look she got from the meditation. She was better at it than me. I found it hard to switch off—battling thoughts to do with recipes for beer and an appointment with the builder.

"I'm sure we won't pop it on at family get-togethers." Juni tilted her head, making my lips curl.

"Oh really? Shit. And here I was thinking that we could gather with the family and watch my son's head popping out of my wife's vagina."

Accustomed to my occasional sardonic take on life, Juni giggled, while Demeter remained stony. I sensed she didn't do irony.

"I think it's a lovely gesture to have family and close friends present," she said soberly.

"Close friends?" Disbelief annihilated what little decorum remained because my waters had broken, metaphorically speaking. "You're fucking kidding me?"

Juni cast me a "be nice" look, which I ignored because we'd hit the limit to what I could tolerate. Breathing exercises, chanting, incense burning, sure… but a fucking audience. No way.

"It's just going to be me, the midwife, and the doctor."

Demeter interjected. "You won't need a doctor, I'm sure."

I looked at Juni to see where she was at and noticed her cheeks draining of color, which always happened whenever we discussed arrangements for the birth.

I took her hand and kissed it. "It's all right. I'll be there to hold your hand."

She smiled tightly.

"What would you like, Juni?" asked Demeter, from whom I sensed a growing hostility toward me.

"I want to have a quick labor, and for my son to be healthy and…" Juni looked at me. "I don't want anyone other than Sam and you, the midwife and…" She bit her lip.

I squeezed her hand. Juni was not her typical determined self. Around Demeter and even Scarlett, she was reduced to being docile and malleable. This being susceptible to suggestion was fine around lifestyle choices, like fads and diets. But to my mind, giving birth was a serious matter.

"Tell me, how are you feeling?" asked Demeter, sounding almost like a hypnotist with that gentle tone that contradicted her determined if not obstinate attitude.

Juni bit her lip and shrugged.

Demeter pointed to the sofa. "Why don't we sit here and watch a home birthing using these same techniques."

This time the blood drained from my face. And that wasn't me weirding out by experiencing sympathetic pregnancy either. The muffin I'd eaten before arriving performed acrobatics in my gut. I'd never been good around watching any kind of medical procedure. I was still getting over the trauma of having witnessed a car crash once, and those gory reality hospital shows that I'd accidentally watched on a hard-to-miss TV screen while sitting at a doctor's surgery. I couldn't understand why they'd even show such a program, which to my mind was akin to an airplane disaster movie being screened during a flight. What it did tell me was that surgical procedures made me squeamish.

Noticing that I'd turned pale, Juni asked, "Are you okay?"

Before I could respond, Demeter had her television turned on. Although great at dishing out advice on empathy, the woman had very little herself where queasy fathers-to-be were concerned.

A woman doubled up in pain holding her heavily pregnant stomach was being massaged by her partner. Demeter stood by, reassuring her with that soft, calm tone. I think I must have crossed my legs a thousand times and tried to block my ears by willing them to squeeze shut as the woman's screams vibrated off the screen.

I looked at Juni, whose unshifting frown told me she was not enjoying it either. One would need to have been a masochist. And the worst was yet to come.

Helping the mother-to-be into a tub, her partner joined her in order to massage her tummy, while Demeter stood on the side telling her to breathe. After ten minutes of primal screaming, which caused my earlier muffin to rise up my esophagus, a baby's head appeared.

I turned my head, and Juni's hand squeezed the blood out of mine.

"I can't watch anymore," she said.

My body slumped with relief before springing off that couch like a newly inflated basketball.

Juni grabbed her bag. "That's the most frightening thing I've ever seen."

Noticing her legs trembling, I took her hand. "Let's get out of here."

Juni looked at Demeter. "I'm sorry. I can't… I need modern medicine."

"Not an epidural," said Demeter, looking distressed as if she was the one having the baby.

"I'll have my baby any fucking way I want," screamed Juni, charging to the door. I followed along, trying hard not to smile, more out of relief than anything more sinister. As much as that had been a harrowing fifteen minutes of footage, it had achieved what I hadn't been able to do.

When we were on the street, Juni, who hadn't regained her composure, had tears running down her cheeks.

"I'm sorry you had to go through that. She's a fucking evangelist."

"Don't insult Scarlett's friends like that," she returned, pushing out of my arms.

Her violent response shook me. "But you just ran out of there."

"I need to go to visit Scarlett. Can you drive me there?"

I opened my hands. "What about Malibu?"

"No… I need some space. You'll make a joke about everything. And I feel like shit." Her voice went up a decibel as we stood on the busy sidewalk.

"Juni… I'm sorry. I didn't mean that. I just don't like her."

"I don't much either. But… I don't know what to do. Everyone's giving me conflicting advice… After watching that, I don't even want to become a mother."

JUNI

The horror on Sam's face mirrored my own. He had a point. Demeter's determination for me to go all natural and drug-free had chilled me to the bone. Even though she had my best interest at heart, Demeter had never given birth, and neither had Scarlett, and suddenly I was being dictated to. If I could turn back time, I would. Although I knew without any doubt that I loved Sam more than anyone I'd ever loved, at that moment, I hated him, something I couldn't quite understand. But I think I hated everybody at that moment.

"You're not going to do anything stupid, are you?" Sam asked.

"It's my fucking body. I'm sick of you and everyone telling me what to do. I want to go home and sleep."

Sam fingered through his hair. I cringed at how dramatic I sounded, but it was as though a monster had taken possession and was pulling my strings.

"Please, Sam, take me home," I said, quietly. I was too tired to argue.

"Of course," he said. "Come on." He took my hand, and we walked silently to the car.

In many ways, a few days' break from seeing each other was what we needed. I needed that space to distract myself by working on my orders.

Sam kept calling me to see if I was okay. He made me Skype him, for he needed to see my face, he said. And when I saw those dark-ringed eyes, despite him looking sexy as sin, I melted. Hope pumped blood to my face and flushed me with excitement and anticipation. That handsome, at times silly man was going to be my husband. What the fuck was I worried about?

From deep depression to elation, the shift was almost jarring. The sudden bounce in mood even made me wonder if I'd lost my mind.

"Are you okay now?" he asked.

"I'm better, thanks. I spoke to Mom. She reassured me that all would be fine. And that these mood swings were part of being pregnant."

"The voice of calm reason, that's your mom. She's lovely," he said.

My cheek spasmed, and then tears dripped down. "I'm sorry, Sam. I'm a mess."

"Me too. I hate not having you here. But I can see that you need some time. And I can't take my hands off you whenever I'm around you."

I laughed through my sobs. "That part's fine. It's reality that's freaking me out."

He nodded. "I'm with you there. It's a serious business being alive." He paused, and a sad smile filtered through. "I hope I wasn't too out of line with Demeter. Just…"

I interjected, "Hey… I would've reacted just as you did. You're right. She's very black and white in her views, which doesn't allow for all those other variables."

"I'm sure you'll do just fine, Juni. I'll be there to hold your hand, and your mother's a picture of health. You are physically very alike."

"That was a bit dramatic of me, earlier. I do want Miles. I do."

"It's all good. As long as you're okay now. And Joe, he's the designer, nearly had a fit when I mentioned salmon pink for the walls. He suggested cream or pale gray."

"Gray? How awful. Life's too short for colorless walls, or anything for that matter."

He laughed. "I knew you'd say that. Anyway, he's got a chart. I'll bring it with me so that you can study it."

"I look forward to it. I love designing, as you know. If I had more time, I'd even do it for you. That's if you'd want me to."

He sat forward and showed me his beautiful face, which put a smile on mine. "I would love to have you on board. I have nothing but faith in your excellent eye. I just thought you were weighed down, what with your designs and orders…"

"I am. But I'll find the time if you like."

He nodded slowly. "Sure, maybe you can have a chat with Joe."

"You look exhausted, Sam," I said.

"And you look fucking sexy. You're not wearing a bra, are you?"

I had to laugh. My body heated up though. I couldn't deny being turned on by those hooded eyes. "No, I'm not."

"Then, maybe… you could…"

I took off my T-shirt.

Sam groaned, and then I heard his zipper.

Inflamed by a pleasant moistening throb, I asked, "Are we going to do this?"

"You bet. Play with your nipples, Juni." His rasp impaled me.

I palmed my nipples, which were already hardened by Sam's aroused leering. "Is this working?"

"What do you think?" He pointed at the screen. "Keep touching your tits."

As he pulled on his cock, my tongue dripped with saliva. "Why don't you stand up, Sam," I said.

"Only if you lie on the bed and take your panties off and touch yourself."

"Are we really going to have Skype sex?" I asked.

"Yeah… nice," he drawled.

Placing my laptop on the bed, I lay down. "Can you see me?"

"Uh-huh. Rip off those panties," he said.

As I popped my fingers inside my cotton underwear, an element of delicious shame washed over me. Instead of it putting me off though, I was drenched with desire, especially with Sam's deep breathing coming through loud and clear.

I removed my panties, and after spreading my legs, I touched myself, rotating my finger over my thickened bud. "I want to see your dick, Sam."

He repositioned himself. His hand moved up and down his enormous shaft. A flood of blood engorged my clit.

"Fuck yourself with your fingers," he said, barely able to speak.

Our connection intensified at that moment, for I would never have dreamed of doing anything so filthy before. But hell, it was hot.

"Ah…" Sam growled as fluid squirted out.

In response, I trembled through that mushrooming warm drenching that only deep arousal and passionate attraction could deliver.

The next day, Jess popped in to discuss her dress as maid of honor.

"Who's he?" asked Jess, pointing to our new farmhand, shirtless as always, raking leaves.

"That's Jason. He's Cam's replacement."

"Oh, I bet he's brokenhearted," said Jess, referring to my besotted neighbor.

I shrugged. "Shit, Jess, my life in the spate of fourteen weeks has changed so dramatically. Can you believe it?"

"Me too. I've got news." Jess's toothy smile was contagious.

"You're marrying Scotty?"

She shook her head. "He hasn't asked. But I'm pregnant too."

My mouth fell open, and we looked at each other and laughed. "How great is that?" I paused to study her. "It is, isn't it? I mean you're happy about it?"

"You bet. At first, it freaked me. But now we're both really excited."

"Yay. Our children will grow up together… Although…" I looked at Jess with a sad smile. "I'll be in Malibu. But it's a huge house. You can stay for as long as you like."

"About that," said Jess.

"What?"

"Sam's asked Scotty if he'd come and work at the brewery for a while. And there's a dinosaur theme park close by that have asked him to put together a display. So it seems that we're moving there, too."

I jumped up and down. "Oh God, that's great news. And with me opening up a boutique, you can come and work there with me. We can bring our signature kooky wear to all those cashed-up celebs."

We shared a giggle and hugged.

"Who would have thought this could be happening," I said, with a tear sliding down my cheek.

In the distance, I noticed Jason carrying a stack of chairs into the wooden rotunda that as a girl I'd dance around in, channeling that scene from *The Sound of Music*. Silly really. It seemed like only a few days had passed. Now I was a grown woman. In many ways, it was my overactive imagination and obsession with fairies growing up that had led me to chain myself to Oscar in a bid to keep those stories alive.

"Yeah. One big beautiful tree down, and one big beautiful new life growing in its wake," she said.

"True. That's so profound," I sang.

"Speaking of your tree, is your brother coming to the ceremony?"

"I rang Lee to invite him. I haven't heard. I don't think so. He's not part of the family anyway. Strange, isn't it? I explained to him that it was because of him that I was getting married. That definitely got him talking, which he rarely does."

Jess nodded thoughtfully. "Oh well, one can't choose one's family."

"Too right." I smiled, thinking about what life would have been like growing up in a normal family. Whatever that meant. It was a question that had crossed my mind on occasion. But then had anything been different, there would never have been Sam.

"Let's go and check out those dresses," said Jess.

"Sure, and then you can help me decide what I'm going to wear."

Jess stopped walking. "Your wedding's two days away, and you haven't decided on a dress?"

"I know. It's crazy. I've been thinking about it though. I didn't even have a bachelorette party." I thought about Scarlett's horror when I'd passed on her invitation for me to be part of a ritual, followed by a party.

We entered my studio, where the full extent of my hectic existence came into view.

"Shit, what a mess."

"Tell me about it. I'm just finishing off the last lot of orders."

Jess picked up a dress I'd added applique dots to.

"This is so cool."

"Yeah. It's very sixties." I'd been inspired by Clarissa Thornhill's incredible collection of vintage clothes, especially through the combining of bright colors.

"My God, purple and green, that's outrageous, but yet it works," she said.

I tilted my head and studied the dress through squinted eyes and had to agree.

"A green empire-line bodice with a purple flounce. It's gorgeous." Jess held it up against her body and stood before the mirror.

"When I'm all settled and I've set up my shop, I'll gift you one," I said.

"It's going to be great. You're going to do great, babe," said Jess.

My mouth trembled. "Sorry, I've become so teary since becoming pregnant."

"All those flooding hormones. I found myself crying after watching *Pretty Woman* for the first time."

"For the first time?" I asked incredulously. Despite not watching much TV, even I'd seen that movie.

"I've had a busy life," she said.

"Haven't we all." I sighed. "It's not just tears." I raised a brow as I reverted to our former subject of hormones.

"No… I get what you mean. I'm so goddamn horny all the time," she said with a giggle.

"Yeah…" A contented breath escaped my mouth. I was still going all gooey thinking about that Skype session with Sam.

"I only have to wiggle in my chair and I feel an orgasm coming on."

I had to laugh, having been there myself.

"Okay then, back to business," said Jess. "Show me what you've got and what you'd like me to wear."

I led her to a rack of dresses.

"Oh, this is going to be so much fun," said Jess, rubbing her hands together.

As I nodded, smiling, a flurry of butterflies invaded my tummy. I'd decided to remain apart from Sam for two days until our big day. Sam had called and asked if we could at least meet for one night. Each day apart seemed like a week, despite our having only been together for ten weeks, not including that initial nail-biting month, when I'd gotten ready to join a single mothers' support group.

Rubbing the antique ruby and diamond engagement ring Sam had given me, I held it up to the light, as I'd done numerous times since he'd placed it on my finger. The ring had belonged to his grandma. Staring down at it as though it possessed magical powers, I felt excitement rush through me as I thought of spending a lifetime with Sam.

SAM

We couldn't have asked for a better day. The late afternoon sang. Literally, as birds chirped away. Even Pablo, prancing about asserting his authority, paused ceremoniously as the guests passed his way. And I could have sworn that Miss Prissy understood what was happening, for she looked on with a little glint in her eyes.

It was a small affair, which was how Juni and I wanted it.

The Thornhills were there with their cherubic children, fascinated by Harmonious, who predictably caused a bit of a stir, with each guest retreating sharply.

My father didn't seem too fazed for a change, which was surprising, but then he'd mellowed. I could only assume that he'd taken to munching on some of my mother's special chocolate. Or maybe after learning about Julia and Marie, he was relieved that at least I was marrying a woman, who happened to be from a very wealthy family.

Scarlett had insisted on being the celebrant. Apparently, much to my surprise, Juni's aunt held a license to conduct weddings. Although I expressed some concern, she assured me that Scarlett wouldn't summon a pantheon to bless our union or even invite her cavorting coven to chant invocations. Even her dress was somewhat subdued; instead of those typical black or purple flowing robes, Scarlet wore an elegant pink gown and a flower in her hair.

I'd opted for a tux, even though I'd toyed with the idea of something more stylish, like a white jacket, and blue slacks, but Juni made me promise I'd wear a black tux. And who was I to argue? I would have turned up in my dinosaur pajamas if Juni had insisted. My soon-to-be wife could almost make me do anything.

My mother kissed me on the cheek. "You look so handsome, Sam."

"Thanks, Mom."

She wiped her lipstick off my cheek. "It's lovely out here." She pointed to the old oaks piercing the blue sky and languid willows whose mushrooming canopies looked almost magical in the sparkling afternoon sun. Butterflies and dragonflies buzzed about and settled on flowers. In many ways, it looked like a Disney animation but without CGI airbrushing nature's perfect flaws.

I couldn't have wished for a better location from which to marry the love of my life.

"I'm happy," I said.

"You are. I can see that. It's been a long time coming. I was worried there for a while. You rarely used to smile. I'm so happy for you," she said.

"You like her, don't you?" I asked.

"Oh, I do. She's a beautiful girl. She's got a big heart."

"Just like you, Mom."

She brushed my cheek. Noticing a sheen of emotion in her eyes, I squeezed her hand affectionately.

We moved in among the guests so that I could greet them.

When Scotty approached me dressed in a seventies suit, I shook my head. "I did mention this was a wedding, didn't I?"

He adjusted the ruffled cuff of his white Elvis shirt and tugged on the pale-blue, wide-lapelled jacket. "It belonged to my dad. Jess suggested it. Is it a bit loud?"

"For someone who wears the same clothes all year round, you chose this day to camp it up?"

He laughed at my quip. "Hey, it could've been worst. I was going to do a *Starsky and Hutch* and wear a safari suit."

I hissed behind gritted teeth at that thought. "I'm glad you didn't. I'll remember this, Scotty."

"Meaning?" he asked, grinning.

"Mm… I was rather fond of *Hawaii Five 0* growing up."

"Ha… Good one. We're actually thinking of a beach wedding."

"Perfect, then. I'll come in my swimmers."

We looked at each other and laughed.

Scarlett swanned over. "Are we ready?" she asked.

"I am."

I cast an eye over at Luna, who'd set up her harp in front of a magnolia tree. Resembling a fairy queen, she gracefully plucked her instrument. The enchanting notes floated through the air and added that special magic to a day that I was sure would be memorable.

The seated guests chatted and laughed among themselves. I studied the scene with amusement and a deep sense of satisfaction. An indelible smile made my face ache as I marveled at the disparate array of people there to witness our big moment.

Seated next to Clint, my father smiled as Juni's grandfather leaned in to tell him something, probably one of his dirty but very amusing stories. If anything could wipe the scowl from my dad's face, it was a smutty joke.

Just to add to the comedy, I noticed Julia and Marie teetering toward me. Their heels were sinking into the ground, making it hard for them to walk.

"Good to see you here," I said, offering Julia my arm to help her along.

I regarded Julia then Marie and flashed a supportive smile. It was a courageous gesture for the women to arrive with linked arms.

"Don't worry. Compared to most of the people here, you're both the pinnacle of normality," I said to Julia after I'd spied her chewing into a nail.

"Mm… There's a little too much grass for my liking."

"I hope you won't sue if you break into a rash," I said.

She stuck her middle finger up at me with a mock scowl.

"Thanks for coming, by the way," I said.

"Who's the blonde Morticia on the harp?"

"That's Luna."

"Now, how did I not guess that?" said Julia, casting a little grin at Marie.

"Be nice, sis. She's my mother-in-law."

"She's talented. Freaking hell. She's playing Satie," said Marie.

My brow scrunched. "You've heard of Satie?"

"Hey, I'm not a complete bimbo."

"I would never have called you that," I defended. "More a vixen."

Julia chimed in. "Careful, that's my wife-to-be you're talking about."

My grin ironed out. "Hey. That's really cool. I mean. It takes balls."

"And mine are bigger than yours, right?" Julia smirked.

"If you say so, sis."

A smidgeon of warmth reflected from her. It was a touching moment for me. We'd come a long way. A little mutual respect was finally giving us that little glue that brought families close. Not too much, I hoped, given that we'd invested a lifetime in ribbing one another.

"I better get out there," I said. "Scarlett will have me on the sacrificial altar otherwise."

"Is she licensed?" asked Marie. "She looks like someone's fairy godmother. Has she got a wand?"

I sniffed. "No. But she parked her broom somewhere."

"Why didn't you tell me it was fancy dress? I could have worn my Cat Woman outfit."

"You would've fit in perfectly. But you look lovely anyway. You both do." I bowed my head and left them to find a seat among the motley guests.

My heart started to beat faster. Even the mellifluous harp notes couldn't relax me.

Juni came toward me, her arm linked into her father's. She seemed to glide. Covered by her long dress, her feet seemed to hover above the ground.

She'd worn a turquoise gown that fluttered in the gentle breeze, making her sylphlike, sensuous, and breathtakingly beautiful,

Her golden hair was up in a bun with flowers sprinkled about.

I couldn't believe that angel was going to be mine to have and to hold.

Juni's lips trembled slightly as she smiled at me. I recognized that expression well enough and hoped she'd worn waterproof makeup. Knowing Juni, by the ceremony's end, she would have cried, and the photos of her looking like a crazed, beautiful clown would make for alarmingly humorous wedding pics.

A lump settled in my throat, and I had to think of all kinds of funny things in order to remain calm and collected.

That afternoon, with dappled light flickering through the leaves and gentle sunny warmth caressing my face, couldn't have been more perfect for the most important day of my life.

Juni settled by my side, and everything then became a blur. Only Juni existed as I fell into those bewitchingly complex green eyes.

We held hands, and after Scarlett recited a sonnet by Shakespeare, I mumbled through my vows, which were brief but heartfelt.

After Juni's "I do" kissed my airwaves, Scotty passed me the ring. As I muttered, "With this ring…" while sliding it on Juni's long, slender finger, Jeff turned up.

In his mouth was a bone. But not just any bone.

Scotty's "He's got *the* bone" blasted through the air. Jeff remained there before us with his teeth clasping a very large bone that glistened with his slobber. His big eyes remained innocent and oblivious to the disruption he was about to cause.

"Oh, my God. It's *that* bone," exclaimed Juni, who still had the moistness of my lips on hers.

Before we knew what was happening, Scotty had lunged for Jeff, who, having figured that we were after his prized possession, bolted.

"What's happening?" murmured from the crowd as their heads turned collectively in the direction of my best man scrambling into the bushes.

My father stopped me in my tracks, and demanded, "What's going on?"

"That bone belongs to Scotty's T-Rex."

"What?" Having never met Scotty, my father, along with the other guests, was left baffled by my abridged explanation.

I looked at Juni, whose face had warped with disbelief. I returned a quick shrug with my hands splayed in apology before charging off in search of Jeff. As I raced ahead, I touched the ring on my finger.

We were married, and therefore we had the rest of our lives together.

I turned and found Juni by my side, panting.

Barefooted, she bellowed, "Jeff!"

Harry also joined in the hunt.

Jeff had gotten the better of us and disappeared into a clump of bushes, which were hard to penetrate and therefore had left us standing about scratching our heads.

Juni shook her head in disbelief. Her crinkled forehead smoothed out and her lips curled. Her contagious giggle made me laugh uncontrollably at how bizarre the whole situation must have seemed to the guests, who, having helped themselves to food and drink, were all talking at the same time.

Jess joined us. "Oh my God, we must find that bone. Scotty's working his butt off for one just like it."

I took Juni's hand in mine. "Should we keep searching, dear wife?"

"You bet, husband," she said with that go-getter attitude that had made me fall madly in love with her.

Aidan Thornhill came up to me. He'd removed his jacket to join the hunt.

"So, what's special about that bone?" he asked.

Clarissa was by his side. Their children swept into the madness of the moment, raced about chasing butterflies.

"My best man, Scotty, is a paleontologist. He needed that one bone to finish his T-Rex. I bought it for him. It's the radius…"

Juni, looking guilty, finished off my story. "And I stupidly confused it for a gift to Jeff and gave it to him."

Aidan, whose eyes slid to Clarissa, looking a little bewildered, asked, "The radius, as in the arm bone?"

Emulating the T-Rex's limp-armed pose, Juni pointed to her forearm.

"Oh, it's that part," said Clarissa, grimacing.

Juni nodded in sympathy. "It's definitely creepy. I've seen it."

Out of the bushes, Jeff appeared without the bone.

Juni went up to him. "Where's the bone?"

In the next minute, Harry came up carrying a plate of canapes.

"How can you eat at a time like this, Dad?" asked Juni.

"They're not for me," he replied. His panting canine stood before his master, tongue dripping with appetite. Harry held up a piece of ham. "Where's the bone, Jeff?"

"The dog's named Jeff?" Aidan asked while following me into the thick scrub.

JUNI

ONE YEAR LATER…

The opening of Oscar's Place had a streak of glamor in that half of Malibu's celebrities, who'd taken to Sam's beer with the thirst of sailors, were there.

I sat outside with Clarissa while Miles lay in his bassinet, sleeping blissfully.

"He's such a good baby," said Clarissa, sipping a glass of wine.

"I know. I'm blessed. He sleeps through the night."

"Oh, God. You are blessed," she said.

"Having him was anything but easy, though," I said, touching my belly. "How long did it take for your stomach to flatten?" I asked.

"Maybe two months or so." She wore a sympathetic smile. "Don't worry, you'll be fine."

"I also took up Pilates. That helped."

I brushed back a stray strand. "I'm a little rushed off my feet at the moment."

"I found having a nanny helped," she said.

"I might have to, what with the boutique and everything else."

"I love your new range. And the baby clothes are inspired and so needed. Babies' skin is very sensitive."

"My thoughts exactly. That's why I designed them, mainly for Miles."

Clarissa looked at my beautiful boy dressed in pajamas that Jess had screen printed mythical creatures onto. She'd originally chosen dinosaurs, but I didn't want to frighten him, so she opted for a Beatrix Potter approach—partly human with cute animal heads. I'd named it the Zoomorphic range, and they were selling like hotcakes.

"He's such a beautiful big boy."

"Yeah. He weighed over nine pounds."

She whistled. "Oh my God."

"That's why I had to have a cesarean in the end. It was hell."

"Poor Sam."

"Poor Sam?" Clarissa frowned. "More like poor you."

"Yeah. It was a difficult labor. Hours and hours." I smiled wistfully, visualizing Sam running about calling the doctor every two seconds, his hair sticking up from endless fingering, holding my hand and nearly squeezing all the blood out of it. The crescendo had come when I screamed at him to get me an epidural. Biting into his cheek, Sam stood meekly and said, "But you made me promise you. Made me swear not to…"

"I don't fucking care!" I'd yelled. I could still see Sam's popping eyeballs.

He mumbled something or other, which was quickly drowned out by my shrieking demands. He stopped at the door and, with a slightly shaky voice, asked, "You won't be pissed off with me afterward, will you?"

I couldn't believe that he was thinking about that and bellowed, "Call the fucking nurse. Now!" After it was all over, Sam recounted that he'd half expected my head to spin in circles around my neck just like Regan's head in *The Exorcist.*

Clarissa touched my hand. "You look really beautiful and healthy."

"Thanks, Clarissa." I touched my belly. "I feel so unsexy though."

"Don't say that. You're glowing."

Sam came toward me with Aidan by his side. They were holding pints of beer and having a laugh.

My husband bent over my shoulder and planted a kiss on my cheek.

"Beer. Ick." I wiped my cheek and smiled. "I don't understand the appeal."

Sam looked at me as if I'd admitted to hating sunsets or anything that was universally admired. He pointed toward the café, which was overflowing with people enjoying the jazz quartet while savoring the variety of ales on offer. "Do they look as though they're not enjoying our brew?"

I shrugged. "I guess not." We looked at each other and smiled.

"It's brilliant," said Aidan. "A great drop."

"It must be their Viking roots," said Clarissa quietly. "I'm not into it either."

A smile claimed my mouth as I imagined my tall, well-built husband wielding a battle ax and wearing horns.

"Here's to Oscar," said Aidan as he clinked bottles with Sam. A baffled expression touched his handsome face. "Who's Oscar, by the way?"

Sam and I looked at each other and giggled.

"It's a long story. We met when Juni chained herself to a tree named Oscar that my father's developing firm was about to fell."

"Then you started off as enemies, I suppose," said Clarissa.

"We did. I hated him," I admitted, casting Sam a teasing smirk.

"Not me though," said Sam, placing his arm around my shoulder. "The feistier she got, the more smitten I became."

"How interesting. You'll have to write a story about it," said Clarissa.

"Mm… maybe in my next life," I said. "This one's already taken."

SAM

Aidan tickled Mile's belly, making him laugh. We lounged about on the terrace I'd recently had repaved by the pool. The Thornhills had dropped in for a late-afternoon drink. At Clarissa's prompting, Juni had brought out a few of our wedding photos that recently she'd had printed.

Opening a box, she looked up and, wearing a grin, Juni asked, "Which would you prefer to look at: the pretty ones, or all the others?"

My brow lowered. "All the others? Meaning not so pretty?"

A mischievous smile grew on her face. "Here, judge for yourself."

She passed me a handful of photos.

The first image was of Juni, who looked as though she'd been in a battle, her face streaked with mud and her bun collapsed. I flicked to the next few shots, all of me in a stained white shirt, wearing a sweaty face streaked with mud and a scowl. As I studied them, I laughed.

"Who shot these?"

"Scarlett," said Juni. "While we were all scrambling about, my aunt, taking delight in what had become a circus, had the good sense to capture it all on photos, and I'm told there's a video that Javier shot. I did notice her holding up her phone. At the time, I wanted to scream at her, but now I'm so glad she did." Juni laughed as she passed me another photo.

"That fucking bone," I said with a hard-to-shift smile, as I studied those madcap shots.

I flicked over to an image of Aidan with his hair tousled and his shirt ripped, holding the bone as if it was a trophy.

"Ah… the hero." I held up the photo.

Aidan's head pushed back. "I'm not sure if I deserve that, even if it was a crazy chase through brambles and slightly rugged terrain."

"It seems fitting that someone who fought for the Special Forces saved the day," I said. "And hell, the look on Scotty's face. I'm sure he was about to plant you a big sloppy kiss had I not stepped in."

We all laughed.

Juni showed me a picture of Scotty in that ruffled, dirt-streaked seventies shirt that was more befitting an Elvis impersonator than a best man. His spectacles hung crookedly as he exited the bushes, looking defeated.

"What a wedding ceremony," I said.

"It was great fun," said Aidan.

Juni and Clarissa nodded.

It had been great fun.

As was my life with Juni.

Strange but beautiful.

THE END.

https://www.facebook.com/JJSorel/

soreljj@gmail.com

https://jjsorel.com/

Printed in Great Britain
by Amazon

60859839R00255